MURDER IN PIGALLE

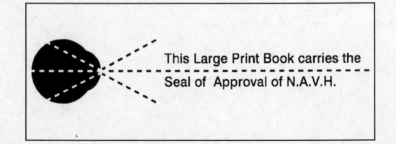

This Large Print Book carries the
Seal of Approval of N.A.V.H.

MURDER IN PIGALLE

CARA BLACK

THORNDIKE PRESS
A part of Gale, Cengage Learning

GALE
CENGAGE Learning·

Farmington Hills, Mich • San Francisco • New York • Waterville, Maine
Meriden, Conn • Mason, Ohio • Chicago

LIBRARY OF CONGRESS CATALOGING-IN-PUBLICATION DATA

Black, Cara, 1951–
    Murder in Pigalle / by Cara Black. — Large print edition.
        pages ; cm. — (An Aimée Leduc investigation series) (Thorndike Press large print mystery)
    ISBN 978-1-4104-6983-0 (hardcover) — ISBN 1-4104-6983-2 (hardcover)
    1. Leduc, Aimée (Fictitious character)—Fiction. 2. Women private investigators—France—Paris—Fiction. 3. Teenage girls—Crimes against—Fiction. 4. Serial rape investigation—Fiction. 5. Large type books.
    I. Title.
    PS3552.L297M7987 2014b
    813'.54—dc23   2014007332

Published in 2014 by arrangement with Soho Press, Inc.

Printed in Mexico
1 2 3 4 5 6 7 18 17 16 15 14

For my mother and
the ghosts

Nothing weighs on us so heavily as a secret.

— JEAN DE LA FONTAINE

Paris, June 1998. Monday, 1:15 P.M.

Stepping into the shadowed cool of Passage Verdeau, Aimée Leduc welcomed the reprieve from the late-June heat — but not the barrel of the Uzi blocking her way. Stifling a gasp, she clutched her stomach, felt a flutter.

"Mind lowering that?" she said to the CRS riot officer standing in her path.

Dim light filtered through the nineteenth-century passage's glass roof and onto the cracked mosaic under her heels. The smell of old books hung in the narrow passage, heightening the faded charm of the shop fronts.

"Use the other exit, Mademoiselle . . . er, Madame."

What was disrupting traffic this time? Another demonstration? World Cup fever igniting riots? Pre-Fête de la Musique revels? End of exams? There was so much

9

to choose from this week.

She shouldered her secondhand Birkin bag, prenatal vitamins rattling against the mascara tubes and Beretta summer catalogs. "What's the problem?"

"Aimée?"

She blinked, recognizing the voice and the face under the riot helmet. "Daniel! You had training wheels on your bike the last time I saw you." It was her godfather Morbier's nephew. Fond memories returned of pushing him on a rope swing at her grandmother's Auvergne farm. "Seems you've graduated to new toys."

"And you're pregnant, Aimée." Daniel smiled, slung his Uzi behind his shoulder and kissed both of her cheeks. "Never thought you'd join the bourgeoisie. Married, eh? Someone I know?"

"It's complicated." She averted her eyes. Melac, her baby's father, didn't know she was pregnant. He'd taken leave from the Brigade Criminelle to go back to Brittany and sit at his daughter's hospital bedside — she had been in a coma since a bus accident four months ago.

"Still working, too," Daniel said.

"Cyber crime never takes a holiday." Thank God for that, or Leduc Detective would be out of business. "Don't tell me it's the sewer workers demonstrating again?" A sigh escaped her as she imagined the choked traffic and tar fumes from the hot pavement.

"Nothing so pungent," he said. "Security detail."

Aimée's eyes widened. In CRS speak that meant there had been a security threat, patrols and surveillance. "A bomb threat?"

Daniel's eyes veiled. "Nothing that exciting."

"*Allez,* Daniel, you used to play with my Lego. Spill."

Muttering under his breath, he said, "The powers that be don't relish the City of Light being tarnished by corruption . . ."

But she didn't catch the rest, as the commander barked an order to advance. His CRS unit continued forward, toward the Grands Boulevards lined by leafy lime trees. Their thumping boots trampled the fallen blossoms, emitting a waft of citrus.

As Aimée waited at the bus stop near the Opéra, her impatience mounted. Shoppers and office workers filled the zebra-striped crosswalks, traffic clogged the boulevards and, *comme toujours,* middle-aged hookers plied their trade on rue Joubert behind the Printemps department store. By the time she reached her office building on rue du

Louvre, a fine sheen of perspiration dotted her upper lip.

The shaking wire-cage elevator wheezed up to the third floor. Fishing out her compact, she checked her lipstick then stepped out onto the scuffed landing. Leduc Detective's frosted-glass door was open.

René had ordered new shelving for a wall module to make room for the crib, and there was a strange man in overalls tapping away at her office wall. Aimée stifled her irritation. All the baby preparation had become a bone of contention between her and René — like a lot of things these days. It was like he was the one having her baby — eat this, not that; exercise, don't lift.

Hot recycled air spun from the old fan under the office chandelier, and lemony afternoon light slanted over the parquet floor. She couldn't wait to nudge off her peep-toe kitten heels, put her feet up and drink something cold. Shuffling noises came from the rear.

"René?"

A head of curly red hair popped up from behind Aimée's desk. It belonged to Zazie, the thirteen-year-old daughter of the café owners on the corner. A worried look shone in Zazie's eyes. "René's gone to the tax office, Aimée. Said you should start praying."

Aimée groaned. René had spent all last night calculating their revenue. If they didn't figure something out quickly, they'd have to pay a penalty — with what money, she didn't know. The curse of the last week in June!

The worker in overalls set his hammer down by their printer. "Tell Monsieur Friant I've taken the measurements," he said as he left. "Delivery tomorrow."

She could do with an iced espresso right now. And taking a load off her feet. The hottest June in years! She caught her breath.

"Are you all right, Aimée?" asked Zazie, her eyes big.

"Fine." She let herself down into René's ergonomic chair and kicked off her heels. The cold wood floor chilled her feet. Almost six months pregnant and still nausea in the morning. "Wait *une seconde.* Why aren't you in class?"

Zazie played with the red tassel on her backpack's zipper, averted her gaze.

"What's wrong, Zazie?"

When she met Aimée's eyes, her lip quivered. "Mélanie, a girl in my school, was . . . attacked."

"Attacked?" Concerned, Aimée took Zazie's hand. "Sit down. Tell me what happened."

13

Zazie took a school binder labeled SUS-PECT W and pulled out a newspaper clipping. The headline read, TWELVE-YEAR-OLD *LYCÉE* STUDENT SEXUALLY ASSAULTED IN HOME AFTER SCHOOL.

Aimée blinked, horrified. "What is Suspect W? Is this some grotesque class project? I don't understand."

"Mélanie's not the first." Zazie's voice quavered. "She's in the clinic, but she told me things, terrible things."

"This is your friend in the article?" Aimée shuddered. "Zazie, how frightening . . ."

"Not just frightening. But . . ." Zazie hesitated. "There's more." She showed Aimée another clipping dated from last December. TWELVE-YEAR-OLD VICTIM OF BRUTAL SEXUAL ASSAULT DISCOVERED BY PARENTS. "It must be the same person," Zazie said. "Shouldn't someone do something to stop it, Aimée?"

"But you don't know they're related," Aimée said, although her mind was turning. A serial rapist preying on young girls?

Her skin prickled as she remembered that long-ago afternoon, a hot, humid June just like this one, when she was eight years old. It was soon after her American mother had disappeared. On Ile Saint-Louis a man had followed her after school. He'd offered her an ice cream at Berthillon's on the corner — she could almost taste the *cassis-limon.* But something in the man's smile, the way he stroked her bare arm, had made her shiver. "Can't I tickle you?" She backed away, ran down rue des Deux Ponts around the corner to the quai and into her courtyard.

Her mind came back to the present at the *rrrrrr* of Zazie's backpack zipper, which the girl was still playing with anxiously. Two similar attacks in a short period of time, both on girls about Zazie's age — one of them Zazie's friend. Could Zazie be right? Could it be one man? Had the *flics* put it together yet, and if not, might there be other victims? Aimée's stomach clenched.

"You have to be careful, Zazie. Never let anyone follow you home."

Zazie chewed her lip. "I have to do something."

"*Bien sûr,* support your friend, she needs you right now."

"Don't you get it, Aimée?" Zazie shook her head. "*Mon Dieu,* I want to stop him. The police aren't doing anything. If they were, they would have caught him before he hurt Mélanie." Her eyes shone with anger. "If the *flics* aren't paying attention, then I have to find him."

Not again.

"Playing detective, Zazie? Don't be silly. We've talked about this." She strengthened her grip on Zazie's hand. "*Attention!* Do you know how dangerous someone like that can be? You can't take on someone like that on your own."

Zazie thrust a FotoFit, a computer-generated image culled from composite descriptions, into Aimée's hand. "That's what he looks like."

Small, deep-set eyes, thin mouth, wearing a cap. He could be anyone. "How do you know?"

"Mélanie described him to the *flics.*"

"So the *flics* are working to find him, then." Aimée shuddered. "They can't get him off the streets too soon."

"The *flics* haven't put it together, Aimée. They made this composite, but they're not moving fast enough. Mélanie was attacked three days ago, and they have no leads! He's got a pattern. He'll attack again." Zazie's face was set with determination. "No girl's safe until someone finds him and brings him right to their door, but I know who he is. I recognized him from the FotoFit. Now I just have to prove it's him."

Alarmed now, Aimée decided she needed to reason with her. "Whether he's the one

16

or not, it's the *flics'* job to find him. Not yours, Zazie. If you think you know who this man is who attacked your friend, you tell the *flics* and then you stay away from him. Do you understand me."

"All the parents went to the Commissariat for a meeting, even the teachers came," said Zazie. "The *flics* talked about the *mec*'s constitutional rights, harassment without evidence. Mélanie's mother was crying. Can you imagine?"

She could. The burden of proof wasn't always fair. She'd seen it too many times. She looked into this child's eyes and saw a budding young woman with the world's weight on her shoulders. Innocent, but for how much longer?

Her eye caught on the papers in Zazie's open SUSPECT W binder. "Wait a minute, what's this?" She pointed to a black-and-white photo of a street scene. "This photo looks like it was shot with a telephoto lens."

Zazie nodded. "My friend's got a good camera. It's surveillance, like you and René do. The suspect goes to this bar on rue Pierre Fontaine in Pigalle."

Aimée stifled a gasp. The photo was a night shot — what had this child seen? She knew that street in Pigalle, and it was no place for Zazie after dark. In the daytime, the area below Place Pigalle was a peaceful world of families, fishmongers, *boulangeries* and shops; costume ateliers that supplied the vibrant theatrical scene in the thirteen theaters dotting the *quartier;* actresses with their children at the park. But at night it was another world entirely: drugs, prostitutes, hustlers, pimps, sex shops, massage parlors. A red-light district.

"How do you know he goes there?" Aimée said carefully.

"I followed him to the NeoCancan."

Aimée wanted to spank Zazie, but she was too big. "Followed him, Zazie? What were you thinking?"

"He hung around outside our school."

Goosebumps rose on Aimée's arms. She reached out and touched Zazie's cheek. "That's too dangerous. No more, Zazie. Please promise me."

"If I promise not to go myself, will you check out the bar?"

"Moi?"

Zazie's goal all along, she realized. But she recognized herself in Zazie — that striving to be taken seriously. Her father had always taken time with her, his patience insurmountable. But right now Aimée didn't feel that she could live up to his example and take on Zazie's little investigation. She had to pee every half hour, her ankles swelled, there was the nausea in the morning. She'd like to smack the next person who told her morning sickness ended with the first trimester. Then this damned tax . . . This was a job for the *flics*, who, it seemed, were already working on it — although privately Aimée shared Zazie's doubts. She knew how good the *flics* were at listening to witnesses, and if this FotoFit was all they had to go on, they really didn't have much.

Not that Zazie had any more than they did, whatever she thought.

Aimée heard the hum of a cell phone on vibrate. Zazie pulled a purple phone from her jeans pocket. Just turned thirteen and she had a cell phone?

"When did you get a phone?"

"My uncle's letting me use his," she said, pride creeping into her voice. She glanced at the display and put the unanswered phone back in her pocket. "I'm late, got to study, finish my class project," she said. "Can you help, Aimée?"

Help her? What could Aimée do, other than tell Zazie's parents to ground her after school and make some calls to a *flic* she once knew in Vice?

"Just look over my notes, please?"

"On one condition, Zazie," she said, taking the binder. "Study for your exams, and leave this alone while I get up to speed on your . . ." Aimée searched for the right word. "Report."

Zazie's eyes widened in thanks. She jotted her cell-phone number on the binder. "Then we'll compare notes tonight, *d'accord*? Later, Aimée." With a wave, Zazie had gone out the door.

Deep in thought, Aimée ground the last of René's beans and powered up their espresso machine, watched the chocolate brown drip into the *demi-tasse* cup. A little girl hunting the rapist of her schoolmate — compelled to help her friend since the *flics* were making no progress. What was the world coming to?

Zazie wore lip gloss and a touch of mascara these days, but Aimée remembered the young Zazie, sitting behind the café counter and coloring with crayons. Aimée had watched her grow up over the years. Telling Zazie flat-out to stop this would get her nowhere. She'd deflected her for the present, but Aimée knew it was only temporary.

No ice in the suitcase-sized fridge. With a sigh Aimée plopped two brown sugar cubes in the *demi-tasse,* stirred.

Even now, years later, she vibrated with fear remembering how the man had continued following her, standing and waiting on the quai outside their apartment. She remembered the hot wind blowing the curtain as she'd stood in the window and pointed him out to her father when he got home, then a *flic* at the Commissariat.

"That one? Good girl, Aimée," he'd said. "Go finish your homework."

She'd never seen the man again. And her father had upped her allowance. "In case you want ice cream."

Now Aimée punched in the café number. She needed to speak with Virginie, Zazie's mother, and warn her about Zazie's project. Busy. She was about to slip back into her heels and go down to the corner café in person when Leduc Detective's phone lines lit up. Clients needed attention, networks needed security, virus scans needed running. Crunch time, like every year in June — impossible to avoid since, as contractors, they were always the last to be paid. René always had only a short window to add the last-moment revenue and compute their estimated taxes.

By the time she looked up again, the shadows on rue du Louvre had lengthened. Almost 7 P.M. and still no René. The butterscotch glow of the evening sun reflected on the mansard windows opposite — the sun set late in the summer, and there were at least another two and a half hours of daylight.

Aimée satisfied her latest craving from the stash in the small fridge in back: cornichons, capers and kiwis. Didn't that cover at least three food groups?

Still more scans to monitor, but she'd run out of *décaféiné* espresso beans, and she needed to speak to Virginie tonight before Zazie took things too far.

But when Aimée entered the bustling café she didn't see Zazie where she would normally be on busy evenings, helping at the counter. The *télé,* a new addition for the World Cup, showed a play-off game, and the café was filled with shouts and the smell of spilled beer.

"How you feeling, Aimée?" said Virginie, making change for customers at a window table. "Got over the morning sickness?"

She wished. "Not yet." The malted beer odor filled her nose, but her stomach stayed in place. For once.

"Don't I remember," said Virginie.

Warm air rippled in from the street, and a dog barked outside the open door. Aimée caught Virginie's eye. "Can we talk before

Zazie gets back? It's important."

"Zazie's late."

Aimée felt a prickling up her spine.

One of the flushed-faced World Cup fans walked up to pay.

"Verez," Virginie said. "Do me a favor and make two *cafés crèmes* for those ladies down the counter? And help yourself to an *express.*"

"Pas de problème," she said. Not the first time she'd barista'd. She whacked the grinds out from the stainless steel, frothed the milk with a whoosh and dolloped foam. The steaming brown–black liquid dripped *serré,* double strength, for her.

Sipping her *express décaféiné,* she followed Virginie behind the zinc counter to the unventilated back kitchen. Steaming heat came from the stove. "You're working by yourself tonight?" Aimée asked.

"Pierre's gone for more wine, the baby's with my niece." Virginie wiped her face with a towel, reached for a tray. "This World Cup makes for booming business. We're run off our feet. Pierre's brother's supposed to help." Virginie sighed. "Don't know why I gave in and let Zazie use his phone when she won't answer it."

Zazie wasn't answering her phone? Aimée made herself take a deep breath. There could be a reasonable explanation. Not the horrific one her mind jumped to. "*Dites-moi,* how late is she?"

"An hour." Virginie glanced at the wall clock. "More. Not like her with exams coming up. She'll have to answer to her father now."

All Aimée could think was that Zazie had gone to surveil the bar again. She was underage, but she would somehow talk her way in. Or watch this "rapist" she thought she'd tracked down from the street.

Aimée pulled out her phone, scrolled to the number she'd entered for Zazie. "Let me try her."

No answer.

"She could be in the Métro and have no service. Stuck in a —" She caught herself before she said dead zone.

Virginie blinked. A momentary stillness settled over her and then she grabbed Aimée's arms. Irritation mixed with fear in her eyes. "She's told you about Mélanie's assault, hasn't she? Her silly plan. I forbade her to get involved."

"That's why I wanted to talk."

"She said she was going to study with Sylvaine tonight." Virginie emanated an almost palpable tension. "It sounded perfectly safe, but now she's so late and not answering her phone . . ."

This feeling piercing Aimée's gut told her Zazie had another agenda. Calm, she had to stay calm for Virginie. "Do you know Sylvaine's number?"

Footsteps and someone entered the café. Hope and anger fluttered in Virginie's eyes. "There she is. About time."

But it was Pierre, her husband, wiping his forehead with a bandana and pushing a dolly loaded with wine cases. "Zazie's still not here? Tables five and six want to order. Number seven needs their bill."

On the board above the sink Virginie took down the business card of a cheese shop on rue de Rochechouart. "Sylvaine's family run this shop and live above it. I'll call them."

"Does Sylvaine have a cell phone, like Zazie?"

"Impossible. Georges, her father, is old-fashioned." Pierre winked.

"And *très religeux* — the whole family is," Virginie said. "That's why Pierre thinks Sylvaine's a good influence on Zazie."

Aimée wiped her perspiring brow, wishing for a whisper of air in the hot kitchen. Standing next to Virginie, she listened to the ringing and ringing. "*Zut,* they won't answer this late . . ."

But Aimée heard a click. Muffled sounds.

25

"*Allô*, Georges, it's Virginie," she said. "What? Say that again." A whisper of fear went up Aimée's neck. "An ambulance?"

Virginie dropped the receiver into the sink. Time slowed for Aimée as an explosion of Persil soap suds and brown-stained espresso cups burst from the sink, the foamy spray arcing as if in a freeze-frame — and she knew this moment would be imprinted on her consciousness forever.

Aimée recovered the phone, shook it hard, and wiped it off with her scarf. The line was still live. "*Allô*, we're looking for Zazie. Isn't she studying with Sylvaine?"

In the background she heard crying.

"Monsieur, what's going on?" The phone clicked off. Her heart thudded. *Non, non,* she screamed inside. "What did he say, Virginie?"

Virginie's shoulders were shaking. "An ambulance, but I didn't understand."

Aimée fought her terrible feeling. "Neither do I, but I'm going to find out if Zazie's there."

"I'm going with you . . ."

Aimée hugged Virginie. Held her tight. Let go and forced a smile. "And leave a café full of patrons to serve? What if Zazie comes walking through the door?" She hitched her bag on her shoulder. "Do you trust me?"

Virginie nodded. "Good. Your place is here. Let me see what's going on, okay?"

She was out the door before Pierre looked up, hurrying as fast as she could, feeling awkward clutching her bowling ball of a belly. Her damn kitten heels kept catching in the pavement cracks. A taxi passed. Full. Then another. Panting for breath, she tried to wave it down. No luck. No bus in sight. At the corner she saw a taxi parked near the crosswalk. Her shoulders heaving, she leaned through the window.

"I'm off the meter," said the driver, lighting a cigarette. "Already did my last run."

"Then how about fifty francs in your pocket?"

"Against regulations."

Perspiring, she grabbed her wallet. There were damp rings under her arms. "Overlook the regulations. I've got to get to a crime scene." She pulled out her father's police ID, which she had doctored with a less-than-flattering photo of herself. "Now."

Inside the taxi she read him the address from the card of Sylvaine's parents' cheese shop on rue de Rochechouart. "Extra if we get there in ten minutes."

He hit the meter. "I'll cut over to rue Lafitte. Faster."

Zazie's face flashed in front of her. Those

27

freckles, the red curls escaping from her clip, those determined eyes.

"Still on the job, eh? When's the baby due?"

October. "Not soon enough."

"Wait till the contractions start," he said, "then you'll sing another tune. My wife did."

It never ceased to amaze her how strangers commented on intimate details of her pregnancy, even touched her stomach in the *boulangerie* without so much as a *s'il vous plaît.*

Traffic slowed to a crawl on rue Lafitte. She tried to calm her nerves. Maybe she'd jumped to conclusions, overreacted. Think, think where Zazie might have gone on her way home from Sylvaine's. Maybe she'd visited her friend Mélanie in the clinic? Zazie could be stuck on the bus in traffic. But who had called an ambulance to Sylvaine's house, and why?

She needed to slow her jumping heart for the baby. Good God, hadn't the doctor instructed against stress?

And René's cell phone was going to voice mail. Of all times! But she left him a message to call her.

Seven minutes later the taxi turned onto rue de Rochechouart — a sloping street of

Haussmann buildings with uniform limestone facades, grilled balconies potted with
geraniums and street-level storefronts. The
Sacré-Cœur's alabaster dome poked up
from behind the rooftops. Behind the taxi
on the narrow street a block away, an
ambulance negotiated its way uphill. She
heard the squealing brakes from the arriving blue-and-white police car ahead. Fear
flooded through her.

"*Voilà,* Madame, you made it in time,"
the taxi driver said.

Not soon enough, she thought, and it was
Mademoiselle. But she thrust a fifty-franc
note in his hand. Added a twenty, hoping to
bank some late-night taxi karma. She hefted
herself up from the back seat, struggled to
keep the heavy taxi door open on the hill.
Just in front, two *flics* were getting out of
their car. Horns blared, and the siren
whined in the blocked traffic on the street.

If Zazie were hurt, she wouldn't forgive
herself for not convincing her to leave this
alone.

She smelled the cheese shop before she
got to the door, where a man wearing a long
white apron paced. Aimée racked her brain
for the father's name. Remembered.

"You're Georges, Sylvaine's father?"

He looked up. Nodded.

"What's happened?"

His thick hands flailed in the air. "Sylvaine needs an ambulance. What's taking so long?" His entire face was pale.

"It's coming. Where's Zazie?" Aimée asked.

"My baby, my baby . . ." Tears ran down his face.

"Tell us what's happened, Monsieur," said one of the *flics,* nodding to his partner. The partner made for the door.

"*Non, non,* Sylvaine needs a doctor. Not you." Georges blocked the *flic*'s way. He swung his fist and punched one in the face, knocked the other one down. Was he suffering shock, unhinged?

No time to deal with Georges. Something bad had happened. She had to quell her fear that Zazie might be involved. She stepped around the scuffling *flics* and into the *fromagerie.* Coolness emanated from the grey-and-white marble counters and the walls. She would bet each one of France's 246 varieties of cheese was represented here; cheese filled the cases, displays, every available nook and cranny. The reek of ripe Roquefort made her stomach lurch.

Behind the counter hung a bead curtain leading to a refrigerated back room. The layout was like all old shops, and she fol-

30

lowed the hallway leading to the upper-level living quarters.

Breathing hard, she took the narrow stairs to the first-floor hallway as fast as she could. On the dark, wood-paneled landing she grew aware of a woman's low voice. Followed it past a parlor and down the dim hallway. "Madame?"

She saw a pink T-shirt and an unlaced sneaker on the hall floor. A mounting dread made the hairs on the back of her neck rise. Beyond, she saw into a girl's bedroom. A woman in a smock — she took her for Sylvaine's mother — crouched on the floor. "*Excusez-moi,* may I help?"

"Only the doctor can come in here," she said, looking up, blinking rapidly. A nervous tic? A gold crucifix dangled from her neck over a white apron.

Aimée looked around. "Isn't Zazie here?"

"Zazie?" The woman looked confused. "You can't come in. Sylvaine's not dressed."

The woman reached for a cloth. Behind her a young girl shivered on the wooden floor, the blanket over her torso not reaching her bare calves. Her jeans were bunched around her ankles. Her blonde hair matted wet to her face. She clutched a ragged teddy bear, her whole body shaking.

Horrified, Aimée noticed the crusted

blood on her ankles, the smears on the floor.
How could it be? Her mind raced. Could
Zazie have been right all along, that there
was a serial rapist on the loose? But how
could the *flics* let such a thing happen in
this neighborhood, so safe and quiet? And
why to this particular girl, this friend of
Zazie's, where Zazie was supposed to be
studying tonight? Her fear almost overwhelmed her. It couldn't be a coincidence.

Facts, she had to get the facts, not jump
to conclusions. She had to calm her
thoughts, get whatever information she
could from this poor girl. She knelt down
on the floor. "Sylvaine, did someone hurt
you?"

A brief nod.

"It's all right," Aimée said, wishing it was.
"You're safe now. Where's Zazie?"

"I'm cleaning Sylvaine up," her mother
said. "With some fresh clothes she'll feel
better. Won't you, *ma puce*?" She took a
washcloth to wipe the smears and blood off
those small ankles.

Aimée cringed. Washing away DNA evi-
dence — the last thing she should do.
"Plenty of time for that, Madame," she said,
putting her hand on the mother's shoulder.
"We need to leave this. Just for now, okay?"
She wanted to search the rooms for Zazie

but didn't dare to leave Sylvaine and her mother alone. What the hell was taking the medics so long? "Sylvaine, can you tell me what happened?"

Sylvaine's body kept shaking. Her breaths were shallow.

The mother threw off Aimée's hand, shot her an angry glare, tears streaming down her face. "Don't tell me how to handle my daughter." She stroked Sylvaine's leg. She wanted to make it all go away. As if it could. "We can't let people see her like this . . . Defiled."

Aimée winced at the mother's word choice. She noticed curled duct tape lying on the floor. Images flashed in her head of the little girl brutally restrained during the attack.

"Did Zazie come over to study with you, Sylvaine?"

But Sylvaine's eyes had rolled up in her head. Convulsions wracked her, throwing off the blanket. Aimée saw red bruises on her chest.

She clutched her stomach, felt the bile rising. Where were the paramedics? She forced herself to feel for Sylvaine's pulse. Weak and thin. Her wrist felt cold.

"Don't touch her," her mother shouted.

Aimée felt a stinging slap on her cheek.

33

"Make way," shouted a medic, bearing the front of a stretcher in from the hallway. Finally. "Give us space."

Aimée rubbed her cheek, watching the medics checking Sylvaine's vitals. Her blackened left eye had swollen shut.

"Who let you in here?" a uniform with a clipboard asked her.

"I'm a family friend," she lied. "We need to find a girl named Zazie — thirteen years old, curly red hair. She's wearing jeans, has a black backpack . . ."

"Why?"

She motioned him to the side in the dark, paneled hall. Fading, pale light from the skylight fell in a rectangle on a music stand, which lay on its side in a pool of scattered sheet music.

"Sylvaine, the girl who lives here, has been raped. And Zazie, her friend, was here studying with her, and now she's missing. We've got to search the apartment."

Georges pushed past the *flic*. "Zazie never comes on Mondays," he spat at Aimée. His eyes were wild. "Today's Sylvaine's violin lesson." Georges pointed to the calendar pinned to the wall. The Mondays were marked by blue stickers in the shape of a violin. "That's why we worked late in the shop — she wasn't supposed to be home

34

until . . . When I came upstairs . . ." His shoulders heaved.

Was there some mistake? Had Zazie lied?

"Maybe the lesson got canceled, and Sylvaine called Zazie," she said, grasping at straws. "Are you sure she wasn't here? Didn't you see your daughter and Zazie come upstairs?"

He shook his head. "*Non,* Sylvaine always comes in through the side courtyard next door, not through the shop."

"So you wouldn't have seen Zazie, or the attacker, as they were coming —"

"We'll take your report at the hospital, Monsieur," interrupted the *flic,* tall and broad-shouldered with short black hair. He gestured to another officer, who escorted the parents down the stairs.

"You are?" he asked.

She flashed her PI badge.

"Ambulance chaser, eh?"

"Call me concerned," she said. "You need to put out a search for Zazie — thirteen years old, red hair," she repeated slowly. Maybe he would listen this time. "The girl who was supposed to be here studying with Sylvaine."

"Didn't you hear what the father said?"

Aimée shifted on her heels. "But look how distraught he is. He doesn't know for certain what Sylvaine was doing this afternoon, and Zazie said she was going to be here. What if she's hiding in the closet or in the cellar?"

"Our team will do a thorough search and question the courtyard residents to see if anyone saw anything. After we assemble the evidence . . ." He paused, checking his phone.

He wasn't taking her fear for Zazie seriously. He would be of no help to her.

"What if she *was* here?" Aimée tried one last time. "What if your team can't find her? Maybe the rapist took her . . ." But she couldn't finish.

"Jumping to conclusions, Madame?" The knowing look he gave her round belly infuriated her.

"She's a minor, not where she said she'd be. Her parents are frantic; she's not answering her phone."

"Sounds like a typical thirteen-year-old. Do you know how many calls like this I got today?" He looked up from his phone. "If the girl is really missing, her family needs to make a *procès-verbal de disparition* at the Commissariat," he said. "*After* the standard twenty-four hours."

Quoting the rule book at her? Filing a missing persons report took time. Time they didn't have.

He nodded to the arriving fingerprint tech with his kit. "Get dusting."

Incredulous, Aimée wanted to shake him. "There's a dangerous man, a rapist, on the loose, and a little girl is missing. Don't you understand? Zazie's never late —"

"Madame, you're not being sensible. You've been told this girl, Zazie, wasn't here. Chances are she's not answering her phone because she's out with a boyfriend or friends her parents don't approve of. The parents enlist us, and she comes walking in the door an hour later."

"Monsieur, I've known Zazie since she wore diapers. She's not like that."

"Open your eyes. She's a teenager, boys and parties everywhere." He lowered his voice. "If she still hasn't returned by tomorrow — after the mandatory twenty-four hours — her parents file the report, and the wheels start turning."

If Aimée's worst fears were right, tomorrow would be too late, she thought with a sinking in her heart.

As they spoke, she stared at the school exercise books and a violin bow scattered on the duvet. She noted the blue backpack, but not Zazie's black one. Could the *flic* be right? Could Zazie have lied to her parents?

A walkie-talkie squawked in the hallway. A

uniformed *flic* tapped the officer's arm, leaned forward and said something in his ear. The officer's fingers stiffened on his tie.

He consulted his cell phone again and punched in a number. Moved to the corner, his broad shoulders hunched. She stepped closer, listening.

"We need *le proc*," he said. The Procureur de la République, the public prosecutor.

Aimée heard a finality in his voice. Saw the look in his eyes when he flipped his phone closed.

"Sylvaine?"

"Her heart gave out in the ambulance," he said. "Be careful where you walk. It's a murder scene."

Aimée gasped. *"Mon Dieu."* She'd witnessed the girl's last moments. Her insides wrenched. "Then you need to treat Zazie as a missing minor right now." She flipped open her phone, scrolled to show him Zazie's number. "She's using her uncle's phone. Track the phone pings from this number."

"You seem convinced she was here."

"Zazie was following a man she thought had raped her classmate." She battled the sob rising in her throat. "We can't just wait for something to happen to her." If it hadn't already.

"Her father needs to make a report at the appropriate time. Like I told you."

"What if Zazie witnessed Sylvaine's attack?" she said, frantic to make him take action. "Can you rule that out?"

"Our priority's the attacker. The murderer," he corrected himself. "Now if you'll remove yourself . . ."

"There's no waiting period to search for witnesses," Aimée said desperately. "Organize a search for Zazie as a witness to the murder." He didn't look convinced. "My father was a *flic . . .*"

"Is that supposed to impress me?"

"To let you know I'm no stranger to procedure," she said. *Or your time-consuming bureaucratic regulations,* she thought, but she kept that back. Time to name drop. "Commissaire Morbier's my godfather."

"Isn't he on leave?"

Morbier, a man who lived for his job, taking leave? "And I'm Marie Antoinette."

Something shuttered behind his eyes, and Aimée was gripped by doubt. Did he know something about Morbier she didn't? Was that why he hadn't returned her calls?

Her phone trilled. Virginie. Aimée's knuckles whitened, clenching her phone. What should she do?

Then something inside her kick-started,

parted the hormonal fog. She would fix this herself. Zazie wouldn't end up like poor Sylvaine. Not while Aimée had breath in her body.

Time was crucial; it must have been three or four hours since anyone had seen Zazie.

"Found her, Aimée?" A nervous timbre in Virginie's voice.

"Virginie, listen to me. First say that you'll listen and just do what we ask, okay?"

"What's happened to Zazie?"

"We don't know. Please listen."

Screaming. In the background she heard Pierre calming Virginie. Then he got on the line.

"Where's Zazie?"

She caught the eye of the *flic,* mouthed please. He shrugged.

"Pierre, I'm handing my phone to a police officer. You'll need to give him whatever information he asks for." She handed her phone to the *flic* standing by her.

Two minutes later, after a one-sided conversation, he passed her back her phone.

"*Allô?* Pierre?"

But he'd clicked off.

"We'll do what we can," said the officer. "Now we're waiting for the Brigade des Mineurs." The squad who investigated crimes against juveniles. "Give your statement downstairs. Leave your number with the officer so I can contact you. Don't forget to give him Zazie's parents' number, and Zazie's, too."

Not the reaction she'd hoped for, but at least he'd taken her seriously. Or so she hoped.

Procedure hobbled the police. But not her.

Outside, quiet had descended over the now-shuttered street. Nothing open, no shopkeepers to question. She turned to the courtyard entrance beside the cheese shop, deserted except for the arriving crime-scene techs tramping up the rear stairs. The windows of the small, two-story ateliers overlooking the courtyard were dark, and the concierge didn't answer.

An old man shuffled into the courtyard lugging shopping bags from Franprix. "*Bonsoir*, Monsieur," she said. "I'm looking for the concierge."

"That's my daughter. She's away." He set the bags down on the cobbles and inserted a key in the door.

"Did you see Sylvaine, the cheese-shop owners' daughter, this afternoon?"

"Eh?"

"Sylvaine . . ."

"Sweet girl," he interrupted. "Today? Think so. Usually she comes through

41

here . . ."

"And her friend, a red-haired girl? Did you see her?"

He shrugged. Adjusted the hearing aid in his ear. "Speak up, will you? But I can't say — it's the World Cup, you know. I'm glued to the *télé.*"

Great.

But she couldn't give up. "Think back a few hours, if you can, Monsieur. Did you notice anyone or hear anything here in the courtyard?"

"Like I said, I was watching the *télé.*"

"What about the other residents?"

"Residents? They're on the beach. Like everyone else. I'm only here because my daughter talked me into collecting the mail for her while she's gone."

"*Merci,* Monsieur," she said, disappointed. For now she'd follow the only other lead she had.

Her phone rang. René at last.

"Where are you, Aimée?"

"En route to the NeoCancan bar," she said. "In Pigalle."

"What? In your condition?"

She had to hurry. "I can't explain now." Glanced through Zazie's notes. "Meet me at Thirty-four rue Pierre Fontaine."

42

Monday, 4 P.M.

Zacharié fidgeted, watching his parole officer's head bent over the file at his desk.
Dust motes drifted in the mottled sunlight
that came through the blinds. No whisper
of air from the cracked-open window overlooking the parched grass below. The office
was stagnant and oppressive, like everything
in his life.

"Staying out of trouble, Zacharié?"

If Faure only knew.

"That firm you recommended called me
back for a second interview," he said, knowing this would keep the old codger at bay.
Parole officers liked to hear about jobs. Of
course, he couldn't let on about the big job.
The one that would finally get him his
daughter back. Get Marie-Jo out of the
custody of his crazy ex-wife, Béatrice, and
her pedophile live-in lover — for good. He
balled his fists at the thought of the creep

43

eyeing his daughter. He wanted to punch something. He took a deep breath, like he'd learned in prison, to dispel the stress. It didn't work.

Faure's phone rang somewhere in the pile of papers on the desk. *"Un moment,"* he said.

Zacharié contained his anger. He would keep to the plan. Marie-Jo's letters to him in prison had caused six months of worry and anguish. And now that he was out, he was struggling to find a job that would pay enough for him to get custody. He needed to take matters into his own hands before something terrible happened. So he'd consented to this one last heist. Not his first choice, but the only way he, an ex-convict on parole, could save Marie-Jo. In three more days, mission completed, he'd spirit her over the Channel to London with their new passports and enough money to buy them a new life.

"Bad news, I'm afraid, Zacharié." Faure replaced the black receiver back on the old rotary phone, ancient like everything else in this high-ceilinged back office, with its dusty photos and *boules* trophies. "Your ex-wife, Béatrice de Mombert, has been charged with driving under the influence. Her license has been revoked."

Fear tore his gut. "Is my daughter hurt?"

"*Soyez-calme,* she was at school. Still, it raises custody issues regarding your ex-wife's competence."

About damn time. Béatrice, an actress, was deep in her love affair with the bottle and pills. He wondered how she still performed nightly. And why a besotted public paid to watch the wreck she'd become.

But it made him think. "She's proved she's an unfit mother. I've been saying that since our divorce. Can't I regain custody? I'm Marie-Jo's father."

"At this point you would have a case: an upcoming job, your apartment. We can request a hearing, Zacharié." His parole officer's eyes narrowed. "Keep straight, get this job, and I'll go to bat for you. The law favors the parent over foster care or a relative."

The cotton-ball clouds parted outside the window, revealing a cerulean spot of sky. A sign. He'd get Marie-Jo back.

A weight lifted from his heart. "*Merci,* Monsieur Faure. My little girl means the world to me." He'd pull out of the heist, stay straight, not jeopardize his chance of obtaining custody. Somehow he'd figure it out. For now he stuffed down his worry. "I will do anything. You have my word."

The truest words he'd spoken since coming into Faure's office.

Out on the street he shooed away pigeons from the fretwork grill at the base of a plane tree. Under the shade of its branches, he clicked on the messages on his phone: Béatrice's garbled rantings about checking into a spa — translation: rehab. Again. Followed by her lawyer's no-nonsense messages — could he pick up Marie-Jo from the Conservatoire tomorrow? His heart beat faster. Her last piano recital was tomorrow. The lawyer suggested Béatrice had reconsidered full custody. Scared. They were scared.

The lawyer knew the judge would declare her an unfit parent. Now they wanted to talk before the hearing. Negotiate. For the first time in years he held the power, knew he could change Marie-Jo's life. His life.

He'd have his daughter back. All he'd ever wanted. The world stopped for a moment; the heat faded; the whoosh of the sidewalk café's milk steamer blended into his thoughts. Her last letter: *Papa, I want to live with you like when I was little. I miss you.*

All he could think of was how he would meet her after school, fix her *croque monsieur,* her favorite, for dinner while she practiced her piano. Zacharié, uneducated, unrefined, had somehow made this little genius, who could translate the black notes on a page into strains of music that elevated his heart.

He'd take that job. Any job. Sweep gutters with a broom. But he'd live straight.

This was his chance.

Jules wouldn't like it, but *c'est la vie.* He'd decided.

He hit Jules's number. Heard him answer and clear his throat. His throaty smoker's cough.

"Took you long enough, Zacharié." In the background he heard muffled voices, then the slam of a door. "We're moving up the schedule."

"What now, Jules?"

"Change of plans," Jules said.

The *salaud* would make it difficult, like always. Every project with Jules doglegged and spiraled. But he hadn't had a choice in prison. Now the situation played out differently.

"We're moving up the schedule," Jules said again.

Zacharié stepped over a splattered cloud of pigeon droppings and braced himself. Time for the tricky part — to extricate himself from the job he'd set up. He'd keep it short, make it a chain of command issue.

"Let Dervier know the new plan," Zacharié began. "He's the one handling —"

47

"Au contraire," Jules interrupted. "You deal with the labor issues. Run your team."

"Dervier's a pro."

"More old-school than pro, *n'est-ce pas?*"

"He's experienced. What this job needs," Zacharié said. Thank God he'd talked Dervier out of retirement. This heist demanded a seasoned pro, with steady nerves. Dervier's forked tongue, split after a territorial gang dispute near Barbès, had put him on the sidelines last year. But he'd heisted buildings with much more complex security systems than this target. "Dervier grew up in the *quartier,* the son of a concierge, knows the sewers and old tunnels like the back of his scarred hand."

"My contract's with you, Zacharié," he said. "Didn't I fix the judges, arrange your parole?"

Zacharié wanted to throw the phone. Stamp it to pieces. Forget this deal and what he owed Jules. If he did this job now, he'd jeopardize his chance of gaining custody of Marie-Jo. He needed to convince Jules of Dervier's skill so he could back himself out.

"Speaking of parole, the officer makes me check in every day, monitors my job interviews," he said, searching for an excuse. His mouth felt dry. Why couldn't he summon the courage and shout no?

Jules gave a small sigh. "Work it out, Zacharié. The job's tomorrow night."

The supplies hadn't arrived. The team wasn't ready. "But we planned on after Fête de la Musique. Everyone goes crazy in the *quartier.*"

"That's why it's perfect timing," Jules said. "Make it work, Zacharié."

"Jules, my parole officer watches me like a hawk. If you move the job up, then count on Dervier. He's perfect. You don't need me. The team's primed. I guarantee it."

There, he'd said it.

Pause. Already he felt better. Jules would see reason.

A horn blared over the phone. But the sound came from the boulevard — a car in front of him. The passenger window of a black Peugeot rolled down in front of him. Jules's smiling face peered out of it. "Get in, Zacharié. You love your daughter, don't you?"

Monday, 8 P.M.

Aimée perched on a sticky leather stool at NeoCancan, a Pigalle bar fronted by a smoked black-glass window with a RECHERCHE HÔTESSES sign. The bar Zazie insisted the rapist frequented, and none too elegant.

She needed to know if Zazie had come here tonight. She glanced at her moisture-clouded Tintin watch face. Hours already since she — or anyone — had seen Zazie.

The dark club's centerpiece, a minuscule black-carpeted stage, was ringed by red velvet sofas with gold tassels. The tables sported rotary-dial telephones — a retro gimmick for ordering champagne. Or maybe they were original, like the cracked, mosaic-tiled floor, she thought.

She kept her fingers off the water rings on the counter. She saw only one client — a florid-faced man with thinning hair, expanding waist and a broad Toulon accent. He sat

50

laughing on a sofa, his tie loose, surrounded by three miniskirted women who kept his champagne flute topped up. Slow night. No one so far matched the FotoFit Zazie had showed her. Where was the bartender?

"Monsieur?"

"Un moment," came a voice from a cellar opening in the floor behind the counter. Cool, mildew-tinged air drifted up from the subterranean depths. She heard cranking and metal grinding as a *monte-charge,* a dumbwaiter, delivered a rack of champagne bottles.

The bartender emerged up the cellar steps, his broad shoulders strained under a tight T-shirt. An amazing arc of pomaded brown hair swept back into a ducktail behind his sideburns. A real Johnny Hallyday wannabe, only now Johnny, the Gallic Elvis, was an aging rock star with tax problems.

"Un Perrier," she said, her throat parched. "And information, *s'il vous plaît."*

"Do I know you?" he asked, a drawl clinging to his syllables. A Marseillais, from his accent — but then most of the bars were owned by Corsicans and Marseilles gangs. Or so the stories went. She flashed her private detective's license with its none-too-

51

flattering photo. At least she looked thinner in it.

He plunked a glass and a green bottle on the counter.

"I'm looking for a thirteen-year-old girl, red hair. She's been seen outside your club." She shoved a fifty-franc note across the bar.

In one quick movement, he flicked off the bottle cap. "Minimum's one hundred."

This would cost. Pigalle's red-light heyday had waned as massage parlors replaced cabarets and clubs. Bartenders gouged anyone's wallet for a simple drink. She put down another fifty francs. "So you've seen her?"

"Not today," the bartender said.

She pulled out Zazie's copy of the computer-generated FotoFit. "Have you seen this *mec*?"

"Not tonight."

"Try stretching your vocabulary." Aimée's grip tightened on her chilled glass. "So last night then? He's a regular?"

The bartender shrugged. "What's it to you?"

She debated telling him. But he needed to work for his money first. "For a hundred-franc Perrier, I ask the questions, and you answer. What do you know?"

But he'd slipped from behind the counter

to serve another bottle to the table with the florid-faced man surrounded by hostesses.

The club's door opened, sending in a current of humid air.

"Always first class with you, Aimée," said René Friant, her partner. He was wearing a straw-colored linen suit, pink shirt and matching tie. His mouth turned down in distaste as he maneuvered himself up onto the barstool. At four feet tall, he was only a little taller than the stool himself. "Don't tell me we're in some under-the-radar, poised-for-discovery, three-star wine bar?"

Before she could explain to René, the bartender returned.

"Go along with me, René," she said.

"Served you before, little man," said the bartender. "Kir Royale, wasn't it?"

René's cheeks reddened. It seemed René had frequented this seedy *bar à bouchon,* where hostesses' salaries were based on the number of champagne corks their clients popped.

"Ah, no doubt you've got a treasure trove of Romanée-Conti and vintage Dom Pérignon stashed in the cellar," René said. His green eyes flashed. "This place was famous during the war. A notorious haunt of Gestapo and high-ranking Vichy. The good old days."

Aimée stared at René. Where did that come from?

"Close, little man," said the bartender, not skipping a beat. "Just give our checkered past a few years to ferment into a titillating historical ambiance. There's still too many alive who remember the jackboots."

"Let's get back to this *mec*," Aimée said, shoving the FotoFit across the counter again.

"Came in a few times." The bartender shrugged. "Like I said."

René's eyes narrowed. "What's this about?"

She nudged René. Gave him the eye to keep his mouth shut. "Can you give me any specifics? His name?" asked Aimée.

"His friend was looking for him earlier today, too."

That could fit — if this was the rapist, maybe he was supposed to meet his friend, and instead he'd followed Sylvaine from school. But where was Zazie?

"His name?"

"Think I'm an information service?"

She willed herself not to throw her Perrier in his face. This bartender might fleece farmers from the countryside, plumbers from the provinces, traveling salesmen hoping the red lights of Pigalle still shone for a racy interlude away from their wives. Or René. But not her.

"I think you're willing, *non,* let's say eager to assist in capturing the rapist who attacked and killed a twelve-year-old girl on rue de Rochechouart this afternoon."

"What?" said René.

She kicked him to keep quiet.

The bartender blinked. "I don't want trouble." He hefted a crate of empty bottles onto the *monte-charge.* Pressed the red button and with a clanking it descended. "*Ecoutez,* we're under surveillance, like all the clubs, checked for anyone underage, licensing regulations. Vice keeps us on a tight leash."

René made a clucking noise. "No wild gangland like the fifties and sixties?"

"Commerce, little man. I operate a business, pay taxes. If we step out of line, we're closed for fifteen days. Next time it's six months, and we're dead. No more club." He grabbed a towel. "We've kept up the tradition since Le Chat Noir opened in 1890. Keep our nose clean and continue shining the red light of Pigalle, Moulin Rouge and the Folies Bergère. All the world knows and comes to see."

He talked the talk. Sounded like the businessman he said he was. But if his "house" was white as pearl, why did she notice the dove-grey shutters?

"You were saying," she prompted, tapping the FotoFit.

"He goes by Nico, if that's who I think you mean."

"A local?"

"A Lille accent." The bartender studied the FotoFit again. The cap, the small eyes, weak chin. "But look." Shook his head. "Too generic. This could be anyone. A dozen *mecs.* Who says it's him?"

"Who says it's not? His last victim — one who survived — came up with this description for the FotoFit."

He hesitated. "Two nights ago two men hung out at the bar. No table. Cheapskates. But if this was him, this Nico, *désolé,* I had no clue. I don't serve pedophiles."

"Have to draw the line somewhere, eh?" said René.

His lip curled. "My daughter's ten. If he's the rapist, then I'll be first in line to nail him. It's a village here," he said. "We watch our own. After closing, my bouncer walks the girls to the Métro."

This bartender had turned helpful. Too helpful? When had she gotten so jaded? Or had she caught René's skepticism?

Laughter came from the table as the

provincial drank champagne.

"Look, the *flics* questioned me about him," said the bartender. "Parents, too. I told them what I told you."

A dead end?

Maybe Johnny Hallyday kept his nose clean. Maybe business was so tough, he was a *mouche,* an informer. Everyone had to survive.

"Here's my card," she said. "I'm looking for Zazie, the girl with curly red hair. She was supposedly studying with Sylvaine, the girl who . . ." Her throat caught. "Didn't make it."

René's jaw dropped. "What?"

"Zazie told me she'd followed this *mec* here, asked me to check on him," said Aimée. "That's all I've got to go on. When do you remember seeing her?"

"Yesterday, I think, after six. A delivery came, that's right. Didn't see her anymore. Nor tonight." The bartender shook his head, his eyes serious. Noticed her baby bump. "Look, I'm a father, too. I live here. Trust me to put out the word."

Outside on humid rue Pierre Fontaine, the lights of theater marquees and clubs glittered in the descending twilight. Shouts came from the bars. The news from a car radio idling at the curb spilled over the cobbled street: *World Cup fever gripping Paris . . . In other news, the Ministry issued a statement denying police corruption and blackmail rumors . . .*

"Why didn't you tell me, Aimée?"

As if she'd had time? "It's all happened so fast. But I need your help. Zazie disappeared close to seven hours ago."

"Zazie?" René's mouth quivered. "But I saw her at the office — what's happened?"

She opened the passenger door of René's Citroën — a DS classic resembling an armadillo — sat and explained. René paced back and forth on the narrow pavement, listening through the open window.

"First, I need to call Saj in to help with our taxes," she said.

"On it," René said. "He got back from Mumbai this afternoon. Already got him reviewing fiscal data and estimates."

A wave of relief flooded her. She was confident Saj, their part-time hacker, refreshed after his meditation ashram, could take that over so she and René could focus on finding Zazie.

"Do you believe this *mec,* who runs a bowl of *merde?*" said René, disgust in his voice.

She didn't care if René had history here. A drunken brawl when he was a student? Some students Pigalle'd it as a rite of passage.

"No doubt he's *un mouche,* an informer, too." She put her hand on her tummy. "René, that's how the *flics* navigate here. Not pretty, but informers . . ."

"Talk for a price," René interrupted. "Nothing's free around here. It might not be the gangland of the fifties and sixties, but Pigalle's still so sleazeville, the peep shows, stripteases, massage parlors."

She'd wondered why René was so ticked off about this place. "My father's first beat with Morbier around here emptied the stardust from his eyes. Corsicans, North Africans and Auvergnats ran a tight network and owned all the clubs," she said, keeping her eye on the street. Hoping for that unmistakable curly red hair. "Policed their own, according to him. *'Entre nous,'* they'd say, settling scores if a pimp was murdered, if there was a jealous boyfriend, a waiter who robbed the till."

"Some noble code?" René snorted. "You make them sound chivalrous."

"We've got to find Zazie, René," she said. "Use whatever works, *non?*"

She noticed the charcoal smudge of loom-

59

ing clouds. Amidst the bars, massage parlors and sex shops across the way, the Moulin Rouge's magic glitter had tarnished. A remnant of the past, if that.

"Can you trust him, Aimée?"

"Until he proves otherwise. Don't read me wrong, René," she said. "Takes a thief to find a thief. With a rapist on the loose, who better to spread the word than a seedy Pigalle club owner? According to Zazie, this is the third girl assaulted in six months."

Concern furrowed René's brow. "So there must be a signature, the rapist's MO," he said. "These serial attackers all have a specific method. A ritual, an obsession. That's what this is, you watch. A serial killer in the making. Not only *l'Amérique* has serial killers, Aimée."

He didn't need to tell her.

"Like Landru," René went on. "He preyed on World War I widows — lured them via the personal ads, raped and murdered them. Then raided their bank accounts."

Not this again. All those thrillers and true-crime books he devoured. The bookcases in his studio apartment bulged. They were supposed to be a cyber detective agency, but Aimée knew René secretly imagined himself as another kind of detective as well.

Meanwhile, she needed to find Zazie. Who

else could she ask for help? She tried Morbier's office. Was put on hold.

A horn blared in the street, and she half-listened to René, who went on and on about serial-killer signature styles over the canned hold music. Her feet hurt. "Your point, René?"

"We're dealing with a pedophile, probably of arrested sexual development, who rapes twelve-year-old girls," he said. "Say the rapist's using the chaos of the World Cup crowds, the Fête de la Musique and the disconnect within the Commissariat branches as a cover for his activities. Say he's an insider."

"Like one needs to be an insider to know the forces don't cooperate?" she said. "Try paying a parking ticket and you discover that."

"There's always more to it, Aimée."

A voice came on the line. "Direct inquiries and messages for Commissaire Morbier to extension two-zero-four, *s'il vous plaît.*"

Gone on leave. The *flic* at Sylvaine's had been right. Worse yet, he'd not told her. Whenever she needed Morbier, he became elusive. They had a problematic relationship — at best. He'd neglected to mention his plans when he'd taken her for lunch last week — a pretext, she'd discovered, for hounding her to register for Lamaze classes over the lobster terrine.

She pictured his napkin tucked under his chin and spread across the front of his brown corduroy jacket, his age-spotted hands working the silver cheese knife.

"Pwah, Leduc," he'd said, snapping his fingers for *l'addition*. He took a last swig of Kir Royale and pulled out his pack of Gauloises. "Aah *non,* secondhand smoke, *c'est interdit au bébé.*"

Champagne and cigarettes, the two things she missed most.

"I hope you read those baby books I gave you and have given some thought to a name."

"What's the hurry?" She sipped an *express décaféiné* and clenched her other fist. For two centimes she'd rip that cigarette packet from his pocket. Take just one puff.

"Have you signed up for that cooking class yet?" He peered down at the bill through his readers, the bags under his eyes darker than usual. Slapped some francs on the tablecloth. Only enough for a tip. She hated how they'd dined off his reputation. Or maybe the waiter was his informer.

"Tell Franck *délicieux, comme toujours.*"

"*Oui,* Commissaire." The waiter bowed and slipped the wad in his pocket.

"You'll get nailed for doing that one day, Morbier," she said.

His drooping basset-hound eyes narrowed. "Leduc, I hope you've redeemed the coupon for Maman et Moi yoga sessions that Jeanne recommended."

Jeanne, his former grief counselor, now his new squeeze. Like two mother hens.

"Have you told Melac yet?"

With a suicidal ex-wife and his daughter in a coma? Tell him as he camped by her hospital bed in Brittany? She kept putting off returning his calls.

"That's my business, Morbier."

"Still haven't, eh? He's the father of your child, Leduc," he'd chided.

A rumble of thunder, crack of lighting brought her back to Pigalle, the heavy evening air. Oppressive, like in that horrific bedroom on rue de Rochechouart. Zazie. She had to find Zazie.

"Earth to Aimée," René said. "Call your hormones to order. Did you hear me? I said this all seems similar to the Guy Georges case — a rapist who goes for a specific type. They're secretive, lead hidden lives."

She shuddered. "René, I saw poor Sylvaine. Her mother lashed out at me, so terrified, so full of shame her daughter would be seen that way. So helpless. So sad."

63

"Of course, it's affected you," René said. "I'm sorry."

"Because I'm pregnant? It would sicken anyone. An innocent child, broken and violated. Dead. And I'm afraid for Zazie."

René grimaced. "What about Zazie's friends, her classmates who might know where she went? Aren't the *flics* putting out a net?"

Aimée gave him more details. "Virginie's calling everyone. The Brigade des Mineurs will search for her — as a witness, not as a missing person."

"What's this?" He gestured to the file sticking out of her bag.

"Zazie's 'report.' "

"How she trailed the rapist?" René shook his head. "Trying to be a detective."

"My fault, René. I should have stopped her."

"Stop a thirteen-year-old? Impossible." René shook his head. "She's like you. When you get something in your head, a tank won't stop you."

The sky opened up. René jumped into the car.

"Where's your police scanner?" She'd given him one for his birthday a few years ago.

René hooked up the console wires under

64

his dashboard and flicked the scanner on. Static and intermittent bursts of conversation accompanied the thwack of the windshield wipers. René switched on the interior light as Aimée moved the passenger seat back and spread the newspaper clippings and Zazie's scrawled notes out on the leather dashboard.

Zazie had clipped articles from *Le Parisien*'s *faits divers* section. In the past six months there had been two attacks on young girls, each twelve years old. The girls attended the Lycée-Collège Lamartine and Collège-Lycée Jules-Ferry, both located in the ninth arrondissement. The attacks showed similar modi operandi. After returning home from school alone, the victims were bound and gagged; unable to call for help, they were left undiscovered for several hours until family members returned.

"Parents let their kids go home alone that young?" René shook his head.

Get real, she almost said. Instead she made a mental note to sign her child up for after-school programs.

"I did. From the time I was eight."

Since the day she returned from school on a rainy March afternoon to an empty apartment. Her American mother had packed up all her things. Left and never come back.

Aimée shivered. Made herself continue reading. "Look here. Discovered blind-folded, mouths taped and tied up."

None of the victims had been able to identify or describe the attacker. No more details.

"I saw duct tape on the floor by Sylvaine," she said, suppressing a shudder.

"That doesn't explain the FotoFit," René said.

"Zazie said Mélanie was able to give some description to the composite artist," she said. "She must have glimpsed him some-how."

Aimée paged through Zazie's grid-lined Claire-Fontaine notebook: notes on Bar NeoCancan, the list of schools. An unfin-ished map sketched in pencil with Xs. No street names, Métro stations or recogniz-able landmarks.

René looked over her shoulder. "Could be anywhere," he said.

She hiked up her black linen agnès b. shift from last summer's sales, glad of the Cit-roën's roof between her and the pounding rain. All they needed was AC.

"Zazie mentioned a pattern. So far, there's their age, the fact they were latchkey kids, the same arrondissement," she said.

René pulled out his large-format navy blue Paris plan, the kind used by taxi drivers. Thumbed through. *"Et voilà."* He stabbed his finger on the page of the ninth arrondissement. "The two schools are here. And rue de Rochechouart, where Sylvaine was attacked, borders the ninth, which makes a triangle. Each school's on the edge of the arrondissement: northwest, southeast . . . and if Sylvaine attended Collège-Lycée Jacques-Decour, the northeast."

She nodded. "A pattern the *flics* didn't notice? But the school parents, from what Zazie told me, had gone up in arms at the Commissariat."

"What do the girls have in common?" said René. "A special type, a look? The fact he knew no one was at home?"

"We need more," she said. "But I know Sylvaine took music lessons. The violin."

René nodded. Excitement in his large, green eyes. "I'll get on it. What if the others took lessons, too?"

Aimée traced her finger on the fogged-up windshield. "Why did the others survive and Sylvaine didn't?" she said.

"He's amped up?" René said. "Something's thrown him off."

Her heart fluttered as she realized something. "Say his timing was off when he attacked Sylvaine. She wasn't alone — Zazie was there. He didn't know, she surprised him, which made him even more violent this time. Or . . ."

"Or she really wasn't there," said René. "Keep that possibility in the mix."

What if Zazie had lied?

But what if she hadn't? Time was slipping by as they hashed this out. René hit the defroster, and she thought hard, watching as the fog began to clear from the car's windshield. She wanted to act. Do something. Now.

"Why hasn't Zazie come home, called, met me when she said she would? That's not like her, René. She wanted my help."

"Don't you remember being thirteen? What if she . . . Let's say with all this World Cup fever, she goes to a party. She's afraid to come home, knows she'll get in trouble."

Excuses. He didn't want to face it. Neither did she. But something niggled at her.

"True, it feels off," she admitted. "What if she's hiding from him because she witnessed something? Or . . ." Or he'd got her, but she couldn't say it.

A burst of techno music blasted from the window of a car, reverberating off the Haussmannian apartment buildings.

René's lips pursed. Then he grabbed

Aimée's arm. "Where did Zazie get this night photo?" asked René. "What if one of these is the man from the FotoFit?"

He held up the black-and-white photo from Zazie's notebook, with the night street scene taken from above: several men, a few wearing hoodies, stood near a Wallace fountain. Boys from the *lycée,* it looked like.

Now she remembered. "Taken with a telephoto lens. Zazie mentioned she needed to use her friend's camera."

René pointed to the Wallace Fountain in the picture. "I'll drive around until I find it."

"Every *quartier* has them, René. It could be anywhere. It's hard to tell the location from this angle." Tall, cast iron and forest green, the Wallace fountains had been donated by a philanthropic Englishman after the ravages of the Commune. They were once the only safe public drinking water.

"Bon," he said, pulling on his driving gloves. "I'll use Zazie's map to identify the streets. You can ask Virginie if any of her friends live on them."

Thank God she had his help. At almost six months pregnant, feeling like a whale in slow motion, she appreciated his taking on this legwork. Meanwhile she'd see if

Mélanie had heard from Zazie.

"I'll take you to the office first," he said.

As if she were an invalid.

"Drop me at the *clinique* on rue de la Grange-Batelière, René," she said. "Zazie's friend Mélanie should be able to shed more light on this."

A few blocks away at the clinic, she hefted herself up and out of the car. The downpour had stopped. Rain-freshened air layered with lime blossom greeted her. She breathed the scent deep into her lungs. Her neck un-knotted.

But the evening duty nurse at the clinic shook her head. "Discharged," she said, checking her screen in the darkly lit reception.

To Aimée's further questions, she shrugged. "Patient confidentiality precludes my giving information."

Great. A wasted trip.

She called the café. Virginie had left to meet with the Brigade des Mineurs, but Pierre, after a breathless search of the kitchen, tracked down Mélanie's address.

Aimée would question the girl at home, hoping against hope that Zazie had con-tacted her. Figuring it counterproductive to score a taxi in the snarled traffic on the tree-lined Grands Boulevards, she took the

Métro. Changed once and exited on the platform at Liège, her favorite station, joining crowds scurrying by the blue-and-white, mosaic-tiled scenes of the old Flemish city.

Near a teeming café *terrasse*, she found the bus stop. Just in time to catch the 68 uphill toward Clichy. It was chock-full of passengers, standing room only. An elder whiskered gentleman offered her a seat, and she didn't refuse.

Heaven. She pulled out her water and prenatal vitamin packets and popped a mouthful.

The bus ground upward in the dark, passing limestone buildings whose pale blue shutters and iron-grille balconies glowed from the lights within. Past the evening crowds under the marquee of the bright Casino de Paris, behind which once extended the Duc de Richelieu's pleasure gardens of Tivoli, home to the long-gone pavilion where Louis XV supped with Madame de Pompadour.

She got off by a weathered building — a nineteenth-century debtor's prison, now apartments with a fruit shop and tailor on the ground floor. Aimée reached her destination, the shadowed rue Ballu, where an almost palpable hush descended. It was a world apart from rue de Clichy, the bustling thoroughfare that had once been the Roman road to Rouen. Rue Ballu was upscale, she noted, and exclusive, gardens and cobbled entry passages leading to lanes with *hôtels particuliers* behind grilled gates.

She'd forgotten to ask Pierre for the building code. Stupid! But she didn't have to wait long before a dog barked. "Done your business? *Bon.*" Footsteps and little sniffs sounded behind her. A figure punched numbers in the digicode.

She pretended to root in her Birkin. "Sorry to disturb you . . ."

A click and the foyer lights flashed on, illuminating a grey-haired woman with a Westie on a leash.

"Forgot the new code again?" she said, irritation in her voice. "Should write it down. It's been three days now."

So right after Mélanie's attack they'd changed the code. Smacked of locking the barn door after the horse bolted. But if everyone was as trusting as this woman, Aimée wasn't surprised the rapist had gained entry.

The woman held the blue metal-grille gate open, and Aimée slipped inside. "*Merci,* Madame." Aimée paused, still rummaging in her bag, until the woman entered a building on the right.

A quick scan of the mailboxes revealed Vasseur at Number 7. Scents of jasmine drifted in the darkness ahead, accompanied by the chirp of crickets. She hadn't heard crickets since last summer in the Jardin du Luxembourg.

Off a cobbled lane to the right stood Number 7, an eighteenth-century town-house, its garden sloping up from the two Mercedes parked in front. Some remnant of the Tivoli, she figured. A welcome mist splashed her from the fountain, which was backed by trellised ivy and surrounded by bulbous orange and pink roses, reminding her of the countryside. Not bad for the center of Paris. A cause for envy for the other few million Parisians who slogged up narrow stairs to a closet-sized apartment with a window overlooking a wall.

A lighted window on the upper floor faced the side garden. About to knock on the carved wooden door, Aimée heard a woman shouting. "I couldn't leave the merger negotiations again!"

A man's raised voice. "That's your answer for everything. She's your daughter, too. But shipping her off to a Swiss clinic?"

A door slammed shut.

So this jewel of an eighteenth-century townhouse didn't bring with it happiness for these high-roller parents and their suffering daughter. The front door opened before she could knock. Streams of light blinded her as a man rushed out. Stepping back, she lost her balance. Felt an arm grab hers.

"Who are you?"

"Monsieur Vasseur?" she said, pulling her heel out of the gravel. Her eyes adjusted to the light, and she kept talking. Bad mood or not, she needed his information. "I'm Aimée Leduc. *Excusez-moi,* but . . ."

"What are you doing here?" The man scowled. Tall, with thinning, blond, side-combed hair and narrow eyes, he wore a rumpled suit.

"Zazie's parents, the Duclos, gave me your address," she said. "Forgive me for showing up like this, but Zazie's disappeared."

"Who?"

"Your daughter Mélanie's friend."

"I'm sorry, but I don't know all of Mélanie's friends. Afraid I can't help you." His voice assumed a gloss. He jingled the car keys in his palm, impatient to leave.

"I wouldn't trouble you, but it's crucial," she said. "I need to speak to Mélanie. Zazie might have called her."

"Impossible." A brittle finality sounded in his voice.

"Another girl was raped tonight. She died en route to the hospital. And Zazie's missing . . ."

"Claude . . . Claude, who's that?" came a woman's voice from the foyer.

"Talk to my wife."

With that, he got into a Mercedes, started the ignition. The window rolled down. "I'm sorry, truly sorry, but . . ." he said. Then pulled out, spitting gravel.

Great.

The tall woman in a designer suit stood silhouetted against the lit doorframe. Mascara streaks trailed down her cheeks.

"Madame Vasseur, I know it's a bad time, but please, we need to talk."

"I'm not in a sociable mood right now," she said, about to close the door.

"I wouldn't describe this as a social call. Mélanie's friend Zazie is missing. Please let me speak with Mélanie. Just five minutes."

"We can't help you," she said. "Mélanie's not here."

Sent to the Swiss clinic already?

"Can you tell me what happened?"

"Like I want to go over the whole thing again? My daughter is traumatized."

"I'm sorry," she said. "But Zazie decided to trail the rapist after what happened to Mélanie. He attacked again tonight, and now Zazie is missing. There's a connection. If Mélanie's rapist took Zazie . . ."

"How do you know it's the same man?" Madame Vasseur interrupted.

"That's what I need to find out. Any information, anything Mélanie told you or anything you saw will help."

Madame Vasseur shook her head. "He violated my daughter, our home . . . I won't relive that."

"But he has raped another girl, and this one didn't make it. She died in the ambulance several hours ago."

Madame Vasseur gasped. She grabbed the doorframe. "You mean . . . ?"

"Do you understand?" Aimée gripped the woman's arm. "Zazie's parents are desperate to find her." Aimée stepped inside. "Please, it's vital you help me."

Madame Vasseur led her into a salon with carved moldings, a chandelier and large abstract paintings on the paneled walls. Taken from the pages of an architectural magazine — a showpiece without a lived-in feeling.

Madame Vasseur poured herself a glass of Burgundy. "Wine?"

Tempted, Aimée shook her head. *"Non, merci."*

She sat down on a maroon-suede couch,

gestured for Aimée to do the same. Took out a pack of cigarettes, lit one and offered the pack to Aimée.

"Much as I'd like to . . ."

"Ah, *d'accord.*" She eyed the bulge in Aimée's middle. "Pregnancy's a bitch, I remember. Then joy of joys, potty training."

A real candidate for mother of the year, Madame Vasseur. She sat back, blew a plume of smoke and kicked off her heels. Talk about rubbing it in. Aimée wanted to tear that cigarette out of her mouth and that wine out of her hand.

A tan pigskin Hermès briefcase lay open on the couch, revealing files and legal documents. The woman tapped her cigarette ash into a blue bowl, distracted.

"Mélanie was attacked three days ago, as I understand?" Aimée said to prompt her.

"My husband, Claude, found Mélanie," she said, her voice hollow. "When he returned from work."

"Any sign of forced entry, anything stolen?"

Madame Vasseur shook her head. "Nothing was touched but my daughter. But Claude blames me because I worked late. I'm prosecuting a huge case. Three years of litigation, and they threatened to bow out. I had to hold their hands."

Aimée's blood ran cold. What about holding her daughter's hand?

"I know it's painful, but can you give me any details of Mélanie's attack?" she said.

"The maid didn't work that afternoon. Claude thinks Mélanie returned at nine P.M. Like usual."

Usual? "Isn't that late for a twelve-year-old to come home?"

"She was coming from her violin lesson," Madame Vasseur said. Aimée thought of Sylvaine's scattered music, the stickered calendar. "Her teacher's not a day person. She takes pupils after school and in the evening. We gave Mélanie taxi money like always. At ten thirty P.M. he found her in the conservatory . . . her music room."

More than an hour alone after the attack before her father found her? Horrible. But it fit the pattern.

"Mélanie couldn't reach the phone? Was she bound or taped?"

"Traumatized, I told you," she said, downing the wine and pouring herself another glass. *"Mais* tied up and her mouth taped, *oui."*

Like the other girls.

"After the medical examination, Claude brought her to the clinic. She wouldn't talk. They told us not to push her or insist."

"But she described the rapist to the composite artist. He looks like this." Aimée showed the FotoFit to her. "Seen him? Maybe a gardener or delivery man at a shop, someone in the *quartier*?"

Madame Vasseur shrugged. "No one I recognize. Could be anyone."

"What did Mélanie tell you?"

"Wouldn't talk about it."

"But she talked to Zazie."

"Red-haired girl, intense?" she asked, with a raise of her eyebrow.

Aimée nodded.

"I know her mother, Virginie. She runs a café, nice. We've met at the *lycée*," said Madame Vasseur, the wine she drank thawing her out. "Claude and I are both lawyers. We work a lot. When Mélanie bonded with Zazie, I was happy. You know, Claude's more *le snob*. But I let Mélanie come home by herself after school. Mélanie said she was too old for the maid to babysit her. I trust her. She's always been a responsible, focused girl. Well, mostly. She's brilliant. A musical prodigy."

Madame Vasseur gestured to a framed photo. In it a young blonde girl wearing an expensive-looking silk dress and grinning to reveal braces posed with a violin beside an older man and a smiling young couple arm-in-arm. "That's Mélanie at her last recital, at a student exhibition sponsored by the Lavignes. Monsieur Lavigne, the elder, with his son Renaud and new daughter-in-law. They're old family friends and supporters of the Conservatoire de Musique. Mélanie is eligible to try out for the Conservatoire this year, and I insisted. No negotiation on that."

Aimée heard a catch in Madame Vasseur's voice.

"Insisted? Do you mean Mélanie seemed reluctant to try out for the Conservatoire, Madame?"

"Think back to when you were twelve," she said, exhaling a plume of smoke. "You rebel against your parents. Everything matters, the way a boy looks at you, or doesn't look at you. Life's heightened, magnified. The world turns on what someone says, on being accepted by your peers — or not."

Mélanie sounded sensitive. But hadn't Aimée felt the same at that age, too?

A few more sips of wine and Madame Vasseur revealed she'd missed seeing Zazie at the clinic last night. She'd found Mélanie asleep and, after conferring with the doctor, sent her to Lausanne this afternoon.

"But what about school?"

"She'll retake the exams in September.

And the violin lessons, well . . . we'll see."

At least Aimée had an idea about where to go next. "What's Mélanie's violin teacher's name and address?" she asked.

"Madame de Langlet, a former professor at the Conservatoire. She's very selective. Her studio's in Square d'Orléans."

Aimée made a note. Not far away. "That's important, Madame. Tonight's victim was also assaulted after a violin lesson."

"N'importe quoi," she replied. "As I told you, Madame's quite selective. She only takes pupils of Mélanie's caliber."

"Selective or not, there could be a link, Madame."

"Then you'd need to speak with her." Madame Vasseur sighed. She opened her mouth as if to say something but took a sip of wine instead. "But I'll fight those battles over lessons when I come to them."

"Battles?"

"Mélanie's so gifted. I want her to continue with the violin."

Sounded like Mélanie didn't.

"Do you think I could talk with Mélanie at the clinic?" Aimée paused. "With your permission, of course."

Madame Vasseur stared at Aimée, almost as if she was seeing her for the first time. "Mélanie's withdrawn into a shell, the doctor said. She won't speak to anyone. Look, on Friday, when I visit, I'll ask her, as long as there's a way to avoid more stress."

Friday . . . too late.

"Does your husband know more about the attack? Would he know what Mélanie told Zazie?"

Madame Vasseur shook her head. "He blames me. He's good at that." She rolled her eyes, which had reddened. "For six months after Mélanie was born, I stayed home, cared for her, put my whole career on hold and devoted myself to her." Madame Vasseur took a long sip of wine. "It sliced me in two to go back to work. I cried for days, wondering if I had made the right decision. Financially I didn't have to, but — you'll face this too — work fulfills in ways motherhood doesn't. And you'll have to choose. No one ever tells you a double standard exists. Women work hard at the job and harder at home."

She let out a sigh. Globed lights outside the tall windows illuminated the garden hedge with a golden sheen. "You're always supposed to be a mother first, no matter what. That's a man's attitude. You're up all night with their colic, then it's bronchitis, the teacher meetings, the clean clothes, the lost homework . . . that's your life. Six A.M.

82

you're up to do it again."

Madame Vasseur, chic in her Dior suit, did not appear to have gotten up at six this morning. Aimée doubted she'd ever made the school run. She wondered about the woman's relationship with her husband.

Fueled by the Burgundy, she grew more maudlin with every sip. "Think I sound like a cold bitch, *n'est-ce pas*? I just wish someone had told me." She gave a little shake of her head. "Another piece of advice. Peach-pit oil works magic on stretch marks."

An angry, driven, unhappy woman. A townhouse in an exclusive enclave, an attorney's power and salary; she was a woman with almost everything. Aimée reflected — could this be her in the future, determined to run Leduc Detective at the cost of her child?

"May I read your police statement, Madame?"

"Claude handled everything at the Commissariat." She waved her cigarette in a dismissive gesture. "My daughter's safe now. Away, nothing to do with this or you."

Au contraire, she almost said. "Just this afternoon Zazie told me Mélanie had shared disturbing things with her. She attempted to surveil this rapist Mélanie described. Asked for my help. Now she's missing, after

Sylvaine was raped and murdered. Don't you see? If there's anything, anything at all . . ."

A phone trilled. Madame Vasseur rifled in her matching tan pigskin Hermès bag and pulled two out, glanced at the display of the one that was vibrating. "A client. I need to take this. I've helped you enough."

She called that help? Time was running out.

"*Bonsoir,* Monsieur Haldane," Madame Vasseur said, "no disturbance at all. *Quoi?* The requisition? It's on my home computer. One moment." She stood in her stocking feet. "You know the way out."

Gracious, too.

But she needed to pee. "May I use your bathroom?"

The woman waved as she walked none too steadily down the hall.

Madame Vasseur's second cell phone peeped out of the bag. Her personal phone. Aimée slid it out and scrolled down the numbers dialed. The third one showed a Swiss country code. The fourth was labeled "M." With her kohl eye pencil, she wrote both numbers on her palm, then nicked one of Madame Vasseur's business cards.

This house gave off an antiseptic aura. Expensive art on the walls, Philippe Starck furniture, period detail — but it felt lifeless. For show. In the state-of-the-art kitchen, she searched for photos and found one attached to the stainless-steel refrigerator by a red magnet: a blonde girl barefoot in the garden wearing pink Levi's and matching pink sunglasses — the same smiling girl from the photo Madame had showed her. The only other evidence of Mélanie.

As she closed the front door, her mind reeled through what she'd discovered, trying to piece together connections — cheese-shop owners and high-ticket lawyers, both with daughters who attended *lycées* in the ninth arrondissement. So far she'd learned Mélanie's music teacher's name and that both girls studied the violin, were blonde and wore pink.

Zazie attended school in the *quartier,* she was a redhead, and she played video games, not the violin. If the rapist had a type, which it seemed he did, Zazie wasn't it.

But could she be a hostage, taken because she knew too much? Murdered?

Hurrying down rue Ballu, she punched the Swiss number into her phone. After a series of rings, a recorded message came on: "You have reached Clinique Berzeval. Please call back during business hours from nine A.M. to noon and two P.M. to six P.M."

She tried the number from Madame Vasseur's list that had been labeled *M,* hoping it was Mélanie's. The phone rang once. "Message box is full." If it really was Mélanie's number, the clinic might have put her in psychiatric lockdown, cutting off her contact with the outside world.

Both numbers led nowhere fast. Questions — that was all she had.

A girl had been raped and murdered; Zazie still hadn't made contact, and there was no trace of her to be found. Aimée wanted to throw something. If she had known Zazie would immediately break her promise not to go investigating, Aimée would have made her do her homework right there in the office where she could keep an eye on her. Talked some sense into her.

Worry roiled her stomach. Intent on Madame Vasseur's phone, she'd forgotten to pee.

At a café downhill on rue Blanche, she made her way to the WC, past the crowd waiting for the quarterfinals on the *télé.* On France2 a news bulletin flashed:

Reggae star Jimmy Cliff will perform an open-air concert during the Fête de la Mu-

sique in honor of the Jamaica versus Argentina match. In Marseilles, a curfew was announced after violent confrontations between British and Tunisian football fans, provoking an all-country security alert and extra CRS patrols in Paris.

All resources were focused on rioting football fans. What about the little girls being raped? Welcome to World Cup Paris 1998, she thought, disgusted.

She put a franc down on the counter as a courtesy, since she hadn't ordered anything. Her wrist was grabbed by an old lady perched on a café stool who was ignoring the blaring *télé.* The old woman's red-rimmed eyes bored into Aimée. "You know where rue Blanche's name came from?"

Aimée shook her head. Extricated her hand from the woman's cold and dry, claw-like fingers. Too much to drink, lonely, crazy or all three?

"The gypsum, as white as my hair," said the old woman. "The Romans used to cart it down this street from the Montmartre quarries."

Aimée had learned that in school. Before the old woman could expound more, she snuck out.

Outside, she punched in René's number.

"René, we've got to follow up with a Madame de Langlet, Mélanie's violin teacher." She ran down her encounter with Madame Vasseur and gave him the information.

She heard him sucking in his breath. "I'm afraid things are verging on ugly. There's trouble here in Pigalle."

"Trouble? But I'm near Pigalle."

She heard shouting in the background.

"What's going on, René?" she asked, uneasy. "Has something happened to Zazie?"

"Parents taking things into their own hands."

"Gone vigilante?" She'd been afraid of this. The *flics* should have put two and two together much earlier.

"Seems you inspired the owner of the NeoCancan to stir something up all right. A witch-hunt."

"Like I should feel guilty?" she said, walking faster. "Time someone took notice and did something."

"More than notice . . . they're by Place Saint-Georges, chasing this *mec* down."

She froze in her tracks. "They found the rapist?"

"Forget it, Aimée," he said. "The area's not safe."

88

"The hell it's not safe. What about Zazie? If this *mec*'s the one . . . we'll find Zazie."

She glanced at her Tintin watch. Nine thirty P.M. Ahead, a few slick-haired barkers were enjoining young men to step inside a club. Only a few steps away in a rose-trellised courtyard, she saw children kicking a soccer ball, smelled frying garlic from an open window with lace curtains. The streets buzzed below Pigalle in the hot night.

"I'm en route." She clicked off. Three and a half blocks downhill the streets changed, steam-cleaned limestone facades rising above chic Place Saint-Georges, the round-about featuring a statue of Gavarni and ringed by upscale *hôtels particuliers*.

Off to the left, down an unrestored cobbled street, she spotted René. As she approached the corner, she heard shouting. People congregated, a jeering crowd spilling onto the street, and she made out smeared blood on a stone wall.

René caught her arm. "Don't go up there, Aimée," he said. "Not wise to get close."

But she had to see.

Several members of the crowd were kicking a man crumpled on the pavement beneath the flashlight glare provided by others. Blood streamed from his shaved head onto the cobbled gutter. His clothing was torn. "Filthy pedophile," said a woman and spat on him. "Gutter's too good for you."

"That's a lynch mob," Aimée said, shivering. "We've got to stop them."

"I tried. Long past the point where we can help now."

The mob's elongated silhouettes bounced off the stone wall, the beating a horrific shadow play. Sirens wailed up the street.

"Time we take the law into our hands since the police haven't," a man shouted, lifting up a wallet. "He's got pictures of little girls here, thinks he's going to do it again."

Someone else yelled, "The animal raped my neighbor's daughter. Killed her." More dull thuds as people kicked the moaning figure.

It was medieval. All they lacked were torches and rope. The sweat dried cold under her arms.

"Call the *flics,* René," she said.

"*Zut,* I have, Aimée. Let's go."

But she moved forward, shouldering her way through the crowd with René following, trying to tug her back. Somehow she had to make them stop. To reason with them. "We need him to talk," she shouted into the crowd. "To tell where he's taken another girl. You'll get your justice."

"Fat chance," a woman said.

She heard a sickening crunch as the heel of a boot landed on the man's bleeding, cracked head.

"Stop, don't you understand? He has to talk," she said. "A girl's life is at stake."

The man's body spasmed in the gutter. Sirens wailed closer.

"Merde, the *flics,"* someone said. The crowd scattered. A hush fell. The only sound was the water trickling into the gutter and pooling with blood.

Aimée stepped back in horror. René pulled her arm. "Come on, Aimée."

"But I think they . . . we've got to get him help."

"Too late. We need to get the hell out of here."

"But if he knows . . . knew where Zazie is . . . there might be something . . ."

René grabbed her. "Listen to me. Village justice, mob violence — call it what you want, but you can't be implicated, understand? That won't help Zazie."

It made sense. The discarded wallet lay by the streetlamp, wallet-sized photos of little girls spilling out.

"See, Aimée, he's a pedophile. But it's not our business."

She used her sleeve to pick up the soggy pictures and turned them over. *Tessa aged seven, Tessa aged nine, Tessa at confirmation* . . . A horrible taste filled her mouth. "René, look." She pulled out his *carte d'identité:* Nico Destael. "He's from Lille, a merchant seaman."

René grabbed the wallet from her with his handkerchief, rubbed it off just in case, and threw it back on the ground. Sirens echoed in the canyons formed by the dense Haussmann buildings. He dragged her around the corner and pushed her into the Citroën, switched on the ignition and ground into first.

Terse messages erupted on the police scanner. "Alert . . ."

She felt numb. Useless. It was all her fault.

"I'm not condoning mob mentality, Aimée, but they dispensed their own justice," said René, checking his rearview mirror. "Now let them deal with it. He attacked their children. It's their battle."

That didn't make it right — especially if they had picked the wrong man. She felt sick to her stomach.

Sweat beaded René's brow. He pulled his Glock from his pocket and opened the glove compartment.

Aimée gasped. "René, tell me you weren't going to use that."

"Didn't have to," he said.

"What happened tonight?" she asked. "Where did that mob come from?"

"They held a candlelight vigil in front of Sylvaine's. Things got out of hand." His knuckles whitened on the steering wheel. "He raped and killed a twelve-year-old girl. Put yourself in the parents' place. Don't tell me you wouldn't do the same thing if you had to."

She had a little life stirring inside her. Part of her wondered what she would do to protect it. And it scared her.

"First I'd find out where Zazie is. Then . . . I don't know."

But guilt invaded her. It had already been a powder-keg situation, and she'd lit the fuse, fanned the flame by showing the FotoFit around, pointing out the man to the NeoCancan owner. Doubt gnawed in the back of her mind.

"René, those pictures . . ."

"You're saying what, Aimée?"

"What if they were his daughters?"

"That's up to the investigating team."

"But what if he's not the rapist?" she said. "What if Zazie was wrong?"

Monday, 10 P.M.

Cold air didn't keep the sweat from trickling down Zacharié's spine in the vaulted stone cellar where his team had rendezvoused. The cellar was a former foundry nestled underneath rue Condorcet's wrought-iron shop, a purveyor of cast-iron plaques cast made from sixteenth-century Versailles molds. Firebacks and wrought-iron railing samples were piled by remnants of the old smelter. No one would ever think they had planned a heist down here.

"*C'est normal.* Changing the plan ups the price," said Jules, matter-of-fact. "So I'm offering to increase your take twenty-five percent."

Not that Zacharié was here for the money — not anymore. Jules had threatened Marie-Jo; Zacharié had no choice but to cooperate until he could figure out how to extricate himself. His plan was to try to demonstrate

94

the crew's expertise to Jules firsthand — he still hoped to take himself out of the operation.

"Ten thousand spreads the butter. Up front," said Dervier.

Dervier's three-man team — Tandou, the digger; Ramu, the locksmith; and Gilou, the trust-fund bobo who sidelined in *explosifs* — nodded. They were the best at what they did. Zacharié knew; he'd gone to school with them — *la classe de crime,* they'd joked. This Pigalle *quartier,* where the affluent lived amongst blue collars and émigrés roughed the edges, hadn't changed since they were kids — apart from the flocks of trendy bobos moving in and upscaling rue des Martyrs. The now aging *ancien régime* generation still rented out their upper-floor *chambres de bonnes* to the poor, only now the latter didn't work as servants, they just slaved to pay rent.

Jules took an envelope from his suit jacket. "*Bon,* show me your plan. Here's a deposit."

Gilou counted the bills with his manicured fingers. He looked up with a smile and nodded to Dervier.

"*Alors,* it's a simple in and out," Dervier said and pulled a map down from the wall. Zacharié tried not to wince at Dervier's lisp or the spittle on his chin that accompanied

95

it. But then outlining the break-in plan with a split tongue couldn't be easy.

"Can you explain how you'll navigate this segment here?" Jules pointed to the underground sewer on the map tacked to the wall.

Tandou, the big-shouldered *mec,* frowned. "I've got it covered."

These professionals hated dilettantes who contracted a job then questioned their expertise. Zacharié shot a warning look at Jules.

"Making a fuss over a simple question?" Jules said.

Why couldn't Jules leave it alone?

"The segments that appear blocked," said Dervier, "connect Gare Saint-Lazare via the old Banque de France rail tracks. Once they were used for transporting bullion, but they've gone unused since the war. They're forgotten shunting tracks."

"A fascinating historical detail, but how . . . ?"

"All you need to know," Dervier said, "is that my boys and I can navigate your several-block radius underground — in and out — in under twelve minutes."

Jules nodded. "Impressive."

"Now all I need you to tell me is how much weight we're transporting. Not ballpark — specific to a kilo, more or less."

Ten minutes later, Zacharié stood upstairs with Jules in the old shop, which was hotter than a furnace. He'd made nice with Jules, introduced the team — obvious professionals — and outlined the heist plan. Hadn't Jules said he was impressed?

Time to stand up and get out of this. Now.

"You're in good hands, Jules. Now time for me to bow out. I can't draw attention to myself. It's too dangerous, with my parole officer sniffing around. Look, the team's professional, the best there is. Consider your favor repaid, Jules."

"Repaid?" Jules shook his head. "You've just begun to repay me, Zacharié. Remember our deal? These thugs provide the window dressing. It's your expertise that makes this work."

"Count me out, Jules," he said. "My daughter's important, and I can't —"

"Let your parole officer get a sniff of this?" Jules sighed. His voice lowered. "But he'll get a big sniff if you don't. A letter from a new witness, a phone call from that old employer, and you can kiss parole adieu."

"But you can't . . . you wouldn't. That implicates you, too."

"You were inside too long, Zacharié." He gave a snort. "A little magic took care of that. I'm clean."

97

Magic? More like bribery and corruption. His stock-in-trade.

Zacharié cursed the day he'd weakened. The day he'd acted like an imbecile and gotten involved with Jules again in a moment of greed. But the man was so convincing. Zacharié had gotten caught, and now he owed Jules for his parole. Maybe Jules had planned this all along. Got him sprung for this job, which was just a front for the real nugget. Jules's take from this heist sounded more than big.

"Of course you love your daughter," Jules said. "Now prove it."

Monday, 9:30 P.M.
René idled the Citroën on Avenue Trudaine under the double row of lime trees. The quiet oasis from the red lights of Place Pigalle a few blocks away was threaded by an island row of greenery. They listened to the police scanner buzzing with static.

Hot, humid air filled the car. "We left just in time," René said, taking off his linen jacket.

"Au contraire." She wiped her brow and rooted in the back seat for a bottle of water.

"You think if we'd found the rapist first . . . what? He'd talk?"

"Un peu difficile to talk now, with a broken jaw and skull fractures, eh? René, that's assuming he's the one."

"He matches the FotoFit, Aimée."

"For now, stick to what we know — from his papers, this *mec*'s a merchant seaman from Lille. Was he stationed in Paris when

99

the attacks took place?"

"The *flics* will find out if he's on shore leave, leading a secret life in Paris, why he gets off on attacking little girls. Who the hell knows, Aimée?"

René turned up the police scanner volume. Disjointed voices, static.

"We can't sit on our behinds until he talks," she said, pushing her doubts aside. "We've got to find Zazie."

"Any more ideas?"

"Mélanie's in a Swiss clinic, traumatized and not talking. But her teacher, Madame de Langlet, is nearby on Square d'Orléans."

"It's late, Aimée," said René.

"And she's a night person, according to Mélanie's —"

"Clueless mother, from your description?" René interrupted. He gestured to the public phone cabin, getting rarer to find these days. "Better to call first."

She didn't agree — time was of the essence, and in person worked best. But he'd lumbered out of the car onto the cobbles. He was unable to reach the phone, but in the glare of the car headlight she watched him thumb through one of the directories hanging on a chain. Not for the first time it saddened her to think of all the daily obstacles he faced with his short legs. She

100

saw him punch a number into his cell phone.

A moment later he rejoined her and hit the defroster button.

"Madame de Langlet isn't answering at her *atelier de musique*. Sounds ancient, from her answering machine. I left her a message." René pointed to the map showing Place Gustave Toudouze, a block from where the beating took place. "Looks like this might be the Wallace fountain in Zazie's photo." René put the photo up on the dashboard. "And there's the kiosk and that tree. So let's say he's at the café, watches Sylvaine, I don't know, and follows her."

Aimée wiped her forehead. "But Sylvaine wouldn't come this way from the *lycée*. She'd go home down rue Turgot."

René shrugged. "Since when does any kid go right home after school?"

"You're right, she'd gone to a music lesson."

"And he sees her en route home but say she's met Zazie and . . ."

Aimée's phone trilled, and she glanced at the number. Her heart leapt. "René, it's her."

She hit answer. "Zazie! Zazie, are you all right?"

"Mademoiselle Aimée Leduc?" said a

woman's voice.

"Oui." Her throat caught. "Where's Zazie?"

"We need you to answer some questions."

A cold chill crept up her neck.

"Who's this?"

"You're familiar with the Commissariat on rue de Parme?" But the voice wasn't asking a question. "We'll expect you within ten minutes."

"Has something happened to Zazie?"

"There's a patrol car in the area," the voice continued. "Off Avenue Trudaine. If you would prefer us to escort you."

Aimée's heart was thumping so loud she thought the drunk snoring on the Commissariat bench would wake up. Why hadn't the *flics* told her anything? She sat in the Commissariat on rue de Parme, a former townhouse behind Gare Saint-Lazare, where the streets were named for European cities: Bucharest, Moscow, St. Petersburg.

The drunk shifted and drooled. From a cubicle she heard a man's raised voice, his German accent becoming more pronounced as he related his being pickpocketed in the Métro. All suspects in the district were routed through here. That hadn't changed since her father's time on the beat nor had

102

the old wire-cage holding cells filled to capacity.

A quick knock on the open-doored cubicle and then a woman in her early forties, a Madame Pelletier, from her badge, of the Brigade des Mineurs, entered and sat at the desk. She wore a Jean Paul Gaultier striped sailor shirt, jeans and espadrilles. Summoned back from holiday or going for the beach look, Aimée thought.

Madame Pelletier kept her eyes on the file she was consulting. Silent apart from a perfunctory *"Bonsoir."* The aroma of fresh-brewed coffee vied with the odor of stale cigarette rotated through the room by the ancient wall fan.

"Refresh my memory about your movements this afternoon, *s'il vous plaît.*"

Again? "You've got my statement already. I gave it to the officer at the scene of Sylvaine Olivet's attack on rue de Rochechouart a few hours ago."

"D'accord," she said, thumbing through the pages. The woman was playing catch-up, no doubt, and had just received the file herself.

"But where did you find Zazie's cell phone?" Aimée asked. At least they'd found some trace of Zazie. Score one for the *flics*. "Do you have a suspect?"

"We're proceeding in our inquiries. A man

was beaten up."

With a guilty start, Aimée realized someone had reported seeing her at the man's beating. An undercover officer?

Admit nothing, the first rule with *flics*. She looked at the police officer blankly.

"Tonight a merchant seaman was a victim of a brutal mob attack," said Madame Pelletier. "He appears to match the rapist's description, or at least the crowd thought so. So we've got a possible suspect lying in critical condition at Hôtel-Dieu. Unable to give a statement."

Her heart sank. But she'd tried to stop the crowd. What if he died?

"Why am I here?"

"I'm checking for any discrepancies in the crime-scene report on Sylvaine Olivet."

That had to mean the arriving police officer's scribbled notes didn't mesh with the crime squad's findings. Or evidence had been compromised. Bottom line: the *flics* had botched it. Minus two points.

"Zazie, I mean, Isabelle Duclos, had been en route to study with Sylvaine, the young girl who was raped and murdered this afternoon," said Aimée. "I last saw her at two P.M., and no one's had word since then. Caring for minors is your job. She's a thirteen-year-old in danger. Missing. That's what you should be investigating. Don't you understand?" She picked up a police flyer labeled KNOW YOUR QUARTIER and fanned herself. "I think Zazie witnessed Sylvaine's attack," said Aimée. "Or hid, and the rapist found her. Kidnapped her to prevent her talking . . . or worse."

"That's all conjecture at this point," said Madame Pelletier.

Like she didn't know that?

"But she's a missing minor, a possible witness. That should make her a priority. Look, my godfather's Commissaire Morbier. If he were here, he'd tell you —"

"How to do my job? Doubtful. Morbier's in a different branch. *Mais oui,* I know about you." A sigh.

Meaning the *flic* had warned her.

"Get real, Madame Leduc."

"It's mademoiselle."

"Then I'll get to the point, Mademoiselle." About time.

"Sylvaine's father denies Zazie came to study with her this Monday. Or ever. Zazie lied to her parents."

Aimée wanted to push that aside. Couldn't. Yet even if Zazie had lied, it didn't explain her disappearance. "Even if that's true . . ."

"We're treating Zazie's disappearance as

105

an unrelated case. One that isn't under our jurisdiction yet because she hasn't been missing twenty-four hours," Madame Pelletier interrupted. She tapped her pen. "The fact that she was caught in a lie tells us something about Zazie. Her parents confirmed she's lied about going to her friend Sylvaine's every Monday. There's no evidence that she ever went to rue de Rochechouart."

"Because no one saw her?" Aimée's fist clenched. "No one saw the rapist either. You can't discount the possibility that he took her as a hostage."

The officer sighed. "Nine times out of ten, missing teenage girls turn out to be runaways, or they met a boy," she said. "We found her phone on the number sixty-seven bus. Probably fell out of her pocket."

"Isn't a thirteen-year-old who might have been at the scene of a rape and murder a priority?" Aimée pulled out the newspaper clippings from Zazie's file. "Look at this, please. Zazie was following a man she thought had raped her schoolmate Mélanie Vasseur. A serial rapist who'd attacked two other girls in this arrondissement."

Madame Pelletier glanced through the clippings. Nodded. "I'm aware of these, but I can't speak to them or about our ongoing investigations." Her tone flattened. No doubt she'd said this many times. "We respond to and investigate reported crimes against minors, and in the case of Isabelle Duclos, there isn't such a crime, at least not at this time. Consult the public record, but I'm sure you know our mandate."

The standard line.

"But now there's a murder she might be connected to as a witness," said Aimée. "That's the Brigade Criminelle's turf."

"Up to *le proc* in a case involving a minor." Madame Pelletier checked her watch. "Look, back off and trust our team on this matter of the rapist, and give your friend Zazie time to come home on her own. We're professionals. The whole team is on the ground, canvasing and investigating. Let us do our work."

Tired, Aimée nodded. They had more contacts than she and René. Rape and murder cases didn't involve rocket science — just grinding work like every other case, plodding, checking details, rechecking alibis, observation, rooting out evidence, suspects, motives, and putting it together. Time-consuming legwork. Precious time lost when there was a disappeared child. She had to fire this woman up, shake the doubt out of her eyes.

"I've known Zazie since she was little," Aimée said. "This is just not like her. She's in danger. Something's very wrong."

"Everything's complicated with all the out-of-towners here for the World Cup." Madame Pelletier leaned forward. "Here's a little advice for a woman in your condition . . ."

"My condition?" Aimée sat up. Cut the condescending *merde,* she almost said. "I'm pregnant — not ill." Apart from morning sickness, cravings for kiwis and cornichons, her swelling ankles and that terror waking her up in the middle of the night.

Madame Pelletier reached forward, took her hand and patted it. "Listen, we've got team members who are parents, of course. Life goes on. It's about not letting your emotions get in the way, keeping focused. Our work deals with children, innocent victims of life's ugly side. To do this job well, you've got to compartmentalize."

She remembered the work her father brought home, the files piled on his desk and his tired smile in the morning. How he'd change the subject when she asked him about a case.

"You're blinded by your personal connection right now, and not thinking clearly about what's best for the general investigation or for the well-being of the victims. Pick your battles, Mademoiselle. This isn't one you should fight."

"That's why you called me in here? To tell me this? Warn me off?" She pulled her hand back from the condescending woman.

"We found your number on Zazie's cell phone," said Madame Pelletier, consulting the report. "Correction, her uncle's cell phone." Pause. "Okay, let's say you're right, and Zazie's involved," said Madame Pelletier, leaning back in her chair again. "You're going about it all wrong. Your sniffing around sends witnesses or informers underground. The last thing we want. After this man's beating, much of the forensic evidence we hoped to recover has been contaminated and compromised. Who knows when, or if, we'll obtain his testimony."

All her fault.

"We discover and compile evidence for *le proc.* She won't green-light a case without evidence."

Aimée got why they wanted her to stop. But she wouldn't.

"Zazie's not a criminal. She's a victim."

Her collar felt damp. Her peep-toe heels' leather instep dug into her skin, and she wanted to kick them off. The fluorescent light strip flickered over the cracked linoleum floor.

"Now get this in your head," said Madame Pelletier. "We're doing all we can and more. Top priority is tracking down the rapist. He is the only thing that would lead us to hostages, if there were any. Stay where Zazie can contact you and don't shout her head off when she rolls in at dawn sheepish and afraid." Madame Pelletier locked eyes with Aimée. "But be assured, finding her whereabouts is a high consideration for us right now."

Aimée nodded acquiescently. But her mind spun.

"By the way, Mademoiselle," Madame Pelletier said. "A woman matching your description riled up a Pigalle bar owner earlier. He in turn incited the mob, resulting in the violent chain reaction that has landed this man in the hospital." The police officer looked her in the eye. "Consider this a warning, for your own sake."

"I get it," Aimée said, wanting to kick something.

"Let us do what we do our way," said Madame Pelletier. "No informant wants to draw attention. They lay low. But we depend on them, and if all this ruckus drives them away, it will hamper our investigation. Let us do our job, and you'll see how it works.

The *quartier*'s united on this. No one likes a pedophile."

"Is the suspect conscious? Has he confessed?"

Madame Pelletier shook her head. She glanced at her phone.

"So for you it's a waiting game? But there's no time."

"We're proceeding with the investigation, Mademoiselle," she said. "Go home."

"I assume you've contacted all the numbers on Zazie's phone."

"You're mixed up, Mademoiselle Leduc. You answer questions here, not the other way around."

What else wasn't Madame Pelletier telling her? Aimée yearned to read those conflicting reports and see Zazie's cell-phone log.

Madame Pelletier looked her in the eye. "And now it is my duty to inform you that Madame Olivet, the murdered victim's mother, wants to press charges against you."

Aimée blinked. "Me? Why?"

"She claims you prevented her from taking care of her daughter."

Saddened, Aimée realized the grieving woman was trying to take control the only way she knew how. "She's devastated. Distraught. I understand. I only tried to talk her out of wiping away possible DNA

111

evidence. She lashed out and hit me." Aimée touched the still-red mark on her cheek.

It had taken all this time for Madame Pelletier to make her real point.

"Forewarned, Mademoiselle. This could turn nasty."

"Nasty? We should be focusing on her daughter's murderer now." Calm down. Act helpful. She'd learn more using her brain than her mouth. "But you're right. *Désolée.*" She aimed for contrite. "On my way out I'll copy Zazie's notes and this photo for you." She stood.

The woman expelled air from her mouth. "The copier's only for official police use. May I see them now?"

Aimée passed Madame Pelletier Zazie's folder so she could page through. Drunken shouts erupted in the hallway near the cells. The fan kept blowing hot, stale air, and she needed to pee. Again.

After taking a few notes, Madame Pelletier handed the folder back to Aimée. *"Merci,"* she said, sounding preoccupied. "That's all."

So she could have the information shuffled to the bottom of the report?

Before Aimée could protest, Madame Pelletier had stuck the file in the desk drawer and taken her jacket from its hook. "I've got a team meeting."

Blocked. So far she'd learned little besides the fact that Zazie's phone had been found on the 67 bus, that Madame Pelletier wanted her to butt out and that Sylvaine's mother was ready to press charges against her.

"I'll accompany you to the front desk," the policewoman said.

Like hell she'd be shown out.

"Nature calls," Aimée said and patted her stomach. "My condition."

"Down to the left." Madame Pelletier pointed. "Second door around the corner."

Aimée headed to the left. By the time Madame Pelletier's espadrilles hit the corridor, Aimée had edged back into the cubicle, her palm-sized digital camera in hand. She slid the drawer open.

Monday, 10:30 P.M.

Nelié's last note quivered indigo in the hot air under Madame's high-ceilinged studio. The note rose, melting into mauve before dissipating in a mellifluous fade amidst Madame's applause. Nelié blinked, the colors of the music gone now, her fingertips throbbing. Madame hadn't stopped her once, had let her make her way through the whole first movement of Paganini's first concerto for violin, the piece she'd been working on for months.

The clapping continued from the courtyard. Not again. That person stood by the topiary tree at every violin practice. At least a month now. Annoying.

She flexed her fingers, rubbed them against her thumb one by one, feeling blood rush into the grooves made in her finger pads from pressing on the string.

"Très bien, ma fille." Madame de Langlet,

114

white hair pulled back tight in a bun, stepped toward Nelié's music stand and tapped her trimmed fingernails on the score. "Give it just a touch more on the crescendo, *et parfait.*" High praise from Madame, a former *directrice* of the Conservatoire, who tutored her gratis. "We worked late tonight, *ma fille,* but it's paid off."

Nelié pushed the stray wisps of her blonde hair behind her ears and packed her violin into the case's velvet interior. Like always, she felt the aura of greatness that imbued Madame's studio, which was once Chopin's apartment — perhaps it was the master's hallowed presence.

"Keep working on it, but you're ready," said Madame. "I'll recommend you for the Conservatoire audition."

Nelié tried to contain her excitement. She kissed Madame, whose rose-flower eau de toilette hovered like a pink cloud, twice on both cheeks. "*Merci beaucoup,* Madame."

Nelié clutched the violin case, swung her messenger bag over her shoulder and ran down the studio's marble staircase into the night. All the practice on the Paganini piece had paid off. Happiness bubbled inside her. Madame said she was ready — finally — for the audition. Papa would be so proud. He couldn't afford the Conservatoire, but

Madame told her to worry about that later.

A wave of damp heat hit her as she crossed the dark, shadowed Square d'Orléans. She paused at the fountain, letting the spray hit her face. Madame had told her Chopin's lover, the writer George Sand, a strange *baronne* who wrote books under a man's name, often crossed this very courtyard to listen to him play. Paganini himself had been here to visit the composer Berlioz, who'd lived nearby. Sometimes after practice Madame would pour herself a glass of wine and Nelié an Orangina and tell her stories like this.

But now she had to rush home. She felt like she flew through the quiet streets, the bright waves of colorful music in her head lifting her like wings. Everyone was at home glued to the *télé* or crowding the bars to watch the World Cup quarterfinals. Not her papa. Tonight, as every night, he worked at l'Opéra as a stagehand. He would be home after the ballet performance and stage-set adjustment.

Dinner . . . that's right, she'd almost forgotten. So much had filled her with color tonight. After the lesson running so late and the excitement, she mustn't forget to stop at the corner Arab shop. Scramble up dinner for them, *comme toujours*. And spring her good news.

116

A few blocks away, the sky opened. Dark blue then a wash of pewter. Stupid — she'd forgotten her umbrella. Just like that, a torrential downpour flooded the hot pavement. Nelié took refuge in a doorway. She couldn't let her violin case get wet. But the Opéra's employee lodging, where they'd lived as long as she could remember, was several blocks away.

Footsteps splattered behind her. A figure darted into a doorway.

Suddenly uneasy, she pulled the messenger bag over her violin case and made a run for it.

The footsteps started again, splashing behind her in the puddles on the dark, deserted street. The silver pings of raindrops on the dark cobbles and the splashing pewter footsteps blended into a charcoal haze. She grew increasingly aware of a metallic-hued vapor, fought panic as she realized the footsteps stopped when she did to seek shelters in doorways.

Her heart jumped. That's when she knew she was being followed. The figure from the courtyard. He was following her.

Monday, 11 P.M.

Back at the Leduc Detective office, Aimée tacked up the Brigade des Mineurs reports René had downloaded from her camera, blown up and printed. Disappointed, she noted the preliminary and cursory details of the crime scene. Sketchy at best.

The first twenty-four hours meant everything in an investigation. Just this afternoon Zazie had stood in this office, only hours before her friend had been raped and murdered. Aimée glanced at the time. Nine hours and counting.

She switched on the green glass desk lamp, which sent an oval of light over Zazie's scribbled notes. Seething with frustration, she took a gulp of Badoit, hoping the carbonation would quell her rising nausea. "Why don't they have more information on the other rape victims?"

"Kind of obvious the *flics* didn't connect

the cases," René said from his ergonomic chair. "They didn't see the pattern. Your tax francs at work."

He'd enlarged and printed a map of the ninth arrondissement, highlighted the *lycées* and *collèges* in blue.

"Nice work, René."

She X'd the Olivets' cheese shop on rue de Rochechouart, the Vasseurs' home on rue Ballu. Studied Madame Pelletier's reports again. "Score one for the Brigade, who pinged Zazie's cell phone. We've got a location."

René rolled up his sleeves, determination in his green eyes. "I think the Wallace fountain photo was taken overlooking Place Gustave Toudouze." He pointed to her map. "Here."

"That's where the call to Zazie came from. It was . . . hold on." She consulted the phone log. "One thirty." Her heart skipped. "That was when she was right here, talking to me. The little minx knew all the time."

"Knew that her friend Sylvaine would be attacked?"

Tired, Aimée rubbed her eyes. Her fingers came back covered with mascara clumps. She must look a sweaty mess.

"That she'd keep investigating, René," she

said. "Even though she promised to wait until this evening and talk with me. She was hiding something even then." She passed him the police report. "From this we know Madame de Langlet gave violin lessons to Sylvaine as well as Mélanie. That's the connection."

"Even so, we don't know if these two other girls were Madame de Langlet's pupils."

"True. We'll follow up with her tomorrow," said Aimée. "Meanwhile, let's prioritize."

"Figuring out his profile — that's key."

Profile? René read too many true-crime books.

"Okay, René, let's put things together," she said. "Say he's a music aficionado or a musician picking girls because he's fixated on their talent. The rapes take place in the *quartier* and stretch back six months — he's local, knows the girls' movements, the families' schedules. And he's free in the evenings."

René pulled his goatee. "Aimée, these attacks concern power. Power over a child, the only person he can dominate."

Let René psychoanalyze. "*Bon* . . . but that doesn't rule many people out. What else do we know about him, specifically?"

"We know he tapes and binds them," said

René. "Calls the shots. He needs to be in control. He probably attacks little girls because it's the only time he feels he is."

"But what does that have to do with music, René?"

"What if their talent threatens him?" said René. "Forget him being a connoisseur — he hears them play and feels inadequate. Resents such talented young prodigies. Say one rebuffed him. He sees them as little snobs needing to be taken down a notch. Only a twelve-year-old satisfies him. That's key."

She nodded. René's profile sounded all too believable. But without any suspects, she had no one to apply it to.

Make a timeline, that's what her father used to do. She remembered those charts in his office at the Commissariat.

"The first thing we have to do is use what we know to track her movements," she said.

On the map below, she wrote in *Leduc Detective, 1:30 P.M.*

"When I got to the café at about seven, Virginie said Zazie was already almost an hour late." Below that on the map, Aimée wrote *Due home 6 P.M.* "Figure Sylvaine's father discovered her close to seven, since the ambulance arrived when I did."

"What about Zazie's phone?" René loosened his tie.

"Her uncle's phone." She checked the police report. "Discovered by the driver on the number sixty-seven bus a few hours ago, according to this. The number sixty-seven stops out front on rue du Louvre."

René nodded and drew a red line of the bus route on his map of the ninth. "So we have her going toward Pigalle. The bus stops at rue de Navarin — that's above Place Gustave Toudouze, where we pinpointed the call. And where there is a Wallace fountain that matches her picture."

She pulled out her bus map. "Rue de Navarin's more than midway to Pigalle," she said. "Zazie could have gone a block down to Place Gustave Toudouze, where the call came from and where she'd taken this picture, or two blocks in the other direction, to Sylvaine's on rue de Rochechouart."

"Her photo of men in this square is all we've got right now. Think, Aimée."

She sat up. "That's right. Zazie said she'd borrow her friend's camera again. What if her friend lived there? We have to talk to Virginie."

"Hasn't Virginie already called all Zazie's friends, talked to the parents? No one saw Zazie." René had checked in with a distraught Virginie in the café while Aimée sat in the Commissariat.

"What if Virginie overlooked someone? Look at this call log from the police report. Here's the number that called Zazie at one thirty."

"If Zazie kept secrets from you, she'd keep them from her mother, *non*?"

She tried the number. Out of service.

Her shoulders knotted. Teenager or not, the Zazie Aimée knew would have called home by now. Aimée could only imagine the worst. But to keep the horrific thoughts at bay she had to keep moving.

"Any other ideas, René?"

Rue du Louvre's streetlamps blurred pale vanilla over the glistening black pavement. The freshness in the air after the thunderstorms eased the headache building in her temple. But it did nothing to ease her mind.

In the café she and René sat across from Virginie. Pierre stood behind the counter serving late-night customers with his cell phone to his ear.

"See, Aimée?" Virginie said. "I listed everyone. René faxed the list to the *flics*. They'll follow up in the morning."

Virginie kept rubbing a towel over the spotted marble-topped table, her eyelids red-rimmed and her gaze distracted.

"That didn't stop me from calling every single parent myself, *mais non.*"

Aimée looked at the checkmarks Virginie had made next to all the names but two. "What about those two girls?"

"Didn't answer but I left their parents messages."

"That's good, Virginie."

But who wasn't on the list? Who did Zazie hide from Virginie?

"Can you think of a friend with this cell number who lives near Place Gustave Toudouze?"

Virginie stared, then shook her head.

"What about your husband?"

While Virginie showed Pierre, Aimée checked her own phone. No message from Morbier. Uneasy, she rang his number. Disconnected. She didn't know what to make of it. She had to put Morbier out of her mind. Concentrate on Zazie. "Morbier's phone's disconnected, René."

"Haven't you've got another connection in Vice?" René said. "You know people, *n'est-ce pas?*"

She racked her brains. A lot of them had retired. But apart from Morbier, she knew someone who would know someone. Suzanne, Melac's team member, formerly in Vice. Transferred to his elite unit that was so hush-hush he couldn't tell her what he did.

Virginie sat down, gripping her dishrag. "Pierre's on the phone with the *flics* again. He can't file a missing persons report until tomorrow."

Aimée reached out and held Virginie's damp fingers. "But they put out an alert for her as a potential witness, Virginie," she said.

"Thanks to you, I know that." She squeezed Aimée's hand.

"When did you last see Zazie?"

"She made herself a coppa tartine, then stood at the bus stop outside. I watched her until the bus came — like usual . . ." Virginie's lip quivered. "Say two P.M."

"*Bon,* she'd come to my office just before and mentioned her friend who had a camera. Any idea who that could be on your list?"

"Camera?"

"High-end with a fancy telescopic lens?" René said.

"I'm trying to think. Besides her school report, that research she had to do for it, all she talked about was Mélanie."

"Was she still in contact with her old friends from *l'école maternelle?*" said René.

"I wrote down everyone I could think of."

"But she was friends with Mélanie and

Sylvaine, who were both attacked," said Aimée. Coincidence? "If Zazie didn't take violin lessons . . . did she know them from some club at school?"

Virginie gave a quick nod. "*Tout à fait.* The girls worked together on a *quartier*-wide science-fair project in spring. Became friends. But look at my list, Aimée, I spoke to all the parents except those two."

Aimée thought back. Tried another angle.

"Didn't Pierre ground Zazie about a month ago after she stayed out late with a friend?"

"That girl's out of the picture," Pierre said, joining them. "That actress's daughter. Screwed-up family."

"You're sure?"

"Screwed up as in a father in prison, mother's a druggie actress with a younger live-in lover," said Pierre. "A younger lover with a title, according to *Le Parisien* the other day."

René shot her a look.

"But I called them already. The house-keeper hadn't seen Zazie."

René nudged her under the marble-topped table.

"Have her address, Pierre?" asked Aimée.

"Somewhere on rue Chaptal. I wrote it down, think it's in the back."

She had to pee. Again. "While you look, Pierre, I'll hit the WC."

She'd forgotten about the old, cracked Turkish squat toilet. Each day it got harder to bend down. She pulled the chain and stepped back before the water gushed over her peep-toes. Research . . . Zazie's words about research kept coming back to her.

"Found it, Pierre?"

But he'd gone out front to serve a customer. Aimée scanned the kitchen counter, sink at one end and cluttered paperwork space on the other. Virginie tabulated their accounts and Zazie did homework here. There was Zazie's report, labeled "Madame Toullier: Resistance Agent in Corrèze."

Why hadn't she taken that report to Sylvaine's? Feeling naïve, Aimée realized Zazie had had no intention of studying. How could she have been so stupid?

Aimée riffled through the papers for more. She found a postcard for Le Bus Palladium. She and Martine had clubbed there in the '80s.

A worn, leather-bound book, *Resistance and Espionage in 1942*. Colored Post-its on different chapters highlighting dead letter boxes, invisible ink, surveillance techniques, evasion, chalk markings.

For her class project?

Aimée shook the book and a paper came out. Written in Zazie's hand she saw:

Go to plan B

Zazie had some plan and a backup for when it failed. But what it could be Aimée had no clue.

"May I borrow this tonight?" she asked Virginie. She'd picked up Zazie's report, the book.

Virginie nodded.

René had the Citroën idling in front of Leduc Detective. Thunder rumbled. She ran to the passenger door and climbed in before the rain started.

"Pierre gave me that bad girl's address on rue Chaptal," he said. His wipers slashed the fat raindrops pelting the windshield. "But first I'm taking you home. Got to think of the baby, Aimée."

"As if I don't?" she said. But she had little energy to argue. Her time would be better spent going over Zazie's report and rereading her notes. "You're okay, René?" Although he never let on that he was suffering, she knew dampness and rising air pressure aggravated his hip dysplasia, common in dwarves his size.

"I can handle this. Tomorrow we'll see how creative Saj got on the taxes."

She rubbed her stomach and felt an answering flutter. "It moved, René."

René's face broke into a smile. "*Voilà,* the Bump has spoken. It wants to go home."

She sat back. Thought. "While you're at rue Chaptal, show this photo of Zazie to the bouncer at the disco Le Bus Palladium."

"What?"

"Ask about the . . ." She racked her brain. "What's it called, something like *la nuit du teenybopper.*"

"Zazie's underage, Aimée. They wouldn't let her in."

"Then why did she have this Bus Palladium postcard for a boy-band concert?" She waved the postcard. "They had those groups when Martine and I were at the *lycée.* The club switches over to adult and open bar after ten P.M."

René shook his head. "Don't be scatter-shot. Keep your focus."

Plan B. She had to figure out what Zazie meant. But with the passing hours the danger she was in increased.

"Every avenue needs exploring. I've got homework of my own," she said. "Maybe it's nothing, René. But it's on your way. Matter of fact, the disco's around the corner from rue Chaptal."

Ten minutes later the rain stopped, and
Aimée walked Miles Davis, her bichon frise,
along the dimly lit quai. Miles Davis was
sporting his new Burberry rain apparel.
Algae odors rose from the gurgling Seine
and mingled with the smell of wet leaves.
She stood lost in thought as Miles Davis
did his business under the dripping lime
tree. But she needed to walk to think, and
Miles Davis needed exercise. Her steps took
her around the corner of Ile Saint-Louis to
the church she'd been christened in. Her
christening outfit sat boxed in an armoire
— but she couldn't think that far ahead.

Several members of the evening choral
practice group clustered at the wooden door
to the Saint-Louis-en-l'Ile church. Candles
sputtered, and she heard the chant of a
novena. She picked up Miles Davis and slid
into the last pew. The smoking incense, the
red glass lanterns and the drone of prayers
took her somewhere else.

Her mind cleared. She said a little prayer
for Zazie. Patted her stomach. Dipped her
fingers in the holy water font, touched them
to Miles Davis's paw and slipped out.

Now to decipher what she'd found in the
café kitchen.

■ ■ ■ ■

Swathed in a cotton duvet and propped up by feather pillows, her one indulgence until tax time, she spent ten minutes reading the musty, yellowed chapters of the Resistance book Zazie had marked.

Code names, dead letter boxes and dry narrative. Techniques for secret communication. For surveillance.

Then Zazie's note fell out again — *Go to Plan B.*

Had her surveillance of the so-called rapist stemmed from this school project? Was there some hint here of how she had trailed her suspect?

Why the hell hadn't Zazie told her everything?

The church bell on Ile Saint-Louis rang midnight, muted and dulled by the Seine gurgling outside her open window. She hated calling people so late, but there was no other choice. She reached for her cell phone.

"How serious, Aimée?" Suzanne said. "Look, I just walked in the door and paid my babysitter. We're short with Melac gone. But of course you've heard, *non?*"

131

She'd left Melac's messages unanswered, not ready to deal with his decision to stay in Brittany. She understood deep down, and she knew if she told him about the baby, his life would change. He didn't need that right now with his daughter in a coma.

"Child endangerment. A twelve-year-old rape victim murdered. Serious enough for you, Suzanne?"

"*Zut!* Let me take off my wet shoes . . . ahh, better. Okay, give me a quick run-down."

Aimée did.

"The Brigade des Mineurs's priority's the rapist," said Aimée. "Zazie's peripheral."

"Standard procedure, Aimée," she said. "Doesn't mean they're not working that angle, too." A sigh came over the line. "The team's fifteen people, specialists all trained in psychology, family dynamics. And trained first as police, for God's sake. They know the field. Deal with the perverts on a daily basis."

"No doubt, Suzanne, but they're playing catch-up. Don't ask me how but I saw the reports."

"Good, because I'm tired," she said. "And it's too late for me to arrest you tonight."

"Who do you know who works Vice in the ninth?"

A pause. In the background she heard a child's voice. "Maman, I'm thirsty."

"It's late, *désolée,*" Aimée said. "But look, you've got kids. Help me out here. Zazie's mother's frantic. I promised her I'd pursue anything I could. And please don't tell me Zazie's a teenager and that's what they do."

A little laugh.

"Right now I'd love her to walk in the door and to hear everyone tell me 'I told you so,' but *vraiment,* Suzanne, if Zazie hasn't returned by now, in my gut I know it's because she can't."

"Hold on, Aimée," she said. "Let me see what I can find. Vice assignments changed. Let me check on a *mec* I know."

A moment later Aimée heard water splashing, little footsteps. "*Ma puce,* back to bed, story in a minute."

Was that how her life would turn out? A crying baby in the night, a toddler and playdates in the park, then down the road a headstrong teenager?

She envisioned a hazy future — her trying to run a business orchestrated around this little Bump. Would there be enough Dior concealer in Paris to blot out the dark shadows under her eyes?

She heard Suzanne come back on the line.

"How do you do it all, Suzanne? Work,

133

kids, keep a relationship?"

"Do it all?" Suzanne snorted. "Why would anyone do it all unless they had to? Being a parent today comes with built-in worries: vaccinations, the right school, doing enough or not enough, giving up your career or your time with your child . . . I'm so sick of my friends debating this guilt in the sandbox all the time."

Aimée thought of the mothers chatting over pastel macaroons in the Jardin du Luxembourg — it looked idyllic until it erupted in sand-throwing.

"You just do it, because that's how things work. It's what we've always done," Suzanne was saying. "Think about it — our mothers, grandmothers and great-grandmothers raised families while helping on the farm or in the shop, *non*? They did what they could with one, two or ten children, and everyone survived. Mostly." She paused. "Think about your mother. You turned out all right, right?"

Because she had her father and grand-father.

"Does this mean you and Melac might . . . ?" Suzanne hesitated.

"Look, it's late. I'll let you go. But did you find that name in Vice?" she said quickly, afraid she'd blurt everything out —

134

Melac's departure, her fears, how she'd avoided returning his calls, how uncharted this all felt. No one to guide her. If only her mother . . .

Crazy to want help from a woman who left her when she was eight years old.

"Tell Beto I know you, that's important," Suzanne said, and gave Aimée his number. "Call him suspicious, but it's kept him alive. Counterterrorism background. He owes me."

Aimée's knuckles whitened on the phone. "*Attends,* you and Melac worked counter-terrorism?"

"Can't speak to that, but Beto's cover was blown, so he's undercover Vice. Got the nickname after his course at Quantico — some Brazilian Ponzi-scheme strategy."

"*Merci,* Suzanne," she said.

"My life's a balancing act, Aimée," she said, her voice blurred with tiredness. "We make it work. Thank God my husband's mother and my sister help out, or I'd jump off the Pont Neuf." A pause. "But I wouldn't trade what I have for anything else in the world."

Clicking off the call, Aimée shifted on her side and readjusted her pillow to support her stomach and relieve the pressure on her back.

Suzanne's words spun in her head. Why would you want to do it all? Should she cave in to that up-and-comer Florian, head of Systex, who emailed her once a week with the same proposal — join computer security forces and expand delivery systems? Then she could take a decent maternity leave and later work part-time. Should she put the baby on a waiting list for a *crèche,* which Martine insisted she should have done on conception? Should she move to the country, make marmalade, be a full time *maman* and go stark raving mad? Should she consider putting this baby up for adoption?

Or should she put her swollen feet on the cold wood floor and get a Badoit before the creeping nausea overtook her? A few gulps later, she stood at her window overlooking the dark, misted Seine. Burped.

Relief at last.

Miles Davis curled at her bare feet as she punched in Beto's number.

"Who's this?" Trance music thumped in a languid wave in the background.

"Suzanne gave me your number. I'm Aimée Leduc."

Pause. "So you say, *chérie.*"

"Check me out. Then I'd like to talk."

"And I'd like the Mercedes parked across the street. We'll see."

136

He clicked off.

Out working undercover, she figured. Anyone worth their salt would verify her identity. All she could do was wait. And hope.

She tried René.

"Before you ask, the bouncer remembered seeing Zazie last week. End of report. Go to bed."

She was about to tell him she was sick of people telling her to go to bed, but René had hung up.

Monday, 11 P.M.

Zacharié played Marie-Jo's message. "Papa, this man says he'll take us to you. Should I believe him? But my friend thinks he's lying . . . where are you?" Marie-Jo's voice quivered. *Non, non,* don't go, he wanted to yell. Then what sounded like chairs or a table scraping across the floor. "Put that down," and the phone went dead.

Panicked, he punched in her number. Out of service. After trying his ex-wife's flat, where the phone rang twenty times, he remembered she'd gone to rehab. Again. He paced back and forth in the rain on rue Chaptal. No lights showing from the third-floor windows.

His ex-wife's restraining order hadn't been rescinded. Only a matter of time, he knew, since he'd gain custody of Marie-Jo. Still . . . he had to chance it. What if someone burgled the house, or what if it was this rapist he'd heard about on the radio this evening?

He pressed the buzzer. Nothing.

"Monsieur? *Vous me permettez?*" He recognized the middle-aged woman, Cécile the concierge, unfolding her umbrella next to him in the doorway.

Would she recognize him? Report him to the lawyer?

"Ah, Monsieur, quite a long time," she said with a smile. She unbuttoned her raincoat. A gold cross glittered around her neck.

Make the best of it. Use this.

"*Bonsoir,* Madame," he said. "I'm dropping off those forms for my ex-wife. She told you to give me the key, *non?*"

Doubt flashed across Cécile's face. "*Mais non,* but *entrez,* come in out of the rain."

Dripping wet, he stood at the doorframe of the concierge *loge.* A crucifix above the minuscule brown sofa, a galley kitchen and brown tiles. Mail slots and keys to the left, in the old style. He wondered how much longer the building would pay for a concierge.

"*Désolée,* I've been at Saint Rita's — I volunteer for the procession," she said. "It's every year, you know, in honor of Saint Rita, the patron saint of hope. It's organized by us fallen women." She gave a grin. "I once walked the streets. But Saint Rita saved me."

A born-again convert. The worst.

Zacharié nodded. "But Marie-Jo . . ."

"That's the thing," she interrupted. "Marie-Jo promised to come down and help out at Saint Rita's like last year. So sweet, your daughter. She took those beautiful photos of the shrine for us after we'd decorated. But she couldn't stay, said something had come up. Apologized for having to leave."

"Leave?"

"With her classmate, the red-haired girl, and that nice man, that friend of yours who was waiting for them."

Zacharié clutched the doorframe. Jules had taken his daughter.

"Which way did they go?"

Tuesday, 6 A.M.

Aimée blinked awake to soft, cream sunlight streaming over the herringboned wood floor. The warm wind rustled her bedroom curtains. Her phone trilled, startling her.

She sat up, pushed aside the Resistance book and reached for her phone on the rococo bedside table. Her eye caught on Zazie's black-and-white photo. The men in the square.

Her hand froze.

She thumbed the book open again to the third chapter Zazie had marked. Slid a piece of paper in to mark the place and glanced at the phone. A number she recognized.

"So you feel like talking," she said.

"That's one way of putting it," said Beto.

"*Bon,* where do we meet?"

"How about answering your door?" Beto said. "I've been ringing your bell for ten minutes."

141

She shook off her duvet and ran to the armoire. Not much in it fit her anymore. She'd been getting by with a slouched silk blouson and the oversize Gucci jacket, layered over a Dior skirt *sans* zipper. Soon she'd have to break down and find maternity clothes.

But for now she pulled on black leggings that came up to her hips and Melac's old oversized T-shirt from a jazz concert at the Olympia, stepped into her red heels and scraped her tousled hair into a clip.

On the black and white tiles of the landing stood a bear of a man with stubble on his chin and black hair pulled into a ponytail. Butter smells wafted from the *boulangerie* bag he held. Delicious.

"Those still warm?"

He nodded. "I figured you'd provide the coffee, *chérie.*"

Typical *mec* working Vice and *les stups,* she thought, rough around the edges but trained in the art of waking a woman up.

"*Entrez.*" She gestured him inside. Miles Davis sniffed his jean cuffs and growled.

In the kitchen she started up the espresso machine, took out the butcher's packet for Miles Davis. She spooned the horsemeat into his chipped Limoges bowl and a wave of nausea rose.

She emptied the bag of brioches into a basket on the table. Not a good idea. The smell of butter wafted through the close kitchen. *"Excusez-moi."*

She backed out of the kitchen.

"What's the matter?"

No time to answer as she ran, her heels clattering in the hallway to the bathroom. Just in time. She heaved. Then again. When the shaking and nausea had subsided, she washed her face, squeezed the last bit of Fluocaril toothpaste from the tube and brushed her teeth.

After a swipe of Chanel Red and a quick brush of mascara, she felt better.

In the kitchen he'd helped himself to coffee.

"Do you always greet guests this way?" He plopped a brown sugar cube in his *demitasse.* Stirred and swigged it.

The whiff of butter made her gag.

"Or only the ones you want favors from, *chérie?*"

The queasiness hit again, and the words caught in her mouth. How stupid — why couldn't her body cooperate?

"Then I'll finish my coffee and leave."

"Non, désolée," she managed. "Forgive me . . . I can't eat . . . in the morning."

He put his cup in the sink. "I don't waste

time with hangovers, *chérie.*"

"*Mais non* . . . it's morning sickness."

His dark eyes lasered the bump under Melac's T-shirt. "So it's true."

Her heart hammered. Did Melac know? Had Morbier opened his big mouth?

"What do you mean?"

"*Rien,* not my business, *chérie.*"

"Then keep it that way. You know nothing, *compris?*"

Flustered, she opened her suitcase of a fridge. Cornichons, capers and kiwis. Not even marmalade for his brioche.

He checked his phone. Yawned, revealing big white teeth. "I'm going home to bed. I thought it was urgent."

She nodded, wiped her damp forehead. "Off my game for a moment, *désolée.* I need your help finding a missing girl." Aimée briefly outlined the situation. "Zazie's disappeared. I think it's connected to the attack on Sylvaine Olivet. Zazie'd been surveilling a *mec* she thought was the rapist in Pigalle. That's your turf, right?"

"A little redhead?"

Hope sparked in Aimée. "You've seen or heard something?"

"I'm repaying Suzanne a favor," he said, chewing a brioche. A flaky crumb caught on his chin stubble. "Consider this a one-off. No more." He poured himself another coffee. "The sailor the crowd beat up last night looks good for the rapist."

She figured in Vice speak that meant *le proc* had sent the case to the *juge d'instruction.* Which indicated evidence, a solid base of investigation and a quick trial. Child rape and murder got the green light.

"So there's DNA, and he confessed?"

"History of priors," said Beto. "They're checking his merchant seaman records. Ports of call. Ships' logs. Takes time, some are out at sea. But he looks good for it."

"Why does he choose girls in the ninth ar-rondissement?"

"They discovered he bunks with a retired seaman who lives . . . let's see . . . on rue Cadet. His friend likes kids, too. They found lots of photos. Checking evidence at the flat."

"But if he's admitted . . ."

"The *mec*'s unconscious," he interrupted, checking his expensive sports watch.

She couldn't let him leave — not before she learned more. "Say he's in a coma for days or never comes out of it."

"Got to go," he said.

Unease ground in her gut on top of the nausea. "Please. Zazie's missing, and no one knows for a fact this seaman from Lille's the rapist. No actual proof or evidence."

"Not yet," he said. "Lab results and DNA take twenty-four hours. They're compromised, from what the Brigade des Mineurs said. But trust me, if you'd seen his priors . . ."

"But what if he's the wrong man? By the time the DNA comes back, it will be too late." She held up her hand to stop him from cutting in. "Zazie's been missing since two P.M. yesterday. You know how important the first twenty-four hours are when a child is in danger."

"I'm telling you, this seaman looks good for it. Figure her disappearance is coincidental." Beto poured himself more coffee.

"But you admit it's possible."

"*Mais oui,* possible. But more like doubtful. And what do you want to do about it, *chérie*?"

Aimée took a Badoit from the fridge, twisted off the cap. "I'd appreciate details on the other victims. These rapes started six months ago." She swallowed a packet of prenatals from her bag, washed them down with a sip of Badoit.

"You don't ask much, do you?"

"But easy for you to find out, *non*? In Vice I'm sure you keep tabs on sexual offenders out on parole in the ninth."

"The Brigades des Mineurs pulled them all in, believe me."

Madame Pelletier had made a move after all.

"The rest is above my pay grade." He brushed the flaky crumbs from the counter into her porcelain sink.

"Quoi?" He had to say it twice before she understood. Some Americanism he'd picked up at FBI training at Quantico.

In the meantime he'd accepted a third cup of coffee.

She reached in her drawer for a knife to peel a kiwi, selected a Laguiole with the signature bee on the handle.

His eyes widened. "You keep a Beretta by your spoons?"

She nodded. "Handy. I don't forget where I put it."

"You might need to work on baby-proofing," he said, stirring the sugar.

That and a million other things.

"True," she said. "But you could ask around the squad, mention Zazie."

"Chérie, I could do a lot of things," he said, stifling a yawn. "The suspect came too easy, that's what you're thinking?"

So he had doubts, too.

"I'm asking where's Zazie?" she said. "All the energy's focused on this suspect, yet

147

she's still missing. I promised Zazie's mother I'd find her. Can't you sniff around, please?"

"Your promise, your problem. You figure out your own case, *chérie.*"

She peeled the kiwi, clammy hands gripping the bee handle. At least her stomach had quieted down.

"I know this," Aimée said, watching as the peeled brown skin revealed a dark emerald. "With ten francs and a Métro pass in her pocket and a school report to turn in today, she didn't run away."

He nodded. "*Chérie,* I just got off an all-nighter. I need my beauty sleep." Hadn't she reached him at all? But she had, because he went on, "Right place, wrong time, you're thinking? Zazie saw him, and he's keeping her quiet?" he asked. "Any ransom demand?"

Virginie would have told her. She shook her head.

"I've furnished you with what I've heard. *C'est tout.* Now I've paid my debt, *chérie.*"

But she'd known most of that, except for the unconscious man's priors. And then he'd left her kitchen, headed down the hall.

She called after him. "Do you have children?"

Beto paused at the double doors. "Don't

go there. I owed Suzanne a favor."

"You do." She heard the turn of her doorknob. "Tell me what you're thinking."

"Let's say he hasn't killed before, so he's got a dilemma," he said. "How to keep her quiet and what to do with her. That's supposing he hasn't . . ."

Her mind spun. Cellars, attics, abandoned warehouses in the *banlieue.* Anywhere.

"If you're right — not saying you are — there's something else to consider, *chérie.* If the rapist is really still out there. School ends soon, so before his victims go *en vacances* he might strike again." He paused. "So if I sniff around — not saying I can — you'll feel up to brioches next time?"

She chewed the inside of her cheek. Nodded. She'd just realized there was one *lycée* he hadn't struck yet.

Tuesday, 6 A.M.

René yawned as dawn haloed the mansard rooftops. The street cleaner's broom scraped the wet cobbles, and water trickled in the gutters. He put down the binoculars and rubbed his chin. He needed a shave, a double *café crème* and a trip to the doctor — his damn hip was acting up again. Instead all he had were leg cramps and an estimated tax bill Leduc Detective couldn't pay. Plus a full day ahead of him after an all-night surveillance. And still no sign of Zazie.

Next to him on the leather car seat lay his open copy of *Noir: The Real Cases of Paris Crime.* Not only *l'Amérique* had serial killers, like he'd been trying to tell Aimée, although she hadn't seemed to be listening to him. But serial attackers had a specific MO for cornering their victims. He'd been telling Aimée about Henri Désiré Landru, the serial killer who preyed on World War I

150

widows via the personal ads. Later, during the Occupation, Dr. Marcel Petiot kept an office down the hill by Printemps. He'd promised wealthy Jews papers for Argentina from his office above La Chope, the Auvergne bistro, and given them "vaccinations." Afterwards he emulated the Nazis and burned their bodies in his building's furnace. Petiot, like Landru, took advantage of the wartime chaos, knowing his victims wouldn't be missed. And Thierry Paulin, known for his bleached blond Afro in the '80s — a nice piece of work who specialized in robbing, torturing and murdering old ladies.

René shut the book. The history lesson hadn't led him to Zazie.

Frustrated, he glanced at the time. Almost sixteen hours since her disappearance.

Time for *le petit déjeuner,* to stretch his legs and question people he hadn't questioned last night.

The blonde waitress served him on the *terrasse* outside the café on Place Gustave Toudouze. Petite, but legs to forever, like Aimée's, under a denim miniskirt. Her face was fresh, unlined, with a pink lip-glossed mouth like a rosebud. She winked. "Long night?"

He smiled. "Too long." A grinding came

151

from inside the café as the juicer pulped oranges.

He'd spent the night parked here watching the building on rue Chaptal, photographing everyone who went in and out. All of six people.

Just then, a young woman came out of the double doors of the building next door and waved to the waitress. "Madie, I left the laundry to dry. Your turn next batch."

Madie waved back to her. "When I take a break. *Pas de problème.*"

So Madie lived here on Place Toudouze. René didn't need coffee to suss out that she'd know the *quartier,* have a view of rue Chaptal.

He pulled out his camera. Flicked through the digital photos. "May I buy you a coffee?"

"Non, merci."

"I'm a detective," René said, hoping she'd bite. "Wondered if you'd look at some photos to help in my investigation."

Madie's eyes popped. She glanced at the empty *terrasse,* the deserted café. "But I'd love a *jus d'orange.*"

Tuesday, 7:30 A.M.

Aimée sipped a Badoit at the café counter to settle her stomach. "You're sure the Commissariat mentioned Zazie?"

"*Mais oui,* like I told you, the Commissariat called about an hour ago." Pierre's younger brother Dizca, a club DJ, wore bibbed overalls and a tank top. He looked like he'd been up all night as he wiped the zinc counter down with a cloth. "Virginie ran out all excited, saying they needed her for an interview. Hope I get my phone back. But what do you expect with a thirteen-year-old?"

"Your phone . . . ?" How could he not be more worried? Could Zazie be at the Commissariat — could it all be over this easily? Where had she been?

Three street cleaners in jumpsuits rolled up to the counter demanding beer. This early? Before her stomach rose in protest at

153

the smell, she paid and left a message for Virginie.

Outside at the kiosk, Maurice, the one-armed Algerian veteran she always bought papers from, grinned. "What about *les Bleus,* Aimée?"

Even Maurice had caught World Cup fever. He had never been one for sports, but now he wore a bright blue T-shirt and had stuck a French flag near the editions of *Soccer World* that a stream of early morning commuters lined up to buy.

Then she remembered Pierre's comments about Zazie's friend's mother being in the newspaper. The girl they had banned Zazie from seeing. "Any dirt today on a druggie actress . . . ?"

"Which one?" His business was booming; she didn't have much time to pick his brain.

"With a titled younger boyfriend." She put down some francs and took a copy of *Le Parisien.*

"Old news. Yesterday, I think. Might have copies if I didn't return the lot." The line snaked across the pavement. "Check with me later, Aimée."

Up in Leduc Detective, Aimée nodded to the carpenter at work on the shelves. She tried to ignore the humidity pervading the high-ceilinged office and the whine of his

154

drill. Bright sun splattered the walls and glinted off the framed sepia photograph of her grandfather sporting a waxed handlebar mustache. It had been taken circa his *sûreté* era.

Saj sat cross-legged on his tatami mat in the adjoining office, at his laptop with headphones nesting in his blond dreads. A coral earring stood out brightly against his tan, and turquoise and sandalwood prayer beads hung over his Indian shirt. He looked up from his laptop, raising his index finger — *une minute* — and went back to tapping on his keyboard.

Today's *Faits Divers* section of *Le Parisien* contained only a brief mention of last night's homicide and an alleged suspect in the emergency ward. Nothing about Zazie, of course. But Virginie and Pierre were at the Commissariat right now; she prayed they would bring Zazie home with them.

How could she focus on work with the incessant noise and heat? Or the reality that she had a sonogram appointment this morning and that she'd be going alone? Martine, her best friend since they were at the *lycée* and guaranteed moral support for most occasions, had canceled on her, claiming a deadline. Aimée couldn't budge her. Even with the offer to go clothes shopping,

Martine's forte — and Aimée could use Martine's help with the dreaded maternity wardrobe.

Not that she should be shopping now, even if she wanted to, with their looming tax bill. She'd keep uncinching waistbands and go for the layered look until she blossomed into the whale look.

She tried to focus on running the day-to-day scans. Concentrate on work — the rent wouldn't pay for itself. Neither would Miles Davis's horsemeat, nor the Italian stroller that resembled a Gucci-print rocket capsule that René had insisted on.

She'd wasted hours yesterday trying to find Zazie, and all she'd learned was that peach-pit oil prevented stretch marks.

She wished the thought of the cold jelly on her belly and the radar pinging her unborn baby on the screen didn't terrify her. Why couldn't she wrap her head around it, why the doubts all the time? The combination of hormones and not having her own mother figure, she surmised, would do it to you. Could she, should she . . . ?

"René filled me in this morning," Saj said. "So it's all over for the rapist sailor, eh?"

She hoped not. "Suspected rapist, Saj," she said. "He's in critical condition."

"Like our accounts," said Saj. "We're still

waiting on three outstanding invoices — make-or-break amounts for the number crunchers at *le fisc.*"

That bad? On paper Leduc Detective was in the black and solvent, if these clients paid on time. Yet as independent contractors, getting money from clients was harder than chewing granite.

Zazie and now taxes!

"Let's try a creative approach, Saj," she said, thinking.

"I'm listening. But the paint's dried, the brushes worn out."

Plan B. Always have plan B. And then it hit her — she hadn't discovered Zazie's plan B.

"The deadline's midnight, Aimée. Twenty percent interest fine if we don't make it. Compounded with what we owe . . . almost six figures."

Six figures they didn't have. She hated her plan B. Not perfect or her first choice and not necessarily legal. But a fallback.

"Check the balance in this Luxembourg account," she said quietly, cocking her head at the carpenter installing the new fixtures. She opened her desk drawer, consulted the contents of a manila file, jotted down a bank account number and handed the paper to Saj. "Verify it's kosher. Then arrange and re-route a wire transfer."

Stunned, Saj mouthed something, but the drill whine drowned him out.

She put her finger to her lips.

With a little shrug that sent his prayer beads clacking, Saj returned to his tatami mat.

Should she tell Saj? She'd kept it from René. But even she didn't know for sure — just that gut feeling. The messages all arrived by diplomatic pouch. The last one from Dar es Salaam.

A firm set up in Luxembourg, Andiamo Limited, an obvious shell company, listed her as the trustee and beneficiary of all company funds. The first pouch arrived with debit and credit cards in her name and a key to a safety deposit box. Up till now, she'd put it aside. Hadn't wanted to touch it.

Only one person in the world would do this.

Her mother. She must have escaped Interpol.

Saj looked up from his computer and gave a thumbs-up. There was enough in the account.

Terrorism, blood money? What if her mother had killed someone for it? Illegal, any way you put it — and someday, somehow, would there be repercussions, a link back to her?

And her choices — let her business go bankrupt with a little mouth to feed soon, or deal with the consequences later? Her shoulders tightened.

"Withdraw the funds and reroute a wire transfer now," she said. "Reroute as in creatively, *compris*?"

"You mean as in avoiding jail time?"

She put her finger to her lips again, shook her head. "I'll explain later. Don't want to be late for my first sonogram appointment."

She checked her Tintin watch. Grabbed her bag.

Saj stopped her on her way out the door.

"First we pray to Lord Ganesha, the elephant-headed god of wisdom, who removes obstacles," said Saj. "After he's been invoked, we pray to the Goddess Garbarakshambigai, the mother goddess, protector of pregnancies and the womb. She's manifested as the Goddess Parvati, Lord Shiva's wife."

Saj sounded serious. Maybe he knew something she didn't.

He took off his orange scarf, which was imprinted with Hindu mantras, and looped it around her neck. "From the Tanjore temple in Tamil Nadu."

"Sweet, Saj." She hoped that didn't mean he would insist on chanting. "Later, okay?"

Her nerves fluttered. A creeping dread — of what? Bad news about the baby's health?

Aimée slipped into her ballet flats and out the door. On rue du Louvre she caught the 67 and rode the bus to Pigalle. Like Zazie.

She took out a new red Moleskine notebook, her attempt at organization and more professional than scribbling on the back of her checkbook. What would she do if Zazie was not at the Commissariat? Even if she was, what about her own hunches about the rapist? Could she just step aside and leave it up to the *flics*? She'd decide later; for now she was only making notes. She thumbed to the to-do list, and after *Maman et Moi yoga* and *Cooking classes* she wrote down *Violin teacher, Madame de Langlet* and then *Zazie's report — surveillance? Check with schoolteacher.* Aimée needed to find out if all this snooping was somehow related to a school project, and if not, figure out a way to discourage dangerous playing at detective. Guilty, she realized that Zazie had just been copying Aimée. Some role model.

Outside the bus windows, the gold-tipped facade of l'Opéra passed by, the teeming Grands Boulevards and crowds surging into Galeries Lafayette. Several stops before Pigalle, she disembarked by the back door. Took a deep breath, gulping air tinged with diesel fumes. Not the best idea. Pulled out a Badoit from her bag and stepped into the maternity clinic on rue de Maubeuge.

Tuesday, 9 A.M.

Aimée felt the cold jelly lubricant on her stomach, the rolling scope pressing on her pelvis. Near the bed, the sonogram machine made bleeping noises. What if something was wrong?

"*Voilà,*" said Dr. Weil, a grinning, grey-haired woman. "Now you can see your baby."

Aimée turned her head, following the doctor's finger to an off-white moonscape on the screen. "Where?"

Dr. Weil pointed to a pulsing blob. "See, that's the little heart working. The legs, the head. *Bon,* makes it real, *n'est-ce pas?*"

Aimée gasped, just like women always did in the movies. But there it was, a real baby. Something melted inside her.

"That's why I prefer waiting until the second trimester for a sonogram," Dr. Weil said. "Not all my colleagues advise waiting.

162

But the baby's formed, and you can see that everything is going well."

A little hand floated. Moved as if waving. The tiny fingers like jewels.

So sweet it made her heart ache.

"Little Leduc's facing away, so we can't tell the gender. Everything looks fine. Think I'll ask the lab to run more tests." Dr. Weil smiled at Aimée, putting her stethoscope back around her neck.

"Tests like what?" Aimée asked, sitting up. The cold jelly lubricant was sticky and damp on her bump.

A machine whirred into life, printing out the sonogram image.

"Standard tests." Dr. Weill tore off a lab request slip from a pad. Handed it to Aimée. A whole column of tests checked off. "Did your mother experience difficulties during her pregnancy?"

"*Non . . .*" Aimée said, taken aback. "I mean, I don't know."

What were all these tests for? Her one year of premed hadn't approached obstetrics. Was the doctor keeping something from her?

"Doctor, you don't order a full-course menu like this for nothing . . ." As soon as she spoke, she wished she hadn't. She didn't want to know. Encephalitis, some rare blood disease, deformity?

Coward.

"Just to rule things out, Aimée. I like to be thorough." The doctor smiled again. "Based on your age, balanced nutrition, exercise and lifestyle, everything should be fine, but it's a good idea to prepare, especially since you're considering a water birth."

She blinked. No way in hell. Water birth was René's crazy suggestion. She wished he hadn't opened his mouth about it to Dr. Weil when he'd insisted on accompanying her to her last visit. And then she understood — Dr. Weil thought René was the father. These tests were for chromosome defects associated with dwarfism.

After explaining her situation to Dr. Weil, she added, "I'm also exploring other birthing options, Doctor."

"No hurry to decide," the doctor said. "Meanwhile, keep that blood pressure down. And exercise. And talk with your mother."

Fat chance.

Congenital heart defects, a gene disorder recurring every so many generations, God knew what else — how could they deal with possibilities if no one knew her medical history? Or what to look for and treat?

Noticing her expression, the doctor smiled

again. "This is routine for ninety-nine percent of my patients, Mademoiselle Leduc. Even one who jogged into her eighth month. Gave birth to twins."

Calm down, she needed to calm down. She still had her father's old trunk at home with her vaccination records from those childhood Port Royal clinic visits, so hazy in her memory. She'd see what she could find. But he'd burned all of her mother's things.

On the pavement in the hovering humidity, she kept to the dappled shade of a plane tree. The drifting mist from the water fountain felt delicious on her bare legs. She checked her phone, which she'd put on silent for the appointment, and saw the voicemail icon. Before she called in to listen, she checked her call log. One missed call from Virginie, one from René.

Good news? Her hands trembling, she hit the voicemail number.

"We've been at the Commissariat since dawn. The suspect's deep in a coma." Virginie's tired sigh. "They're questioning his cohort. Tearing his place apart, Aimée. If there's any trace of Zazie, they'll find it. The *flics* think she's run away. But . . . I don't know what to think. I'm at home taking care of Lucien. He's sick." Defeat and exhaustion seeped into her voice.

Click. End of message.

Her heart skipped. No Zazie. Nothing new. The next was from René.

"Aimée, the violin teacher's gone until this afternoon. I checked . . ."

Merde!

". . . but . . . I heard on the police scanner . . ." His words chopped off. ". . . reported attempted rape." Horns honked in the background. ". . . last night on rue Lamartine. The girl got away." More horns. He must be driving. "She's at the Commissariat this morning — her father took her to make a report. They're treating it . . ."

The message cut off.

Rue Lamartine. Aimée pulled out Zazie's map. In the ninth arrondissement.

She called him back. Only voicemail. "Find out who the girl is, René, and then find the father. We must talk with him —" The message cut off.

Great. Nothing for it now but to try to sweeten the sour taste of her last encounter with the Brigade des Mineurs. She dialed, and a woman answered the phone.

"Madame Pelletier?" Aimée tried.

Sounds of conversation in the background. "Can I take a message?"

And waste time? "The girl attacked on rue

Lamartine last night — the one who's giving her statement with her father right now —"

"Who's this?"

"Is she blonde, and does she take violin lessons?"

"Why?"

"Just tell me, please . . . blonde? Takes violin? I'm wondering if it's my neighbor's daughter."

"I can't give out names, Mademoiselle. Security issues."

"*Mais oui,* I understand," she said, thinking hard. "I'm concerned. After all, I live on rue Lamartine. I want to help them if I can."

"Best if you wait to speak with Madame Pelletier."

"Please, for peace of mind . . . just yes or no. I used to babysit her. She'd be twelve now. *Mon Dieu,* I hope it's not her."

Pause. *"Désolée . . ."*

"Please, can't you just say . . . ?"

"She's blonde. Carried an instrument case, but I can't verify any more."

"Merci." That was all she needed. The merchant seaman from Lille wouldn't tell them anything when he came out of the coma, if he ever did. He wasn't the rapist.

Despite René's message, she called the violin teacher, Madame de Langlet, again.

Only answering machine. Didn't people answer their phones anymore?

Maybe she should sit down at that corner café and plan, work out every possibility, go into painstaking detail then plot a course of action. Get Madame Pelletier to listen and then leave her Brigade and *les flics* to it. The two forces who, combined, still hadn't put the rapes together?

She'd promised Virginie she'd find Zazie. Her instinct was to tackle it in her usual way — dogged, persistent, single-track mode.

But now her back ached, and she had to stifle a yawn. So tired.

Still, if it were her child who was missing, wouldn't she want someone to make good on that promise?

She could follow her to-do list, hail a taxi, try one more time to trace Zazie's steps. Or maybe she should listen to her body. Go home, put her feet up and catch some delicious sleep.

She hailed a taxi.

The Lycée Jacques Decour incorporated the former abattoir of Montmartre into part of the gym. The portico'd walkway of the nineteenth-century school's courtyard enclosed a garden of shooting purple hollyhocks. The school exuded a convent-like ambience — apart from the clumps of teenagers, the running and yelling and the piercing bell. A blur of movement, pounding footsteps, and then the testosterone and chaos evaporated behind high classroom doors.

After a five-minute talk with the *gardien* through the window to the wood *loge,* Aimée knew which classroom to look for. Finding it, she discovered, was another matter. Staircases on the far side of the courtyard led to an upper floor with long corridors and a warren of rooms. A bit like her old *lycée* in the Marais.

Salle A led to *Salle A1,* which led to a roomful of students bent over exercise books. Those low wood desks and chairs were exactly how Aimée remembered them, gouged with initials and murder on her long legs. Two teachers stood conferring by the chalkboard. One wore a peach scarf, the other a sundress — no doubt ready for *les vacances.*

"*Pardonnez-moi,*" she said. "Is either of you Zazie Duclos's teacher?"

"That's Monsieur Sillot. *Là-bas.*"

A small, trim middle-aged man wearing a red vest, bow tie and rimless glasses stood in the corridor, intent on checking off

169

something on a clipboard with his pen. He made clucking noises accompanied by frequent shakes of his head. He reminded her of a nervous robin counting crumbs for the winter.

"Monsieur Sillot," she said. "I understand you're Zazie Duclos's teacher."

"I can't talk to you," he said, giving her a once-over with his sharp, black eyes. "Confidentiality."

"Monsieur, I'm not a *flic* . . ."

"That much I figured out," he interrupted. "A journalist, *non?*"

Tempted to lie, she shook her head. "A concerned friend. I've known her since she was in diapers."

"Zazie's absent today. That's all I can say."

Her attempt at ingratiating herself didn't work. "She's missing." She flashed her PI badge. "Her parents, my close friends, hired me to find her."

Not that she'd ever charge the Ducloses. They struggled to break even on the café.

"The *flics* asked us a lot of questions." He shrugged. "Again, confidentiality issues preclude my speaking to you about students." A flick of his gaze took in the corridor, the stairway. Instinct told her he had something to share.

Aimée nodded. *"Bien sûr."* She stepped

closer, sensing a thaw in him. "Zazie's mother shared with me the latest in the *flics'* investigation. It's not much. Zero."

Angling to give him something he'd be willing to comment on, she followed a hunch. "Zazie's class project fascinated her, she told me." She pulled out Zazie's report. What did she have to lose? "I think I can find her," she said. "There's a link between the surveillance techniques in Zazie's project and the ways she tried to trail the rapist. The rapist who murdered Sylvaine Olivet yesterday."

His birdlike eyes darted down the corridor again. The bell drilled. Aimée felt the reverberations in the soles of her feet.

"My neighbor, Tonette, *une vraie héroïne,* visited our class," he said. "She inspired this end-of-year project. The *flics* showed no interest in questioning Tonette, although I suggested it."

"How's that?"

"Tonette is a Resistance hero. She told my students about how children their age were involved in the Resistance, about how they filled their days during the war and communicated with each other without getting caught. She bet them they couldn't last a week without video games or phones or computers."

Somehow this tied in. But how? Down the hallway she spotted a trio of uniformed *flics*. Great. She needed to squeeze something out of this teacher fast.

"And that relates how, Monsieur?"

"From what I understand, Zazie and Tonette formed a friendship. Zazie became very interested in the Resistance, chose it as a topic for her final project. I know she spent some time with Tonette after school to learn more." He paused. "We're about to inform our students of Sylvaine's passing now, at the assembly," he said. "*Désolé*. I can't say any more."

Students lined up in the corridor, ready for attendance check off.

"So how can I get in touch with Tonette, Monsieur?"

Giggles came from the girls, pointing from the boys, all fresh faced, full of energy, like Zazie. Self-conscious, Aimée realized the lip-smacking noises were aimed at her . . . "His wife . . . *non,* his *chérie.*"

"Silence!" Monsieur Sillot commanded. A hush descended. In a swift movement, he wrote Tonette's address on top of Zazie's report. Winked.

At least this no-nonsense teacher had given her a place to start.

■ ■ ■ ■

"Madame Tonette?" said the concierge, shaking a rag on the pavement. "Gone out. You just missed her." She stepped back into the shadowed *porte cochère.*

"Where did she go?" Aimée wiped sweat from her forehead. "Shopping, the market?"

"On Tuesdays she works," the concierge said. She picked up a wet cloth, draped it over her mop and set to wet-mopping the stone *portail.* So early and already humidity clung to the air like a wet sheet.

"The address, please," Aimée said.

"Who wants to know?" The concierge's eyes narrowed.

Aimée flashed her PI badge yet again.

"Funny, you don't look like those PIs on the *télé.*"

"We never do, Madame."

The concierge shrugged. "Rue de la Grange-Batelière, the street *d'antiquaire.* Le Vieux Lapin."

Ten hot minutes later, she wound down narrow rue du Faubourg Montmartre past Au P'tit Creux du Faubourg — Dédé, the owner, served the best *prix-fixe* lunch in the *quartier,* attested by the regulars who always

173

crowded the place. The old wood, the mirrors and the smells emanating from within, where the staff were preparing for lunch, were still the same as she remembered. Like her *grand-père*'s time. She felt a stirring of hunger. Farther on she waved at Monsieur Arakian, one of the many *diamantaires*, diamond merchants, whose shops speckled rue la Fayette. In this *quartier* they were all Armenian. She had him to thank for the two-carat studs that never left her earlobes.

Ahead was a *mélange* of philatelic shops and Hôtel Drouot, the auction house — her *grand-père*'s old haunts. He frequented them all, a hound for antiques. The Louis XV tables, Aubusson rugs and chandeliers in her inherited seventeenth-century flat on Ile Saint-Louis were evidence of that.

Growing up, she'd trailed him through the Hôtel Drouot galleries filled with jumbles of treasures and trash: a taxidermied muskrat, Belle Époque escritoires and '70s plastic cube chairs. She even knew the auction-house porters, all from the Savoy region, known since Napoleon III's time by their distinctive red collars, their profession handed down from Savoyard father to son.

She made a left and found Le Vieux Lapin mid-block, one of many antique shops on the street. Dealers smoked on the pavement, and she heard snatches of conversation drifting — ". . . belonged to the Rothschilds . . ."

Le Vieux Lapin's interior, dim and cool, gave off a wax-polish smell, just like what *grand-père* used.

"Bonjour," Aimée called, her eyes adjusting to the low light.

"Talking to the whore again?" said a woman's voice from the shadows. "About that Watteau? *Zut!* Forget it." Aimée heard a phone slammed down on the receiver.

"Excusez-moi, but —"

From the dim interior emerged a young woman with prematurely white hair pulled into a beehive. Maroon lipstick on a smooth, made-up face, lime green cigarette pants, red heels and a white blazer. Right out of *Vogue.*

"Oui?" she said, her voice clipped.

Aimée pulled out a card. Glanced around the showroom filled with antiques — walls lined with cracked oil paintings; eighteenth-century portraits of powdered, bewigged men; countryside scenes of rolling green and winding rivers.

The woman surveyed Aimée's card and snorted. "Here about some insurance claim? I'm not a fence. That's the territory of the red collars, those Savoyards."

She remembered her *grand-père* negotiating with the red collars amid winks and exchanges under the table. Hence his "deals." *"Non,"* Aimée said, "I'm not here to see any fences."

"It's like that saying," the woman said, eyeing Aimée with a smirk. "Drouot resembles a wonderful old whore — you know she's corrupt and full of flaws, yet you keep going because she's charming and funny and she gives you lots of pleasure."

She had that right. "I'm here to see Madame Tonette."

"Busy." Crisp, to the point, end of discussion.

On closer inspection the woman appeared older; a hint of crow's-feet, smoker's lip lines. But Aimée wished to God she could have fit into those cigarette pants. A scallop shell of red embroidery on the seam, last season's Lacroix.

"Monsieur Sillot, the *lycée* teacher, recommended I speak with her."

A little expulsion of air. *"Et alors?"*

She had to appeal to this woman. Somehow. How else could she track Zazie?

She lowered her voice. "His student, Zazie Duclos, whom Madame Tonette knows, is missing. I need Madame Tonette's help, *s'il vous plaît.*"

Concern crinkled the woman's brow. A moment later her heels clicked on the hardwood floor. From the rear door to the office Aimée heard, "Tante Tonette, you decent?"

A muffled reply. The woman beckoned Aimée.

"Don't tire her out," she said. "She's got a *cinq à sept* tonight."

That meant one thing only. A lover over *apéros* between five and seven.

Unsure of what to expect, Aimée smiled. *"Merci."*

A well-coiffed, white-haired woman, seventy if she was a day, sat at an ebony desk spreading Tarot cards, her trim figure encased in a white linen sheath. A fuchsia *foulard* was knotted around her neck, matching her Chanel sling-back heels.

Fashion genes in every generation in this family.

"Excusez-moi, Tonette?"

A bat of her mascara'd lashes at Aimée. Then a wave of her hand as she scooped up the Tarot deck.

"You're not here for a card reading," she said, her voice graveled and deep.

A fortune-teller. Another surprise. But then she realized she didn't understand a lot of what had happened since Zazie disappeared.

"Madame, if I could, this concerns —"

"Aah, *pardonnez-moi.*" She'd pulled on her tortoiseshell reading glasses. "Now I can see better. You're the attorney representing the Ziegler heirs."

"Heirs? But . . ."

"I prepared," said Tonette, reaching for a worn, leatherbound ledger. "You can see the sale documents of my father's purchase of Monsieur Ziegler's shares in the *antiquaire.* Papers, all the Jews needed papers, for Aryanization, you know. So we kept everything for the Zieglers, but they didn't return. Now it's ready for the heir claimants."

Aimée gave a sigh. "Madame Tonette, I think you've mistaken —"

"*Attendez,* please hear me out," she said. The woman wanted to talk. "The ledgers detail every transaction, tax paid. It's all here," she said. "For fifty years and up to date." Tonette shot her a look. "*Dénoncés,* you know. Denounced by their neighbors."

The Occupation, and what the French did to the French during that dark time, remained as vivid as the present in those shrewd eyes. But Aimée hadn't come to dip into the sad past.

"You've confused me with an attorney."

"*Mais oui* . . . But you look like her. You're both pregnant."

Aimée handed her a card, sat down.

"Aah, *la détective,* the one Zazie goes on about."

Encouraged, Aimée perched on a fragile gilt and red upholstered chair, hoping it would hold her, and spread out Zazie's map, the report.

"Zazie's teacher said you inspired his class's end-of-year project," said Aimée. "That you and Zazie spent time together. I'm hoping Zazie told you about her subject, a man she practiced surveillance on. Can you help me understand more?"

"Aaah, to catch le Weasel." Tonette took off her glasses. "Her teacher and I, we had a bet. Challenged the students to get by without electronics, like we did during the Occupation. We encouraged them to partner and communicate. Like a game of spies, to make it fun. Surveil someone in the *quartier* — with their permission, of course. Using techniques of keeping a log, photographing, following and writing a report."

Now it made sense. "The way you surveilled people in the Resistance, *n'est-ce pas*?"

"Resistance? That's an overused term." Tonette shrugged. "I was thirteen in 1943

179

— Zazie's age, *vous comprenez*?" A faraway look entered her eyes. "Flirting with a boy in *les communistes*. To us it was game. At first." Under her rolled-up sleeve, Aimée noticed scars. "Ravensbrück," she said, noticing Aimée's gaze. "No tattooed numbers by then. The Nazis didn't have time. We were on the last convoy in and the last to be liberated." Her light brown eyes flickered. "Zazie's so impressionable, such a sweet, smart girl. We met several times, but I hoped after she came to see me yesterday . . ."

Aimée sat up. Her stomach hit the desk. She turned in the delicate chair, tried to keep it balanced.

"What time, can you remember?"

A bell rang in the shop. "Tante Tonette, a customer for you."

"I'll come right back," said Tonette, rising.

Aimée reached and put her hand on Tonette's thin arm. "Time's important. When did you last see Zazie?"

"Yesterday afternoon. Now if you'll let me help my customer?"

"Her classmate was raped and murdered, and now Zazie's missing. You might have been the last to see her," said Aimée. "Isn't that more important?"

180

Tonette gasped. Her hand flew to her mouth. After a moment she pointed to rue Notre-Dame de Lorette on the map. "Here, at my place. After lunch we met for tea. To go over her report, but . . . she didn't bring it. And she was in a hurry."

"Around two thirty?"

Tonette nodded. "She left maybe three P.M."

"No one's seen her since."

"Le Weasel, she talked about le Weasel, their suspect, she called him."

So Zazie had tracked le Weasel, the man she took for the rapist. The real man in the FotoFit?

"Who's 'they'?"

"I'm not sure of her friend's name."

"Didn't she mention Sylvaine?"

"A Marie-Jo, maybe. Yes, that's who she talked about."

"Did Marie-Jo, this friend, live on rue Chaptal?"

"Close by, that's all I know," said Tonette. "Somehow I thought the man they were tracking was her friend's mother's boy-friend."

"Why?" Aimée leaned forward.

"That's who they chose to surveil for the project." Tonette shrugged. "Although I know they didn't like him. I got the idea

181

they were hoping to catch him at something." Suddenly her eyes widened. "You
think he's this rapist? I read about the attack. Horrible."

"Please, Tonette, it's vital . . . why did they
pick him?"

"I don't know."

The pieces clicked together in Aimée's
head. If Marie-Jo was the friend on rue
Chaptal Zazie's parents forbade her to see,
the girls must have used a Resistance-style
system, *sans* phone, to communicate.

"How did you help Zazie track le Weasel
and communicate with her friend?" Aimée
said.

The younger woman called again. "Tante
Tonette?"

Aimée pushed Tonette's fuchsia bag toward her on the desk. "Better yet, you'll
show me. Tell your niece you're taking the
afternoon off."

Tuesday, 10 A.M.

The police scanner crackled in René's Citroën as a garbage truck cut in front of him. *Merde!* He braked and pulled into the first place he could, the open gate of Cité Malesherbes, an elegant lane of townhouses. Listening carefully to the scanner, René took his pen and noted the latest victim's father's name and details in the margin of the true-crime book.

Thank God he'd caffeinated and scored another meeting tonight with the waitress. Now to buttonhole this father, who'd finished his police interview and returned to work. But right now René had to cool his heels, stuck until the garbage truck moved. Sun beat down on his streaked windshield. A crow, its body glinting like shiny black satin, cawed from the roof tiles.

After spending all night in the car, his calves ached and his spine felt out of alignment, like his heart. He had to start a new *ardoise* — a clean slate, get over his feelings for Aimée. Melac could reappear, want to support Aimée and be a father to the new baby. Who knew?

Yet he couldn't help — in secret — graphing costs of cloth diaper services versus the price of disposable. Enrolling in Lamaze as her partner. Studying the benefits of breastfeeding on infant growth charts.

His phone bleeped. Aimée.

"Any luck, René?" she said, breathless.

"What's wrong? You're out of breath."

"Walking up a hill with a sixty-eight-year-old and I can't keep up with her," she said. "Good exercise. And you?"

"The father of the latest victim has finished up with his police interview." The garbage truck's loader whined. Pungent aromas drifted through his window. Forget this. He turned the key in the ignition. "I'm off to question him."

"Where's that, René?"

"I'm going to l'Opéra."

René walked out of *le parking* at Place Edouard VII into an impasse of steam-cleaned limestone buildings festooned with carved nymphs and a naked woman or two — the alabaster almost glowed. Wrought-iron balconies overflowed with pink and red geraniums. Picture *parfait.*

Beyond the zebra-striped crosswalk, René glimpsed the Palais Garnier, Napoleon III's gold-cuppola'd, rococo and Empire-style opera house. His detractors derided it as over-the-top, as had the ice-cart delivery-men, who complained that the time it took to circumvent the "monstrosity" to reach Café de la Paix melted their ice slabs.

Artistic furor died down over the years, but not so the grumbling over traffic jams, first from the horse-drawn trolley drivers, then later from motorists and bus drivers. Haussmann had discouraged revolutionaries by demolishing alleys and twisting lanes that were fertile ground for street fighters, with no thought of practical traffic navigation.

Yet in indigo summer twilight, *la vieille dame,* no stranger to controversy over the centuries, was bewitching.

René loved it.

Now the orchestra had decamped to l'Opéra Bastille, but ballet performances thrived. Les Rats, the corps of young ballerinas, rehearsed in the attic, and a beekeeper attended the beehives on the roof. There was a whole world here: costumers, make-up artists, lighting technicians and stage-set designers, stage crew and in-house firemen.

Courtesy of Saj's connections, René had obtained an *entrée* backstage, where the latest victim's father worked.

"I'm looking for Monsieur Imbert?" asked René

A rail-thin arty type wearing a *bleu de travail* and the typical loose work jacket, appeared under hanging chandeliers. He was carrying antlers and chewing the pencil hanging from his mouth.

"That you?" asked René.

A shake of his head.

René tried again. The antlers looked heavy. "They told me Monsieur Imbert works here in props."

The arty type renegotiated the antlers to rest on his hip and stuck the pencil behind his ear. "Imbert's gone fishing."

Fishing?

Maybe his daughter's attack was grounds for taking time off. Of course, how upset the whole family must be. Not a parent, René hadn't thought of that. He'd need to work on developing his paternal instinct. Especially since Aimée had hinted she'd chosen him for godfather.

"I understand he gave a statement at the Commissariat this morning after his daughter was attacked."

"His daughter's at her grandmother's." He gave a knowing nod. "Whole thing stressed him out. He goes fishing when he needs to think."

"You mean along the quai of the Seine?" The only other fishing spot René knew of was along the Marne outside Paris. He hoped that wasn't where Monsieur Imbert had gone, or tracking him down would involve bumper traffic on the *périphérique* — meaning this could take all day.

"It's important?"

"Otherwise I wouldn't be taking your time," said René, impatient. "I'm investigating a missing girl."

"Behind makeup," the man said. "Twelve floors down. *Salle A*, then the stairs. You'll find it."

"Find what?"

"Our cistern." He grinned. "You know, the supposed Phantom of the Opera's lake. The firemen dive train down there. We drain it every ten years."

"Like they'll let me down there?"

"Tap in the code 'Fantome1900.'"

Twelve floors of stairs. René groaned inside. All night in the car and now this.

The cistern under the Opéra was a dark and vaulted channel. Not the fabled lake —

187

Gaston Leroux had made that up. René inhaled the algae and water smells while feeling for footholds on the slippery, wet stone. He grasped the wall and looked for a ledge. How did people get around beside swimming or a boat?

Then everything plunged into darkness. Damned timed light had gone off.

René's foot slipped. Those expensive handmade leather soles weren't famous for their traction. He grabbed out and heard splashing.

"Monsieur Imbert?"

A yellow beam of light illuminated the semi-transparent, greenish water. René noted white catfish, their whiskers lazy swirls in the water. There stood a man in hip-high waders attached by suspenders and a bicycle helmet mounted with a flashlight.

"Who wants to know?"

"Hit the lights and I'll tell you," said René.

Imbert's chuckle echoed off the damp stone vaults. "No lights down here. Just the fish. They're blind."

René edged back a few centimeters at a time until he reached more solid footing.

"You accompanied your daughter this morning when she gave a statement at the Commissariat," said René. "I'm investigating the disappearance of another girl, Zazie

188

Duclos. I'd appreciate your help, Monsieur."

"Why didn't you say so?" He pointed to a niche with a carved stone ledge. René hoisted himself until he'd maneuvered inside, perspiration beading his upper lip.

"A detective, eh?" said Imbert, reading René's card in the beam of the flashlight. "I guess you come in all sizes these days."

Imbert told him his daughter, Nelié, had sensed the attacker's presence and known to run. She heard him following her home from her violin lesson but never saw his face.

"Did she see anything at all? His clothing, shoes? Or hear his voice?" asked René.

Nothing. In the dark and the rain, she'd concentrated on getting away. Zazie? He'd never heard his daughter mention her.

Despite the dank cistern and his wet socks, René was determined to prolong the conversation. He knew there had to be something. He just wasn't asking the right questions.

"Smells? Did he wear cologne or give off the smell of alcohol?"

The rapist hadn't gotten that close, thank God, Imbert said. "Nelié feels the world differently. It's lucky she noticed the attacker because she can't always process other people's presences like we do. She said he gave off a color, like anthracite — cold,

189

hard. You see, my Nelié, she's got this synesthesia." He paused, searching for the words. "Her music teacher says it's a gift. She sees colors for letters, numbers and musical notes. People give off a color to her. The doctor calls it a neurological condition."

René nodded. He knew many artists experienced synesthesia — Berlioz, Billy Joel, some argued Vuillard.

"She could play the violin before she could read. Played by ear. Won every scholarship they have. Such a gifted girl, my Nelié. Her teacher's suggested her for the Conservatoire de Musique."

"Madame de Langlet?"

"The old dame herself."

René needed to speak to this woman.

"But the attacker knew our place on Cité de Trévise."

"Eh, how's that?" asked René, recalling this secluded, narrow, passage-like enclave with a fountain festooned with nymphs. A chic address. "Do you mean he'd watched your daughter and knew her schedule?"

Like the other victims?

"No doubt, especially as the concierge found paper wedged in the gate to prevent it from closing."

Another example of methodical planning.

"Le salaud!" Imbert's tone hardened. "L'Opéra offers workers' housing so we union members can live nearby, on call, you know. For our sake I insisted Nelié make a police report. We need to dot the 'i's and show the bureau, or they won't change the codes and locks. Heighten security. I hate that Nelié goes home alone, but what else should I do? I can't deny her these free lessons with Madame, even if they are late at night, after her paying pupils are done. It would break her heart."

René heard the man's anguish. Not a choice a father would want to make. Impending godfatherhood, René realized, came with responsibilities.

A slapping sound, and in the yellow beam René noticed Imbert's net with a wriggling catfish.

"Edible?" he asked.

"Served with a light hollandaise sauce and a sprig of tarragon, *parfait.*" Imbert put his fingers to his mouth and smacked his lips.

After making Monsieur Imbert promise to ask his daughter if she knew Zazie, René started to make his way up the dripping, slick stairs.

"I remembered one thing, Monsieur Friant," Imbert called after him.

René turned, careful not to slip.

"Someone clapped after her playing."

"I don't understand."

"Nelié says it wasn't the first time she heard someone, a man she thinks, clap outside the window at her violin lesson."

A stalker? The rapist.

"Does Nelié think he's the one who followed her?"

"It was the humming. My Nelié said he hummed."

"Any tune she recognized?"

"The Paganini piece she's practicing for the Conservatoire de Musique tryout. The piece she'd just played."

René shivered, and the chill that ran down his spine didn't come from the damp, sweating walls.

Tuesday, 11 A.M.

Aimée, drenched and winded by the time they reached the wedge of park behind Place Saint-Georges, noticed Tonette hadn't broken a sweat. In the shade of green-leafed branches, blue delphiniums and hollyhocks framed pink, trellised roses. A true breath of paradise, Aimée thought, this secluded oasis between the nineteenth-century limestone buildings.

"Zazie wanted to hear the old stories," said Tonette.

Aimée hoped this went somewhere. "You mean for her report?"

"All of it." Tonette's gaze locked on a hovering blue-purple dragonfly. "How we *lycée* students marched under the Germans' noses to the Arc de Triomphe on Armistice Day in 1940. A small protest no one talks about." She shook her white head. "We took to the Grands Boulevards, just near here, forty-one of us singing *La Marseillaise* and flying the tricolor until the police appeared. Can you imagine? But that's what you do when you're young and foolish. We started a clandestine one-page newspaper, printed in secret in our school's cellar. Even distributed copies using special signs, signals and drop boxes until our principal caught us. My story fascinated Zazie."

Tonette unfolded the story her way. Aimée tried not to squirm with impatience.

"So you inspired Zazie to use your techniques," said Aimée, fanning herself in the heat. "Ways that informed her surveillance?"

"I wouldn't call it that," said Tonette, rolling her eyes. "Well, maybe a little." A shrug of her elegant shoulders. Children ran over the grass. The blue-purple dragonfly fluttered by the rose trellis. "Later we mostly distributed anti-Fascist pamphlets from clandestine printing presses — all run by communists then — at cinemas just before the German newsreels. We threw them from balconies. They floated like butterflies. Then we ran. Kids."

So far Tonette's tale had told her little.

"We all went to the cinema then." Tonette's gaze softened. "Truffaut grew up right around the corner, you know. We would have been almost the same age.

194

Everyone lived in the cinema. During the Occupation, theaters were heated. At least for the first few winters. But '40 and '41 were cruel. No wood or charcoal — the Germans took it, courtesy of French racketeers. Trying to obtain food and rations dominated our lives. In 1942 a D ration ticket got you a half kilo of potatoes. For a K ticket, workers got a liter of wine. Depended on who you knew." She gave a knowing nod. "My mother heard Mistinguett sing before German troops at the Casino de Paris; a ditty about her cold apartment and empty stewpot. The next day Mistinguett received five bags of charcoal and six lamb gigots. She sold them. *Mais alors,* everyone did."

Aimée's collar stuck to her neck. This heat. "Our history teacher once told us Mistinguett said, 'My heart is French but my ass is international.' "

Tonette shook her head. "That's Arletty. Mistinguett said, 'A kiss can be a comma, a question mark or an exclamation point. That's basic spelling that every woman ought to know.' "

Aimée grinned. No wonder Zazie had connected with Tonette. Kindred spirits. And Tonette must have seen her former thirteen-year-old self in Zazie.

"Oh, and butter," Tonette continued, "color was the only way you could tell if it was the real thing. My mother detested the butcher, a black-market profiteer." She pointed to an *antiquaire* shop visible outside of the park. "Gone now. But back then women lined up in the cold, waiting. I remember seeing my teacher shivering — no one had stockings, scarcer than diamonds. But she'd stained her legs with *brou de noix,* walnut-hull juice, to look like she did. Like a lot of women."

Old stories of the dark years, as this generation and every generation since had termed it. She needed to listen and focus on what Zazie had gleaned and used.

Tonette shrugged. "We were so hungry, my mother contacted her fifth cousin on a farm, the snob who she hadn't seen since before the war. Ah, then *la cousine* became my mother's closest member of *la famille.* She furnished us with eggs, once in a while a chicken. We were lucky. We ate."

They were walking now. "You told Zazie all this?"

"If we don't inform the next generation, who will?" She waved her hand at the garden, the townhouses surrounding them. "Until twenty-some years ago, all this lay derelict, boarded up."

196

Aimée stared.

"Hard to believe, eh? But there by the old *lavoir* is where we hid underground papers."

Aimée noted the open-sided washhouse holding stollers and tricycles.

"And clothing for stranded RAF fliers," Tonette was saying, "men escaping from *service du travail obligatoire* in Germany."

"You brought Zazie here?"

"I showed her how to make a drop. See. That's hers."

Under a weathered stone support Aimée saw a smudge of chalk. An X. Yet Aimée found nothing in or near the stone.

"Only use a place once, I told Zazie," said Tonette, noticing Aimée's frustration.

"So they did follow, surveil and drop off info about this man le Weasel? Marie-Jo's mother's boyfriend?"

"Zazie said something about proving le Weasel wasn't who he said he was, something like that."

Le Weasel . . . the rapist? Was that Zazie's connection to the attacks? What about the violin lessons? How did they fit in?

"I wish I could help you more," said Tonette.

Something niggled in Aimée's mind. Something Zazie had said, something that chimed with Tonette's story . . . If only she could hold a thought in this humidity.

Tonette, oblivious to the heat, pointed to a church spire peeping over *grisaille*-blue tin rooftops. "We always met in *bistrots, musées,* department stores with more than one exit. Irony of ironies, in the building on Boulevard Haussmann, the Nazis' office was on the third floor, above Simexco, a cover for the Red Sympathy organizers."

Their walk took them back to Tonette's building. Its dark green double doors could fit a horse-drawn carriage, and once had.

Aimée's mind went back to le Weasel. Did the rape boil down to something close to home? Suppose the girls had discovered in their surveillance that this boyfriend, le Weasel, had assaulted their schoolmates?

"Don't you want to come upstairs? Take a load off your feet? Drink something cold?"

Aimée nodded, grateful for the invitation.

But her legs balked at the winding Charles X staircase. Eight flights up at the dome-ceilinged last landing, Tonette reached in her mailbox and came out with a stack of envelopes. A slip of paper fluttered onto the black-and-white checkerboard tiles, landing at Tonette's Chanel fuchsia sling-back heel.

Aimée picked it up. "Yours?"

Tonette shook her head.

Aimée recognized it as a receipt from the

photo shop on Boulevard de Magenta. It was for a roll of Ilford black-and-white, high-speed film. Her mind went back to Zazie's black-and-white telescopic photo of men standing around the Wallace fountain.

At least the receipt gave her an address to check.

"You trained Zazie well. May I take that, Tonette?"

"Bien sûr," said Tonette. "Some things never change."

Aimée stopped at the one-hour developing shop on Boulevard de Magenta. The girl behind the counter shook her head. "Not ready, *désolée,* professional film like this takes two days. The customer was told that."

"Ah. Do you remember her?"

"I started this morning," she said. A big smile. "Ready tomorrow," she said, trying to be helpful.

Aimée retraced the route she'd taken with Tonette, alert at every corner, shop doorway and intersection for a trace of Zazie.

The humidity and the heat — a cotton-like layer of dense, still air — wilted the irises and melted her mascara. All the walking, getting nowhere. She felt a sharp cramp. The baby turning? Better sit down.

Back in the square behind Place Saint-Georges, she checked her messages. None.

Lost in thought, she watched a young woman pushing a stroller, a toddler in a yellow dress clasping her other hand. A bouquet of red balloons was tied with red ribbon to the stroller handle.

Her eye caught on the smudged chalk X she had noticed earlier on the stone. But that could have been yesterday. Still, she checked the area again: riffled through the soil, under leaves and gravel. Nothing but dirt under her fingernails.

And what good would that film at the developer's do if it showed more scenes of the same?

Yet she couldn't assume anything. This was all moving like drying glue. Her hormones, this heat . . . she wanted to kick something.

Police procedure, plodding investigation, waiting, checking, matching took too long. All of the many reasons she hated this kind of work. Almost twenty-one hours had elapsed since Zazie's last sighting by Tonette.

She took Zazie's map from her bag, dotted in pen the points she and René had marked on the map he'd enlarged. Now she added dots for the locations Tonette had showed her.

But she needed to try Madame de Langlet, leave a message even if the woman was away. She punched in the number René gave her.

Several rings later a woman answered with a breathless *"Allô?"*

Finally.

In the background Aimée heard violin notes. "Madame de Langlet," she said, "I'm Aimée Leduc. Last night your pupil —"

"I don't talk to journalists," she interrupted.

"Smart, Madame. I'm a detective."

"I don't talk to detectives."

"But Madame Vasseur told me to speak with you." In a manner of speaking. "It's important, please, your pupils have been attacked. I'm sure you're more than concerned about the connection."

"Connection?" Pause. "I'm teaching right now."

She hadn't denied it.

"And I'm sorry to bother you, but Sylvaine's death —"

"Horrendous," she interrupted. "A tragedy. The *flics* questioned me this morning."

Merde! Instead of listening to René last night, she should have listened to her gut and tracked the woman down. "But now four of your students —"

"I don't understand."

Of course you do. Or you don't want to.

"Weren't the other two victims also your students?"

"I'm not supposed to talk about this," she said, her voice quavering. "*Désolée.* I want to help, but I can't now."

"The investigators told you that, Madame?"

"I'm teaching. Must go."

Strains of a violin rose in the background.

"Can we meet when your lessons finish, Madame?"

"I can talk tomorrow."

Aimée had to persist. "Madame, it's important. Another girl has disappeared. Just a few minutes of your time."

A sigh. "Call me later." Then Aimée heard a click. She'd hung up.

She wanted to throw the damn phone. Crucial time passed with no leads to Zazie.

Frustrated, she studied the map again. The location dots formed a pattern, like the facets of an eight-carat stone. Zazie had to be in this hexagon. She felt it in the marrow of her bones.

A child's crying interrupted her thoughts. The red balloons had become untied, escaping. *"Maman!"* The balloons hovered above the toddler in the yellow dress, floating out of her reach.

Aimée caught two, reached and caught another that was stuck in the lime-tree branches.

"*Merci,* Madame," said the mother. "You saved the birthday party from disaster."

"Good exercise." Aimée's eyes caught on the tiny pink toes peeping from the stroller. A little ball in an orange onesie.

The woman sat down next to her on the bench. She was brunette, thin with tan legs. "I'm Sybille. Your first?"

"That obvious?" Aimée patted her stomach.

"You have the look." Sybille grinned. "Boy or girl?"

"Doctor couldn't tell." And she wanted to share it with this smiling mother. Yearned for a moment to forget Zazie, the horror, yearned to bask in the baby smells of fresh laundry and talcum coming from the stroller. Admire those pink toes.

Aimée pulled out the sonogram image. It took her breath away. This little thing growing inside her.

"Ah, fifty-fifty either way." Sybille pointed to the whitish blob Aimée had seen pulse on the screen. "Strong heart. My two looked like alien pods, big heads but full of brains."

Her toddler daughter tugged her sleeve. "*Oui, mon petit chou.* But look how beautiful they turned out."

"People give me advice about the birth . . ." She hesitated but figured why not ask a stranger something she'd always wanted to ask a woman? "So it really hurts?"

"No picnic." Sybille leaned closer. "Far as I'm concerned there's a reason drugs were invented, *alors!*"

Aimée smiled.

"Take all the help you can get. Like letting other people bake for you," Sybille said, pointing to a basket with a *boulangerie* purchase glistening with apricots. "You think I made this tart?"

A woman after her own heart. Hunger lapped in her stomach. She needed to eat.

"I'm a *resto* critic. Work at night when they're asleep," Sybille said. "Her father," she said, indicating the baby in the stroller, "left when I was six months along. Babette" — she nodded to the toddler — "her father takes her every other weekend. Those bobo-chic Left Bank *mamans* who look like they have it all, with six kids and a career? They neglect to say they've got staff, an army of nannies and cleaners."

"I'm raising mine on my own, too," said Aimée. "I run a business. Try to, at least."

"Then you need a posse. Never too early to get one in place. I wish someone had told me that."

Aimée took out her red notebook. "Go on."

"And I wish someone had warned me about breast milk leaking at meetings," Sybille said. "Never wear white silk, at least for the first six months."

Aimée wrote that down. The little girl handed her a curled, green ginkgo leaf with a dust of lemon pollen. "For you," said the toddler.

"My little Babette loves leaves. You're special." Sybille, still smiling, turned to Aimée. "Here's free advice. On *télé* talk shows they gloss over what it's really like for a woman to work and raise a family. But I did hear one woman from Toulouse who was interviewed on the radio in the *hypermarché* speak about how it feels being a *maman. Cela,* it felt real. She'd lost her son in the aisles for three minutes, but it felt like three years. What mother can't relate to that? That's daily life, three minutes feeling like three years, because you worry so much and love them so much and feel so alone being responsible for their world. Don't picture motherhood as those perfect, coiffed career *mamans* jogging. They aren't real people. They never breast-feed."

Reaching people, real people. Now she knew what to do. How to kick-start this investigation into high gear. She needed to reach lots of people, like the woman on the radio.

"You've given me an idea," said Aimée, putting her notebook in her bag. And she'd catch the Métro at Saint-Georges, by the theatre . . . all good exercise. "*Merci* for the great advice." She stood up, adrenaline coursing. "Enjoy the birthday party."

"I see it in your eyes," said Sybille.

"And what's that?"

"Like you want to turn vinegar into honey," Sybille laughed. *"Bonne chance."*

On the way she called Martine.

Tuesday, noon

"Lunch at Printemps, your treat? That's an EMERGENCY?"

Across the table from her at the Printemps rooftop café, Martine speared a yellow beet with her fork. Martine, a journalist and Aimée's best friend since the *lycée,* wore vanilla gauze layers that offset her tan. The vista from the department store's roof *terrasse* spread from the Grands Boulevards to the tour Eiffel to the Parc des Buttes Chaumont.

Starving, Aimée ignored the view. She gulped down the shooter of cold leek vichyssoise then started on the grapefruit, avocado and shrimp salad before attacking the *saumon fumé.*

"How can you eat so much in this heat?"

She'd gained four kilos. Right now she didn't care. "Eating for two." With any luck she wouldn't throw this up. Sated, she took a breath and noticed for the first time that Martine was looking with longing at the woman smoking by the handrail. "Now I know what's different," said Aimée. "You're not smoking." She grabbed Martine in a hug. "Only one thing would ever make you quit. A baby."

She felt Martine's shoulders quiver. Her blonde hair brushed Aimée's cheek as she shook her head.

"What's the matter?"

Martine bit her lip. "Nicotine withdrawal."

"Liar. Did you break up with Gilles?" Finally, and come to your senses, she almost said. Martine's lover had a multitude of children and an ex-wife living below their big flat overlooking the Bois de Boulogne.

"Does this look like a break-up tan?" Martine asked, indignant. "After two weeks on Martinique?"

A fight and make-up tan, then. "What's his ex-wife done now?"

Martine was upset. Even though Aimée had other things on her mind, she'd have to hear it. Martine was her friend.

"Quiet for once," said Martine. "She's got the children in July."

"Then what's . . . ?"

"Your emergency?" Martine interrupted. "I dropped my meeting I was so worried.

Did something happen at your doctor's appointment?"

The appointment Martine couldn't go to.

"Baby's fine. It changed me, looking at it and really seeing it." As she reached for the sonogram, her eye caught on Martine's open agenda sticking out of her bag on the *terrasse.*

A red circle around a date two weeks ago. Martine's indicator of bad news. Aimée noticed she'd lost weight.

"No one loses weight after they quit smoking, Martine."

"I'm not ill." Martine's eyes brimmed. "I'm not being a good friend right now."

A cold shaft traveled Aimée's spine.

"Did I do something?" Again? And she had to ask another favor of Martine.

Pain radiated from Martine's face. "Two weeks ago," Martine paused. "I didn't want to tell you . . ."

"Tell me what?" Worried now, Aimée took Martine's shaking hand.

"Or mar your happiness. I couldn't face you. I had a miscarriage."

A knife pain of guilt lanced her. "*Mon Dieu,* I'm so sorry, Martine."

She should have read the signs. So caught up in her own world of this baby and wondering if she should even have it, how to take care of it — all those doubts she'd shoveled on Martine since the beginning of her pregnancy.

"Martine, you have the stable relationship," she said. "You want a baby and yet here I am, the unfit candidate, moaning about my feet swelling." She put her fork down. Insensitive again and in hormonal overdrive, as René pointed out to her often these days. It seemed so wrong.

She thought of what the woman in the park had said. "You'd be a better mother than me," she said. "And you have a posse to help you." Martine had a mother, tons of sisters, aunts and uncles, not to mention the baby's father on site.

Martine averted her gaze.

Merde — stuck her foot in her mouth again. She couldn't get anything right. First Zazie and now her best friend.

"*Désolée,* Martine, it must be *difficile* for you to watch me go on like this." She grabbed her hand. Squeezed it. "So terrible for you. Forgive me?"

"Really, it's okay, the doctor says I'm fine," said Martine. "We'll try again in a few months."

Thinking of Martine's support system, of her own total lack of one, her head began to swim. How could this be happening? What

210

was Aimée thinking, having a baby? She'd end up like her mother and abandon her child. Or leave others to raise it while she cluelessly doled out money. Like her mother.

"*Et alors,* if I'm the godmother shouldn't I see the sonogram?" said Martine.

Aimée's phone vibrated on the table. Caller ID showed Virginie. "*Excusez-moi,* Martine, got to take this."

She put her hand over one ear to listen. *"Oui?"*

"They haven't found Zazie." Virginie's voice vibrated with fear. Aimée's heart fell. "No trace of her at that suspect's . . . keep saying she's a runaway." But the conversations on the *terrasse* made it impossible to hear.

"*Un moment,* let me call you back when I'm somewhere I can hear," said Aimée. She hung up. "Martine, this is the emergency. What ever happened to that friend of yours, the interviewer on that TF1 show? What's it called? *On the Rue?*"

Martine blinked. "Nadine, the sensationalist? The muckraker?" She blotted her eye with a napkin. "Another *bohème* with a trust fund."

"Like all of them," Aimée said. "But I remember meeting her at that faux Leftist gathering back when you were in Sciences Po together."

She had to reach out to the media via Martine, and she wouldn't let Nadine's mudslinging reputation put her off. Time mattered. As the hours ticked by, Zazie's danger grew.

"C'est ça," said Martine, uninterested.

"Can you call her?"

"She's not a close friend. Why?"

Sunlight blazed and sparked on l'Opéra's verdigris cupola, lighting the gold trimmings on fire. So close Aimée felt she'd burn.

"Ask her if she wants a bombshell interview on the street where a woman's daughter disappeared — how it links to unsolved cases of three twelve-year-olds raped in the same arrondissement."

Martine's eyes perked up. "What's it to you?"

"The *flics* never put it together. Zazie did, and now she's missing."

Martine dropped her fork. "Zazie from the café, your little shadow?"

"Not so little. She just turned thirteen. Her mother's on the phone, frantic. She's been missing . . ." Aimée glanced at her watch. ". . . almost twenty-two hours."

"Haven't the *flics* briefed the press?" asked Martine. "Enlisted the public's help?"

"And reveal how lax and incompetent they've been? Fat chance." Aimée tried to catch the server's attention for the bill. "Easier to label her a runaway. Please, Martine. Either Zazie's locked up somewhere, or . . ." She wouldn't say it. ". . . the rapist tried again last night. Thank God the girl got away."

Martine nodded, determination glinting in her eyes. "Right up Nadine's alley. She loves scraping the cobbles with the police. She'll run after the scent like a rabid dog."

Foaming at the mouth worked for Aimée.

"Plus," Martine added, "she'd owe me some contacts I need."

A journalist to the core.

Aimée threw a wad of francs near her half-finished plate and started to rise. Martine touched her wrist. "Word of caution, Aimée. Nothing's sacred to her — people get singed. But if someone's going to expose corruption, better she does than I do."

"*Exactement.* Down and dirty. It's about finding Zazie now — anything that works."

Martine had already started to dial. "Where and when?"

"Below Place Saint-Georges, corner of Notre-Dame de Lorette and rue Laferrière in the ninth. Can she get there within the hour with a crew?"

"Less. The vans are very mobile. With luck one of the news agencies will pick it up. Maybe a nice little crowd."

She grabbed Martine's other hand. "*Désolée,* Martine," she said. "I'm the one who's not been a good friend, so wrapped up, preoccupied . . ."

"That's what best friends do — give and take, eh? And don't let *salauds* mess with little girls."

Tuesday, noon

Zacharié's head hit the crumbling ceiling in the low, dark tunnel under the Hôtel Drouot. He cursed. He hated the mildew and crusty dirt miasma. His fingers trembled. He balled them in a fist to stop shaking. No good. So he shoved his hands in his jacket pockets.

Time to get his bearings, calm his nerves for the dry run. Otherwise the job would go up in smoke. What else could he do? His shirt, damp with perspiration, stuck to his spine.

"We're done," Dervier said, his forked tongue darting in full view. "Tunneled and drilled last night. Piece of *gâteau.*"

Professionals. Jules wouldn't have needed Zacharié at all. Except for the cherry on top.

The cherry of a job that guaranteed Marie-Jo's release. Zacharié's gang only knew a part of the plan, only part of the risk. For a moment he was wracked by guilt. Not that he had known the whole plan when he'd had them hired.

"And at short notice," he said. "I'm impressed. Good job."

"I know the tunnels," Dervier said. "We'll enter via the cistern chutes that run here like wet dogs." Under the city lay ancient mines, quarries and series of passageways threaded by tunnels. Métro and train systems cut through old passageways hemmed by sewage and gas pipelines — a warren Dervier knew like the lines in his old mother's face. God knew what she'd done down here during the Occupation, with the rumored black market, the brothels and the hiding places for Jews — all available for whoever could pay.

Dervier raised nine fingers.

Nine hours to the heist.

Dervier timed their practice run based on the job's outlined scope — a robbery of the underground vault that should take fifteen minutes once they'd broken in. What Dervier did not yet know was that as the team emptied it, Zacharié would gain entry via the vault into the Ministry's temporary storeroom, in the building behind the one they were breaking into. That was Zacharié's special job. To take the thing Jules had hired him to steal.

Dervier clicked his stopwatch. "Fifteen minutes and forty seconds."

"Ask me if I'm surprised, Dervier." He summoned a grin, nudged him. "You're the best."

Each of the crew had his own motivation to succeed. Dervier faced a mountain of medical bills. Gilou itched for the thrill and getaway. Ramu, gambling debts. Tandou, the tunneler, *zut,* this was how he earned, with three kids and another on the way.

No margin for errors. The "supplemental" plans Jules had given him lay damp against his shirt under his jacket, directing him to the real object he'd been hired to deliver. He'd planned to add the change to Dervier's itinerary at the last minute. He needed to get the team through the beginning of the plan first.

"Forget the big paintings and sculptures," said Dervier. The team nodded in approval. "Remember, we're going for the portable *objets d'art,* silver and jewelry."

No doubt Dervier had his fence lined up. But he'd noticed Zacharié's look. "Don't give me a sad face, Zacharié. Every object's valued and insured. Half of the coots whose names're on the little tags have passed away.

217

Think of it as a gift from the grave to their descendants. Old *grand-père*'s forgotten gold watch suddenly becomes an insurance windfall."

Let Dervier rationalize. Jules had taken his Marie-Jo as hostage. Zacharié had no choice.

In the cold, dank tunnel, he felt a sheen of perspiration on his upper lip, his stomach in knots.

He pulled out the diagram Jules had given him.

"What's this?" Dervier asked, shining his flashlight.

"Just between us. It's an add-on to the plan. I need you to open those back exits, like here and here," said Zacharié, pointing.

"Tell me you're joking, Zacharié. There's fifteen tons of concrete laid there after rue Papillon sunk in the RER excavations," said Dervier. His tongue flicked. "See." Cement supports shone in the bobbing yellow beam from Dervier's flashlight. "They evacuated the whole street, and still people died. Now they run a Fête des Papillons to make people forget. As if they could."

"*Allez*, Dervier, you've got the equipment, work around it. Not that difficult."

"In eight hours?"

Zacharié's hand tensed.

God in heaven, how stupid he'd been to agree to Jules's plan. Yet his only alternative — at the time — had been enduring eighteen more months of prison while his ex and that pedophile decamped with Marie-Jo. Now, with his ex's DUI, he'd have been sure to gain custody of Marie-Jo, but Jules had forced him to jeopardize all that.

At every step he'd racked his brains for a way to pull out yet still satisfy Jules and guarantee Marie-Jo's return. For the life of him he couldn't think of a dodge. Trapped. Like in this tunnel — no way to turn except straight ahead into Jules's web.

"I need this gate opened," he said. "And I need you to figure in twelve more minutes."

"Here?" Dervier's flashlight beam played on the dripping tunnel. "Why?"

"So I can get out via the sewer while you're packing up the vault. *Compris?*"

The whole thing was a tight wire, a balancing act. Deep inside, a sliver of fear vibrated — what if Jules refused to release Marie-Jo? Knowing Jules, hostages were more trouble than they were worth. He pushed that thought down.

Play the chump again. Play right into Jules's palm.

"Something in it for me, Zacharié?"

He'd hooked him.

"This should sweeten it, Dervier." Zacharié put a wad of francs into Dervier's waiting hand.

Tuesday, 1:30 P.M.

Virginie stood on the narrow street, fingers picking at her knotted scarf. Doubt wavered in her eyes. "There's no call-in hotline. You're sure this interview will work, Aimée?"

Aimée groaned inside. She hated to put Virginie through this.

"Nothing's sure, Virginie," said Aimée. "But it stands to reason Zazie didn't go far."

It seemed the best shot yet at finding her. Maybe the only one. With every hour that passed, chances faded.

"Think of it as reaching out to anyone who might have seen and remembered her — the bus driver who found her phone, a concierge, shop keeper, kiosk vendor, mother in the park."

Water spluttered by them, running downhill in the gutter. The curled iron lamplight imprinted its mirror image in shadow on

221

the flat butterscotch stone. A few bystanders had gathered near the corner.

"I've brought her school picture."

"Parfait." Aimée squeezed Virginie's hand. She noticed the parked media vans, antennas sprouting. "Looks like more channels have picked up on this. More coverage. Remember, Virginie, you're appealing for help finding your daughter. Acknowledge the police effort and just say after last night's attempted attack no girl's safe and you're worried. Speak from your heart."

Virginie chewed her thumbnail. "If Zazie's nearby, why hasn't she come home? The *flics* assume she ran away. You think you know your child, then . . ." Virginie wiped her tearing eyes. "But you're going to be a mother. The biggest worry is keeping them safe."

Aimée's insides wrenched. Part of her wanted to stay out of this ugliness and concentrate on her baby. Yet she'd gotten involved. Couldn't abandon Zazie.

Was it wrong to give Virginie hope? Aimée prayed that Zazie was alive. "Virginie, the girl the rapist tried to attack last night was another blonde, twelve-year-old violinist — just more proof Zazie's not his type. I'm no expert, but I think there's more to this story, and we need to figure out what it is. Time's crucial."

A microphone was thrust into Aimée's face. Attached to the microphone was a denim-jacketed arm — a reporter with a bob of black hair and a clipboard under her arm. The woman wore no makeup. She had a pointed chin, small, piercing eyes and a beak of a nose. "I'm Nadine from *On the Rue*. Can you identify yourself for the listeners and tell us why you alerted *On the Rue*?"

Her father's words played in her head — any detective worth their salt avoided the media. Too much exposure. Keep your face out of the paper unless you want desk work all your life. Aimée took Virginie's arm and guided her forward. "This is Virginie, Zazie Duclos's mother."

Irritation showed in the fine lines radiating from Nadine's forehead. "And you? Aren't you Aimée Leduc, the detective who discovered the twelve-year-old murder victim?"

Not what she'd bargained for. A camera crew hovered behind Nadine.

"Speak up, please."

The last thing she wanted was to step into the spotlight. "A terrible thing, yes."

"The murdered victim's mother alleges you interfered —"

"This isn't about me," Aimée interrupted, hating to rise to her bait.

"But the victim's mother's threatening to press charges against you," said Nadine. "Any comment?"

"I'm so sorry for this distraught mother's loss." She had to deflect this to Zazie. Her mind raced.

"Sources say you put together a pattern of rapes in the ninth arrondissement that the local police had missed and the Commissariat had ignored," said Nadine. "Can you tell the viewers how feelings ran so high after your inquiries that a mob of angry parents took the law into their own hands, sending a man to the hospital . . ."

Aimée's own fault — hadn't Martine warned her? A gutter journalist throwing her own spin to smear everyone. Sensationalize. But Nadine had done her homework.

"The mob picked a victim who matched a computer-generated image from a twelve-year-old victim's glimpse of her rapist," Aimée said, trying not to grit her teeth. Hot lights beamed on her in the already sweltering air. Her hands shook.

"Which resulted in the attack on an alleged suspect, a man who hasn't yet been charged," said Nadine. "He's on life support in Hôtel-Dieu, according to the Commissariat."

Did the muckraker side with *flics*? What tactic was this?

Aimée could sense Virginie tensing at her side. Aimée had to get over the personal attack and use it. Use Nadine's reach to find Zazie.

"Let's get this clear, Nadine. With four young victims, one murdered, we alerted you, knowing that the community has to work together, not strike out, to prevent another tragedy. Now another girl, Zazie Duclos, is missing."

"What makes you think they're related?" said Nadine.

"We fear Zazie, who has personal connections to two of the victims, may be a witness."

"Witness? Or a runaway scared of the trouble she'll get in after the drama she's created?" Nadine kept the microphone so close Aimée saw the vapor of her own breath on it.

"Zazie's school report was due today," said Virginie, her hands shaking. "My daughter's got final exams. She wouldn't throw away her whole school year like that."

Aimée took a breath. "Virginie's daughter Zazie has been missing almost twenty-four hours," she said. "She's a victim."

Nadine stuck the microphone closer, almost poking Aimée's lips. "*Alors,* you blame the police and the Brigade des Mineurs for inaction?"

Some investigative journalist. Putting cheap and salacious words in their mouths and complicating the investigation. Aimée had to turn this around.

"Virginie's asking for help — from you and the people of the *quartier.* She's counting on you and your listeners to help encourage the police and the Brigade des Mineurs to set up a tip hotline." Aimée gripped Virginie's arm. "Zazie was last seen here at two P.M. yesterday. We don't know any more. She's thirteen years old, with curly red hair and a great smile."

Camera crews moved forward, surrounding them like vultures.

"We're asking if anyone knows anything or has seen anything, please come forward," said Aimée. "Her mother Virginie will tell you more."

Nadine pushed the microphone into Virginie's face. "Madame, do you want to tell our listeners about Zazie?"

Aimée nodded to Virginie.

Virginie held up a photo. "This is Zazie, my daughter . . ." She began to speak.

Aimée stepped back into the crowd, trying to edge her way out. Her arms quivered as she warded off the microphones thrust in her face. "No comment."

Her phone vibrated. She checked. A voice-mail from René.

"You need to see this, Aimée. Meet me behind the *musée* on rue Chaptal."

She hurried over the cobbled alley, glad of her ballet flats, to the back of the Musée de la Vie Romantique. Behind the ocher walls of a former painter's atelier — once known for a Friday-night salon of neighborhood artists and writers: George Sand, Chopin, Delacroix — nestled a garden blooming with orange and pink roses.

René sat by the rose border at a green, metal café table that came up to his chest. Dark circles puffed under his eyes, but he wore a starched shirt. A steaming celadon cup with a gilded porcelain handle sat before him.

What a relief the cool shade and woody rose scents were after the hot street and the jackal journalist.

"Saj just called. He saw you on TV." René eyed her. "Seems you're a celebrity. Pulled Virginie into it, too? I can't believe you talked to that viper."

Surprised, she wanted to slap him. Instead

she sat down and rubbed her swollen ankle. Stupid water retention.

"*Bonjour* to you, too, René." She took a sip of his *thé citron.* "Hard night?"

A shake of his head.

"Tell me another way to enlist aid of the *quartier,* René," she said. "What about the people who don't realize they know something — a nosey concierge, the prying neighbor, that curious passerby, the garbage collector sneaking a smoke who might clue us in to where Zazie could be. How are we supposed to reach all those people when the *flics* aren't even treating her as missing yet? How else are we supposed to find her if she's duct-taped and being held captive in a cellar? That's if she's even . . . alive." Her throat caught. She blinked to combat the welling tears. And felt that damn knot at the base of her spine. "Go ahead, tell me how, René."

"I'm worried too, Aimée," said René, averting his eyes. "But *On the Rue* doesn't exactly garner you friendship with the *flics.*"

"*Alors,* my fan club diminishes." With all the bogus tips sure to be called in, they'd dislike her even more. Still, it only took one real lead. "Did Saj give you an update on the taxes?"

"All kosher, whatever that means," said

René. "He made the tax deadline. Care to explain how money fell from heaven?"

She owed René an explanation of the fund source. He was her partner, had a stake in Leduc Detective.

But she cut the paycheck. And she didn't want to get into the topic of her mother.

"Later, René."

She felt a flutter and then a sharp jab. She cradled her stomach.

"You all right?" Alarm shone on René's face.

"The Bump kicked. Think it likes the excitement." She took René's hand and put it on the side of her belly. "Feel?"

"Kicking like a soccer player." René's face softened. "Shouldn't you think about a name . . . ?"

Not him, too. Morbier had already suggested a whole list of names for either sex.

"I mean a family name — a father on the birth certificate. Think of school, children can taunt. Everyone in the village took me for the count's bastard. Still do."

Aimée had no idea René had suffered. Wasn't the count his father?

He saw the question in her eyes. "The count raised me as his son. But giving me his name would entail . . ." He shrugged. "A title, family issues, inheritance wars.

Still . . ."

Was René offering to put his name as the baby's father?

Her phone vibrated. She glanced at the caller ID. Her heart skipped a little.

"Aren't you going to pick that up? What if it's about Zazie?"

She shook her head. Bit her lip. "Melac."

René's face clouded.

"It's not the time to deal with him, René," she said. Or to waste time wondering if he'd reject the child growing inside her.

A look she couldn't fathom crossed René's face.

"You found something on le Weasel?" She sipped more of his tea. "That's what you needed to show me?"

"Who?"

She recounted her conversation with Tonette. Brought him up to speed on Marie-Jo and Zazie's project.

"So le Weasel, Marie-Jo's mother's Euro-trash boyfriend, is the top suspect?" said René. "Marie-Jo and Zazie followed him at first to get dirt on him and show her mother, then linked him to the rapes?"

"That's a working theory, René."

"*Ecoute,* last night I staked out Marie-Jo's apartment here on rue Chaptal," said René. "Only these six people came or went: an

230

older couple, these four *mecs.*"

He clicked through the images on his digital camera — his latest expensive toy. No one looked familiar to Aimée.

"You can see le Weasel here in the copy of *Le Parisien* Maurice gave me."

Aimée opened the newspaper to the celebrity page. *Actress Béatrice de Mombert accompanied by Hapsburg noble-cum-model Erich von Wessler — the couple puts on dancing shoes for a night of clubbing.*

Aimée stared at the couple's photo. Béatrice, late thirties, with a glazed smile, drooping eyelids, wearing an off-the-shoulder beaded camisole over leather stovepipe pants.

"Béatrice had been partying a little earlier, *non?*"

René nodded. He gestured with his balled-up fist like he was drinking from an imaginary bottle.

In the photo, Béatrice leaned on the arm of a long-haired, tousled type Aimée figured to be in his early twenties. His close-set eyes and chiseled nose and jaw emphasized his Aryan features. His thin lips formed a pout. Erich le Weasel looked fed up.

"Can't say I'd pick him to match the FotoFit," she said.

"But he's got small eyes," said René.

"Look, he could tuck his hair under the cap. And if the girl's terrorized, only catching a glimpse of him in dim light . . ."

Aimée read on. A small paragraph detailed Béatrice's background: her parents both actors in the Comédie-Française, she grew up in theatre, attended the Conservatoire des Arts Dramatiques, branched into cinema for some unmemorable films then returned to the stage to continue the family tradition.

Next, in a sidebar: *Car accident: The actress Béatrice de Mombert crashed into a lamp post on Pont Alexandre III after last night's performance of* Orphée Unchained. *After sustaining minor injuries, she was released from Hôtel-Dieu. Her press attaché cited the actress's* fragilité, *saying she was suffering exhaustion from nightly performances and indicated she checked in for a Thalasso cure in Biarritz.*

Press lingo for rehab, Aimée figured.

"According to Maurice's tabloid, le Weasel's a spoiled, impoverished Hapsburg descendant whose family branch lost the loot and the castle during the war. Obscure origins — Austria or Poland, no one's sure." René grinned. "He survives here with Dior Homme runway work and occasional *GQ* photo shoots, saves money by shacking up

232

with Béatrice," said René. "My violin's playing."

That made Aimée think. "Madame de Langlet, the violin teacher, promised to talk to me later."

"*Elle est formidable,* that lady, and to the point," said René. "I reached her an hour ago."

"*Et alors,* did she . . . ?"

"Confirm both girls were her pupils? *Oui* — but we knew that."

"How about the other two victims?"

"Let me finish, Aimée — Sylvaine attended her lesson as usual late Monday afternoon but left early. Madame informed me in no uncertain terms that that was all she would tell me. She's only talking to the police."

René had gotten more out of Madame than Aimée had.

"What if she's covering up for the rapist? For le Weasel?"

René nodded. "Madame spent the morning at the Commissariat — she only deals with the police, she repeated. Eh, wouldn't you?" René took back the teacup and sipped. "Say le Weasel appreciates violin. I spoke to Nelié's father this morning. According to him, Nelié heard someone clapping outside the window during her lesson."

Strange for the rapist to draw attention to himself — could that be a red herring? Unless he had been too successful and gotten brazen; or maybe he'd lost control.

"Any chance Nelié recognized her attacker?"

René shook his head. "It was pouring rain. Nelié ran, trying to protect her violin case. But she heard him following her all the way to their apartment on Cité de Trévise. He hummed the Paganini piece she'd been practicing. Terrified, she ran in the gate and shut it behind her."

"What time?"

"Her lesson went late. Eleven P.M."

"After the seaman got beat up."

The same time she'd wanted to drive to the music teacher's — if only they had. If only she'd veto'd René — they might have caught him.

"Two attacks in one evening. Unusual." René pulled his goatee. Thought. "Given his methodical behavior, the secrecy involved in this other life he lives, I'd say he was overcome by some pressure," said René. He traced his finger on the moisture ring of his teacup on the green metal table. "Say an external event's pushing him. He's escalating."

"We still don't know what the crime-scene

team found at Sylvaine's house. What if Zazie walked in and disturbed him?"

René's brow crinkled. "How do we know she actually went there?"

"We don't," she said. "Farfetched, maybe, but if Zazie's captive, he's under pressure, since he's never had to deal with a witness who could expose him. Or . . ." Aimée stopped the thought.

"Face it, Aimée: Even if some pieces of this scenario are true, we might be too late. She could be dead." René hung his head. "*Désolé* but . . ."

Aimée's lip trembled. "I owe it to her family to find her. To find out."

René nodded. "So say last night after it went so wrong with Sylvaine, he needs to clear his head. He goes back to Madame de Langlet's studio, where he hears Nelié's violin. She's his type . . ." René looked up. "Then, frustrated again by Nélie's getting away, he . . . I'm not sure."

Aimée pulled out the map. Added the time, noted the location of Madame de Langlet's studio. "Go on, René."

"So he's a musical fanatic. Paganini pieces are difficult — not anyone could just hum one," said René. "You'd have to know the piece very well."

Aimée didn't know anything about Paganini, but it was a good point — she wouldn't be able to recognize any classical piece, let alone hum it. "Okay. Does anything at all connect le Weasel? Could he be this music lover?"

"If we compare the FotoFit, Zazie's photo of the men on the street, le Weasel's newspaper photo and my photos of the *mecs* entering Twenty-one rue Chaptal last night . . ." René shrugged. "It's hard to tell."

"Try Marie-Jo's mother's number, René."

René dialed. Shook his head. "Only a recorded message. I've been trying all morning."

On the table by the bowl of wrapped sugar cubes, she set the newspaper photo next to Zazie's photo of men standing in the square.

"See a link, René?"

"What are we looking for, Aimée? 'I'm the rapist' tattooed on his arm?"

His frayed temper indicated he was exhausted. She needed him alert right now; his help was crucial.

She studied Zazie's photo. What wasn't she seeing?

"So according to Tonette, Zazie disobeyed her parents and continued to spend time with Marie-Jo, worked on this surveillance project with her. We know Marie-Jo lives here, a few doors down on rue Chaptal with her mother and le Weasel," said René, lining up the sugar cubes in a row. "The girls followed le Weasel to dig up dirt on him. Zazie thought they'd discovered le Weasel was the rapist, based on what she told you, but where's their proof? We still don't know anything about this photo. It wasn't taken from the rue Chaptal flat — impossible since the flat doesn't overlook this scene. Nothing points to le Weasel in this photo."

No way to cement this theory.

And then Aimée noticed the squared toe of the shoe the figure in the photo was wearing, the loafer shape and crest the unmistakable trademark of Polo by Ralph Lauren. "Look at the shoes, René. The figure in the hoodie's wearing the same dancing pair as le Weasel."

She saw the wheels turning in his head. "Maybe at first to prove to her mother that he was carrying on other affairs," he said. "Fits with what Tonette told you, that they were trying to prove he wasn't what he said he was. Classic case of slimeball live-in boyfriend. The daughter wants her mother to dump him."

"She'd go to those lengths?"

René sat up. "What if he hit on her?"

"But how does that fit with the rapist's profile? Secretive, single-minded, targeting twelve-year-old blondes after violin lessons?"

"But that's it. He hits on her school friends. Specifically the ones who take violin."

That only fit if they knew more about le Weasel, sniffed out some musical connection.

"Like I said, he's escalating because he's under some kind of stress." René nodded to himself. "He steps it up now that Zazie's onto him."

"The flat's on this street." She put her phone in her pocket. "Time to ask him."

"No one answers, Aimée."

"But the concierge will." She took a last deep breath of the warm, rose-scented sunshine and stood. "Coming?"

René's phone trilled. He checked the number. "Saj and I need to go over the hiccup in today's virus scan." He pulled out a paper covered with notations. "Takes ten minutes."

Ten minutes she didn't have. "Call me when you finish. You're the backup."

"For what?"

"I have a weasel to catch."

She left René to walk a few doors down rue Chaptal. Pigalle teemed with people. Locals who would normally be packing to head to the train stations and the countryside were staying at home this year, crowding the streets and cafés with World Cup chatter.

Twenty-one rue Chaptal's facade of freshly sandblasted limestone, subtle and solid, breathed wealth. A couple paused before the high, green, carved doors in the arched former carriage entrance. Aimée waited, pretending to consult her phone until the couple hit the digicode. A smaller door in the large one clicked, and they pushed it open. She waited until it had almost shut before sliding inside.

She adjusted her eyes in the cool, paved *porte-cochère* entrance. Trellised ivy climbed the back of the courtyard, still dripping from a recent watering. The concierge's *loge* held a sign: FERMÉ.

There went that idea.

She found de Mombert on the nameplate — TROISIÈME ÉTAGE, GAUCHE. They were more security conscious here, with a solid Fichet lock to the glass door, behind which she could see a marble floor and twisting staircase.

She continued into the courtyard, where the carriage house and stables had been converted into garages. Like everywhere around here. She looked up at the massive backs of the buildings and realized the sixth floor held small windows for the *chambres de bonnes,* maid's rooms. From the looks of the ten or so small, dust-colored mailboxes, the former maid quarters were now rented as single rooms. But these buildings had stairs for the help — *escaliers de service.* So there would be a back door — one likelier to respond to her lock-pick set than the Fichet.

Inside she saw garbage bins tucked under winding stairs so steep and narrow elves would feel at home. There was no locked door to the stairwell — in fact there was no door at all. She climbed, pausing to catch her breath as she pulled herself up the almost ladder-like stairs.

On the third-floor landing, jutting off to the left, lay a narrow walkway lined by an old hinge rack with just enough space to store sacks of coal — a common practice. She didn't envy the help who had to carry up those sacks.

She hit René's number. "Try de Mombert's number again, okay? No need for surprises."

Pause.

"Wait *un petit moment,* don't tell me you're breaking in?" René said. "Think you'll find le Weasel sleeping it off, Zazie locked in a closet?"

"Something like that."

"Alone? With a dangerous *mec* who's —"

"The reason I asked you for backup, René," she interrupted. "Make the call."

She clicked off, put her ringer on mute. A moment later she heard a phone ringing from deep in the apartment's bowels, but after ten rings, no answer.

Her neck damp with perspiration, she reached into her bag. Under her prenatal vitamins she found her mini lock-pick set, which she kept in her Dior sunglasses case. Inserting the pick and switch clip, she toggled up and down until she heard a click. The half-glass-paned back service door yielded, and in less than two minutes she had checked the walk-in pantry, cupboards, and cabinets under the old-style porcelain kitchen sink. No Zazie.

Not much cooking done here, either, evidenced by the Chinese take-out cartons in the trash. The refrigerator held yogurt and a glass bottle of capers. Nice and pickled, but she resisted the temptation. On the wood trestle kitchen table was half of a stale baguette and a bowl of *café au lait*. Cold, a beige skin floating on the surface of the milk. She sniffed. Not curdled, so from this morning.

She needed to work fast. The apartment's rooms were laid out along a parquet-floored hall. So far all she had heard behind any of the doors was the flushing from the pipes above.

A loud buzzing disturbed her thoughts. She froze.

In her pocket she felt her phone vibrating. *Merde.* She'd thought she'd silenced it, but she'd only put it on vibrate. She checked the display.

René.

She stepped behind the door to the salon — formal, with period furniture and wall tapestries. Unused, by the look of it.

"What?" she whispered into the phone.

"Buzz me in. I'm downstairs. You're not doing this alone."

"Then hurry up."

She tiptoed to the front door. Pushed the button for PORTE, waited a few seconds, then pressed the second buzzer, ENTRÉE.

By the time René came puffing up the stairs, she'd done a cursory check of the whole apartment. "If he was here, he's long gone, René."

"So you've checked the armoires, the closets . . . ?"

"We have to dig deeper. Any information about le Weasel or Marie-Jo . . . You take

242

the left side, and I'll do the courtyard side."

He rolled up his sleeves.

The apartment phone rang. René jumped. "Good God, what are we doing here, Aimée, besides getting arrested for breaking and entering?"

"Shh."

After nine rings the answering machine clicked.

"Monsieur, the dry cleaner on rue de la Rochefoucald won't give me your suit without the ticket. Pff. So don't wonder why I'm late to work this afternoon, eh?"

The housekeeper.

"That's two blocks away," said René. "Sounds like she expects him to be here. Maybe he's stepped out for cigarettes."

Any moment he could appear. If they were going to confront him, it couldn't be in this flat they'd broken into. They needed some kind of proof first.

"Quick, René." She pawed through her bag. Where was her bug? Finally her fingers closed around it. "If you find a computer, use this."

"So that's where my scramble tracer's gone!" He shook his head. "Concentrate on the girl's room. Figure we've got less than ten minutes."

Through the second door she found a

teenager's room — clothes on the floor, photos of boy bands on the walls, a few schoolbooks on a maple-wood rolltop desk. She scanned notebooks — only schoolwork — and then she found the camera. A high-end Nikon with a telescopic lens. No film inside.

She stepped back and surveyed the cluttered floor.

"Aimée, let's go . . ."

On the floor by her foot, peeking from below a hoodie, she saw a red tassel. The red tassel she'd last seen on Zazie's backpack.

Her heart cartwheeled, flipping from relief to fear. Zazie had been here.

But where was she now?

"Now, Aimée! Or do you want to get arrested?"

"Head through the kitchen to the pantry — the service stairs," she said, scooping the tassel into her pocket. "I'm right behind you."

But her feet refused to take her past the foyer. Zazie had been here and gone. There had to be more. Footsteps sounded outside the front door.

Her palms moistened in a hot sweat.

The shoes. A pair of scuffed Polo loafers, just like in Zazie's photo, sat under a

244

coatrack with a man's linen jacket.

A key turned in the front door. Perspiration dripped between her shoulder blades. She reached in the linen jacket's pockets and snatched the contents.

Moments later, breathing hard, she'd shut the back service door and was padding down the steep, winding stairs. Reaching the courtyard, she took deep breaths, focusing on the breeze blowing over the stone wall and trying to still her thumping heart.

Men always left things in their pockets. Incriminating things. Le Weasel proved no exception: the dry-cleaning receipt and a coat-check ticket she recognized from the Cercle de Jeux casino below Place Pigalle. There was also a rolled-up twenty-franc note — snort material.

René waited by the ivy, checking his phone. "Hurry, Aimée."

The blurred outlines of le Weasel came into focus: a gambler, careless enough to leave white crystals on the rolled-up note in his pocket.

"Look what I found in le Weasel's pocket."

René face soured as he scanned the items in her palm. "With pedophiles it's not unusual for them to have families, professions, even be pillars of the community. It's about a double life. Power."

"Yet gambling wouldn't necessarily fit the profile of a serial rapist," she said.

"Unless the screws tightening up in the *quartier* stressed him, he's gambling, amping up. What's the red tassel?"

"Proof." Aimée's palm shook. "This was on Zazie's backpack the last time I saw her. But the *flics* need more for a case."

"We don't," said René, taking the Cercle de Jeux ticket from her. His jaw set. A single-minded focus in his green eyes. "Now we know Zazie was here. Time le Weasel coughs up her location."

A woman's voice carried over the pavers. The apricot light streaming into the arched carriage entrance sharpened her figure into a dark silhouette — a woman not much taller than René, a chignon atop her head and what appeared to be a long apron tied around her ample waist.

The voice, not the one she'd heard on the answering machine minutes before, sounded familiar. She knew that woman's voice. But from where?

Time to find out.

"*Bonjour,* Madame. You're the concierge?"

Startled, she fumbled with her shopping bag. Red and white radishes — reminding Aimée of little torpedoes — fell on the cobbles.

246

"You've no business here," she said, irritated. "It's private property."

"*Excusez-moi,* Madame," said Aimée, bending down with difficulty to recover the radishes. Soon she'd need a crane for such a maneuver.

The low smoker's voice was at odds with the woman's clear complexion and bright grey eyes. "But you're Leduc's daughter, *non?* The big eyes, skinny legs — you're taller now. Grown up." Her eyes narrowed. "And a bun in the oven, as they say."

Now Aimée remembered Cécile. A Pigalle working girl whose pimp Aimée's father had put in prison. Instead of turning informer, as he'd counted on, or showing him any gratitude for freeing her from the life, she'd found another *macquereau* — so named for their sardine-shiny flash suits. Would the woman be friendly to her now or hostile?

"Cécile." She smiled, bent down to brush both cheeks. "You're looking even younger than the last time I saw you, if that's possible."

"I found *mon Sauveur,*" she said, tugging the gold cross around her neck. "In Saint Rita's chapel."

"You look happy," Aimée said.

"I've made my peace with the past. How is Leduc now?"

Aimée looked down at the worn pavers. Almost ten years gone, but the memory seared like it was yesterday.

"He died in a bomb explosion in Place Vendôme," she said.

"Désolée," she said, glancing at Aimée's stomach. "He won't see his grandchild, then. You know, I made my peace with everyone but your father. I always wanted to." She shrugged. *"C'est dommage."*

"Can you help us, Cécile?" She folded Cécile's hand in her own. "Marie-Jo's friend Zazie's missing. She'd been following the rapist."

"That pig who murdered the little girl above the cheese shop?"

Aimée nodded. "Maybe if you could help me find Zazie . . . Think of it as some way of making it up to Papa."

Cécile glanced at René. Her brow furrowed.

Impatient, René was tapping his hand-made Lobb shoes on the cobbles. She noticed his balled-up fist clutching the detritus from le Weasel's pocket, the other jingling his car keys. "Cécile, where's le . . . I mean, Monsieur von Wessler?"

"Him? If he didn't answer the door, some modeling job or out gambling, I expect. *Comme d'habitude,* these days."

248

René shot her a look. "*Excusez-moi*, Madame. Talk to you later, Aimée."

Gung ho, René headed to his parked Citroën, which glowed dark green in the sun. Where was he going? To try to track down le Weasel? She wished they'd had a chance to discuss a plan, but she would call him when she'd gotten more information from Cécile.

But before she could, the phone rang in the concierge's *loge*. "I'm busy, and with any luck that's the plumber."

Before Aimée could press her, she'd gone into the *loge* and shut the door.

Aimée's bad feeling mounted. She hesitated on narrow rue Chaptal, the afternoon sun melting into dim gold reflections on the mansard windows. Did René believe he could force a confession from le Weasel in a casino? René had taken off like a shot, unprepared and without thinking things through, just like he often accused her of doing. He was tired, too. The purple-tinged rings under his eyes worried her.

She knew Zazie had been here, that Zazie had trailed le Weasel and was after the rapist — but had she ever found out they were one and the same? Or just assumed?

In the fog of her pregnancy brain, she'd missed something with Cécile. She couldn't let this unease in her gut go. Cécile had to know more.

"*Zut alors,* I've told you all I know," said Cécile peering out from the concierge's *loge.* She made a *tsk* sound. "But you can't let things go, eh? Like your father."

Her father's lopsided grin flashed in front of her; his tired, smiling eyes over a bowl of *café au lait* in the morning, poring through police files at the kitchen table. His bath-robe, the musk and fresh laundry scent it carried, her father's smell. The ache of missing him never went away.

But she wouldn't let Cécile fob her off again. "It's more than that, Cécile," she said. "Zazie's in danger. What more can you remember? There must be something."

Cécile glanced at the time. Untied her apron.

"Red hair?"

Aimée stepped closer. "Curly and red. You saw her, Cécile?"

"Marie-Jo and this Zazie went out yesterday afternoon. With this nice man, a friend of her father's."

Alarm flooded Aimée with this new twist. Wasn't the father in prison?

"Were the girls struggling? Upset?"

"*Mais non,* not at all."

Aimée felt a tightening in her chest. Who

the hell was this "nice man"?

"What time was this?"

She thought. "A bit after five. Something like that."

The most recent sighting of Zazie by several hours. "Can you describe him?"

Cécile shrugged. "Polite."

"His clothes, color of his hair?"

"I had to sign for a package. Too much going on to notice."

"Can you just look at these and see if you recognize him?" Aimée pulled René's camera from her bag, showed her the small screen, clicking each photo. "Was the man who took them — the friend of Marie-Jo's father — was he any of these men?"

A shake of her head.

Standing in the heat, feeling her ankles starting to swell and at the end of her rope, she pulled out her last shot, the FotoFit. "What about him?"

Cécile blinked. "Jean-Michel!"

Aimée's heart caught.

"So you know him. Where does he live?"

"Live? But he's in Marseilles. Talked to them this morning. He's my nephew."

"You're sure?"

"My sister's boy. But his eyes are bigger."

Great. The generic FotoFit matched half of the French male population.

"Un moment," Cécile said. "Show me the ones in the camera again."

Had this jogged her memory?

Aimée clicked forward.

"Go back. *Mais oui,* this one, that's Marie-Jo's father. Zacharié."

Aimée saw a side view of the man's face, black curly hair.

"Did he take the girls?"

Cécile shook her head. "He asked me which way they'd gone. He seemed worried."

Aimée filed that away. Now she had to press Cécile while her memory stirred.

"Did this nice man have an accent? Try to remember. Young or middle-aged?"

"Didn't look like a rapist to me," she said, dismissive.

"See, you noticed something. Then what did he look like? How did he strike you?"

"Like I said. Polite."

"But you'd seen him before, right?"

"A long time ago, perhaps. *Non,* I'm not sure. So many people come through here."

All working ladies typed men instantly. That was part of their trade and negotiations.

"Neighbor, shopkeeper? Lives in the *quartier*?"

"Come to think of it, he wore pressed

jeans, like some of them do."

"Some of who?"

"Off-duty *flics*." She shook her head. "I don't know. We only spoke a few seconds."

She turned the concierge sign to FERMÉ and grabbed her handbag.

"I'm late for Saint Rita's."

Aimée's head spun. Cécile's observations of a nice man in pressed jeans like an off-duty *flic* didn't fit with what they'd learned. Someone else had abducted the girls.

Who?

Meanwhile René had run off half-cocked to nail le Weasel.

She punched in René's number. No answer. Tried again.

Frustrated, she started to leave a message, but the voice mail cut her off. When she tried again, his message box was full.

Merde!

Thoughts swirling, she made toward the bus stop. The dense heat hovered, caught in the valley of tall sandstone buildings. She realized she'd gone the wrong way on rue Chaptal. *Merde* again.

Retracing her steps, she noticed a man loitering at the now-closed doors of Marie-Jo's building. He rocked on his heels and checked his phone. Marie-Jo's father — she recognized him from René's camera.

From the corner bar came loud cheering. "Score!"

She had to jump over a gutter rushing with last night's rainwater. "*Excusez-moi,* but you're Zacharié, Marie-Jo's father?"

He started. "And you are?"

"Looking for Zazie, her red-haired friend." She pulled out her card. "Please, she's the friend Marie-Jo left with yesterday, around five o'clock."

Something like pain crossed his face. He glanced down the street, moved away from her.

"Who's your friend the girls went with? Where's Zazie?"

"Not my friend."

"But who? What's happened to her?"

Fear and anger battled in his eyes. "Stay out of it. You have to stay out of this."

"And leave them in the hands of a rapist?"

His jaw quivered. "What the hell does that mean?"

"Don't you understand? The girls were trailing a rapist who murdered a twelve-year-old yesterday, and now they've disappeared."

A taxi pulled up on the street. "I think you're climbing the wrong tree." He jumped in the back seat.

"Wait!"

But the taxi took off in a splash of scummed gutter water that sprayed her ballet shoes. She ran, her feet sopping wet, trying to see the taxi number — too late. It disappeared down the hill into a winding street.

Tuesday, 6 P.M.

René glanced at Aimée's name on his call list. Three times already. He wished she'd take a nap.

Blue smoke spiraled toward the casino's Art Deco stained-glass ceiling. Low conversations carried through the clink of *glaçons* in whiskey tumblers, a swish from cards dealt onto the baize tables.

Behind velvet curtains in the private, roped-off area, le Weasel lit a cigarette on his maroon leather chair at the felt poker table. Gone through a pack already, evidenced by the butts in the ashtray. In front him was a dwindling pile of chips. Le Weasel played *le punto banco* — small stakes — and relentlessly. René couldn't wait for the *salaud* to wise up — not that he ever would — and quit the game and lead him to Zazie.

Fat lot of good the tips René had dispensed had gotten him so far. The casino, all wood and brass with a wall-sized, Art Nouveau stained-glass window backlighting the nine poker tables, listed itself as a "social club" with a large membership fee to skirt the gambling regulations.

He'd slipped the smiling bouncer a "spectator" fee, indicating he'd like to get a feel for the place before he joined.

"*D'accord,* Monsieur." The man had smiled and held out his hand.

But that was as far as René had gotten. "*C'est privé,* Monsieur," said a short, sparse-haired waiter, barring René's way past the bar. "Members only."

"*Bien sûr.* Could I have a word with Monsieur von Wessler?"

"Not allowed, Monsieur." The waiter indicated he should wait at the bar.

He'd have to bide his time until *le salaud* got up from the table.

Doubt hit René. Would a serial rapist waste time at a gambling table? Was his own impatience clouding his logic? Le Weasel glanced at his phone, then back to his cards.

René joined the mixed clientele: a few men in blazers, a woman in *un jogging* with pearls, Asian men with gold-link wrist chains, a leather-jacketed rocker he recognized from the guitar shop around the corner. The woman in pearls shook her head and exclaimed, *"Tout sur rouge!"* as she clicked a pile of gambling chips to a red nine.

The casino gave off a low-key vibe — casual, almost homey. Everyday gamblers a world apart from the Deauville Grand Casino milieu.

His phone vibrated again. Madie, the waitress in the café, who'd promised him information, was waiting at the *bistrot*. He'd forgotten. Too bad.

He looked up. Saw movement at the *punto banco* table. But with his short stature he couldn't see over the shoulders of the crowd. He tried edging his way forward through the gamblers.

An older woman sat at le Weasel's place. He'd gone. *Merde!*

René grabbed his jacket.

Tuesday, 6 P.M.

Aimée had changed out of her sopping clothes, and now her damp feet were drying in the sun by Leduc Detective's window. Her chipped, neon-green-lacquered toenails were in dire need of a pedicure.

The office was anything but peaceful. Horns blared in the street, and boos and cheers drifted from radio broadcasts from the cars below. The carpenter's unswept sawdust was piled in the corner, making her sneeze.

So far no word from Mélanie at the clinic in Lausanne. Nor had René returned her calls. The FotoFit image lay on her desk, troubling her. This suspect had a cap without hair showing; le Weasel a full head of hair.

And what did Marie-Jo's father mean that Aimée was climbing the wrong tree? He'd appeared worried, gone to the apartment, no doubt tried Marie-Jo's phone. He knew this man who had been seen with the girls. Zacharié was the key.

How could she find him?

On her laptop she searched for the Actors' Union's database. In five minutes she'd bypassed the firewall and maneuvered into the directory, searching for de Mombert.

The biographies of an illustrious acting family spilled onto her screen. Béatrice's career was not so illustrious. Still, roles at Théâtre Charles Dullin and the Théâtre de Nesle. A sporadic résumé, with gaps between engagements. Her marriage to a Zacharié Plessis had ended in divorce a year before.

Now that she knew Zacharié's last name, she ran a search through a prison database Saj had turned her on to a month ago. A shortcut for finding anyone's history in the penal system.

Zacharié Plessis, born in 1970 at Hôpital Laboiserie. Last residence 21 rue Chaptal; convicted for what amounted to *criminalité en col blanc* — white-collar crime. He'd been released on parole a week ago.

Just a week ago.

Serving six months of a two-year sentence, then out on parole? Only prisoners who pulled strings served minimal time like that.

How did that fit into the equation of the girl's abduction?

Somehow this all connected. Vice?

She tried Beto's number. No answer.

A moment later her phone rang. "Didn't I tell you I'd repaid the favor, *chérie*?" said Beto.

"True, Beto," she said, "but you also said that the rapist would strike again before school let out."

Beto cleared his throat. *"Et alors?"*

"I don't know how this fits," she said, "or if it does, but with your contacts in the *quartier . . .*"

"My contacts?" he interrupted.

She heard the *rabatteurs* — strip-club barkers — loud and distinctive, shouting in the background, "*Cherchez les femmes* of your dreams . . . no drink minimum."

"*Chérie,* make it quick."

And she told him about the "nice man." "I need to find him."

"That's too vague a description," said Beto. "All you know about him is that he wore jeans that reminded Cécile of a *flic.* There's nothing to go on, no reason to think she's even right."

"True." But Cécile's former-working-girl intuition hadn't left her. "Wouldn't it be

261

worth talking to the owner of the NeoCancan for a tip? Fish around and mention
Cécile's description."

"The Johnny Hallyday wannabe, that one?
Why?"

"He's an informer, *non*?"

She heard Beto's intake of breath over the
phone. "He intimated that?"

"*Mais non,* but I figured like all the bar
owners he informed to keep on your good
side." Quiet as the bars kept it, rumor went
they also paid *sécurité,* a percentage of earn-
ings given in a weekly envelope to the
controlling network of the moment to keep
their doors open.

"He's got a record."

Cymbals and guitar sounded in the background. The Fête de la Musique, celebrated
on the eve of summer solstice, had begun.

"What's on his record?"

"Statutory rape . . . but you didn't hear
that from me."

She remembered he'd led the lynch mob
to the Lille seaman. A foil to take the
suspicion away from himself? Had René
been right to suspect his motives?

Her mind went back to the dumbwaiter in
his cellar floor. A gasp escaped her as she
pictured his jeans. Long shot, but worth a
try.

"Why don't you visit the NeoCancan's cellar?"

"Just like that, out of the blue?"

"Health violations, contraband liquor, prostitution," she said. "You'll think of something."

He snorted. "Why risk my neck?"

"Several reasons," she said, rubbing her belly. She wished she hadn't eaten that last cornichon. "It sounds like you're in Pigalle."

"Along with a quarter of Paris, *chérie,*" he said.

"Two young girls could be held down in NeoCancan's cave, you're in the *quartier* and my Beretta's back home."

"I don't know." His tone turned serious. "It's all circumstantial."

She wanted to spit. Instead took a deep breath to calm down. Covered the phone and burped. "Could you live with yourself if you didn't check it out?" she said. "Or deal with me on your back for the rest of your life?"

On his back . . . she wondered what he wore to bed. Or if he wore anything at all. Where had that thought come from? Down, girl.

"I forgot about irrational pregnant women," he said.

Did she care what he thought? Or his tone

of condescension? Or more that he had big, protective arms and knew how to wake a woman up?

Time to put the brakes on her hormonal overdrive.

"So humor me," she said, trying for charm. *"S'il vous plaît."*

"Promise you won't throw up pastries again."

"Deal."

He clicked off. Good thing he couldn't see her wide grin.

A knock came from the door. "Aimée?"

"Entrez." She pulled her now-dry feet in from the window ledge.

Pierre entered with Zazie's brother, little Lucien, in his arms. "Virginie's upset," he said.

The toll and strain showed on Pierre's furrowed brow.

"*Ecoutez,* I apologize for putting her through that interview, but . . ." Aimée trailed off, feeling at sea. "We needed the quickest way to get word out and find Zazie." More than twenty-four hours had elapsed now. "Pierre, I'm sorry, but believe me, time's crucial." Keep it positive, forward-moving. "Any word yet?"

"The Brigade des Mineurs established a hotline. Got a call. There's been a sighting."

The hair rose on Aimée's neck.

"They're telling us not to raise our hopes, but . . ."

"Where?"

"A warehouse near *le périphérique.*"

Not what she had been expecting. "A creditable tip, Pierre?"

Lucien squirmed in his arms. "They think so. Dispatched a team."

For once she kept her mouth shut and nodded.

"The Brigade wants you hands-off, Aimée. *Désolé,* but we can't risk jeopardizing this operation."

Warned off by Marie-Jo's father and now Zazie's. She realized Virginie couldn't face her and had sent poor Pierre in her place.

"It's gotten *compliqué,* Aimée."

Life threw complications at you when you loved your child. You'd do anything to co-operate, no matter how tangled or messy. Listen to whoever you believed could save her.

But an operation out in God's country, way out on *le périphérique*? This smelled. A ruse to get people out of the way. Deflect attention.

But right now, she didn't have much. She had le Weasel's computer tracked — worth little after Cécile's information and no contact from René. All she had to work with was proof Zazie had been at rue Chaptal, Cécile's sighting of her leaving with a "nice man," Zacharié warning her off. The only thing she was certain of was that she had to find this "nice man."

"I understand, Pierre," she said, glad not to lie. "No fear I'll jeopardize the operation."

She would run her own instead. If you could call it that.

Her cell phone rang. She didn't recognize the number. When she looked up, Pierre had gone.

"*Allô?*"

"My daughter Mélanie left me a message," said Madame Vasseur. No *bonjour,* and her voice in a low whisper. "But I don't understand it."

Aimée sat up.

"Mélanie sounded upset. It's garbled, but if you can understand . . . ?" Pause. "The FotoFit tech got the rapist's description wrong."

"Wrong how?" Aimée reached for a pen. A chord of anticipation rippled her spine.

"Maybe it will help Zazie."

"Mélanie left a message on your cell phone?" Aimée said. "Let me listen."

"What do I do? All these dual functions

but . . ." Beeps, the sound of her hitting the keys. "Sorry, Mélanie knows how to do that. Not me. But I'll try."

It must have cost the woman to call her. Touched, Aimée'd never expected any help from this *haute bourgeoise* professional. Maybe she'd misjudged Madame Vasseur. Or Madame Vasseur had hit cement and was scared, didn't know where else to turn.

At last, Aimée heard a buzzing, muffled voice. Inaudible. She needed to hear it in person. "Where can I meet you, Madame Vasseur?"

"I'm in contract negotiations. Impossible."

"What time do you finish?"

"But I'm a cosponsor of the Conservatoire de Musique benefit tonight." What sounded like a pen clicking came over the line. "Must go. They're starting again."

Talk about complicated. But she couldn't let this go.

"Give me the address." Silence. "Please, it will take, what, a few minutes?"

"Madame Vasseur, we're waiting . . ." came from the background.

"Ten rue de la Tour des Dames. Eight P.M."

Two hours. Which would make it twenty-seven hours since Zazie was last seen.

■ ■ ■ ■

Aimée spent an anxious two hours on her laptop trawling Zacharié Plessis's penal history and gleaned precious little information, only that his charge was "corporate theft" in the court documents and lawyer's statements.

To her it appeared someone had expunged his court records, picked through the documents and combed out every nit. Alarms sounded in her head.

Pressure exerted by his ex-wife's influential family? Friends in high places? Béatrice de Mombert's father, a member of the Comédie-Française, had been awarded the Légion d'Honneur. Smelled like the *crème de la crème* didn't want their reputation curdled.

Too bad they couldn't muzzle their daughter and keep her antics out of the papers. Or maybe after so many incidents even the press couldn't be bought.

Not Aimée's business.

Still . . .

She'd found zero on Zacharié's present address or a contact for him. Yet he knew this "nice man," had warned her off. Right now he was the only avenue to pursue — if she could find a name, a contact, then meet Beto and give him the information . . . Back inside the penal database she checked his release date again — just last week. He'd report to a parole officer, of course.

Stupid. She wished she'd twigged on that right away. She'd wasted more than an hour.

It took twenty more minutes to locate his parole officer, a Monsieur Faure, and his office number. It was late, but she thought up a story. But Faure's voice mail answered. Didn't public servants have to perform the public service of answering their phones? She slammed the desk with her fist. Then left a message stressing the urgency of reaching Zacharié Plessis concerning a lucrative job offer for a man of his skills. If that didn't a get a call back, she didn't know what would.

Frustrated, she entered Zacharié's info in her red Moleskine, giving him a full page after the "formula vs breast milk" benefits comparison René had made for her.

She tried René. Only voice mail.

René stood fuming on bustling rue des Martyrs next to the fishmonger's — he'd lost le Weasel. Zazie could be locked up . . . buried. Shame and anger at himself prevented him from answering Aimée's call.

Money, always follow the money, he thought, desperate. That was Saj's second-favorite mantra, after the Hindu one tattooed on his wrist. How would a gambler refresh his funds? Pay debts without a ransom demanded for kidnapping?

Forget that, he realized. Le Weasel had been living off his druggie actress girlfriend, but he couldn't count on that now with her in rehab. Just a male model for *GQ,* caught clubbing in the pages of *Le Parisien* . . .

A trumpet blurted from the corner, a crash of cymbals — the damn Fête de la Musique had started. He couldn't hear himself think.

As he turned he hit his head on a door handle. Cursing and rubbing his temple, he happened to catch sight of the tabloids used for wrapping fish at the fishmonger's counter. If paparazzi could track him, then so could René.

Think like a paparazzo.

Five minutes later he got through to the head booker at Stylisme — the model agency *à la mode.* "Erich von Wessler doesn't wake up for less than a thousand francs a day," said a bored voice.

"I'm not booking him," said René. "Something fell out of his man-purse at the photo shoot. A delicate item, *compris*? I'd like to show him before we publish."

A long sigh. "I detest you paparazzi."

"*Non,* you love us," said René. "We make him bankable. Indiscretions cost, remember, and drive his price up."

"He's under contract. We'll take you to court," said the voice, alert now.

"*Non,* you'll give me his number," said René. "I'll work it out with him."

"Why should I believe you?"

"He's small fry, but these allegations could stick to his lady, Béatrice de Mombert. Can you risk not giving me his number?"

"He's booked all week. Busy. All I can do

is pass your name and number to him."

Booked? He'd just lost him at the casino. René consulted his map, trying to figure out how to lure him. "Tell him to meet me at ten rue de Parme, the café."

"He's busy."

"He'll make time. I'll be waiting. Tell him I know about Marie-Jo."

Fifteen minutes later René sat in the café on rue de Parme across the street from the Commissariat. Le Weasel would have a short walk to justice. Without any actual proof against him, René would use one of Aimée's tactics. Lie.

Le Weasel strode into the café alone. Despite dark circles under his eyes and the fact that he was wearing those damn monogrammed velvet loafers, he still looked like *GQ* material.

He sat down at René's table and snapped his fingers at the man behind the counter. *"Un express."* Several men stood watching the match on the *télé* over the counter.

Le Weasel's quick glance took in René's short legs. He moved the water carafe and set down his man-purse. "I recognize you from the casino," said le Weasel. "You want me to cough up, *non*?"

Chalk one to le Weasel. Chalk minus two

for René's surveillance technique.

"Then you know," said René, "you've been identified. The last victim provided your description."

"Eh? Cut to the chase, little man," said le Weasel. "Where's Marie-Jo?"

"Nice try," said René, disgusted.

He gave a weary sigh. "How much this time?"

"What?"

"So she's run off with a boy, partied, and now, *quoi,* she's hiding in some basement squat with a hangover? The usual?"

This wasn't going how René had planned. "Where's Zazie?"

"Who knows?" Le Weasel waved a pinkie-ringed finger, dismissive. "What does it take to keep Marie-Jo off the front page?"

Le Weasel acted like René knew more about Marie-Jo than he did. Did he really believe she'd run off? Or was le Weasel bluffing to hide his guilt?

Why did René feel tongue-tied? Why did he almost believe this dandy with mono-grammed velvet slippers?

"You scum always turn up," said le Weasel. "But one only three apples tall takes the prize."

Three apples tall — René hadn't heard

273

that since a bully's taunts in the village school.

Something snapped inside René. The smirking, long-haired Eurotrash's insolence, his aching hip, his fear over Zazie — it was too much. Up like a shot, René planted his feet in the offensive karate position. They never expected a dwarf to be a black belt. Aimed and kidney-kicked the surprised fashion sensation off his chair, spun and twisted his arm until he was down to the tiled café floor.

"I call half-men like you scum, preying on little girls," he said. René pressed the groaning man's arm back. "You're going to tell me where Zazie is and then we're walking across the street to a cell. *Compris?*"

"What are you? Some *demi-tasse flic?*"

"First I'll break your arm, then I'll work my way down."

The waiter stood by the table, tray in hand, and shook his head. "*Attendez,* I want no trouble in my café. Take it outside."

"After this pedophile talks," said René, his breath coming in short gasps.

"I'm not a pedophile," le Weasel shouted, squirming on the floor.

"What, you prefer child rapist and murderer?"

Before he could answer, René took a café

napkin and stuffed it in his mouth.

"*Ça alors,* that one who attacked little girls after school, him?" The café owner's face darkened. "Didn't they catch the *salaud*?"

"*Non,* he's face down on your café floor. So let justice take its course," said René. "Go back to fixing him an espresso. Make it extra hot."

The waiter gave a long look, then nodded. "It's always the ones you'd never suspect. Sick."

René took the napkin out of le Weasel's mouth and used it to bind his wrists behind him.

Le Weasel sputtered and spit. "Let me up."

"As soon as you tell me where Zazie is," he said. "Start with last night. Where did you take her?"

"You're crazy, little man. I went to Marie-Jo's grandparents' place to meet Béa's lawyer. Look in my pockets."

René reached in the blazer's pockets. A used round-trip train ticket to Fontaine-bleau. "That's where Zazie is?"

The men at the zinc counter gathered around the waiter. Not one cracked a smile. He'd use that.

"The waiter's preparing your espresso," said René. "He and his friends will pour it on your face. Scald and burn that *GQ*

275

cover-boy face. Now shall I let him?"

"But you don't understand," le Weasel protested.

"Oh, I understand. What is it about violinists you like so much? Classical music make you want to attack little girls?"

"What? No. Trance and techno's my groove," he said. "What's music got to do with anything?"

"But you're a Paganini aficionado, *n'est-ce pas?*"

"After suffering piano lessons all my childhood . . . I prefer Chopin."

"And twelve-year-old blondes, little girls who play violin get you off."

The men at the counter huddled, listening.

"What are you, some kind of pint-sized avenger? It's against the law, assaulting me like this," le Weasel said, the bravado faltering in his voice. "In public, too. You can't do this."

René gritted his teeth and hoisted him up against the banquette seating. "Then I'll drag you down to the wine cellar. After I finish, it's their turn." He nodded to the murmuring crowd.

René noticed panic flooding le Weasel's brown eyes. Good.

"Going to tell me the truth now?"

Le Weasel nodded.

And then he started talking.

"Béatrice's parents want me to take her and Marie-Jo down south. To start over. But the brat hates the idea, refused to go and ran away. Now I'm stuck here until I track her down, Béa's in rehab, Marie-Jo's gone and her grandparents think I've got her under control. I need her, don't you see? The lawyer insists I show responsibility so Béa can keep custody."

"And you get paid for it."

"We've got to live."

"Gambling?"

"I'm going on a hiatus in my modeling career for the little brat. Why shouldn't I make some coin for my sacrifice?"

Eurotrash.

"So you couldn't report your meal ticket missing?"

Le Weasel shrugged. "She hates me. Followed me with her friend, that redhead, convinced I cheated on her wild mother while I was trying to clean up after her. Taking photos of me, like little spies, trying to set me up and make me look bad to her grandparents. That's the thanks I get."

He flicked his head back to get the stringy hair out of his eyes.

"But we know Zazie was in the rue Chaptal apartment. I've got proof."

"How the hell do I know if she was there?"

"When did you last see Marie-Jo?"

"Yesterday afternoon. We had a fight after lunch, maybe her friend came by later. I don't know. Look, I've been on assignment for photo shoots, not raping little girls. Check my bookings. Four full-page spreads for Dior Homme."

After a while René wished he'd stop talking. Such a pathetic, self-important pretty boy.

Aimée's heels clicked over the cobbles as she hurried through la Nouvelle Athènes to meet Madame Vasseur. The über-wealthy slice of the *quartier* seemed almost oppressive after the vibrant, humming Pigalle and the jazz trio she'd passed on the Grands Boulevards a few streets away.

She turned the corner to see the woman's distinctive Mercedes, but no waiting Madame Vasseur on the dimly lit rue. *Merde!* Not a goddamned café in sight — not in these parts, where one paid half a million francs for a maid's garret.

This dark street, one of the most expensive in the ninth arrondissement, oozed wealth. Ahead of her a gate fronted what looked like a palace. Trees made a canopy over the alley, which was silent except for her beating heart.

Had Madame Vasseur forgotten her promise to meet Aimée before the benefit?

On her cell phone she hit callback, but Madame Vasseur's number went straight to voice mail.

Damn. The woman had stood her up. Two precious hours lost.

No return call from Zacharié's parole officer. Nothing.

Her patience ran thin. She tapped her strappy Valentino sandals on the cobbles. A night bird trilled from the half-concealed garden of a mini-château behind massive metal-grilled gates. But she couldn't wait anymore. Time to storm the château.

She rapped on the gatehouse window. This caught the attention of a man in a dark blue suit, who opened the window a crack.

"*Excusez-moi.* I'm meeting Madame Vasseur at the Conservatoire de Musique benefit . . ."

"You have an invitation?"

A flush of anger rose up her neck. "There's an emergency."

"But this is a private affair." The man in the blue suit had a wire trailing from his ear and looked more like security than a concierge — a retired *flic.* Her father's police ID doctored with her photo wouldn't bear his scrutiny.

Great. She thought quick. Time to flash

the business card she'd appropriated from Madame Vasseur's designer bag.

"I'm her administrative assistant at . . ." She glanced down. ". . . Hachoin Associates. Do we need to have this conversation on the street?"

His expression remained the same. "But that's Madame Vasseur's card, not yours."

Apprehension filled her. What if she couldn't get past him?

"Of course," she said with more bravado than she felt. She needed to get inside, hear the information from the cell-phone message, learn the real description of the rapist and find Zazie. "Madame Vasseur gave me this to authenticate my presence. We've had a crisis at the office."

He stared at her. "Try her cell phone."

"As if I haven't?" Aimée pursed her lips. "But if you want to incur her wrath when she loses a ten-million-franc lawsuit because you wouldn't let me inside . . ."

The low side-door in the gate buzzed open. She walked into the rectangles of light spilling from tall windows over the dark garden and winding driveway. Faint strains of a piano drifted from a balcony.

He opened a door leading into a white-tiled foyer. Hit a button on the elevator panel.

"The Lavignes' reception is on their second floor."

If that wasn't an indicator of wealth, Aimée didn't know what was. But they all put their shoes on one foot at a time, as her *grand-père* would have said.

She didn't even have time to reapply her Chanel-red lipstick in the mirrored interior before the elevator door whooshed open.

"May I help you?" a voice welcomed her from a grand, marble-tiled reception area. Marble columns, marble everywhere. A grand salon was off to the left.

"Aimée Leduc to see Madame Vasseur."

The greeter, a woman in her late forties and wearing pearls, took one look at Aimée's secondhand Birkin bag. Or maybe it was her shoes.

"I'm afraid your name's not on the guest list," she said with a frozen, coral-lipsticked smile.

Aimée almost ground her teeth, but she returned the smile instead. "Then write it in."

"You misunderstand. This benefit's private. Invitation only."

"And there's an emergency. Madame and I made a rendezvous." Aimée peered over the woman's bouffant-haired head to the adjoining salon. She scanned the well-dressed crowd of thirty or so, hoping to catch Madame Vasseur's eye and take her aside.

No such luck.

Aimée stepped around the woman into the cloying scent of blue delphiniums overflowing from the vases in the fresco'd hallway. It was all neo-Renaissance detail, from the gilded *boisieries* to the gleaming inlaid walnut floor. "Please tell her I'm here."

The woman blinked. "I'm sorry, Madame, but —"

"The sooner you find her, the sooner I leave." Aimée leaned closer. *"Vous comprenez?"*

Flustered, the bouffant-haired woman backed away, summoning someone — a security guard? But a petite blonde waved back and mouthed, *"Un moment!"*

Scanning the designer attire for Madame Vasseur, Aimée noticed *intellos* scattered among *ancien régime* types exuding the whiff of old money. Typical of those born into privilege who supported *les arts et la culture* with *noblesse oblige.* Faces from society columns. Not an *arriviste* millionaire in the bunch. It wasn't that they had a lot of money in the bank — they owned the bank.

Not her crowd, but she hadn't come to socialize. Impatient, she nudged through the group, earning irritated looks. No one moved a centimeter. Didn't anyone respect a pregnant woman?

"Excusez-moi," she said, fanning herself with her hand. "Air, please, I need air."

People parted, several eyebrows raised, until she reached the edge of the crowd. On the dais, Madame Vasseur, in a sleek white-linen pantsuit, downed a glass of champagne. Aimée noticed the sag to her shoulders, a weariness that disappeared when she pumped the hand of an old man next to her and turned to smile at the well-heeled attendees.

"Madame!" Aimée waved. "Over here."

Her smile froze as she saw Aimée. A moment later she joined her by the tall window, her back to the crowd. "What right do you have to come here and gate-crash?" she said under her breath.

"You called me, remember? I need to hear Mélanie's message."

"Can't this wait?"

"Didn't Mélanie give you details, some important information for identifying the rapist?"

She stiffened. "There's too much going on right now."

"Right. Zazie's missing, and if you don't —"

Her words were drowned out by a white-haired man standing on the dais. He boomed into the microphone, "Mesdames et Messieurs, allow me to introduce Madame Vasseur, our Conservatoire de Musique committee chair."

She raised her hand and smiled at the white-haired man beckoning her. "That's Monsieur Lavigne. I've been working on this program all year," she said, smiling between clenched teeth. "You will wait and show some *politesse* until I've finished my speech. If you make a scene, I'll call security and have you thrown out."

". . . Madame Vasseur has several wonderful announcements," the old man was saying.

Thundering applause greeted him. Disappointed, Aimée drifted to the back. In the meantime she'd try René again. Check if Beto had left a message.

"Madame Leduc?" said the petite blonde, attractive apart from her overbite and large teeth. She wore a little black dress Aimée figured cost more than Leduc Detective paid in rent.

"Oui?"

Loud *shhhh*es from those around her.

285

"Please, over here."

Aimée followed the blonde into an adjoining salon. More nymphs and cherubs frolicking on the ceiling. A couple, arms entwined, broke apart at their entry, guilty looks on their faces, then beat a quick exit. Several attendees passed through, stopping at a white-linen-draped banquet table for fizzing flutes of amber champagne.

"My father-in-law goes on a bit," the blonde whispered. "But I'm sorry, Madame Vasseur's busy giving the highlight presentation."

Like Aimée didn't know that?

The blonde's brow knit at Aimée's nonplussed expression. "*Désolée,* I'm pinch-hitting as hostess. Only married a few months, I don't know all the ropes." Before Aimée could reply, the young woman gave a smile that revealed her big teeth. "Aaah, you're having *un bébé,* how wonderful." Her smile reached her eyes. "Congratulations. I know we've just met, don't want to be indiscreet, but my husband and I are trying, too. I want a baby so much. Champagne? Oh, silly me, of course not! Some juice?"

She seemed overwhelmed but genuine. Better get this woman on her side.

"Non, merci." Aimée took her hand. It was

286

warm to the touch. "Madame Vasseur's got information for me. A girl's life's in danger."

"Danger?" the blonde said, worry clouding her open face. "Does this have to do with her poor daughter, Mélanie?"

Aimée nodded, looking back into the filled salon. Madame Vasseur spoke, smiling, holding the audience in thrall, thanking donors. Aimée prayed this wouldn't take long, so she could get the hell out.

The blonde leaned closer, her grip on Aimée's hand tightening. "Has Mélanie's condition worsened?"

Before Aimée could answer, a young Asian cellist began playing her instrument to the side of the speaker.

"You've met my wife, Brianne?" A beaming twenty-something man slid his arm around the blonde's shoulder. He had a fresh, angular face and bright blue eyes. His velvet-collared smoking jacket was unbuttoned, a green, leafy stalk of anise sticking out from his shirt pocket. He reached to shake Aimée's hand. "Renaud Lavigne."

He noticed Aimée's look at his pocket and grinned.

"We're babysitting my niece Émilie's pet rabbit. He loves anise, go figure." He gestured to the little girl, about ten, standing by the chamber ensemble in a mauve velvet dress and matching patent shoes. The girl smiled back. Renaud pecked Brianne's forehead. "My wife doesn't want me to forget to feed him."

Brianne answered with a look of adoration.

"Thank you for coming," he said. "My father's endowing a music chair in Madame de Langlet's honor at the Conservatoire."

The victims' violin teacher. The woman hadn't answered again when Aimée had tried before she'd left. "Of course, Madame's here tonight, *non*?"

"She's en route," Brianne said, nodding. "It's all about music tonight."

In a place that could double as a wing of the Louvre, she thought. Morbier's oft-repeated saying came back to her: look to what wealth hides and what it buys. She doubted mention of the poor girls' assaults sat on Madame Vasseur's agenda tonight.

Brianne's brow creased again. "But Renaud, a girl's in danger."

Aimée flashed her PI license. "Look, there's a serial rapist on the loose, a missing girl whose life is at risk. Madame Vasseur's daughter, one of the victims, called from a Swiss clinic and left a message I need to hear, something that could be important to the investigation."

Renaud sucked in his breath. "I understand, *mais encore* . . ." He lowered his voice. "She's welcoming the new board and the benefactors of the scholarships."

Noticing Aimée's pained expression, Brianne took her husband's elbow, her face pleading.

"Can't you do something?" Aimée asked. "Take over for her? Or have your father?"

Renaud's father, the old man who'd introduced Madame Vasseur, had to be in his late seventies.

"The only thing that matters is that I get to listen to the message on Madame's cell phone as soon as possible," said Aimée.

Several distinguished heads turned. "Shhh," came from a dowager sporting medals on her lace cocktail dress.

Laughter erupted, echoing off the crystal chandeliers. Madame Vasseur had warmed up her audience.

"How can I interrupt her now?" For a moment Renaud had a lost look on his face, but it was replaced by determination. "But I'll try to hurry her up."

She grew aware of two older women in designer black leaning closer, listening to their conversation. Felt their palpable disapproval and condescending looks. She wanted to shout at them, but the words died in her throat. This upper crust exuded a glacial frost. Like black crows picking gossip from another's misfortune.

Aimée was overcome with despair. Zazie in danger and all this time wasted.

Renaud stepped forward into the salon and waved to the dais. From across the heads, he caught Madame Vasseur's attention. He lifted his wrist and tapped his watch. Madame Vasseur nodded.

"Merci," Aimée whispered to Renaud. She hoped that would hurry Madame Vasseur up. Now she had to check in with René. *"Excusez-moi."*

She tiptoed past the vulture ladies back out into the corridor. Three young male violinists tuned their instruments in the corridor. She hurried toward a quiet corner in the adjoining room — another salon with oil paintings covering the walls. The crackled veneer and ornate frames testified to old masters and Impressionists, and she didn't know what all else.

A museum, all right.

René answered on the second ring. Finally.

"Where are you, Aimée?" He sounded cranky.

"Me? *Zut!* I've been trying you for hours. It's not le Weasel, René."

"I know." She heard defeat and tiredness

in his voice. "I'll spare you the details. Let's just say I made a fool of myself."

Poor René. She could have told him if he'd answered his phone instead of playing the avenger. But this wasn't the time to scold. "*Ecoute,* René, I went back to jog Cécile's memory."

She gave him an edited version of everything that had happened since they'd parted, including her enlistment of Beto to check out the NeoCancan owner.

Behind her the damn violins were tuning up. She put a finger in her ear.

"Where are you, Aimée?"

"Madame Vasseur's daughter remembered something, left a voice mail."

Pause. She heard car horns blare in the background on René's end.

"Zazie's friend in the Swiss clinic, that girl?"

Aimée looked around. No one was listening. Just a ballerina statue that looked like a Degas.

"Her mother said Mélanie left a message about the rapist's description. The FotoFit tech got something wrong," said Aimée. "I don't know. I'm stuck waiting for her to finish her damned speech."

"Is that the sonata from *L'Arlésienne* playing in the background?"

"You're asking me?" One piece of classical music sounded like another to her.

"Sounds like Bizet, Aimée. A chic soirée. So, this 'nice man.' How can we find him?"

Think, she had to think.

"Or maybe it's too late," René said, a different shade in his voice — grim, determined.

Her heart wrenched. *Non,* not that. Forced herself to try and allay René's fears. To smother her own. Somehow concentrate on the plodding details — all she could clutch at for the moment.

"We have to keep going step by step, René," she said. "I left Marie-Jo's father's parole officer an urgent message. He's got to be in contact."

"You think the father will cough up info on the 'nice man' if he hasn't already? You'd trust a man just out of prison who dodged answering you?"

"Any other ideas, René?" She rubbed her ankle.

"Think he'll tell you if this 'nice man' hums Paganini?" he said. "Get real, Aimée."

"Once I hear Mélanie's message with the rapist's real description . . ." She took a deep breath, forcing herself to ignore the growing knot of tension in her shoulders, this gloom and sarcasm René emanated.

"I'll let you know right away and alert Beto in Vice."

Pause. "You've always said if you hit a wall," he said, "go back to the beginning."

Her father's words drilled into her.

"*Exactement.* With any luck the NeoCan-can bar owner knows more —"

René's sigh interrupted her. "I've got a bad feeling, Aimée."

Her patience exhausted, she wanted to kick him. "So you're giving up on Zazie?"

But René had clicked off.

A male voice spoke behind her. "You appreciate the Vuillard, I see. That's what they used to call the square, Place Vintimille."

Startled, Aimée turned around.

Renaud's father, leaning on his gold-handled walking stick, smiled at her. This family smiled often.

Old men liked to be gallant, *non?* She clutched her stomach. "*Désolée,* I need to sit down."

Alarm spread over old Lavigne's face. "But of course, let me get you something to drink." She sank down into the chair he proffered, a gilded Louis-something museum piece adorned with brocaded velvet.

"You asked if I appreciate the Vuillard painting — but 'appreciate' is a subjective term, Monsieur." She said the first thing that came out of her mouth. Stared back at the painting to study it.

"Forgive me, my dear." He handed her a fizzing glass of *limonade* and cleared his throat. "I thought since you were standing in front of it . . ."

Aimée grinned and tried for charm. "But I've passed that square countless times. Just yesterday." She gave what she hoped came off as a sigh of wonder. "This work breathes. I feel the wind rustling through the linden trees. Hear the leaves scuttering over the cobblestones. Timeless."

The old Lavigne's eyes lit up. "*Exactement.* Vuillard painted from his atelier overlooking the square. Must have painted this scene twenty times over his life."

Madame Vasseur's voice carried from the salon on the microphone. ". . . for young musicians whose careers have been made possible by the generous endowment of our host this evening . . ."

Stupid. Why hadn't she put this together before? This rich old coot might know something. "So Madame Vasseur told you I'm a detective, Monsieur?"

The old man blinked. "*Vraiment? Mais* how exciting! Things have changed since Inspector Maigret, *non?* But I'm only her messenger — she apologizes, instructs me

294

to ask that you wait."

Zazie's life hung in the balance. She ground her teeth and felt like screaming.

"But Monsieur Lavigne, with all these attacks, aren't you concerned? Your young protégés, the ones who you're endowing with scholarships, whose futures you've invested in?"

"I'm horrified," he said. "These girls burst with talent. They're close to my heart. But what do you mean?"

"Can't you see the connection, Monsieur?"

"Connection? But these were isolated attacks. The *commissaire* assured me," he said. "Believe me, I've raised the issue with him."

She caught herself before she slapped him. With this *laissez-faire* attitude, no wonder the rapist got away.

"Think again, Monsieur. The one thing all those girls have in common is your Madame de Langlet. Four girls have been attacked after violin lessons in six months. At least some of them were scholarship students of the fund you're raising money for tonight." She didn't know that for sure, but it had to link.

Worry crossed his brow. "You think I should have offered a reward? But they caught a suspect. I heard that on the news."

Before she could answer, another seventy-ish man, this one with a white walrus mustache, had entered and embraced old Lavigne. "Ready for my tour, *mon vieux*?" His accent was a burred Languedoc.

"*Excusez-moi,* but I promised to show Gerard around."

Great.

Old-man Lavigne pointed with his cane and tugged Gerard forward to his wall of paintings. "My father collected works by the locals here." His voice swelled with pride. "Vuillard, Degas, who met with Pissarro and Manet just around the corner, Gauguin, Delacroix, Ingres, Renoir, Toulouse-Lautrec, though only because his doctor lived below . . ."

He droned on. It was obvious the old man relished the opportunity to expound on his collection to a semi-captive audience. She stifled her impatience, crossed her legs.

Gerard nodded, gave her a wink as if to say, *humor the old man.* She checked the time again. Fumed. If she didn't hear Mélanie's message soon, she'd scream.

Oblivious, the old man carried on. The lecture had moved on to connecting painting with music, two related forms of symbolic art. "Take Debussy's violins in *La Mer,* conveying the rising storm waves as a string of color," Lavigne was saying.

Her dress chafed her expanding stomach. She'd give anything for a cigarette. Or a nicotine patch. She craned her neck toward the salon, checking on Madame Vasseur's progress. Lavigne paused, noticing her look. "Forgive me, it's my passion."

Was he tasked with keeping her occupied so she didn't disrupt the reception?

Gerard mopped his brow with a handkerchief. How could she grab the conversation back with *politesse* and glean more while Madame Vasseur toadied up to her benefactors?

Gerard glanced at the champagne. Helped himself to a flute. "*Santé.* To Renaud and his beautiful new wife," Gerard handed Monsieur Lavigne a glass and clinked his to it. "Going to carry on the tradition and family business, eh?"

"Renaud was our unexpected blessing late in life," said Lavigne. "His mother passed away when he was a child."

Translation: spoiled, privileged brat expected to continue the dynasty. Yet given Renaud's rarefied upbringing, he seemed down-to-earth. She'd liked him and Brianne.

"Ah, Gerard, there's not enough music in

the world." Old Lavigne raised his cane, moved it back and forth across the polished parquet in time to the violin quartet.

Maddening.

"But of course you know this piece — from Bizet's *Carmen,* Madame?"

"It's Mademoiselle." But play along with him. She pretended to recognize it. "Ah yes, of course."

"You hear, yes?" His mouth pursed. "But do you feel it?"

She gave a quick nod. Parched, Aimée sipped the *limonade.* She saw Madame Vasseur on the dais, awarding certificates to benefactors amid applause. When would she finish? In the meantime Gerard checked his cell phone, bored, no doubt, and timing a getaway. "*Désolé.* I've got to take this call."

Gerard disappeared. She wished she could join him instead of enduring the art and music lesson. But now that he was gone, she could try to get something new out of the old man. Her father's words sounded in her head: never leave an interview without a name, an address, a hair color, a type of tree — even the most insignificant-seeming details, he'd drummed into her, would add up. Instead of stewing until Madame Vasseur ended, she needed to try a hunch.

"Is the actress Béatrice de Mombert, your

neighbor a few streets over, one of your Conservatoire benefactors?" Maybe there was a link to the "nice man."

"De Mombert? I knew her father."

"I'd imagine Béatrice's ex-husband Zacharié and his business associates must donate."

"Never met him." Old Lavigne shrugged. "Or her."

Another dead end.

Yet she had to reach him somehow. She went back to their earlier conversation, determined to press harder.

"But the rumors must concern you, the implications that the Conservatoire's bright talent is being targeted by the rapist."

Old Lavigne looked confused for a moment. "Rumors? Targeted? But the attacker is in custody."

"Last night another girl was followed after her lesson at Madame de Langlet's. She escaped, thank God."

"That's news to me." Old Lavigne shook his head. His cane wavered on the floor.

"The attacker's loose. Still on the street." She took a gulp of fizzing *limonade*. "The girl remembered him humming her Paganini piece. Madame de Langlet's been questioned by the police."

His face reddened. "Terrible. But why? I

can't understand this . . . *Non,* I don't believe there can be a connection. Impossible."

Denial.

She wanted to explode. Instead, she took a deep breath, wished she could burp and rubbed her stomach. "Madame Vasseur's daughter's traumatized," Aimée persisted. "But of course she's told you."

He nodded, and weariness settled in his face. "It sickened me," he said. "We've offered all our support to Mélanie's family. But Madame Vasseur's a trouper, keeps soldiering on for the Conservatoire."

And neglects poor Mélanie, shipping her off to a clinic.

"It's a village here," he said. "We met with the Brigade des Mineurs, offered to help in any way we could."

And look where that led. Nowhere. Another do-nothing unit whose captain assured Zazie's mother she'd run away or gone partying. No break in the rape case. All static.

His thin shoulders sagged. "It is troubling, though . . ."

"More than troubling, Monsieur," she said, leaning forward to relieve the pressure on her back. "How can you think there's no connection? Madame de Langlet won't answer my calls. She's afraid."

Understanding shone in his eyes. The light gone out of them, he looked his age. "I promise I'll talk to Madame de Langlet," he said. "She'll confide in me . . . but I don't want to spoil this evening for her."

"Where is she?"

"Delayed." He shrugged. "How can I get back to you?"

She thrust her card into his hand.

Brianne approached the salon with Madame Vasseur, helping her with her white jacket. About time. Behind them she saw Renaud mounting the dais, leading the applause.

"Monsieur Lavigne, I've been called back to the office," said Madame Vasseur. "Renaud's stepped in. Sorry to run short."

Short?

Aimée followed her out, tried to keep her impatience down as they reached the elevator. She needed to hear this message and question the woman in private.

But a duo of *branchée* sisters, both with heavy seventies-style bangs, boarded the elevator with them. In loud voices they gushed over the event all the way to their taxi at the gate, talking about how excited they were to support the Conservatoire. In a whoosh they'd gone.

"Now if you'll let me listen to Mélanie's message —"

But Madame Vasseur already had the phone to her ear, deep in a conversation with someone else. Looking agitated, she shook her head. Aimée caught the words "stalled negotiation." Couldn't this woman even give her two minutes?

Aimée kept up with her as she strode along the pavement. The dusk had turned the street into a shadowy canyon of buildings. No Fête de la Musique quartets playing on street corners here, no impromptu courtyard concerts — quiet reigned. No ballyhoo of rabid World Cup fans drinking at bars in this part of town.

Her damp collar stuck to her neck. Madame Vasseur stepped out into the narrow, cobbled street, heading toward her black Mercedes.

"Let's talk in your car," said Aimée.

"No way, I'm running late as it is," said Madame Vasseur. Her voice was tight. She rooted in her Hermès bag. "Can't find my damned car keys."

"How can you say that?" Aimée said. She was hot and tired of wasting time. "I've waited for you for almost three hours, come all this way to hear one voice mail that may save a child's life! I'm asking for two minutes of your time here."

"You know what, forget it!" said Madame Vasseur. "Between you and talking to the *flics* over and over — I can't deal with any of this."

Aimée grabbed her arm. "How dare you?" She'd had enough. "How would you like all your music friends to know you didn't help find a missing girl? A girl taken by the same man who raped your daughter?"

Madame Vasseur backed away. Surprised, Aimée realized her eyes were brimming with tears. "Shame," she said, her voice low. "I can't deal with this shame. But my daughter's safe now."

For a moment she felt sorry for this woman. "You think sending Mélanie to a Swiss clinic will make it go away?" said Aimée. "Your daughter needs you, her mother."

Madame Vasseur stood helpless, tears dropping into her purse. Was there something else? Was she holding back? Afraid?

In the sudden silence, Aimée felt a chill. The quiet street was too quiet.

"Give me your phone." She reached out, and Madame Vasseur relinquished her phone. "Where's Mélanie's message?" Aimée asked, flicking through the log. "Was the rapist familiar to her? You said she mentioned his hair . . ."

A motorcycle revved, shattering the quiet. Out of the corner of her eye, she caught sight of its headlight, bright and steady. So out of place on this shadowy street. The blinding headlight made it impossible for her to read the cell phone's display.

"What's wrong?" Madame Vasseur asked.

"Let's drive to the Grands Boulevards. We shouldn't linger."

"Why?"

The motorcycle was coming the wrong way down the one-way street. A wave of fear hit her. "Get in the car. Now."

Madame Vasseur stood by the door, still digging for her keys, as the blinding light got closer and closer.

"Watch out." Instinct took over, and she yanked at Madame Vasseur's arm, trying to pull her out of the street.

But too late. She heard a low pop so distinctive it chilled her blood. Only a gun with a suppressor made a sound like that.

"Get down!" she yelled, pulling at the woman's shoulder with one hand and shielding her stomach with the other as they hit the pavement. The woman shook off her grip as Aimée rolled on the sidewalk toward the shelter of a massive doorframe. Another *pop pop* followed, echoing in the street.

Metal pinged, glass shattered by her ear. A stinging in her shoulder, then a cold, oozing wetness.

When the revving of the motorcycle had faded away, Aimée pushed herself up to her hands and knees. In the dim streetlight, she saw something glinting under the car. Bullet casings.

She reached out, grabbed the door's metal carriage protector and crawled, keeping low. Madame Vasseur sprawled on the cobbles. Blood seeped from the grey-ringed holes in her white linen jacket. Her eyes were wide open to the night sky. The last whine of the motorcycle echoed, and Aimée turned to see the red brake light disappear.

"Non, non," she gasped. With shaking fingers, she felt for a pulse. Faint but beating. "Hold on . . . stay with me." Despair and frustration mingled with regret for this difficult, sad woman.

Where was the woman's cell phone? She needed to call for help. Frantic, on all fours, she crawled on the dark pavement looking for it. Her fingers came back wet and sticky.

Had the shooter been after Madame Vasseur or her? Cell phone, where was the damn phone? When Aimée tried to stand, waves of dizziness hit her.

"Mesdemoiselles, mesdemoiselles," came a

drunken shout. Two men were coming down the narrow street. Laughing. "Join us for a drink."

Aimée's vision blurred. Doubled. The two men were now four men. "Can't you see? She's been shot. Call an ambulance."

Why didn't these men respond? Why were they staring at her, backing away?

"Now!" she yelled. "Call eighteen."

She tried to stand, staggered against the side of the Mercedes, clutching her stomach. But her hands were red, sticky. Blood.

Pain choked her, and everything blurred and spun. "Oh my God, my baby . . ."

Tuesday, 9 P.M.

Zacharié paced across the old tiled bath-house in the shadowed courtyard, alert to car horns, a muted saxophone, high heels clicking on the pavement. His neck was tense with fear. He squeezed the cell phone so tight he thought he'd break it in half, cursing Jules for the millionth time.

He'd tried every crony and gotten nowhere. Either Jules had paid them off, or they owed him silence. And the piece of *merde* wouldn't answer his cell phone.

His palms were wet, perspiration beaded his lip. Dervier and the team, right on schedule, entered the misty courtyard, followed by Jules's driver, the Corsican with a scar-rippled eyebrow.

Zacharié froze. The Corsican had never been part of the plan.

"What the hell are you doing here?"

"Boss's orders."

Insurance.

"Where's my daughter?"

The Corsican shrugged.

The team was disappearing one by one into the old water workers' entrance at the side of the bathhouse. Dervier looked back. "Let's go, Zacharié."

"I don't go in there until I hear from my daughter," he said to the Corsican. "Call her."

"You know I can't. Cell-phone towers will triangulate this location."

"Like I care? I don't go in until I talk to her."

The Corsican hit speed dial on his cell phone. Zacharié grabbed it from his hand.

"Jules? I want my daughter."

"Soyez calme," said Jules, "she's right here. Go ahead, talk to her yourself."

He heard fumbling, scratching as the phone was handed over.

"Marie-Jo? Are you all right?"

"Papa! Papa, get me out of here." A gulp. "I'm scared." Marie-Jo's voice broke. "Do something, Papa. Zazie's hurt. Help us."

Zacharié's stomach clenched.

Muffled noises, then Jules's voice. "Finish the job, Zacharié. We'll meet you afterward, as planned."

His mind went to the arranged rendezvous

spot, the flower stall at the east exit of the Gare de Nord. Originally he'd planned to take the Thalys from there, and he and Marie-Jo would have breakfast in Brussels. A new life.

"I don't go in and do your job until I see her, Jules."

"With a rapist on the loose, the area's crawling with *flics*. You can't be too careful."

Zacharié bit his lip so hard he tasted blood. "What's that supposed to mean?"

"Watch the news, Zacharié." Jules sighed. "That hot female detective's face is all over the place, looking for a red-haired girl."

And then the woman with the big, intense eyes flashed in his mind. That leggy pregnant looker on rue Chaptal searching for Marie-Jo's red-headed friend. He hadn't told her that Jules had abducted his daughter and the redheaded girl and was going to use the rapist to hide his tracks, because he hadn't understood until now.

Zacharié wanted to kick the stone, smash the metal drain-pipe.

"You complicated everything by kidnapping Marie-Jo and her friend. Stupid, Jules. Not like you. What about the repercussions?"

A sigh. "Bad planning, I admit."

Zacharié sensed an element of desperation in Jules's plan. That was a first. "Someone's got you by the balls."

Pause. "I need this, Zacharié."

And now that other people were searching for the girls, too, Jules was risking everything on this little kidnapping insurance scheme. What about this file Zacharié was supposed to steal was so precious that Jules would go to these lengths to ensure Zacharié saw the job through to the end?

If the woman twigged on the girls' abduction and got too close . . . He couldn't worry about that now.

"Do the job and we're done, Zacharié. Think of your new passports, new country, a new life."

A thin red laser beam danced on the worn stones. Dervier's signal — the team were in their positions along the dry vestiges of the ancient river Grange-Batelière. Zacharié needed to hang up the phone now and finish this job — he had no choice. It was beyond his control.

In one last hopeless attempt, he said into the phone, "You want the job done, you bring those girls. Now."

A deep sigh came over the line. "In fifteen seconds I'm going to shoot off Marie-Jo's toes, then work my way up unless you perform the job as planned."

The phone clicked off.

The Corsican smiled and grabbed the phone. "Satisfied?"

"Get the hell out of here."

In several long strides, the Corsican crossed the damp pavers and disappeared into the street.

Bile rose in Zacharié's throat. He wanted to spit the sour taste out of his mouth. He was stuck.

Tuesday, 9:20 P.M.

The bright glare hurt Aimée's eyes. Her shoulder stung and throbbed. Her head reverberated with the whines of the ambulance's siren and the beeping from the machines. Her hand flew to her stomach, and she saw the tube in her arm. She moaned into her oxygen mask.

"Blood pressure a hundred and fifty-five over eighty-six," said one medic to the other. Both *sapeurs-pompiers,* firemen, always the first responders. "Pregnant woman, gunshot wound to the shoulder," he said into his radio. "Alert: Emergency. Possible preterm labor."

Preterm labor? Fear scorched her. "My baby, you have to save my baby." She was shouting. Her words, muffled in the oxygen mask, vaporized with her breath.

She wanted to kick herself free, but restraints strapped her ankles to the gurney.

312

The stark ambulance lighting glared whiter than daytime; the medics poked and read from the machines. What was wrong with these idiots? She thrashed her arms, yanked the mask off. Wetness spread over her legs and ankles; her arms were streaked with blood.

"Check my baby," she said, gasping.

"Calm down, Madame. We know what we're doing," said the frowning medic. "First we have to stop the bleeding. We're about to apply a compression bandage."

"Then compress, for God's sake." Just one year of premed but she knew the signs: jumping heart rate, elevated blood pressure, all putting her and her baby at risk. She panted. Wild-eyed, she looked around. She needed to center, get control. Something beside her was whirring, and she recognized a smaller version of the ultrasound machine her doctor had used.

"You're listening to my baby's heart?"

"First things first," said the red-cheeked one. "You need to calm down. Leave it to us."

"Don't talk to me like an *idiote,*" she said, trying to breathe deep. What if the trauma stimulated uterine contractions? Why were the first-response team always men?

Oh, God . . . calm down, she had to calm down.

Cold, viscous gel was rubbed on her exposed stomach, the rest of her covered by a white cotton sheet. She felt pressing on her stomach. Heaviness.

The medic strapped the mask back on. "Breathe deep, again and again," he said. "No spotting. That's good. Relax. Keep still so I can listen to your baby's heartbeat."

She felt pressure. More heaviness.

"Give me the other gel," said the medic.

"We're out," said his partner with a quick shake of his head. The siren rose, drowning the rest of his answer.

The ambulance made a sharp turn. Stopped with a screech. Cymbals, a wheezing accordion then shouts over the siren.

"*Merde!* And now a traffic accident, too?" he said. "We need a Doppler to check fetal heartbeat. This one only checks blood flow."

"You mean it's not the right one?" she shouted. The mask fogged. She tore it off again. "My baby's not even six months. Give me something to prevent contractions."

The medic sucked in his breath. Not good, she could tell.

"We need to prep you."

A throbbing cramped her stomach. She

314

shook her head as he tried to put the mask back on her. Bit down hard on his finger.

The medic yelled out in pain.

"I feel a contraction." Tears brimmed her eyes. "You've got to save my baby."

"This will shut her up." She felt a jab in her arm.

The rest happened in a cold, white blur.

Tuesday, 9:15 P.M.

Sweat beaded Zacharié's forehead in the moist, decaying air. The team's headlamp beams bobbed over the lichen-encrusted stone. Water dribbled down the walls, and rats scurried in the dark. Layers upon layers, centuries of muck and detritus surrounded them in this narrow tunnel. Dervier had tunneled into the ancient sewer and excavated with precision. In single file, they stepped over the jagged concrete into a storeroom.

Their headlamp beams caught on silver tea sets, old masters in antique frames and jewelry filling glass display cases. This subterranean storeroom of Hôtel Drouot, the auction house, reminded him of a glorified pawnbroker's, overflowing for the upcoming auction.

Ramu grinned, took out the tools from his bag. "Like old times, eh?"

Ripe for the team's picking. And three minutes ahead of schedule.

"Hurry up, old man," said Tandou, wiping his hands. He was grinning, too.

The cavern storeroom was lined with shelves of porcelain dinner plates, bronze statues, silver bowls, paintings, more display cases of jewelry and even a nineteenth-century mattress-delousing machine. Dervier's men got to work filling the canvas sacks with the jewelry and smallest items first.

Zacharié spotted his destination, a metal door lit by a lantern. Dervier had already snipped its padlock with his wire cutters — they would replace it on their way out — and Zacharié followed him to a second old, rusted padlock on a second metal door. With a quick tug, Dervier opened the door to reveal a mildewed *abri,* a bomb shelter from the war. Peeling notices dated March 1942 indicated a thirty-person capacity. Seconds later Dervier cut the third door's rusted padlock, rubbed olive oil on the door's hinges and pulled it open. Ahead, a short series of concrete steps led up to the courtyard.

Two key cards were slipped into Zacharié's hand.

"The yellow for the *rez-de-chaussée* entrance and the white for the top floor."

Dervier checked his watch. "You've got ten minutes from when I disable the alarm. Then I padlock all three doors and trigger open the courtyard exit."

"I knew you could do it, Dervier." Zacharié hit his stopwatch. "See you in nine minutes."

While he went into the next building, Dervier's crew would be stocking up on a haul worth a good number of zeros to waiting auction houses in Bordeaux, Strasbourg, Aix-en-Provence and Nice. By next week, when the items were discovered missing, Dervier would have re-cemented the tunnel hole and replaced the re-rusted locks on the metal doors.

The added beauty to their plan was that once Dervier disabled the alarm with his remote, Zacharié would be able to enter the temporary Ministry storage depot via the subterranean bomb shelter, only crossing through the building's unmonitored courtyard, without leaving any trace on the video cameras stationed in the front foyer or street entrance.

A quick in and out.

His goal lay in the temporary repository of Ministry files that had been stored here after a basement had flooded. While his team busied themselves emptying the auction house's cavern, he'd remove the file Jules had hired him to steal.

There'd be no connection between the jobs. If later, during inventory audits, the file couldn't be found, it would be assumed it had been misfiled, misrouted to another location in the usual bureaucratic fashion. At least that's what Jules was counting on.

It took him a minute and a half, according to his stopwatch, to reach the top floor and slide the white key card into the storage room's lock. A tiny click, and he entered. The grey room smelled of damp and wet paper. Consulting Jules's diagram, he bypassed cartons, boxes, shelves of files as innocuous as in a doctor's office. His headlight beam revealing the labels, he located iixx.450dsM, a box like all the others. The Ministry file. He flipped it open with his gloved fingers.

Clipped on top was a note: *Addendum in ixx.451dsM1.*

Better take that, too.

He slipped both inside his jumpsuit.

He crossed the ivy-covered courtyard to the sewer access door — oiled and left unlocked by Dervier. Once he'd gone down the steps and was back inside the old sewer, Zacharié checked his time in the dripping tunnel. Four minutes ahead of schedule.

He heard a shout followed by a series of muffled pops coming from the auction house's cavern down the tunnel. His pulse thudded. Shots? This wasn't part of the plan.

Had the *flics* appeared?

Zacharié hunched down, terrified for his team, that he'd be next, the job ruined, his Marie-Jo . . .

A figure climbed over the jagged cement hole out of the cavern. From the silhouette he recognized the Corsican, who was clutching a duffel bag and headed his way.

No way was he supposed to be down here. He should be waiting in the car to move the goods. Zacharié's hands shook. It all came together now — Jules had used the Corsican to betray them.

But Zacharié had the file Jules wanted. His mind raced, debating whether he should escape, make a run for it through the sewer. Risk everything?

But that would put Marie-Jo in more danger and catch him up in a world of revenge. He had no weapon, no way to defend himself. Seconds, he had seconds to decide.

The Corsican paused, as if listening. Zacharié tried not to breathe. If he ran, he'd be heard the moment his feet splashed through the puddles.

But the Corsican stepped back into the hole.

No way could he trust the Corsican or Jules. He had to act. Wasting no time, Zacharié edged behind the metal sewer door, careful to keep it half open, as Dervier had left it.

A moment later the Corsican's running footsteps splashed in the water, headed toward the door. Zacharié heard metal on metal, the snick and click, the unmistakable sound of a cartridge loaded. The Corsican was going to kill him, would already have killed him if Zacharié hadn't been running so far ahead of time. Sweat streamed down Zacharié's neck. He held his breath, kept his body rigid until he heard footsteps go through.

Un, deux and on *trois* Zacharié slammed the sewer door shut behind the Corsican.

He tried to flip the bolt back. But it stuck and wouldn't lock. Pounding and muffled yells sounded from the Corsican on the other side. His arms strained, pushing the bolt down, progressing a centimeter at a time. Grunting and heaving, he felt it wedge into place.

The Corsican would have to scale the two-story stone-walled courtyard to escape, or enter the building and set off the alarms. Zacharié had put him out of commission for now.

Panting, Zacharié ran back to the auction-house cavern to find his team. He skidded on the old tiles, sticky with blood. Horror-struck, he found his childhood friends sprawled among the jewelry glittering in his headlamp. Gunshots to the backs of their heads.

A sob rose in the back of his throat. Jules had betrayed him and his friends, hired the Corsican to seal their deal permanently. Zacharié would have been next. The traitor had escalated from felony to group murder.

Fear ground in his gut. How could he trust that Marie-Jo would be safe? He'd never known Jules to go this far, to take such risks — what was in the file that made him so desperate?

His only bargaining chip was the file in his overalls. No way would he give it up unless he had Marie-Jo. He held the only thing that would keep Marie-Jo alive.

In the Corsican's duffel bag he found a pair of night-vision goggles, an extra ammo clip, gloves, an alternative lock, cell phone, folded sheets of plastic and even rags to clean up the blood spatter. A pro. Hired to erase all traces. The *salaud*.

Zacharié shook with anger. Helpless. Why had he believed Jules again? Why didn't he ever learn?

Groaning came from the floor. Tandou blinked, a death rattle in his chest. "Your daughter . . . never part of the plan. Believe me . . ."

A traitor, too? In league with Jules, scheming behind his back?

He knelt down at Tandou's side. "Why, Tandou? Why betray me? He's got my baby."

Blood trickled from Tandou's lips. "Never meant . . ."

Zacharié cradled his old friend in his arms. "Where's Marie-Jo? Where's he keeping her?"

Tandou's labored breathing tore his heart.

"Tell me. I've got to . . ."

"Get him." Tandou's chest heaved. "Dervier's bro . . . broth . . . in . . . knows the . . ."

And his lungs gave out. He'd gone, leaving a wife, three children and another on the way.

Zacharié stuck the Corsican's cell phone in his front pocket. Goddammit. He'd find his daughter. But he needed help.

What had Tandou been trying to say? Brother? Dervier only had a sister. Think, he had to think. Brother-in-law? Was the sister married? He thought he might have met the man at some holiday meal once; a picture of a chunky man in a turquoise shirt floated through his mind.

The Corsican's phone kept lighting up with calls from an unknown number.

Jules.

He needed to let Jules stew, let the scenarios play in his head. The Corsican hit man had made two errors — miscalculating their timetable and leaving behind his phone. Now he was trapped in the courtyard until regular business hours. Jules wouldn't know anything that had gone down, wouldn't even know Zacharié was alive.

He had to use this advantage. Leverage it to find Marie-Jo.

He'd get that big-eyed pregnant one with the long legs to help him. The minute Zacharié appeared, Jules would send more goons. What better cover than a pregnant woman?

But he was covered in blood. Tandou's blood. A sob caught in his throat.

No time to mourn this senseless carnage, cry over their betrayal. He needed to save his daughter. His hand shook as he rooted through the Corsican's bag. He made himself take off his bloody shirt and put on the windbreaker the Corsican had brought for that very purpose.

Along the way he threw his bloodied shirt and overalls in a dumpster behind Monoprix. Sweating, nerves frayed, he battled through the laughing crowds and street musicians clogging the humid streets of Pigalle. It took forever to reach the guitar store on rue Victor Massé.

Rigaud, the long-haired guitarist who let him sleep in his *garçonnière,* bachelor pad, above the shop, gestured to the *télé* screen behind the cash register. "Sick, I tell you, sick. Can you believe this happened just a few streets away? During Fête de la Musique?"

Zacharié tensed. Had the Corsican escaped, the *flics* discovered his friends' bodies . . . ?

"And right after the *fromager*'s daughter was murdered by the rapist," Rigaud went on, tuning his guitar. "What's the world coming to, I ask you? Shooting a pregnant woman!"

Intent, Zacharié stepped past the Fender amplifiers and closer to the screen to process what he was seeing on the *télé:* the yellow crime-scene tape on the cobbled street, the flashing red lights. It couldn't be, it would be too much of a coincidence . . . Damn. Had she been shot? Had Jules gotten to her first?

325

Tuesday, 11 P.M.

Aimée woke up to the rustle of fabric as the curtains parted. A honey-complected boy with hazel eyes took her hand.

Was she dreaming? Could this be her baby, born and grown? Confused for a second, she squeezed his hand. Warm. Tried to speak but nothing came out. Her tongue was thick, mouth dry like sandpaper.

"*Grand-père* got a call," he said. "He's your emergency contact on your medical card. We got off the train and came back."

Finally she recognized Marc, Morbier's half-Moroccan grandson. He had shot up like a wild sprout. Only nine or ten, but he reached his grandfather's shoulder.

Morbier, in a crumpled seersucker jacket and loosened shirt collar, looked none too pleased to see her. "Careless and downright stupid, Leduc. Getting shot again? Consider your pregnant heels curbed." He turned to

326

the arriving *flic.* "Make sure there's a uniform at her door as soon as she's moved to a room," he said, gruff. "Meanwhile I'll take her statement."

The *flic*'s eyes widened. "The Brigade Criminelle chief sent me, but . . . is that an order, Commissaire?"

"We called it that when I graduated from the Police Academy," said Morbier. "Has anything changed?"

The *flic* pulled out his cell phone. "*À votre service,* Commissaire."

Morbier palmed some francs into Marc's hand. "Why don't you find some chocolate in the cafeteria?"

As Marc left, Morbier sat down with a sigh. Fanned himself with a train ticket. "Another fine mess," he said. "What the hell's the matter with you, Leduc? You've got a baby to think of."

She swallowed. Found her voice. "They knocked me out with an injection. Don't let them give me more drugs." She pushed herself up on her elbows. "Promise me, Morbier."

A nurse with flyaway blonde hair loomed at the bedside with a chart. "No drugs?" She snorted. "Does topical antiseptic bother you? I'd call you lucky."

"Getting shot's . . . lucky?"

Morbier stood and moved to the side as the doctor entered.

"Your companion, the other victim, bled out." The doctor's bald head shone under the white cubicle lights as he checked her chart. "But good news. We halted your contractions with a shot of Terbutaline. The Kleihauer–Betke blood test showed no fetal blood cells in your circulation. The sonogram shows a healthy heartbeat. Your cervix hasn't elongated."

She blinked. "So my baby's okay?"

A nod. "We're monitoring you for concussion, shock, fetal disturbance, anything that could affect the baby. We'll err on the side of caution."

She shivered, remembering. The gunshots, Mélanie's mother crumpled on the cobblestones, the blood, the shock. How close to losing the baby she'd been.

"You're sure my baby's not injured?"

"We're going to watch out for pain in your womb, chills, fever, dizziness, fainting, headache, swelling in your fingers, vomiting, bleeding." The doctor ticked off a checklist. "So far you're strong as an ox. The baby too. But we still have to remove the bullet, treat your gunshot wound, get you some stitches and prevent infection. You'll stay here tonight under observation."

He swabbed more gel on her stinging shoulder. "Ready?"

"For what?"

"Breathe." She felt a sharp poke, digging, then fire erupted in her shoulder. She gritted her teeth, determined not to cry out. But she did.

"Voilà." The doctor held a bullet between surgical tweezers.

He dropped it in a kidney-shaped metal pan with a ping. With a deft motion, the nurse reswabbed the bullet wound and stitched it closed. "We'll check on you later." A whoosh of antiseptic air, padding on their soft, rubber-soled shoes, and they'd left.

Morbier took a latex glove and baggie from his inside jacket pocket. Dropped the bullet inside and examined it. He whistled. "Don't see many like this anymore."

"Like what? Explain, Morbier."

"Nine millimeter. Can't read the casing number without a magnifier. Vintage, I'd say. A Luger?"

"From the war? You mean a German Luger?"

"So you're ticking off Nazis again." Shook his head. "Don't you ever learn, Leduc?"

She ignored his taunt. Wondered how this fit in. And how the hell Morbier could identify it like that. But ripe pickings for Serge, her medical pathologist friend, to analyze.

"Morbier, get this to Ballistics, priority. And copy Serge at the morgue."

"Telling me how to do my job?" But he'd gone to the door, had a word with the *flic* guarding her room. By the time he returned and sat down heavily on the plastic chair, he'd taken off his jacket and dabbed his perspiring brow with a wrinkled handkerchief.

"Why not tell me you were going on leave, Morbier?" she said, that little girl inside her bursting out. Why did she always feel like a child with him, craving his attention? Stupid. "*Zut!* It worried me," she said, attempting to recover. "Couldn't reach you. Why disconnect your phone?"

"There goes my keeping it on the quiet, Leduc," he said. "I took a week's leave. Wanted to keep it from the pencil pushers who calculate retirement."

Since when did Morbier, a senior *commissaire divisionaire,* take leave on the sly? Didn't add up. She sensed there was more to the story. Hadn't he moaned about the roadblocks in his ongoing investigation last week, the upper echelon's pressure to shelve it?

"Did this sudden trip stem from your corruption investigation? Things got too hot?"

Morbier gave a start in the plastic chair. She could have sworn guilt and something like fear crossed his furrowed brow. Then it disappeared. His sagging jowls, the day-old beard gave him a haggard look.

"Not for you to worry about, Leduc. Not in your condition."

But his pinhole pupils were sharp in those brown basset-hound eyes.

"*Mais alors,* you got into a shootout," he said, "in your condition."

As if it were her fault? "A shootout is a mutual armed exchange," she said, fuming. "Not an innocent woman gunned down in the *rue* as she is getting into her car. Get your facts straight."

"Ever thought the shooter might have been aiming at you instead of this Madame . . ."

"Vasseur? The mother of Zazie's friend, the rape victim?" Aimée shook her head. But could Morbier be right? Her spine prickled. Was she responsible for Madame Vasseur's death?

"Your face plastered all over the *télé* didn't help, Leduc," said Morbier. "Why would you get mixed up with that gutter-press sensationalist who calls herself a *télé-*

journalist? Unleashed a can of crazies. Typical. You act before you think."

Morbier had a point. A uniform guarding the hospital room gave her some comfort.

"But this means the rapist's cornered, desperate. That's the whole point, Morbier. Force him out in the open so we can find Zazie."

Poor Mélanie, first attacked and institutionalized, now motherless, left with a widowed father who had complained his high-powered wife put her law career before her daughter. Now even more than before, Mélanie was in his hands.

Guilt stung her. Mélanie's mother had tried to help. Where was her phone?

A smiling medical attendant with a mustache appeared with a new clipboard.

"Commissaire, we're moving the patient to the Obstetrics ward."

"I'll join you." Morbier shuffled to his feet. Nodded. "After I stop in at the cafeteria."

Upstairs in a room redolent with bleach and disinfectant, Aimée rubbed her stomach. She hated the hospital smell. Her open window overlooked darkened rails glistening in a night rain shower.

Marc lay curled asleep on an adjoining

hospital bed, the covers pulled under his neck. Morbier took a bite of *céleri rémoulade* from her green tray. "Not bad, Leduc. Try some."

"Hospital food?"

But hunger clawed, and the Bump needed to eat.

"Open wide . . ."

She almost batted the plastic spoon of glistening celery slivers back at him. "Quit treating me like an invalid."

She finished the whole plate, and a second.

"Ready for my statement, Morbier?"

Wednesday, 8 A.M.

Madame Pelletier stared at the files on her desk. They went back five years, but what she was looking for wasn't here. That incident niggled in her mind.

She pushed her cup of steaming *tilleul,* lime-blossom tisane, to the side of her desk. Her *vacances* put on hold thanks to the backlog of cases and now the rapist terrorizing the ninth. She'd come in early this morning to catch up. Quiet for once — at least she could concentrate.

What if that Leduc had been right? Not that she was happy about the media pressure, how the woman had painted the police as inefficient. Leduc's scenario — that her missing young friend, the thirteen-year-old redhead, had something to do with the rapist — hadn't sounded realistic to her. Yet now the girl's story bothered her. Madame Pelletier's own daughter had run away when she was thirteen. Had she been projecting her own experience on the distraught parents — something she'd been trained not to do?

After the divorce, her daughter had decided to live with her father. Almost relieved, Madame Pelletier had agreed. She didn't miss the yelling matches — *you're never home, it's not like you'd miss me.*

Now her daughter lived in the Cévennes, raised sheep, chopped firewood in the bitter winters. Never mind that she'd married a man who was the mental equivalent of a barn post. They grew what they ate and slaughtered their own meat, and they were expecting . . . Her daughter, now happier than she'd ever been, begged her all the time to visit.

There she went again. Projecting.

Quiet as they kept it, with the Brigade's huge log of investigations — infant- and child-abuse cases, incest, child pornography — missing thirteen-year-olds like Zazie went to the bottom of the priority list.

Before the unit meeting, she'd pull up a few more years of files. She had to scratch that itch, make up for . . .

What was that name?

"Need you," her commander barked from the doorway.

"But I came in early to work on that case."

"Now, Pelletier. There's been a sighting of the rapist and two missing girls. We had a false one last night, but this looks real."

"Where?" she said, reaching for her cell phone.

"A warehouse. On the outskirts of Ivry."

A tough industrial suburb, more than an hour away in morning traffic. She grabbed her jacket.

Wednesday, 9 A.M.

Miles Davis licked Aimée's ankles at the concierge-*loge* door. Madame Cachou's lips turned down in disapproval as she handed Aimée a shopping bag labeled "maternity" that had been left for her by Martine. Hand-me-downs from her fertile sisters who, according to Martine, had populated a good sixteenth of France.

Thank God. And designer goodies, too. She'd outgrown most of her armoire.

"Careful, I just waxed the foyer."

Madame Cachou had always had a soft spot for Miles Davis — not so for Aimée. But since Aimée's pregnancy the concierge had thawed, almost to lukewarm. She'd bring up the mail, slip in an article on prenatal nutrition or tips on *bébé*'s first months.

"Left another package for you upstairs by your door."

"*Merci,* Madame."

Aimée leaned forward to take off Miles Davis's leash, and Morbier's borrowed jacket flapped open. Madame Cachou's gaze caught on her yesterday's worn clothes, stiff with blood. The bandage.

"What happened this time?" Shock mingled with concern in her tone. She wagged her finger. "An accident on that scooter? A woman in your condition . . ."

Quit sounding like my mother, she almost said. But her mother hadn't said that, because her mother wasn't there.

"I saw you on the *télé* in the appeal for that young girl."

Her and the rest of the world. The rapist, too.

Apart from getting herself shot at and Mélanie's mother murdered, where had the news appeal got her? Zazie was still missing. The "nice man" rang no bells with the owner of the NeoCancan, and no girls were held captive in his cellar, according to Beto's message. No brioches this morning, either, because of his double shift. No word from Zacharié's parole officer. And neither Madame Pelletier at the Brigade des Mineurs or Madame de Langlet had answered her calls.

"My baby's fine."

"Always in trouble, and now with a little life inside you . . ."

And the shooter still out there. Where was the police protection Morbier had promised her?

"No one's heard from Zazie in two days. There's a rapist on the loose." Her shoulder stung.

"And why is that your business?"

"A little girl I've known since she first started talking? I can't rest until I find her." She looked the concierge in the eye. "Could you?"

And with that she left an openmouthed Madame Cachou. Mounting the worn marble stairs more slowly than usual, she pulled out her cell phone and called Virginie again.

"I'm sorry, Aimée," said a breathless Virginie. "So many tips have been called in."

Aimée leaned on the scrolled metal filigreed banister, rooting for her keys. "Anything concrete?"

"Every tip's being checked out. The *flics* promised."

About time.

"Got to go, Aimée."

Not even a "how are you feeling?" . . . but then Virginie wouldn't know about what had happened last night. Or would she? And the *flics* had warned her against contact. She couldn't worry about that.

She checked her messages as Miles Davis scampered up the stairs. A missed call. Serge, her friend at the morgue. So Morbier had come through and asked for a ballistics report.

She hit callback. "*Allô*, Serge?"

He cleared his throat. "We're awaiting the final report, but the bullet's a match for the victim, Commissaire."

One of the staff had to be in the morgue with him.

"That's all, Serge? Didn't you notice anything out of the ordinary for a nine millimeter? The casing grooves? A magnifier would show."

"Commissaire, you're referring to the ballistic prelim?" said Serge. "It showed the bullet's from a Luger. A 1942 German standard issue for the Wehrmacht."

The shooter was smart. Lugers had no serial numbers, and making a definitive match would be difficult.

She heard water splashing in the distance. The whine of a bone saw. Tried not to cringe imagining Serge, with his black-framed glasses outfitted with magnifiers and his black beard muffled by a mask, leaning over a half-dissected corpse on the stainless-steel autopsy table.

"Thanks, Serge."

"Now if you'll let me get back to my autopsy," he whispered.

"Wait, Serge," she said. "Have you autopsied Sylvaine Olivet, the twelve-year-old rape victim?"

Pause. "What's it to you?"

"Yes or no?"

She heard a door creak. Footsteps. He'd stepped into the corridor. "A hard one, Aimée. Children are the worst." Serge had twin preschool boys.

"Was her convulsion brought on by the rape, her injuries?"

"Not what comes to mind, but I'd have to check my notes. Why?"

She had to think.

"I asked what's it to you, Aimée?" He cleared his throat again. "I've got a whole queue of bodies — multiple gunshot wounds, suspicious asphyxiation, and that's just before lunch."

"But I found her, Serge, with her distraught mother, on the floor . . ." She paused, the scene playing in her mind, Sylvaine's cold limbs. "Any traces of sedatives, drugs in her blood?"

"Does this have to do with you on the *télé*?"

"Long story, but yes, and Zazie might be another victim. Please, Serge, I'll take the twins for their vaccinations."

He hated to do that. A medical pathologist who couldn't face seeing his own children poked with needles.

She heard a door shut. "Sir, the magistrate's waiting."

"I have to go," he whispered. "And you owe me big time, Aimée. Vaccinations and the boys' summer camp physicals." He clicked off.

She groaned inside. Never mind taking them to the doctor, the boys were bad enough just to babysit — they never sat still for longer than a minute.

But a German Luger from the war? She filed that away. Right now her bladder called. Again.

Her seventeenth-century flat, bone-chill cold in the winter and stifling in the summer, welcomed her with stale air and the tang of lemons from the silver bowl on the dining table.

In front of the door, she'd found the package Madame Cachou had mentioned, which was addressed in René's handwriting. More pregnancy books and Lamaze pamphlets. She'd promised he could be her Lamaze coach, whatever that meant. But she guessed she'd find out by studying this new batch of material.

First she had to get the bloody clothes off, wash up and think about next steps — what favors to call in. Favors she didn't have. She'd just have to figure that out.

Steam fogged her gilt-framed Directoire bathroom mirror. In the tub she kept the bullet-wound area dry and sponged around the stinging in her shoulder. Only two stitches. She swabbed on the doctor's ointment, attached an Asterix bandage over it.

Just as she was pulling a towel around her expanding middle, she heard the front door click. She froze, prickles running up the backs of her damp legs.

No one, not even René, had a key anymore.

Her cell phone sat in her bag by the door, her Beretta in the kitchen spoon drawer. Had the shooter followed her back from the hospital? Lock-picked his way in to finish the job?

Taking no chances, she grabbed her heated hair-straightening wand and manicure scissors and stepped behind the red-lacquered Chinoiserie dressing screen.

She took slow breaths.

Raised her arm.

The footsteps paused in the hall. The tall

bathroom door creaked open. Her heart beat so hard she thought it would jump out of her chest.

She gauged the distance. Waited until he got within range. Swung.

A cry. The smell of searing flesh. She kicked the Chinoisierie screen over. She just had to make it through the hallway and reach her gun in the kitchen. Using the screen as a shield, she almost made it to the door, where she slipped. The intruder wrestled her to the ground. Her ankles were caught, and she jabbed out with the pointed manicure scissors.

But her wrists were caught in a steel grip. She was pulled down, hot breath on her neck. Melac's perspiring face grimaced in pain.

"Still like to be on top, don't you?" Melac sucked in his breath.

"Next time remind me you still have the key." Her body went limp. "Morbier sent you, didn't he?" His familiar citrus scent made her heart clench.

"You okay, Aimée?"

"Almost wrestled you down, didn't I?" No point in telling him her shoulder stung like hell. "Don't tell me you're my police protection?"

"You're carrying my child," he said. "Or

did that slip your mind as you were kicking high-heel ass and getting shot?"

"So it's my fault I got gunned down in the street?"

He waved his hand in dismissal. "Why does someone else have to tell me about our baby?"

As if she hadn't wanted to tell him? Sort of.

"I called," said Melac. "Left you messages. *Ecoute,* Sandrine suffered a setback. Intensive care. I got caught up. But what's the problem?" Surprise filled his face. "We planned all this, talked about fixing up my father's farm, raising children together in Brittany."

Once, one midnight, after too much champagne. "That was months ago. And you just assumed . . ."

"But you agreed, remember?"

Had she?

"Every morning I work with my old friend Paul — he's buying a bigger fishing boat. The farm's almost finished. There's a perfect room for your office, but now it will be the baby's room."

There he was, tanned, muscular and so vulnerable on her bathroom floor. And brimming with crazy ideas. "My life's there now," he said. "Yours, too, and the baby's.

You won't be alone raising a child."

They hadn't spoken for months, and he expected her to move to Brittany?

"Do you know how lucky you got last night?" His grey-blue eyes narrowed in concern. "You can't just think of yourself now. There's a new life growing inside you."

This again? "You call a bullet lucky?"

He kissed her shoulder. "I'm worried. Think of the baby, Aimée. The farm overlooks the sea, the air's clean and the only crime is poaching in the forest. You can learn to cook."

Cook? Another reason they didn't get along. It would always be this way with him.

He sighed, maybe realizing she wasn't going to just say yes to him. "Zazie's been sighted," he said then. "Two units have staked out a warehouse. All under control."

Her heart leapt. "How can they be sure? What if it's just a ploy?"

"According to my friends on the force, no one appreciates your interference," said Melac. "The chief of the Brigade des Mineurs is handling this case personally. Let them do their job."

Interference? Would they even be looking for Zazie at all if she hadn't gone to the lengths she had? "And you're the messenger to warn me off?"

346

Melac pulled her towel off. "Beautiful." He ran his hands over her stomach. "Son or daughter?"

"It's a surprise." She glared at him. But he'd pulled her close, his body heat enveloping her, his lips on her neck . . . his tongue licking her ear.

He smelled the same, that same citrus scent.

"I've missed you, how I've missed you."

She couldn't pull away. Then she didn't want to.

"How long has it been?" said Melac.

"Four months and fourteen days, but who's counting?" Immediately she wanted to take those words back.

Melac grinned. "So we've got a lot to make up for."

Why did she want him to keep stroking her stomach? To keep feeling his hot breath in her ear? Why couldn't she ignore that shiver she'd missed so much?

She woke up on top of the duvet, Melac's tanned leg over hers. Delicious. A breeze rippled the gauze curtain, carrying in the scent of the lime trees below.

"Can't beat making up like this," he whispered and nuzzled her neck. She realized he was cradling his cell phone to his

347

other ear even as he was nuzzling her. "Listen, the care nurse comes recommended. Trust her, Nathalie."

Aimée sat up. Talking to Nathalie, his ex-wife. And she realized it would always be like this with him — his life dominated by his suicidal ex, who never stopped calling. A man stretched in all directions.

Right then she knew she wasn't ready for a new role: moving to Brittany, working long-distance and figuring her baby's life around Melac's fragmented idea of a relationship. Always preoccupied and at the beck and call of his daughter and her health; his fragile, unbalanced ex who required so much maintenance.

She watched those blue-grey eyes, felt his warm hand on her thigh, but . . .

Stuck in Brittany? Think again. Maybe if she cared enough, but inside she didn't know if she did. He had left her to go back to his first family, just put her to the side, and he would do that with their child. She'd always play second fiddle. No, she needed something more. Time to turn the page on the kind of freewheeling relationships she'd had before, the kind she just let happen to her.

He was pulling on his jeans, in the middle of an argument with his ex. Miles Davis, at the foot of the bed, cocked his head.

On the bedside table, she removed her key from his key ring.

"*Désolé,* I have to catch the train at Montparnasse." He pulled on his jacket. "There's a problem with the nurse."

And you just had great goodbye sex.

He noticed her look.

"Aimée, we'll make it work. I want to do the right thing."

Do the right thing like in an old Balzac novel, make an honest woman of her? Or more of a duty, like flossing every night? "Marriage?"

Melac averted his gaze. And when those blue-grey eyes looked up, he shrugged. "I meant give the baby my name."

Stupid. Yet she wished her heart would stop shuddering, that she'd caught herself before blurting that out. "Marriage wouldn't change anything, not that I would marry you," she said, recovering. "As for wanting to be the father, give the baby your name — get in line."

"What?"

"René's already offered," she shot back.

"René?" Melac shook his head. "Can you be that blind? Open your eyes, he's —"

His phone beeped.

"My best friend and Lamaze coach," she

349

shot back. So involved she could swear she'd noticed him suffering sympathy back pain when she complained the other day.

"I can't miss this train," he said.

Duty called.

"I've never asked you for help," she said, "and I've no intention of starting now."

He checked his phone again. "Try to understand. I've got to deal with the hospital, rehab, getting the house adapted to move Sandrine in."

"You're spread thin," she said. "I do understand. But it's not for me."

"You're having my baby, who needs a father."

A father who'd love it, be there for it — and for her. This would never work. But she'd felt that from the get-go.

"We'll invite you to the christening."

"Stubborn like always. But I'll —"

"Miss the train if you don't hurry, Melac."

She shut the door behind him, locked it.

She felt a kick. "You want me to kick him down the stairs?" she asked the Bump. "Be nice." She rubbed her stomach.

Aimée watched Melac walk along the tree-lined quai until he disappeared under the green leaves. Left alone, sadness overwhelmed her about what had happened last night, poor Mélanie who'd lost her mother, the desperate dead woman who'd prioritized her work to hide her shame. Guilt layered on top of guilt — Aimée'd judged this woman who was now on a slab in the morgue.

And now Zazie. She said a little prayer that the *flics* would rescue Zazie alive. Right now all Aimée could do was wash down her prenatal vitamins and the mild analgesic the doctor had given her and sip her *espresso décaféiné.*

Her eye caught on a man on the quai. Something about him was familiar. He saw her at the window and waved, then pointed to the green bench. A taxi, red brake lights on, idled at the curb.

Yes, she recognized him. The man on the bench was Marie-Jo's father. Morbier had warned her to stay inside, the shooter still at large. But were the shooter and rapist one and the same? And could they be this man, this ex-con?

Right now the *flics* were going after Zazie at the warehouse. But if Marie-Jo's father was connected to the man who abducted the girls, no way could she ignore his involvement. Or his possible ploy to pull her in.

Reason told her to stay inside, let the *flics*

do their job. Yet her gut told her to trust him. She lumped a second mound of horse-meat into Miles Davis's bowl. Took her Beretta from the spoon drawer, checked the clip. Full.

From the bag of Martine's sisters' pregnancy clothes, all of them splattered with high-end labels, she picked out a pair of black leather pants, buttery-soft pigskin, stylish and with an expandable waist. Paired them with a silk Dior tunic that hid her bandage. A minute later, mauve metallic ballet flats on, scarf trailing, she locked her door.

Cool breezes ruffled the Seine below into frothed white caps. The leaves *shhhoo*'d and trembled in the wind. A dry heat hung in the air this morning, the humidity gone.

"I need your help," said Zacharié, Marie-Jo's father and the former husband of Béatrice de Mombert.

"To catch the nice man who took the girls from your ex-wife's apartment yesterday?" She felt for her Beretta in her secondhand Birkin bag. "The man you're in league with?"

Surprise crinkled his brow. His fingers worried the buttons on his shirt.

"I'll bet he's into music. Marie-Jo plays

violin, doesn't she?"

"Piano. I don't know what you're getting at, but I know where Zazie and my daughter Marie-Jo are being held."

Old news. "They've been sighted at a warehouse in Ivry," she said. "Two units were dispatched."

She noted the grim set to his mouth. He shook his head. "That's a diversion," he said. "They're in Paris."

The hairs on her arm rippled. "I don't understand. They've tracked the rapist —"

He raised his hand. "Forget him. He has nothing to do with this."

Neither girl was the rapist's type. But then how did the attacks connect to Zazie's circle of friends? Could it be just a coincidence? "The rapist's not involved in the girls' disappearance?"

He shook his head. "And I can't tell you any more."

"Fine." She made as if to stand. "I'm leaving."

He grabbed her wrist. "To keep them alive we need to move now."

Her fingers trembled. "You expect me to trust you? Just like that? Tell me why I should."

"It's complicated." His voice cracked. Serious. He was serious. But he was holding back.

"You're on parole, your ex-wife's in rehab, you know this man."

He averted his eyes.

"Why should I believe you?"

"My daughter's . . ." he took a breath. Looked toward the taxi. "They're both pawns."

"Pawns in what?"

He hesitated.

"If this man's holding something over you, why not go to the *flics*?"

"You know I'm on parole. I can't. That's why I came to you."

This put a new spin on it. But she needed more. "Tell me who took them."

"Do you really want an answer? Or do you want to rescue the girls?"

A nervous energy emanated from him. Intense eyes. The eyes of a father. She hated to, but she believed him.

"Why me?"

"Everyone trusts a pregnant woman; together we'll be able to get in without arousing suspicion. Plus you're a detective, I checked," he said. "I saw you on the *télé* — you want to save them as much as I do."

He had that right.

"But last night's murder . . ." Her throat caught. "Were you involved in the shooting

354

of that woman? Is that related to whatever this is?"

"*Non. Pas du tout.*" He stood. "But your choice. Either you take the chance and believe me, or you wait to find out the Ivry warehouse is a hoax and lose two hours."

He was already hailing the taxi, which started up its engine.

"Coming?"

Wednesday, 11 A.M.
Pigalle. The morning street sweepers'
brooms raked the detritus from the celebra-
tions into the flowing gutters. The scraping
over the cobbles sounded not unlike fingernails on a chalkboard to Aimée — her
nerves were acting up. Parents walked
children to school on the narrow pavement.
The neon club signs looked naked in the
sunlight.

"Follow the plan, okay?" said Zacharié.

A makeshift plan involving a reputed lead
to an old crony's brother-in-law, but she
put on her Jackie-O sunglasses and readjusted her spiky black wig, the one she
kept in the pocket of her oversize bag.
Thank God the leather pants' waist was
expandable. "I'll call you."

"What?"

"If there's an obstacle, we go to plan B."

"What's plan B?" said Zacharié.

356

"Improvise."

She left the taxi in front of the disco Le Bus Palladium, the "temple of rock" when she and Martine clubbed there in the early nineties. Or had it been the late eighties? The white facade glared starkly in the daylight.

She was overrun by doubts about Zacharié's plan. But she knew one thing. If Zazie was here, she'd find her.

"Bonjour." She smiled at the young woman barring her way with a vacuum cleaner. "I'm late. But he's waiting for me."

"Who?" The woman stood her ground, readjusting her paisley headscarf.

"Like I said, he's expecting me." Aimée scanned the vacant box office, the deserted, red-carpeted foyer. She remembered the layout: beyond the ground floor's closed double doors lay the dance floor. That wouldn't help. To the right was a short staircase leading to a *resto.* Directly across from the *resto* she saw a sign: OFFICE.

The disco, a former theatre, hadn't changed except for the DJ names on the posters. She'd never heard of any of them. A new generation and it made her feel old.

"He's waiting for me in the office."

"No one's up there, Madame," she said.

"Only the cleaning crew comes in this early."

"And you're so efficient. He couldn't run the place without you." She tried to step around the woman towards the stairs.

"No one's allowed upstairs."

"Chut!" Aimée pressed her finger over her Chanel red lips. "Let's keep this between us. Woman to woman." Aimée pointed to her stomach. "His wife doesn't know yet. But she'll understand, I tell him. All the nights he spends away, here with me."

The young cleaning woman blinked. "Raoul?" She pointed to the color photos of staff on the wall. "That Raoul?" A balding, fifty-something man in thick glasses squinted at the camera. He wore a floral shirt.

"L'amour." Aimée sighed.

The woman shrugged. Aimée took the stairs two at a time and knocked on the office door. No answer. It was locked. *"Bonjour, chéri,* it's me," she said loudly, for the benefit of the cleaning woman.

With her lock-pick set, she inserted an upper and lower prong into the door lock and toggled. A moment later she turned the handle. A dark, empty office.

She hit the lights. Desk, posters of Johnny Hallyday and Depeche Mode, a brocade

358

chaise in need of reupholstering.

No Zazie.

No closet, no back room. She wanted to kick the legs off the ugly chaise. Stupid to go along with Zacharié's idea, to think that this Raoul would lock the girls up in an office, with the *resto* so close by. But he'd been so sure, so adamant that Raoul was key.

Key.

The desk's third drawer yielded to her lock-pick. Paper clips, business cards, and three sets of color-coded and labeled key rings: yellow backstage door, red stage entrance, blue lighting loft.

She took all three. Picked up the yellow-handled flashlight from the desk and noticed a receipt under it. Bottled water, toilet paper, apples from the nearby Monoprix — the receipt was dated last night. She stuffed it in her pocket. Parched, she twisted the cap off the Evian bottle from her purse and drank in the hot, airless room.

She had to find something else, something more, and quick — before the cleaning woman got curious or Raoul showed up. She opened and went through every drawer again — there were only three — then lifted the faded Turkish throw rug, peeked behind the posters, emptied the metal-wire trash bin. Vacuuming sounds came from the stairway. As she was about to give up, her eye caught on something red tangled in the bottom of the overturned trash bin.

A red tassel. Like the one on Zazie's backpack zipper. Like the one she'd already found in the de Mombert apartment.

Her pulse raced.

Outside in the hallway she studied the evacuation diagram required in every building for the fire brigade.

She hit Zacharié's number. Let it ring once. Clicked off then rang again.

"Oui?"

"I've got Raoul's keys. Meet me at the backstage entrance."

"Where's that?"

"Rue Pigalle." She clicked off.

The closed *resto* dining room, converted from one half of the old theatre stage, sported retro decor with a splash of old polished silver and fifties turquoise glass. More *branché,* catering to the *bourgeoises- bohèmes* rather than the rockers downstairs.

The back stairs from the kitchen led down to a door. She tried six keys from the red key ring before she got the right one.

She stepped out onto a dim, sloping stage, passed the DJ apparatus — turntables, microphones. At the backstage door, she let

Zacharié in.

"Find them?"

"Just this." She showed him the red tassel. "It's Zazie's."

"Marie-Jo has one, too."

"How would you know?" she said. "You've been in prison."

"Think we didn't communicate? That I don't know what's going on with my daughter?" His gaze swept the seats, the balcony. "We wrote each other every week. She sent photos. She had a backpack with a tassel like that."

"So they were here," Aimée said. "We've got three options: backstage, stage entrance, lighting loft."

"Lighting," said Zacharié without skipping a beat.

"Why?"

"You said you'd trust me."

She nodded.

"Raoul's in charge of lighting." He took the flashlight and headed toward the spiral staircase on the right. "Stay down here."

She hiked up the waistband on her leather pants. She hated heights. "Like hell I will."

The high catwalk, rimmed with colored gel-filter spotlights, swayed like a tightrope, making her feel like she was on a high-wire act with no safety harness or net. Only a top rail, thin metal planks and a toeboard between her and the orchestra pit below — and the whole outfit in serious need of welding.

She snuck a glance down at the stage. Big mistake. Dizzy, she grabbed the narrow rail, made her feet move, shuffling one forward after the other. Every breath of the hot, dense air was a struggle.

Under the rafters nested a cockpit-like glassed-in booth. When she followed Zacharié inside, it turned out to be larger than it appeared. More hot, stale air, a flat console with toggle switches and buttons, an overflowing ashtray. An empty bottle of Ricard sat on the unswept wood floor.

Raoul's lighting nest in the eaves stifled her. She gasped, finding it hard to breathe. Zacharié cursed and kicked the stool over. "I know Raoul's got them. Give me the keys. I'll search backstage, under the orchestra pit."

She'd climbed up this high — she was going to spend longer than one minute examining it. And catch her breath before the long way down. "Impatient type, eh?" She took the flashlight from him. Shone it on wall shelving filled with plugs, odd bulbs and tools. "The color's different here."

"Et alors?" He'd turned and headed to the walkway. "There's no time to waste. They're in danger."

Her frustration mounted. "Quit the runaround. What kind of danger?"

Zacharié's lips pursed. She could see the conflict behind his eyes. "You don't want to know. If not for yourself, think of that baby inside you."

His words sent a shiver down her neck.

She played the flashlight over the shelves once more, more carefully. This time, the beam revealed a chalk mark, faint and smudged, but distinctive: an X.

Her throat caught. She'd seen that chalk X in the park. Zazie's sign. "That's from Zazie."

"You're sure?"

"Help me move these shelves aside."

That done, they saw a light-colored plywood sheet, hung at the side with hinges, like a door. A door no bigger than a suitcase.

He pulled back the hinged door, then propped it back with a power strip. Going onto her knees, she studied the crawl space. The air was even denser than in the stifling lighting booth. But if Zazie was here . . .

She hunched down and crawled. Her hands pressed against swags of dank velvet, and cobwebs clung to her damp arms.

363

She emerged on her knees into a stale, musty room. Bright mid-morning sunlight seeped through the closed shutters and softened the dust-swaddled edges of a Second Empire-style salon.

"Zazie? Where are you?" Her voice echoed off the high *boiserie*-molded ceilings.

The place looked deserted. Had they walked into some kind of museum?

Disappointed, she strode past a stuffed ostrich, framed paintings and a writing desk piled with old letters bound with ribbon. She walked over to a mirrored dressing table covered in perfume bottles and ivory-backed hairbrushes and picked up a gold lipstick case. Ruby-colored lipstick inside with a cloying sweet scent.

How long ago had it been abandoned? Like something from a Proust novel, from another era. A past long gone, frozen in time.

She and Zacharié searched every nook and cranny from the enamel, claw-footed bathtub to the large brick-and-iron coal furnace in the kitchen. She checked the walk-in pantry and found a yellow matchbox and a portrait of Maréchal Pétain.

Dust everywhere. Patches disturbed on the kitchen floor, the carpet in the salon. Random or a sign?

"No one has lived here for a while," Zacharié said, wiping his finger over piles of yellowed newspapers dated 1940.

"We've missed something," she said. She paced through the rooms. In the library she noticed more mashed footsteps in the dust on the faded carpet. Behind a gilded chair she discovered a six-pack of water bottles and some toilet roll — the only evidence of the modern day.

Frustrated, she leaned against the wall. "They've been here. Look." She pulled out the Monoprix receipts. "Bought yesterday."

Alarm filled his eyes. "Then we're too late. He's moved them."

"Who's he?"

"Better you don't know."

"Quit playing games. You've got what this man wants, right? Your daughter's the pawn for it. And Zazie." She leaned against the bookcase. "Why don't you call the shots? Threaten to expose whatever he doesn't want exposed?"

It seemed simple to her.

"I can't."

"Or won't? Got a better idea?" She shook her head. The man had told her nothing, expected her to just go along with him. "I don't care what the hell you've done. But quit keeping me in the dark. Tell me what else he's holding over you."

"That's unimportant. Just say he knows too much."

"I'm guessing you do, too," she said, putting it together. "He, whoever he is, hired you."

He blinked, clutched her arm. "Shut up."

But she wouldn't. She'd hit a nerve.

"He kidnapped your daughter to keep you on task. But Zazie got involved. So give me the information."

Zacharié nodded. Hung his head. "He killed my partners. I was next. But I escaped."

Shivers went up her arms. And that was the man who had Zazie?

"We can't trust him. He's desperate," said Zacharié. His jaw quivered. "He's killed already to keep people silent. The girls' lives are at stake."

Zazie held by a sadistic criminal — a man who kills to make sure no witnesses survive? Fear clamped her stomach. Breathe, she had to breathe in this hot, dense air and figure this out.

"What do you have that's so important? State secrets, blackmail?"

"Something like that." He jangled the key rings. "But he won't get what he wants until I find Marie-Jo."

"What does that mean?"

But he'd turned to go back through the crawl. "Coming?"

Instinct told her not to leave yet. Something spoke to her here, and she didn't know what. Her father always said to listen to the crime scene. Let it speak to you. Didn't old Second Empire buildings feature concealed alcoves, secret built-ins? Nooks to hide trysts from the inconvenient arrival of *les domestiques* or the spouse? She remembered that from some de Maupassant story.

The carpet's dust was most displaced in front of a bookcase full of worn leather volumes. She ran her hands over the bookcase's period molding and came back with sooty fingers. Nothing. Her fingers traced the ridges and burls in the bookcase's wooden interior. She rose on her tiptoes to reach the high shelf, her bump pressing on the volumes below.

Something shifted. She felt a book give way against her stomach — the dark maroon leather Bible. The bookcase moved, sliding back to reveal a chamber. She gasped and took a step inside.

Perspiration-laced used air and darkness greeted her. "Hand me the flashlight!" she called.

No answer. No Zacharié. Impatient, he'd gone.

She pulled out her mini-flashlight from her bag. The beam wasn't as strong as the other would have been, but it illuminated a round, vault-like room with peeling wall-paper. She saw pink toenails peeking out from behind a box — a bare foot with a chain around its ankle. She leaned down. A girl, her mouth duct-taped, squinted into the glare. Matted black hair plastered with sweat to her forehead. She wore a tank top and jeans.

"Marie-Jo?"

She nodded. Her chained feet thumped the floor.

Aimée took out her Swiss Army knife. "I'll get you out of here. Where's Zazie?"

Her feet thumped again. Moaning came from next to Marie-Jo. Aimée followed the sound with the beam, catching on curly red hair and Zazie's flushed face.

"Zazie!" Her pulse raced. Good God, she was alive. "Hold on, this will sting." She ripped the tape off Marie-Jo's mouth, then Zazie's. "Thank God . . . please tell me you're okay," she said, working to free their bound wrists from the duct tape.

Marie-Jo spit. "Thirsty."

"I knew you'd . . . you'd find me." Zazie's

368

lips quivered. She reached up and hugged Aimée tight the moment her wrists were free. Her shoulders shook.

"Good job on the chalk mark, Zazie," she said. She pulled a bottle of water out of her bag for them to share. Her shirt, soaked in perspiration, clung to her back. "Now to get you two out."

"That man checks us every three hours," said Zazie. "We timed him. He drinks, but —"

"What's with the bad hair, a wig?" Marie-Jo interrupted.

"Her disguise," said Zazie, admiration in her puffy eyes. "She's got tons of them. Nice pants. Your tummy's bigger, Aimée."

So much for designer maternity clothes. She felt like a whale, swimming in her own sweat.

"We have to hurry." Aimée went to work with her lock-pick set on the padlock chaining them. Two minutes later they were free and struggling to stand. "Can you walk?"

"Of course we can," Zazie said, but she hobbled and gripped the wall.

"Lean on me," Aimée said.

She tried not to wince as Zazie grabbed her wounded shoulder. Dense, engulfing heat made her knees wobble. The damn wig was sticking to her scalp.

"What is this place, besides a time capsule?" Aimée said.

"Some old lady escaped to Nice during the war, that man said." Zazie pointed to an oil portrait covered with dust. "This was her great-aunt's place. She was some kind of *lorette.*"

Courtesans who lived around Notre-Dame de Lorette Church at the turn of the century — nicknamed *lorettes* — were often installed in flats by wealthy lovers.

"The old lady never came back, so no one knows this place, that man kept saying on his phone," said Zazie. "They'd never find us. The front door's bolted."

Her stitches smarted. They had to get out. Quick.

"He's due anytime," said Zazie. Her voice quivered. "He comes in through that crawl-space. Drunk."

Great. If he was armed she couldn't risk a confrontation with the girls.

"Then we'll find another way out."

Places like this always had servants' back stairs. "Let's try the back." With one of Aimée's arms around each of the girls, they made halting progress to the kitchen. The back-stair door held a rusted padlock. Her lock picks worked no magic on rust.

"Where's my papa?" Marie-Jo said suddenly.

"Explanations later." Right now, she had to prioritize getting them to safety. In a kitchen drawer she found a cobwebbed meat mallet. "Here, take a swing and bust the lock."

But Marie-Jo didn't move. "My papa told you where we were. Where is he?"

Of all times. The girl was as stubborn and impatient as her father. "He wants you safe, Marie-Jo. We need to get out before . . ."

"What aren't you telling me?" The hollow-cheeked girl was a bundle of nerves. "That man will hurt Papa when he finds us gone."

"She's right, Aimée," said Zazie, but she took the mallet and swung.

If only the impatient *salaud* had waited instead of searching in the theatre. "He's got a plan," she said, improvising. "We meet him after I get you to safety."

The bolt broke under Zazie's repeated whacks. "Now shove it open," Aimée said. "Go!"

But the door didn't budge. It must be bolted or barred from the other side.

"We're running out of time," said Zazie. "He's late already."

Aimée pulled out her cell phone and hit Zacharié's number. If only he were there to help them force the door. No answer.

Aimée thought quickly. "I'm going back through that secret passage to find your father," she told the girls. "You need to push the kitchen table and those cupboards to block the door. Meanwhile keep shoving that back door. Let no one in, do you hear me?"

"Why can't we go with you?"

"And risk you running into Raoul? And whoever else might come with him? Stay here."

"But my papa —" said Marie-Jo.

"He'll be all right if you do exactly what I say."

"Like I believe you?" Tears ran down Marie-Jo's face, and she tried to push past Aimée. "The man's going to kill him."

Aimée caught her arm and held her back. Damn teenager. She was right.

"But you believe me, right, Zazie?" Aimée said, her glare making it clear Zazie should back her up.

Wide-eyed, Zazie nodded.

Taking no chances, Aimée pulled the Beretta from her bag, loaded a cartridge. She tried René's number. Busy. Next she tried Saj.

"About time, Aimée," said Saj, his voice raised. "René's been —"

"I've found Zazie," she interrupted. "Right now we need to escape. I need backup. Jump in a taxi."

Saj choked. "Location?"

She stared through the grime covering the kitchen window to try to see what was outside. A small concrete courtyard with trash bins five floors down. No balcony, not even a railing with flowerpot geraniums. No way out from here.

"Look for a courtyard exit, on the east side of rue Pigalle, maybe two doors down from the rue Pierre Fontaine corner," she said. "This apartment wall's flush with Le Bus Palladium's lighting booth."

She heard keys clicking over his keyboard. "On it."

"Have you figured it out?" Her breath came in short gasps. "It's the fourth-floor service stairs, and the door's barred."

"Got it. Fifty-nine rue Pigalle."

"Bring your bag of tricks. Call my phone when you get here — I'm giving it to Zazie. She will be the one to answer."

"I'm bringing an ax." Saj clicked off.

She handed Zazie her cell phone. "Keep trying the door. Stay in contact with Saj. Can you do that?"

Zazie nodded.

Marie-Jo averted her eyes.

"Help Zazie if want to see your papa, *compris,* Marie-Jo?"

Marie-Jo gave a sullen nod.

"Now barricade yourselves in."

After shutting the kitchen door, she waited until she heard furniture shoved behind it. She stuck the Beretta in her leather maternity pants' back pocket. Removed her wig, scratched, then took a bottle of water and splashed it over her head. Alert now, she took a breath.

Noises came from tunnel to the lighting booth. Shouts. Her neck prickled.

In the time it took until Saj arrived she had to hold Raoul off and find Zacharié. She crawled back through the hole to the lighting booth. The voices were louder. Zacharié was bent from the waist over the catwalk railing, a man pinning his arms behind him as he struggled. Not Raoul from the photo, but a blond, curly-haired man with broad shoulders, wearing a blazer and jeans. Aimée saw that he'd secured Zacharié's hands behind his back using yellow plastic flex-cuffs.

She ducked behind the partition in the lighting booth.

"Can't you keep to our deal, Zacharié?" the man was saying.

"You call having the Corsican murder my friends part of the deal?" Zacharié gasped. Keys and change rained down from his pockets to the stage below. "You planned it all along. Fool that I am, I believed you. Jules, just let Marie-Jo go and you get the file." He coughed. "Even bonus material."

Jules hesitated, shadowed under the stage lights.

Perspiration beaded her upper lip. Hot, it was so damn hot. And with the shadows she wouldn't have a clear shot.

"Bonus material? Nice touch," Jules said. "Like what?"

"Just let my baby go."

"Look, you think I want to do this? I don't want to hurt you anymore, Zacharié," Jules said. "Cooperate. Easier all round." He let Zacharié up. "Let's go backstage. Marie-Jo's safe and sound, and you'll see her as promised. Now hand over what you owe me."

Liar. She scanned the control panel, looking for the houselights' control switch.

"Marie-Jo's backstage?"

"First the file."

"You think I've got it on me?" Zacharié laughed. "I'm not that stupid."

"*Bon,*" Jules said, checking his phone. "I'm late. This has caused my connection no end of worry. Life will be difficult all round if I don't deliver."

"Someone's blackmailing you and your cronies, that's why you're so desperate?"

Jules blinked. Zacharié had hit a nerve. "Ten years I've worked for this. They owe me in the Ministry. No one's taking it away from me now." Jules gave a long-suffering sigh. "Haven't I always come through for you, Zacharié? When you were young, when Marie-Jo got sick? Made sure you were in the best prison wing, received the early parole. Now I gave you this simple job, with a reward of a new identity, a new life."

Aimée saw the catwalk shift, straining under their combined weight.

Idiots.

"I want that to happen, Zacharié," said Jules. "Cooperate for Marie-Jo's sake. Trust me."

Aimée saw him slide something from his jacket pocket. Then a glint as he raised a knife to Zacharié's neck.

Now. She had to act now. She pulled as many levers as she could reach, praying one would work.

The stage floodlights blazed orange, throwing a fire-like halo on the two men.

Thinking fast, she reached for a thin, stapled packet, a lighting manual, stuffed under the control panel and brandished it for him to see. "You don't mean this, do you? Zacharié left it with me."

Jules turned. His small eyes darted from Aimée to Zacharié and back. "You neglected to tell me about your new accomplice." His mouth tightened. "A dripping Madonna in leather pants, interesting. So Zacharié gave you the file and bonus material?" Jules kept his grip on Zacharié. But confusion flashed in his eyes.

"As soon as you put that knife away, Jules. May I call you Jules?"

Zacharié shook his head. "Don't listen to her."

"Long way down, boys," she said. "And it's never wise to upset a pregnant woman."

Jules snorted. "Is she for real?"

"Want to find out?" Aimée waved the smudged packet.

"She's making that up. I've got the file . . ."

"Jules, he claims I'm making it up," she said. "But how can you be sure? More to the point, how can he trust you after I found Marie-Jo and Zazie tied up and hidden behind the bookcase?"

Zacharié's jaw dropped.

"They're escaping down those old servants stairs. So convenient. Safe. Nothing left to hold over him now, Jules, but if you don't want this file . . . ?" She flipped it open. "Someone else will."

Jules dropped the knife, tightened his grip on Zacharié, and shoved him forward. Smiled. "Aah, a businesswoman. How much?"

She could almost hear Jules sniffing like a dog. Testing her.

"Fifty thousand, don't you think, Zacharié?" she said.

The reflected orange light revealed Zacharié's blackened eye, his shaking body. His foot caught in the plank's rim, shaking it loose. The bar sailed through the air, crashing below.

Aimée shuddered. A long way down.

"Now I understand, you sly dog," said Jules. His eyes narrowed as if assessing their relationship, his options, who to attack first. At least in his position that's what she would be assessing.

"Playing happy families again? She's a looker. And more stable than Béatrice, I hope. Now, Zacharié, keep moving to the cubicle."

Jules's blond curls had darkened with sweat, and they clung tight to his head. He gripped the catwalk rail.

"You know I'm undercover, a *flic,*" said Jules.

■ ■ ■ ■

Shocked for a moment, she grabbed the wall . . . then remembered Cécile's description. Old hookers didn't lie about the law. She'd got his pressed-jeans look correct.

"So was my father," she said, biting her lip before she said, "but he wasn't a snake like you."

"Then you know how the game's played. The bond between *flics*. How it's family, and in a family we help each other."

No family to her, not after they drummed her father out of the force in disgrace. Not after the years it had taken to clear his name. Or witnessing the dead ends in the layers of corruption.

Instead she smiled. "Family maybe, but not a charity. Still, I don't much buy into the family. My father died in a bomb explosion doing 'routine' surveillance. A damn setup."

Jules gave a knowing nod. "Place Vendôme. Enough *plastique* to cinder the van and melt the fence around the column. I remember."

"You?" Lying again. "You're too young."

"Happened during my first month on bomb disposal," said Jules. "You never forget. Or the things that don't add up."

He had the details right. "What the hell does that mean?"

Stalling, the *salaud* was stalling for time. Trying to figure out how to kill them both.

"Word came down to leave your father's investigation alone," said Jules. "That's how I learned the family punishes its own. Your papa played in the dirt; now so do you." He shrugged. "Cut the high and mighty. You know I'm right. So it's business now. I pay, and you provide."

Why was she letting his words affect her? Why was her hand shaking so much she couldn't steady it to shoot him right now, like she wanted to?

Zacharié reached the booth, and Jules pushed him toward her. Ready, she shoved Zacharié down.

"Maybe you're lying," said Jules. Recognition lit his eyes. "Now I remember. You're the one on the *télé.*"

He'd halted, undecided, on the shaking catwalk, so close his cologne and stale-sweat smell reached her. The spiral staircase was right below him. One more step and she'd have him.

"Want to find out?"

"First my checkbook. But I need a show of good faith."

He reached inside his blazer pocket toward a distinctive bulge. Bad move.

She shook the catwalk railing. Threw him off balance. He fell on his knees. Came up with a Sig Sauer pointed at her.

"Naughty," said Jules. "Now put down the file and shove it with your foot."

She shrugged. "You win." She pushed the file forward with her toe, surreptitiously reaching for her Beretta. "Come and get it."

Jules's eyes flicked from her to the file, back and forth as he reached out, the gun in his other hand trained on her.

His left hand grabbed at the file; her eye clocked on his right with his finger curled around the trigger. Aimée jiggled the catwalk, aimed her Beretta and drilled Jules three times in the right shoulder. He jerked, his shots going wild as she ducked. *Thupt, thupt.* Bullets thudded into the rafters and metal pinged. Jules grabbed at the shuddering catwalk rail, yelling in pain, and lost his grip. The file opened and papers spilled, floating and dancing in the orange light.

Jules's shouts ended in a crashing thud. She didn't want to look. But she did.

He sprawled on the stage's edge by the DJ table. The microphone wires splayed around him like a wreath of snakes.

Aimée shuddered. Her palms were wet;

her knees shook. She hated heights. "Let's go." She reached for Zacharié, who stood shaking and mute at her side. "Did you hear me?"

"I'm on parole. Now I'll go back to prison."

Even a bent *flic* "shot in action" marshaled the combined *préfecture* forces on his side.

"Not if they don't find you. Hurry, we'll go out the backstage door."

"But where's my Marie-Jo . . . ?"

She checked her Tintin watch. With any luck Saj had the girls in a taxi right now.

"Safe. Wish I'd known she's as stubborn as you." With her Swiss Army knife she sawed through the plastic flex-cuffs on Zacharié's wrists. She followed him down the steep, winding staircase again to the backstage door. "We'll take his phone and what's in his wallet and put the theatre keys in his pocket." She wiped their prints off the keys with her scarf, then handed the bundle to Zacharié. "Can you do that?"

Zacharié stared at the body. Blood dripped from the turntable to a pool on the floor. "But he's still chained me to him. I'm not free."

"What can he hold over you from the grave?"

"Jules is . . . was my half brother." He

winced. The floodlights cast an orange glow over his swollen eye and the cuts on his forehead.

The rotten half. But no one picked their family.

"*Désolée,* but it was him or you, and Marie-Jo wants her papa."

"Years ago he took care of me, after our mother left," he told her as he pulled Jules's phone and wallet from the dead man's pocket and planted the keys. "He was my big brother, all I had. But later he changed."

A pang hit her. She could relate. Her mother had left, but at least she had had a father to raise her.

A vacuum whirred. The cleaning woman.

"Where's Marie-Jo?" he asked.

"Follow me."

Wednesday, 11 A.M.

Madame Pelletier hung her straw bag over the office chair, glad, after the futile trip to Ivry, to get back to investigating her hunch. She thumbed through the older dossiers filed under *agressions sexuelles,* squinting as the late-morning light glinted on the metal file cabinet's surface. Then the next drawer. Nothing.

Tachet, her boss, poked his head around the door in the Brigade des Mineurs file room. "I'm holding off on calling that girl Zazie's parents."

He hated to give parents bad news. She nodded. "Should I do the follow-up, sir?"

"Follow-up? I'd rather charge the anonymous caller with wasting law-enforcement time and resources," said Tachet. "We'll give it a few more hours." He was more irritated than usual at the expended manpower. Having personally led the squad, he looked

384

angry enough to spit. "All this World Cup mess and we're running around in the suburbs, wasting three hours?"

He didn't expect an answer.

But her frustration simmered. "Sir, we still don't know if a link exists between the rapist and this Zazie Duclos."

Tachet's lips pursed. "That's the Brigade Criminelle's realm now. Follow up on the five-year-old with the broken ribs and cigarette burns. That's on your desk. Handle that."

"D'accord," she said.

"Good news. Your vacation starts tonight. Do what you can to wrap up the ongoing, then shoot them over to me before you leave."

Good news indeed. She wouldn't lose all her deposit on the beach chalet. Maybe she'd invite her daughter.

Back at her desk, she crossed the *t*'s on that final case, arranged the child's interview with the psychologist and sipped on her steaming tisane. Still, she couldn't push away her multiplying questions about the rapist. She had a growing sense of familiarity when she went over the facts — like he'd attacked before, years ago. But when and where she couldn't place.

Had she even been on the force then? Had

she heard about a similar case when she was at the Police Academy? Or did it come from a conversation overheard in *la cantine* or in the incident room — a passing reference? An open secret in the branch, maybe? One of many overlooked incidents — the hands-off files, incidents involving people either too connected or too protected, which a good *flic* knew about and could lean on when needed. That's how it worked and how it always had worked. The beat *flic* knew the score and tallied it. Old-style — the personal touch got you further than any computer or suit-wearing *commissaire* who had quotas to fill. She'd regarded the system as archaic and prone to favoritism. When the Brigade des Mineurs position opened, she'd applied and got in.

Yet everyone depended on the beat *flics,* the eyes and ears on the cobbles, who were often the first to report crimes against children. That never changed, nor did the fact the damn Commissariats didn't communicate with one another. What was all this department reorganization worth if they didn't implement communication? Or, now that the law had been passed, get the FNAEG up and running — the *Fichier national automatisé des empreintes génétiques,* which would authorize a database of sexual predators?

What was it she couldn't remember?

Wednesday, noon

Sirens whined behind them as an ambulance parked by Le Bus Palladium. The cleaning woman had found the body. Any minute the *flics* would pull up.

No sign of the girls or Saj.

"Wear my sunglasses and keep your head down," said Aimée. She relocked the backstage door, then dropped the key ring in the courtyard's slatted drain cover. "We've got to keep moving."

"But where are they? I won't leave without Marie-Jo." His hands shook trying to answer the vibrating cell phone in his hand. "Who's this calling me?"

Aimée spotted her own number on his cell's display. "Zazie. I gave her my phone."

"Where's Marie-Jo?" he said into the phone. He leaned against the wall. Listened. His shoulders relaxed. "*Ma puce* . . . you're okay."

Thank God. She saw a taxi, waved at it. But, spurred by the arriving rush of *flic* cars, it kept going uphill.

Merde.

They couldn't stay here. Determined, she hooked her arm through Zacharié's. She didn't relish the long uphill climb to Place Pigalle with his noticeable limp. Still, her stomach appreciated being back on terra firma.

"Where are they?" she asked him as he hung up.

"At the apartment on rue Chaptal. Your friend Saj said there's a taxi stand by the Sexodrome."

Thank God. But first the hurdle of getting there unnoticed.

"Look, I can't get caught in this," she said. "Nor can you."

"Marie-Jo's going to go home to pack her things," he said, his breath labored. His weight dragged on her arm. "I need to figure out what to do before things hit the fan."

Fugitives. But she couldn't think about that now. By the time they'd piled into the idling taxi just outside the Sexodrome, perspiration was dripping into her eyes.

During a tearful reunion in the apartment

on rue Chaptal, Aimée pulled Saj aside. "Good job. We need to talk."

"Haven't you let Zazie's parents know?" said Saj.

She shook her head. She needed a game plan. Jules's death complicated everything. Plus she felt bile rising from her stomach. Damn morning sickness, or nerves — or both.

"You look pale, Aimée," he said. "Nausea again?"

She nodded.

"What about all our asana sessions, the centering meditation?"

Fat lot of good that did with a gun aimed at her.

From his orange cloth bag, stenciled with *OM,* Saj handed her a paper twist of brown powder. "Sprinkle it under your tongue. Let it dissolve. It's an ayurvedic remedy."

Right now she'd try anything. It resembled dried mud. Tasted like it, too.

"Zazie's safe — thank God," Saj said as she struggled to swallow. "The sooner we get the little troublemaker home the better."

If only. Dry-mouthed, she shook her head. "Events went all sticky. I feel like I got caught in flypaper."

She'd caught René up a minute ago, after

she'd recovered her cell phone from Zazie. The girls were safe, but there was too much still to sort out — her own involvement in a murder, a rapist still on the loose and no leads left to follow. And a stubborn, desperate man who would be separated from his daughter forever if they couldn't figure something out quick. "Listen. I want to help Zacharié."

"But you already have." Saj smiled. "Earned good karma helping each other."

"If only it were that simple, Saj."

Saj's amber prayers beads caught between his fingers. "What did you do now, Aimée?"

She gave him a quick version. Told him about Jules. Minimized the shooting.

"Shooting . . . in your condition?"

"*Zut!* Pregnancy's not a disease. Look, it was either him or —"

"No way whoever contracted Jules for this information will let Zacharié get away," interrupted Saj. "Or you. You're implicated all right."

Her thoughts, too. Fear vibrated through her. "What if the bent cop left insurance?"

"We need to think this through," said Saj.

She pulled out what she'd discovered in his pockets. His phone, the police ID from his wallet — Assistant Chief of Internal Affairs, a *bœuf-carotte.* Saj whistled. "He must have been desperate, or he wouldn't have made stupid mistakes. How'd Zacharié get involved?"

Before she could answer, Zacharié appeared in the doorway. His shoulders heaved. "That's the beauty of it," he said. "Jules used everyone to pave his way from Internal Affairs to the Ministry. For years he's kissed ass, lied, covered up and looked the other way. With the information in the file, he'd seal the evidence. Get his Ministry post. No one could afford for him not to."

Internal affairs and links to the Ministry . . . did that connect to Morbier's corruption investigation?

"Apart from the Corsican, his henchman, only Marie-Jo and I . . ." His throat caught. "Link to him."

She scrolled Jules's call log. One number repeated. "Except this caller. I'd say he's implicated, or a client for the hands-off material."

"*Merde.* I've got to think this through," Zacharié said. "Act smart for once. Outwit the *salaud.*" He glanced back to the bedroom, where Zazie sat talking to Marie-Jo as she packed. "After I married, Jules came back into my life," he said. "He'd risen in the force. Changed. But I had a crazy wife and my little girl. I was weak. Took the easy

way. Let him wrap me around his finger. I
did things for Jules I shouldn't have."

Doubts assailed her. At the end of the day,
she had risked her baby's life to nail a bent
flic. The price of recovering Zazie and
Marie-Jo? Yet she still didn't know anything
about the rapist — who was still on the
loose.

"What did you mean when you told me
Jules created a diversion in Ivry?" Aimée
asked. "I don't get it. The girls were tracking a rapist who attacked their friends. This
must connect."

"Connect?" Zacharié shook his head.
"Apples and oranges. It was convenient
when it came up, so Jules used it. And to
mask a robbery . . ." His words caught.

A bent *flic* to the core, resorting to emotional blackmail. She'd seen it before.

Then it sank in — in saving Zazie, Aimée
had gotten herself implicated in whatever
heist Jules had organized. From the fight
she'd overheard between Zacharié and
Jules, she knew there was a trail of dead
bodies now — and something had been
stolen that was so valuable that Jules had
been willing to kill for it.

"I need to know about this file you stole,"
she told him.

Zacharié pulled it from the back of jeans.

"It's dirt on people. Reports filed on prominent officials, industrialists. People like Jules use the dirt as leverage when they want a cut of the pie or need a favor."

She flipped through the pages. Her eyes popped. "Explosive stuff." She skimmed the addendum closely enough to see it contained details of covert Ministry surveillance and operations abetted by the *police judiciaire.*

"Looks like corruption at the top: the Ministry running operations with no oversight and the *préfet de police* sweeping any fallout under the carpet." She swallowed hard, thinking again of Morbier's corruption investigation.

"Knowing Jules, he's left some detail implicating me," said Zacharié, his face clouded. "That happens and I'll lose my shot at gaining Marie-Jo's custody."

Her nerves jingled. And her? She'd gotten too involved already. Tangled in this web when her only goal had been to save Zazie from the rapist.

Merde. "I never saw you, never met you, *compris*?"

He nodded. "My parole officer wants an update on my job search. It's imperative for the custody hearing." He sagged into a doorframe, anguish in his eyes. "I can't lose

Marie-Jo again. Can't go back to prison."

"May I see that file?" asked Saj. After reading the pages, he looked up. "You know what they say, use it or lose it."

"So I should sell it to the highest bidder, like Jules planned to do?" Zacharié clenched his fist. "Get mired in that muck?" A sigh of despair. "But I already am."

"Did I say that?" Saj ran his hand, henna'd with a Hindu symbol, over the addendum pages. "Interesting. Remember how we handled a similar *doc-sca* issue last year, Aimée?"

She shot Saj a glance. He was making this up as he went along. But he had used their code for portable scanner. So he had brought his bag of tricks. His ultra-thin scanner, as usual, in his cloth meditation bag.

He raised his eyebrow.

She nodded. *"Bien sûr."*

Zacharié's fist unclenched. "What do you mean?"

"Give me a minute to go over this," said Saj, "explore less incriminating options. A way for you to get around this."

"Another reason I like you, Saj," Aimée said. "You have a twisted angle to everything."

"That's why you pay me the big francs,

395

Aimée," said Saj.

She wasn't the only one, either. After Saj had hacked into several Ministry systems, they'd found him too valuable to lock up in prison. So he consulted on an as-needed basis, constructing firewalls designed to keep those like himself out.

Saj winked at Aimée.

"Try to relax, Zacharié," said Aimée with more confidence than she felt. "I think Saj has an idea."

Saj paid the taxi driver and got out in front of the café on rue du Louvre. He bent down to the open passenger window, readjusting his orange meditation bag so it completely concealed the ax.

"Zazie, time flows and cycles in our journeys." He gestured to the café. "Avoiding confrontation only prolongs the circle of Samsara . . ."

"You go see your parents, Zazie," Aimée said, interrupting Saj.

Saj nodded to Aimée. "I'm off to that consultation in Sceaux. I'll send you the scans later."

"Good work, Saj." Maybe she could figure out how to inform Morbier without implicating herself. Maybe she would regain her figure someday. She doubted both.

Saj's dreadlocks bounced on his muslin-shirted shoulder as he headed to the Métro.

"I tried to do the right thing, Aimée." Zazie's shoulders slumped. "We followed a red herring."

Aimée shrugged. "You got sidetracked. But what's fish got to do with it?"

"A detective term. Don't you know?"

She did. But Zazie seemed so wilted. "See? You know more technical terms than I do," she said, trying to make her feel better.

"I'm not a good detective."

"Practice, Zazie. You're bursting with talent. You left clues so I could find you. If you hadn't chalked that X . . ." Her throat caught. Then she pulled Zazie toward her and hugged her hard. "Just never do this again, *tu promets*?"

"Now you sound like a *maman*," Zazie said.

Aimée sucked in her breath. "I have to practice too, don't I?"

"I'm in big trouble, Aimée."

Aimée bit her tongue before saying she'd earned it. "Your parents love you," she said. "Now you're home, and that's what's most important. Tell the truth, Zazie."

"Everything, Aimée? I mean . . . I don't want to get Marie-Jo's papa in trouble. And

397

I was so frightened you'd get hurt."

Aimée brushed Zazie's red curls from her eyes. Cradled her face in her hands, then pulled a café napkin from her bag and wiped at Zazie's brimming tears. "Better to keep to the truth, but some parts . . . *bien,* say you'll talk more about it when you're ready."

Zazie nodded and shot her a knowing look. "Like you do when you don't really want to lie."

"Did I say that, Zazie?"

"But I can't get her papa in trouble," said Zazie. "And we still haven't found the rapist . . ."

"Who might have been caught," Aimée interrupted. She'd left out Mélanie's mother's murder and the shooting last night. Zazie had enough to worry about already. "For now, concentrate on that class report that's due."

"Will you come with me?"

Aimée nodded. "But the café's full. Why don't we enter through the back?"

In the café, Virginie absently rocked Lucien on her hip and stared at the *télé,* which was showing the news. Pierre clutched a bag of oranges with a phone wedged between his shoulder and ear. "What do you mean?" he shouted. "My

398

daughter's —"

"Back home," said Aimée.

He dropped the bag. Oranges rolled over the floor, and the phone fell onto the counter.

"Thathee," lisped little Lucien and clapped his hands. "Thathee!"

Amid the hugs, tears and squeals of delight, Aimée stepped back.

"Are you all right? My God, we thought you were . . . don't you realize . . . ?" Pierre's words died in his throat. His shoulders heaved, and he pulled Zazie to him. "You're back. That's what matters."

Zazie nodded. Her lip trembled. "I'm sorry, Papa . . ." And she ended in tears.

Virginie wiped her wet cheeks with her sleeve. "*Merci,* Aimée. Forgive me for doubting you. But where . . . ?"

Aimée put a finger to her lips. Gave a warning nod.

Understanding filled Virginie's eyes. She hugged her daughter again. "Plenty of time to talk about things later. Are you hungry?"

Time to leave them together.

On Leduc Detective's landing, Aimée felt an ominous rumble in her stomach. The taste of acid bile. Her damp tunic clung to her spine, to her arms. Her shoulder stung.

She reached for the dressing, and her hand came back wet and sticky. Blood. Her stitches had broken open.

She made it past the office door and down the hallway to the bathroom before she felt the heave and nausea overtook. A loud burp erupted and then she lost the coffee all over the tiles. She heaved and panted until nothing else could come up.

Again and again. She washed her face and mopped up the floor. Her fingers trembled applying steri-strips in place of her busted stitches.

Her stomach curdled at the risk she'd taken. Yet if she hadn't, could she have lived with herself? She'd saved Zazie. Done what she'd promised.

Then, like a little fish, the baby moved. She leaned on the small porcelain sink, felt the tension draining from her. Zazie was safe. She kept repeating the words inside her head. Zazie was safe.

Forget the image of Madame Vasseur on the cobbles, the blood seeping through her jacket. Her vacant eyes and slack jaw. That momentary hesitation — as if she'd wanted to say something, and now she never would. What could it have been that the woman was about to say? Who was it that had killed her? Aimée shivered, realizing that Zazie might be safe, but the danger was far from over.

Work was waiting — she had so much to catch up on. With the tension gone, she felt limp, tired. She wanted to put her feet up. That's what she'd do, stretch out on the recamier and get down to reports that needed attention. Run the virus scans she'd promised René, or face mutiny.

Inside Leduc Detective's frosted-glass door, she unwrapped her silk scarf and turned to face Madame Vasseur's red-eyed husband.

"You, you're the one," he said, irate. His linen suit hung from his shoulders. Anger emanated from him in waves. "Hounding my wife, and now she's . . . she's dead."

René, sitting on his ergonomic chair tailored to his height, shot her a look. "I've explained to Monsieur Vasseur that he needs to speak with the Brigade Criminelle."

"Don't tell me what to do," he said.

The man, grief-stricken and angry, was lashing out at whatever target he could. That she understood. Still, guilt flooded her for not saving the woman.

"I'm so sorry, Monsieur," she said. "If it's any consolation, Zazie's home with her family."

"And where's my family?" he said, advancing on her.

Stupid. Not the most tactful reply.

He shook his fist. "Look at you, walking around stirring up trouble. The shooter was aiming at you, and now my wife's dead."

She hated to think that it could be true — she might have brought that danger down on Madame Vasseur. She shook it off. Thinking that wouldn't help either of them now.

"You blame me, I understand," she said. "But shouldn't you focus your energy on catching your wife's murderer? The man who raped your daughter?"

His face twisted in shame. "How dare you?" He raised his arm, ready to strike her. She stepped back, tired, sick of everything that had happened, exhausted by this poor man's gut-wrenching pain and fury. Felt the Beretta in her back pocket hit the copier-machine lid.

"Hitting a pregnant woman won't change what's happened, Monsieur." René stood at the open door of Leduc Detective.

Thank God. She threw him a grateful look.

"My colleague was shot trying to protect your wife," said René. "She's not your enemy here. Think of your daughter. She needs you, Monsieur."

"Yesterday your wife called me," said Aimée. "Wanted me to hear a message Mélanie had left her with more information about the man who attacked her. She thought I might be able to help her understand it. Your wife was trying to help Zazie."

"And died in the process?"

"Your wife wanted the rapist caught," she said. "Zazie disappeared, and we thought the rapist had taken her."

"Didn't the *flics* catch him?" Defeat painted his face, now devoid of anger. "The comatose pedophile who'll never wake up and face justice."

"But another girl was almost attacked," she said. "The answer's on your wife's phone. Mélanie's message with the description of her attacker." Aimée stepped forward. "Your wife hesitated — I think she wanted to tell me something else."

For a moment fear flashed in his eyes.

"Any idea of what she wanted to say, Monsieur?"

"How would I know?" A line of silent tears dripped to his collar.

"Where's your wife's phone?" Aimée asked gently.

But his gaze was unfocused. His collar was wet.

"I don't know," he said, deflated, his voice

far away. "I'm due at the morgue to identify her."

"Ask them for it." Unless the shooter took it. Could that have been the real aim? But she couldn't think about that now. "Have you told Mélanie yet?"

"Don't hound my daughter. I forbid you to contact her. Leave her alone. She's lost her mother."

"Then let me know if you find the phone, Monsieur."

But he'd gone out the door.

René shook his head. "How can he blame you?"

"In a way he's right," she said, saddened. "His wife called me to arrange a meeting, then had second thoughts. Did her best to shake me off, all to avoid . . ."

"The pain of her daughter's rape?" René interrupted.

A frisson went up Aimée's neck. "She said she couldn't handle the shame. Like Sylvaine's mother, who's pressing charges against me."

"Charging you won't take the pain away," said René.

"Displaced grief," said Aimée. "Hurt and shame. Guilt over failing in the responsibility of protecting their children. Put it down

404

to shock, devout religion, but what if . . . ?"
She paused, thinking. "It's just a feeling,
but I think Madame Vasseur was holding
something back."

René rubbed his eyes. He switched on the
espresso machine, and it rumbled to life.
"Don't the *flics* always say look to the family first — it's the husband nine times out
of ten?"

"You're thinking this distraught man shot
his wife, then came to accuse me of . . . ?"

She didn't buy it. Or did she? The woman's second thoughts kept coming back to
her. A midday glow suffused the office's
high-ceilinged carved woodwork. Shafts of
light prismed in the crystal drops of the
chandelier.

"Say Monsieur Vasseur's got a hidden history of incest with his daughter," said René.
"But that's not enough, or he's worried he
won't be able to keep her quiet."

"Where's the proof, René?"

"It's always the ones you don't expect."
He set the *demi-tasse* under the brown
stream. "Don't put it past him."

"Put what past him?"

"He protests too much," said René. "According to the police report, he was the one
who discovered his daughter after she was
raped. Imagine a different scenario — his

grief and antagonism are a cover-up."

She shuddered. "His wife didn't strike me as a look-the-other-way type." Aimée remembered her strident voice, her clear unhappiness in that elegant townhouse. "Her last words were about the shame of it."

René stirred in a sugar cube. "For argument's sake, what if she was ashamed not because her daughter was raped, like you thought, but because she had just realized who the rapist was?"

He paused to let this sink in. She nodded. A possible scenario that made her insides crawl.

"Sad but classic," René went on. "The wife knows inside but hides the truth from herself, throws herself into work. You said Madame Vasseur was obsessed with her job."

"I see where you're going, René." She didn't like this. She hit the wall switch, and the overhead fan lurched into motion. A slow current of tepid air stirred.

"The father's grown insatiable and attacks her classmates," said René. "Easy prey. They know him already, maybe they're friends with his daughter — say the girls practice violin together or overlap at lessons. These young girls trust him, let him into their houses when he follows them home from a lesson, then he frightens them into swearing to secrecy. Or maybe he never lets them see his face, just follows them home to familiar addresses. Sylvaine dies accidentally. He never meant this, but *alors*, the stakes have risen. Now you come into the picture, stir things up and get his wife asking questions. And she's on the point of breaking down and telling you. Cornered, he has to silence her. Like he silenced his daughter, shipping her off to the Swiss clinic."

"But I heard them arguing," she said. "He accused her of sending his daughter away."

"He's a lawyer, *non*? Makes things appear one way, twists them around. We just saw him in action. Blames you — you were getting too close."

"I don't know about that. But I know I got too close."

"Of course, he knew about his wife's big speech last night," said René, warming up. "What if she'd been about to confront him with his daughter's message? Where was he last night, did you ask him?"

"He drives a Merc, not a motorcycle. They both do . . . did."

"But he could have a motorcycle, too. Maybe borrow a friend's?"

He raised good questions. She scrolled

407

through her cell-phone call record, searching for the girl's number at the Swiss clinic. When she found it, she hit dial. Just a message.

The grinding of a fax came from the machine. René picked up two pages as they rolled out. "From Serge."

"More on the ballistics?"

"Not quite."

GET WELL, AIMÉE, OUR SUPERHERO was written in childish scrawl with a crude drawing of her: big belly, arms out and a cape streaming behind her. From Serge's twin boys, whom she was dreading having to babysit.

"They sat still long enough to draw this?" René shook his head. "Aimée, the caped crusader."

Her heart wrenched. She couldn't sit here and run corporate scans after all these questions René had raised.

"This came with it." He passed her a second sheet of Serge's scribbled notes under Sylvaine Olivet's blood panel.

Post mortem — PHENYTOIN with a level of 2 but normal therapeutic range to be 10–20. Abnormal collection of blood vessels, arteriovenous malformation, in temporal lobe with acute bleeding and herniation of brain. Victim's doctor had no CT scan on record. No evidence of sexual penetration. Bruising and lacerations to the eye and chest. Bite marks on tongue, surmise bleeding from undiagnosed AVM with an acute seizure and herniation of brain.

René took the paper and read it. "Sylvaine was an epileptic, is that what this means?"

"*Mon Dieu,* it means he didn't rape Sylvaine," she said. "She had an undiagnosed blood-vessel abnormality that caused seizures. Poor thing. The doctor probably didn't think her seizures had a specific anatomic cause — but since a CT had never been done, he would never have known. Lazy. But they treat seizures irrespective of the cause with Phenytoin — that's the generic term for Dilantin. I'd say her seizure thwarted the rape, and that's why he attacked Nelié the same night. She got away. He's off his game, and there's Madame Vasseur about to expose him —"

"Or he thinks she will," interrupted René. "He shoots her. His own wife." René frowned. "I'd say she suspected her husband."

"Smart, René. Look at this."

She picked up the third faxed sheet, a prelim ballistics report. "The shooter used a German Luger. Wehrmacht issue. How the hell can anyone trace that? But there's a name at the bottom. Jacques Baleste, vintage arms expert."

"*Et alors,* that Baleste?" said René. "But there can't be two." René took a last sip of espresso. His mouth tilted in a small smile as he grabbed his jacket. "We go way back. Baleste owes me a favor. Time I collect, eh?"

Wednesday, 1 P.M.

Little did the tourists at Notre-Dame Cathedral know what lay behind the unmarked nineteenth-century wood door they passed. The police armory, nestled on Ile de la Cité, a stone's throw from the *préfecture*. From time immemorial every *flic* had checked out and returned their weapon here across the same worn wood counter. Hadn't Baleste once commented that any coordinated armed insurrection would succeed, given the time it took for the *flics* to log out their weapons through this narrow, wire-caged counter?

René stepped into the cloud of familiar odors: oil and stale coffee. He heard the radio tuned to the World Cup quarterfinals. "Jacques Baleste, *s'il vous plaît?*"

"*Une seconde.* He expecting you?" asked a pockmarked young lieutenant. He sniffed, looking down on René, whose chin just

411

reached the counter. Too bad the *maître d'armes,* old Voudray, had retired.

He rotated his foot to ease his shooting hip pain. "Tell him it's about the Luger," he said. "He'll understand."

"ID?"

René reached up and shoved his *carte d'identité* over the grooved wood. His fingers came back greasy.

The lieutenant pulled out the duty log, consulted it and dialed a number on the old, black rotary phone. By the book, this one.

"A René Friant to see you, sir." Pause. "Room one hundred and thirty-two, down the hallway."

We go way back, he almost said, former shooting partners . . . Instead he smiled. "I know."

René sucked in his breath as he walked. Their last parting loomed in his mind. But his failure so far to find anything leading to the rapist and Aimée's shooter drove him on.

"Come to gloat, have you, Friant?"

Jacques Baleste, perspiration beading his flushed forehead, sat at a metal desk with his leg in a cast propped on an orange crate.

"What happened?" said René, surprised.

"As if you didn't know," said Baleste,

vibrating with angry energy. Short and stocky, he filled the chair.

René reached in his pocket. "If it's about the firing-range club fees I owed you . . . look, I'm sorry if that got you into trouble."

"That? Pheuff." Baleste waved the francs away. He expelled a gust of air. "You don't know?"

René shook his head, perplexed. "A fight?"

"I plan dinner at Solange's favorite *resto,* bring her roses, and she gives me the heave-ho. Literally." He slammed down his fist. "Down the stairs."

Last month René had fixed up Baleste with Solange, a *coiffeuse* with a passion for astrology and rollerblading.

René stifled a laugh. "Solange kicked you down the stairs?"

"Tripping on the damn carpet didn't help."

Clumsy as usual.

"She blurts out, 'René introduced us, but I can't get over him, Jacques!' and shuts the door in my face, just like that."

He hadn't thought of Solange that way in months. Or ever.

"*C'est ironique.* You're moonfaced over someone else. Women go for you, and you go for the unattainable Aimée."

Was it that obvious? Or too much drinking and talking after the shooting range one night? Unattainable — Baleste got that right.

"Which brings me to the Luger someone shot her with last night," said René.

"Remember that song, 'Love the One You're With'?" Baleste sighed. "When will you ever learn, Friant?"

Learn that to Aimée he would never be more than her best friend? He knew that already. Best friend, business partner and godfather to her child. Uncle René, if she'd let him be.

"Tell me about the Luger, Baleste."

The office was piled with files, walls plastered with black-and-white photos of weapons: Uzis, semiautomatics, Sig Sauers. Baleste pointed to a shelf. "There." Damp, blue sweat rings showed under the arms of his blue uniform. "Get that green binder in the bookcase, the least you can do."

René stood on tiptoe to reach the shelf, pulled the binder and set it on Baleste's messy desk.

"I'll show you what I showed the investigating Brigade Criminelle." Baleste thumbed through the pages. His anger had evaporated now that he had guns to expound on. "But they're on it already."

A wasted trip.

Still, René sat down, determined to take a load off his feet and learn something.

After five minutes of viewing photos of German Lugers, he sat back in the chair, his eyes on the shadows of the tourists crossing outside his window like a fretwork.

"So the shooter ditched the Luger in the Seine, *non*? It's gone?"

"Did I say that?"

Everyone consulted Jacques "Short-Fuse" Baleste, despite his volatile temper, on military arms. His grandfather had worked on the design of the M1909 Benet–Mercie before the First World War, his father on adapting features of the Lee–Enfield in the Second.

"Then tell me what you didn't tell the Brigade Criminelle."

"How can I? It's all conjecture."

"You must have a theory. Any of these Lugers registered?"

"You're kidding, right? No one turned in booty from the occupiers."

So the perfect murder weapon, untraceable.

"The countryside turns these up every so many years — someone finds them in an old trunk or an attic on a farm."

René's mind went back to the count's château in Amboise where he'd grown up. To that WWI rifle the cook had kept in the pantry, the pheasant her husband hunted with it strung upside down in the shed, its plucked feathers carpeting the dirt floor.

"*Alors,* the grandfather dies," Baleste continued, "his heirs discover a Luger in the cellar or the attic or under the floorboards. They think, 'He really was in the Resistance?' Fat chance."

"What do you mean?"

"Look to history," said Baleste. "Who armed the scattered pockets of the Maquis, the loose networks of the Resistance, with Enfield rifles and Sten submachine guns? The British. Rare to find them with German arms."

"*Et alors?*"

"Two years ago in the countryside, a jealous husband took his uncle's old Sten gun and finished off his wife. In the process, the thing jammed — they were notorious for doing that during the war. It recoiled and took half his shoulder off."

René wished he'd get to the point. "Try being helpful, Baleste."

"When the Wehrmacht retreated in defeat, a lot of these Lugers found their way into closets," said Baleste. "These pieces withstood the cold of Russian winters and the heat of the North African desert. Tough.

Built to withstand extremes. Captured Lugers were prized. Why throw this untraceable workhorse away? Even with the bullet-casing striations identifying the piece," said Baleste, "it's impossible to identify the owner."

Damn, René thought, careful and methodical. It fitted the rapist's modus operandi.

"Have any shootings with matching bullet striations been reported before, Baleste?"

Baleste's phone console lit up with red lights. He ignored them and shifted his foot with effort. Grimaced with pain and blew a gust of air from his mouth. "Not in the last five years. I'd remember."

"Why's that, Baleste?" Impatient, René wished he'd cough up some detail, some link to help identify the shooter.

"Five years ago the Ministry of Defense funded our project: a research database documenting and referencing specific incidents involving military firearms." Jacques grabbed a copy of *L'Équipe,* the racing paper, off his desk and swatted at a buzzing fly. He shut the binder. "There's always the chance Aimée ticked off an old Nazi."

"Serge copied you on the ballistics report," said René. "Don't you have more to say?"

Baleste leaned over, winced and eased his

cast-bound leg higher on the crate. "I'll say ten to one this Luger lay forgotten in some old codger's desk. Now, with a good cleaning and oiling, it's no fuss to use. And no one's the wiser."

René'd learned little. As he stood, Aimée's words came back to him — never leave without a name, a place, a referral. He gave it a last shot.

"This happened in Pigalle. Strike any bells from the past?"

"Some gangster heyday tie-in? All moot now. Still . . ." Baleste paused. The tourists' footsteps shuffled, never ending, outside his window. Spit it out, René wanted to say.

"Madame Mimi ran Bar Pigalle," he said. "Years ago she told my grandfather the Nazis left arms in her cellar. 'Left' being a loose term. No doubt Mimi sold them years ago at the flea market or to connoisseurs who go for that." He shrugged. "She's dead now. Her grandson took over, renamed it the NeoCancan."

Could it be? "The Johnny Hallyday wannabee?"

"So you know him?"

"Maybe he deals with collectors," said René.

For the first time, Baleste smiled. "Or maybe it's a fart in the wind."

But in Baleste-speak that meant René was following the right track.

"I'll give him a call. Get back to you."

"Better yet, Baleste, tell him I'll drop by," said René, checking the time.

"He's picking up supplies. Give him two hours. And you can pick up something for me."

"D'accord," René agreed. "*Très gentil* of you, Baleste."

"Not really. He's my cousin's husband. Just grab the bottle of Romanée-Conti the little turd owes me."

Wednesday, 2 P.M.

Jules's damn cell phone vibrated in Zacharié's shaking hands in the *garçonnière* above the guitar shop. The same number flashed again.

The caller was more than impatient, he realized. Downright angry.

But what else could he do with this file? How could he get away with this? This crazy idea that the Rasta–hippie hacker had?

Go transparent, give this to the Ministry. And then go straight back to prison?

Or like that old film — a German spy movie he couldn't remember the title of. Funny, that was all he could imagine — a heap-movie scenario — but hell, it was the same thing. His life was a cheap-movie scenario. Big, bad brother coerces little brother into doing his dirty work, then sabotages him to take the fall. In the film, the little brother outwits him in the end . . .

about to do the hand-off to the bad guy, he gives it to the good guys.

Or *tant pis* . . . give it to this insistent caller, pocket the money, take Marie-Jo and head to Gare Saint-Lazare, board the train to a new, free life. Free and fugitive.

Nothing involving Jules had ever been easy — it could all be another setup.

He had to think of the big picture, the long term with Marie-Jo. School, stability beyond the scope of his crazy ex and her scum boyfriend.

The phone vibrated in his sweating palm.

Marie-Jo stirred on the bed. "Papa?"

"Oui, ma chérie," he said, coming to a decision. "Go back to sleep. I'm going out for an hour. Stay here and I'll bring your favorite tartine. *Tu promets?*" He kissed her forehead.

She nodded and gave a sleepy smile. "Don't be long, Papa."

And it tore his heart.

Wednesday, 2 P.M.

Aimée looked up from her screen as René entered Leduc Detective. "Any joy from Baleste, René?"

"I'm working on it," he said. "The Neo-Cancan's owner's grandmother kept a Nazi cache of arms. Whether any are left . . . I've got to wait till Johnny Hallyday returns."

Her fingers paused on the keyboard, her damp tunic sticking to the small of her back.

"What's wrong?" René asked, giving her a look she couldn't fathom. "Does it have to do with Melac?"

She put her feet up on the recamier, hesitant to dump her non-existent love life on René. Again. She couldn't help it. "The father of my child appears and just like that expects me to uproot to Brittany. Wants to do the right thing, he says."

Doing the right thing, my ass.

She lifted the damp strands of hair from

422

her neck and sighed in disgust. "Then I sleep with him. But he's got to rush back because of his high-maintenance ex and poor daughter's full-time nursing issues."

"But I thought you . . ." René hesitated, choosing his words.

"Funny thing, René. Melac's jealous of you." She rubbed her ankle, wishing she'd had that pedicure last week.

"Moi?" René blinked.

"He can't understand we're best friends," she said. "How involved you've been with the baby."

Was that disappointment on his face?

"But you were debating leaving the business? Taking time in Brittany?"

"Like that will ever happen, René."

René brightened. "You mean it?"

"At least about the going to Brittany part," she said. Going part-time felt more and more appealing as her stomach expanded and tiredness dogged her every worn marble step to her apartment. But she'd never admit it to René. "You're more interested than him in the baby, René."

René smiled. "Of course, Saj and I will helm the ship when you take maternity leave. We'll have the crib, too."

A stab of guilt hit her. The idea she toyed with of selling the business to Florian at

Systex, who'd barraged her with offers to merge. Another thing she'd kept from René.

". . . bring the baby to work . . ." René was saying. But she listened with half an ear as she pulled up her email. Checked for the deposit Saj had requested from the Luxembourg bank wire transfer. Done. Taxes paid. Relief filled her.

But René was one step ahead of her.

"Looks like Saj won the hacker competition and lent us a hundred thousand francs for our taxes," said René, his voice laced with suspicion. "Or maybe you used your hormonal imbalance, welled up in front of the tax adjuster?"

Not this. Not now. "It's complicated, René."

"I spotted this a kilometer away," he said, "not that *le fisc* would. Want to explain how you paid the taxes?"

Should she tell him?

"Working here involves me," he said. "It's my skin, too, Aimée."

So she told him. The mounting feeling that her mother's clout worked in mysterious ways. How the financial information had all arrived by diplomatic courier pouch — the last one from Dar Es Salaam, around the time Agence France-Presse reported a coup against the dementia-ridden dictator by a well-funded rebel group.

René's eyes went round as *demi-tasse* saucers. "Your mother's arming rebel insurgents in Africa?"

"Did I say that, René?"

She recounted that last call from the diplomatic attaché, their hurried meeting on the quai. How when she'd pressed him for info on her mother, his face had shuttered. "I don't know what you're talking about. And if you ask any more, this avenue shuts down. *Vous comprenez?*"

René's gaze swept the ceiling *boiseries.* "Knowing our luck, they're bugging our conversation. Or they've embedded microphones in . . ." He paused and turned on the radio to the classical station.

"A healthy dose of paranoia is one thing, René," she said, "but what's done is done." All of a sudden, tears brimmed in her eyes.

"Don't get emotional on me, Aimée," he said, looking awkward.

"These days I well up at anything," she said, wiping her eyes. "Even the ads for Alouette brie yesterday on the radio. Hormones."

"How can you think of financing a baby's layette with arms-dealing money?" René hopped off his ergonomic chair, grabbed his jacket. "Dirty money your mother's stashed

425

in a Luxembourg shell company?"

"René, I don't see any dirt in those zeros," she said. "That's keeping us afloat until our clients pay up."

But he'd slammed the office door.

Now what had she done?

Her phone vibrated in its charger. Morbier. Filled with mixed feelings, she hesitated before picking up. She wondered if word of Zacharié's half brother's death had traveled. Best defense was a good offense.

"Just thought you'd want to know, Leduc."

"Not to count on police protection?" she said. "Or Melac in my life?" Stupid. She hadn't meant that to come out.

A long sigh from Morbier. "Hormones in overdrive, Leduc?"

"My body's swimming in estrogen," she said, noticing the pregnancy book René had left open to the chapter on the second trimester. If only she weren't so emotional right now. Sleeping with Melac hadn't helped; neither had killing someone in self-defense. And all in one morning.

Calm down. She needed to keep herself in check.

"Why did you tell Melac about the baby?" she said.

"Not me," he said, surprise in his voice. "Worst-kept secret. Everyone knows. But

that's not why I'm calling, Leduc. If you'd
kept your phone charged you'd know about
the suspect in *garde à vue* — looks good for
the rapist."

"Who?"

"A Monsieur Vasseur came up with priors
as he identified his wife at the morgue."

Priors? "But he's an attorney."

"Don't attorneys batter their wives,
Leduc?"

"I mean, how could he practice with a
record?"

"*We're* talking the 'unofficial' files — on
two occasions his wife wouldn't press
charges."

The unofficial files. Just like the files Zacharié stole for Jules. She held her breath,
wondering if Morbier was intimating in his
indirect way that he knew about Jules's
death.

"Not enough for court, I know, Leduc,"
Morbier was saying. "Turns out after the
Brigade Criminelle questioned the neighbors today, a family friend who had given
him an alibi last night at the reception has
changed his 'tune.' "

"Old man Lavigne?"

She heard the rustle of paper, his notes.
"Looks like it."

"Don't the rich stick together, Morbier?"

427

she said. "Have they checked his where-abouts on the dates of the attacks? The murder?"

"Getting to it. The man's a lawyer, after all, and knows his rights."

"And you're telling me so I'll . . ."

"*Dors tranquille,* Leduc," he said. "Zazie's back, the *mec*'s off the streets, so give the little sprout a break." Pause. "Doctors recommend rest during the second trimes-ter, eight solid hours a night and naps."

How could she argue with that? The tired-ness, the guilt of having put the baby at risk this morning. Still, doubt sprang up in her mind. "Don't you think the pieces add up too well, Morbier?"

"Not my case," he said.

Her mind went back to the addendum file Zacharié stole for Jules. The top names she'd seen involved in Morbier's corruption investigation. That was his case. Proof he could use.

Yet how could she tell him without reveal-ing the heist, the murders and kidnapping, her complicity?

"Morbier . . . *alors* . . ."

"Take a nap, Leduc."

He had clicked off.

On her screen another email from Florian at Systex came up. *Reconsidered my offer?*

428

I'll sweeten it with a new Leduc Securité logo, you as acting consultant and board-member position, upping your shares to 42 percent.

When would she get another offer this good?

She checked the letter from the social insurance that covered *profession libérale,* the CANAM, stating that she qualified for paid maternity benefits — a pitiful monthly check.

Her heart thumped. Looking down on her from the walls were the black-and-white photos of her father in police uniform, the original sepia-tinted Leduc Detective license. Memories, that's all they were now. She had a new life stirring in her. More shaken than she'd let on to René or Saj, she knew this offer would clear money issues long-term and erase the need to use the Luxembourg funny-money shell account. She sat back and pondered. Should she give this up? Could she?

Wednesday, 5 P.M.

Tachet stuck his head in Madame Pelletier's office. "Zazie Duclos turned up, like you figured," he said. "Cross that *procès-verbal de disparition* off your list."

A rush of relief. She always felt relief when they turned up. She nodded. "Shall I do the exit interview?"

"Would there be any point in questioning this thirteen-year-old? The parents will no doubt cover up for their little girl's drunken exploits."

"Still, the rapist . . ."

"A Monsieur Vasseur, father of Mélanie Vasseur, one of the victims, is in *garde à vue* being questioned for his wife's murder. And he's a vintage weapons collector."

Madame Pelletier thumbed through the dossiers on her desk. "Vasseur, Mélanie," she said and scanned the case notes. "How does that connect? The girl wasn't shot."

"But his wife was last night. With a nine-millimeter German Luger, war issue. Hand me the file," he said. "Vasseur was the one who'd found his daughter after she was attacked. You know those markers for incest might add up. I'm off to question him."

Disturbing.

He paused in the doorway with the file. "This could wrap up tonight, so go enjoy your *vacances.*"

She remembered Monsieur Vasseur sitting with his sobbing daughter, the icy wife who had only appeared once. The questions the team had had. Statistics in these cases pointed to the parent . . . Still, something didn't add up.

But the name had come to her. The name she'd tried to remember. She pulled her old address book out from her straw bag, searched and dialed his phone number.

The balconied Haussmannian buildings stretched up the *grand boulevard,* filling the horizon. Traffic hummed and mothers pushed strollers into the department store Galeries Lafayette. The vibrations of the Métro rumbled beneath Madame Pelletier's espadrilles as she poured the *vin rouge* into both wineglasses at the outdoor café. She clinked her glass to Rodot's. *"Santé."*

"I'd like to think it's my good looks that inspired you to ring me, but I understand it's to do with an old case." Rodot, a broadchested barrel of a man with a bald head and matching round, smooth face, reminded her of a shorter version of the Michelin man. "Juvenile sexual assault is not my turf."

"More like your memory of ten years ago or so, sir," she said. Sipped. The smooth, full-bodied Bordeaux should open his mind. "Something you'd remember hearing about."

"Rumors, you mean?"

"To be honest, sir, I don't know what I mean. I overheard something at my first posting. I was just an eager rookie then, but I never forgot it. You were stationed there."

"The Commissariat on Place des Petits Pères?"

"That's right." She nodded. "And it's been bothering me."

"Burglaries, bar brawls, domestic disturbances, purse snatching on pension day, gang knifings kept *en famille,*" he said. "Innocent stuff. Not like today, predators attacking young children."

She disagreed. Children had always been victims; incest, beatings, neglect — none of it was new. She dealt with it every day.

"Maybe it sells more newspapers now, sir."

"Sensationalism," he said, dismissive. "A different world these days. Glad I'm retired."

"The case was unusual," she said, persisting. "I think I remember staff talking about it, how it involved music."

"Think it matches the one in the papers?"

"I can't discount it, sir." She took another sip. "Brought to mind a lecture you gave at the academy . . ."

"You mean the 'be yourself, everyone else is already taken' one?"

She smiled. His famous new-recruit lecture, based on a line of Oscar Wilde's for which he took credit.

"Sir, I mean about when a case detail talks to you," she said, persisting. "Something's talking to me, and I can't nail it down."

He shrugged. "Glad one of you listened." He took a drag of his cigarette. Exhaled thoughtfully. "That's right. A young girl raped after her violin lesson. Horrific. Fourteen? *Non,* she'd just turned twelve. Ruined the birthday party. I remember now."

She leaned forward. "Did you work the case?"

"No names, no files that I ever saw." He shot her a look.

"But I can't find a sexual assault case filed

433

at that time."

He downed his glass. Reached for his jacket. "You won't. Both parties involved were juveniles."

She sat up. "All the more reason I should find it at the Brigade des Mineurs."

"Quit thinking like a *flic*. Think like someone with something to hide."

She read between the lines. "So the case was hushed up, buried. *Les X-files.*"

The term for files that never saw the light of day.

"I didn't say that," he said. "Think what you want."

Shivers rippled her arm in the hot air. "I think he's come back, struck again. Four girls, and this time one died."

Rodot shrugged again. He threw twenty francs down on the wet ringed table.

"Check 1998. Disturbance of the peace reports." He winked. "And I never told you that."

Wednesday, 8 P.M.

After several hours of work, Aimée pulled up Florian's email. She took a breath and hit reply. Began to type. Her phone, nestled in its charger, vibrated.

What now — an invective from René, about to quit? He wouldn't have to. But the café number showed.

"*Allô,* Aimée."

"Feel okay, Zazie?"

"Papa said I should apologize," Zazie said, contrite. A sniffle. "In person. But I'm doing my homework."

Aimée hit SAVE AS DRAFT and powered off her laptop.

"Then time for my late *espresso décaféiné.* See you in a moment."

Poor thing.

The Dior shirt stuck to her back. She had to change. In the back armoire she picked one of Saj's gifts, a loose, Indian white-cotton shirt — the soft fabric breathed, thank God. She pulled her short jean jacket over it, stepped into an agnès b. cotton-flounced lace skirt with a drawstring waist-band and slipped into a low-heeled pair of sandals.

Her finger paused on the old enamel light switch. A *tristesse* overcame her. Shadows darkened the office, throwing into relief her mahogany desk, inherited from her father. Should she give this up? Leave the memo-ries and move on? With a bittersweet feeling she set the alarm, locked the frosted-glass door of Leduc Detective and faced the wire-cage elevator. Out of service. As usual.

Zazie hunched over her mathematics book at the café's rear table. "Papa took me to the *lycée* so I could bring the teacher my report. I turned it in."

"Bravo, Zazie."

"Just some math to do," she said.

Virginie set down a steaming *espresso dé-caféiné* and a tall glass of fresh-squeezed orange juice.

Aimée reached to pay, but Virginie stopped her.

"We're putting this on Zazie's tab, eh?"

Zazie nodded, her eyes serious.

"Zazie owes you a debt. She will make it

up to you," said Virginie, hands on her hips. "You're a busy mother-to-be — all this running around and neglecting your business. There's consequences, I've told Zazie. Then getting shot, *mon Dieu.* I'm so sorry, Aimée."

Aimée's sandal strap itched. She felt awkward. Was this that tough love she'd heard about in *Raising Your Child with Discipline,* another book René had given her? Could she do that?

Maybe she should she take notes.

"I need help behind the counter," said Virginie, tapping her feet. "Has Zazie said what she needs to say yet?"

A big sigh and rolling of eyes — Zazie was back in teenager mode. "*Maman,* give me a moment."

After Virginie gave a territorial swipe of her towel around Zazie's textbook, she retreated to a waiting customer at the counter.

"I'm sorry, Aimée. I have to thank René, too. Somehow make this up to you."

Aimée pretended to think. "I might consider letting you babysit after you finish your homework once in a while."

"*Vraiment?*" Zazie grinned. "Deal."

Aimée sipped the fresh orange juice. Heaven. A bit of pulp lodged on her lip.

"Mélanie called me that night from the clinic." Zazie leaned over her book and lowered her voice. "It was after I left. She didn't make sense."

"She was in shock, traumatized. But you can understand," said Aimée.

Zazie shrugged. "I don't know." She closed her book. "She kept talking about his shirt."

"What's that, Zazie?"

"Licorice. His shirt smelled like licorice."

Aimée's hand froze on the glass. Licorice. Virginie beckoned from the full counter of customers.

"Coming, *Maman.*"

If only Aimée'd heard this before.

Outside, under the arcades of rue de Rivoli, she leaned against the limestone. Her mind raced. Just then, her phone vibrated in her bag. The caller ID showed Madame Pelletier.

"Oui?"

"Mademoiselle Leduc, I'm off *en vacances,* and you never heard this from me. *Compris?*"

"Bien sûr," she said, moving into a doorway and pulling out her Moleskine notebook. "What haven't I heard?"

Aimée listened. Wrote it down. No doubt now. The pieces fit together. A minute later

Madame Pelletier clicked off.

Now it made sense.

She needed a plan. Backup. But Saj had gone to Sceaux for a consulting job — too far away. Morbier didn't answer, and his voice mail was full. Typical. As a last resort, she called René. He didn't answer, no doubt still furious with her. But she left him a message, stressed she needed backup and gave him the address.

The buses and taxis clogged rue de Rivoli to a standstill. Dusk hovered, and the twilight rays shimmered off the Louvre's tall windows. Her mouth soured in the air laced with diesel exhaust fumes.

Determined, she got on the Métro, stood most of the way until a young woman offered her a seat, then changed at Concorde for Line 12 toward Pigalle. Three stops later she ascended the Trinité station steps across from the hulking church, its high columns blurred in approaching darkness.

En route, she'd come up with a plan. A plan to lure him out.

She walked one uphill block of rue Blanche, turned right into rue de la Tour des Dames. Her insides wrenched. The scene of last night's shooting, right before her. Yellow strips of crime-scene tape fluttered.

The old Electricité de France building looked proud despite its sagging scaffolding. The cobbled street of elegant townhouses appeared as deserted and lifeless as it had last night.

At the gatehouse, a new guard looked her over.

"Aimée Leduc to see Monsieur Lavigne."

His flushed face and loosened tie indicated he hit the bottle or didn't do well in the heat. Or both.

"Concerning? You have an appointment?"

Inquisitive and irritable, just her luck.

"Last night I forgot my scarf here at the reception," she said, mustering a big smile. "Silly." Patted her stomach. "But there's sentimental value — it was my *grand-mère*'s." She sighed. "She died last week, and it's all I have."

His eyes softened. "Will Madame Lavigne, the daughter-in-law, do?"

You caught more flies with honey than vinegar, as her *grand-mère* said.

"Parfait."

He dialed a number.

A moment later the door opened.

Dusk hovered. Light from the rooms in the townhouse glimmered in the lengthening shadows. Purple wisteria dripped from the trellis in the cobbled entryway. A scent of honeysuckle wafted. From the lighted entry Brianne ran down the curving outdoor staircase, smiling. Again those large, bright teeth.

"I'm just thankful you're all right after what happened. Your baby's safe, they told me." She hugged Aimée. Innocence shone in her eyes. "Tragic. The *flics* asked questions all day. I'm so sorry."

"I need to speak with Renaud."

"*Désolée,* he's gone out. A dinner, maybe? . . . I don't know exactly, but he's coming back late. Can it wait until tomorrow?"

Until another girl had been raped?

"It's important . . . can you call him? There's memorial planning for Madame Vasseur. But her husband's at the Commissariat. In *garde à vue.* It's a mess."

"Mon Dieu." Brianne blinked.

"I'm sure Renaud wants to help. I didn't know who else to turn to."

"But of course. My phone's inside."

Guilt wracked Aimée.

A uniformed maid on the *terrasse* waved to Brianne. "Madame, that phone call from the ship has come through."

"Excusez-moi," she said. "That's my mother. My father suffered a stroke on their cruise to Istanbul. I must take it first, do

441

you mind?"

"Of course, but this heat." Aimée fanned herself with her trembling hand. "May I have a glass of water?"

"*Biên sur,* please." She took Aimée's arm. Walked her up the stairs.

In the state-of-the-art kitchen, open windows overlooking the courtyard, Aimée accepted the tall bottle of chilled Perrier and a glass. "I wondered where you kept the rabbit."

"Rabbit?" Brianne, distracted, glanced down the hallway. "Ah, Renaud put the cage beside the old *jardin d'hiver.*" She gestured out the window to the glazed, gazebo-like Belle Époque affair by the old stables that had been converted into a garage. *"Excusez-moi."*

Brianne's heels clicked over the parquet floor.

With Brianne engaged on the phone, Aimée took the Perrier bottle and slipped back out the front door.

The old stable doors were rolled shut. She saw no one. She kept to the shadows at the side of the building, creeping along until she heard a scratching. She shone her penlight to reveal a sniffing black rabbit with floppy ears in a chicken-wire cage. Beside the rabbit on the tamped dirt and clumps of grass lay half-chewed anise bulbs, their feathered leaves nibbled. The anise gave off a licorice odor.

Now to find more proof. Assemble her ducks in a row . . .

The familiar rumble of a motorcycle came from near the old stable. Her heart immediately started pounding.

Where the hell was René? She hit his number. Busy. Time to get out of here.

She turned and shone her penlight toward the path. On Renaud, who stood wiping his oil-stained hands with a rag. "Shh, don't tell Brianne."

That he liked little girls? She scanned the wall, the shrubs, looking for an escape.

He put a dark, smudged finger over his mouth. "I forgot to feed Basil." He pulled a leaf-topped bunch of carrots from his pocket. Dropped it in the cage. "We'll keep it our secret, *non*?"

Like hell she would. Somehow she had to deflect his attention, call the guard. "It's just that . . ." She clutched her stomach with one hand. Groaned. "These pains, must get to the doctor."

"Afraid not, Aimée," he said. He held the ends of the rag in both fists. Snapped it taut. "I wish you'd left me alone."

Her eyes darted for an escape. He had

blocked the path. Stupid not to plan this out better.

"The guard's drunk. No one will hear you scream."

His words chilled her. Stall him and play for time.

"Renaud, you were a boy ten years ago." She tried to keep her voice even. "I understand. So will Brianne, but you need to get help."

The leaves rustled as he edged closer.

"You sound like everyone else."

"Me? Last night you murdered Madame Vasseur and almost killed my baby."

"But I like babies," he said. "I love children."

She cringed inside. His words sickened her.

"I never meant to hurt you," he said. "But I had to stop her."

His old family friend? Then framed her husband after raping their daughter?

"Why, Renaud?" Her hand gripped the Perrier bottle behind her. "Why this infatuation with young girls who play violin?"

"I grew up on music." He smiled. "My father sent me to violin lessons my whole childhood, until I was twelve. And she played the Paganini piece, exquisite and exciting."

444

"Paulette Destel," Aimée said. "Another pupil of Madame de Langlet. But your father hushed it up."

His eyes went faraway. "I remember those lace curtains in Paulette's parents' salon, that burnished patina of her violin. So hot that afternoon. Paulette's skin flushed pink, those notes . . . I wanted to be with her," he said, his phrasing like an adolescent's. "You know, like my papa was with his mistress. Paulette did, too, but she pretended she didn't. They all do. They lie to me."

His open man-child gaze and matter-of-fact tone chilled her.

"Papa sent me to a boys' boarding school after. It wasn't the same. I don't like boys. Then university."

Her gaze flicked over to the yard, calculating how many steps it would take, how fast she could run.

"Renaud, you're married now," she said, edging away. "Brianne's sweet, beautiful. Blonde."

"Six months we've been married, but she's impatient."

Six months — that was how long ago the rapes had started.

"Papa's pushing us to have a baby, carry on his name," said Renaud, twisting the rag. "An heir and a spare, he's always harping.

445

Then Brianne's constant pressure. She doesn't understand."

He wrenched the greasy rag in his hands.

"So you follow little girls home from their violin lessons," she said. "Relive being twelve years old with Paulette and force yourself on them."

She'd reached the old stable door. Her back pressed against the handle. She could do this, she could get away, keep her baby safe. Made herself breathe and reached the handle. Pulled. Didn't budge. Locked.

Before she could make a break and run, his arm was around her neck. She choked and tried to kick him.

"You need more than help, Renaud," she said. Her words came out in gasps. He'd pinned her to the wall. Her arms stuck behind her. "To be . . . stopped. Stopped before you rape your little niece."

"But Émilie likes to sit on my lap. Wants to cuddle with me."

His eyes went dreamlike again, his short, soft, panting breath hitting her face. It made her insides crawl.

"She's just a child."

Then he stuffed the greasy rag in her mouth. She struggled, but he swooped his leg behind hers and turned her. Panicked, she tried to break her fall as best she could, but he hoisted her shoulders and dragged her back into the bushes, her heels trailing in the dirt. And then in the shadows he stuck the sharp tip of the Luger in her rib.

"I didn't want to have to do this, Aimée," he said. "I like babies."

With all her might she whacked the Perrier bottle at his temple. He cried out in pain but didn't let go. She hit harder at his face until the bottle shattered.

She jabbed the jagged, broken bottle neck in his thigh. Crying out, he dropped her, the Luger falling beside him. He clutched his bleeding head, moaning.

She spit the rag out of her mouth.

A sobbing came from the bushes. Light flicked on behind, silhouetting a shaking figure.

"How could you?" Brianne's shoulders were heaving. Teary mascara streaked down her cheek. "All this time . . . when you won't touch me, making me wonder what's wrong with me."

Aimée's fingers scrabbled in the dirt and pebbles for the Luger's black handle. Had he taken out the guard?

"Waiting for you every night." Brianne's voice rose. Shouting and crying. "Therapy sessions and you lied, lied, lied."

Blood matted Renaud's temple. "Little

girls like when I'm nice to them, Brianne," he said in a whimper. "Try to understand."

"That you're a pervert?" Brianne reached down and grabbed the Luger. "Can't act like a man? But you can't, can you? You'll never touch Émilie."

Aimée vibrated in fear. "Put that down, Brianne."

"Never touch her, you hear me?" Brianne's finger curled around the trigger.

What could she use to stop the woman?

"Aimée?" shouted René. Footsteps pounded.

"Behind the cage," she called. "Hurry."

"You're sick." Brianne's hand wobbled. "A disgusting pervert." Wild-eyed, she pointed at Renaud.

Aimée flung a handful of dirt at Brianne's face. She stepped back, teetering, and squeezed the trigger. A loud crack. Glass splintered from the winter garden, sending gleaming shards over the rabbit hutch.

By the time Aimée managed to grab Brianne's ankles and pull her down, René had grabbed the Luger and ejected the cartridges.

"Sorry I'm late." René stood panting, looking from one to the other. "Johnny Hallyday's *grand-mère* sold Monsieur Lavigne a Luger *comme ça*. I've got the receipt dated 1978, too."

"Why don't you take care of Renaud?" she said, wiping the perspiration from her neck. "Let's get some gun residue on his fingertips."

René gave a grim nod. "With pleasure." He judo-kicked the squirming Renaud in the crotch. Then again. With his handkerchief René wiped off the Luger's handle, put it into a moaning Renaud's hand and fired at the bushes.

She took Brianne's face in her hands. "Brianne. Listen. We have only minutes. You never fired the Luger, *compris*? You discovered your husband attacking me, he confessed that he raped twelve-year-old girls after their violin lessons. That he hurt one so badly she died. He taunted you about your niece. He pulled out the Luger . . . thank God he missed."

"But . . ."

"Do you want him off the street?"

Brianne's shoulders heaved. "What have I done?" Her face streaked with dust and mascara. "He's my husband. I can't . . ."

Aimée wanted to slap her. "Wake up. Ten years ago his father paid off the police and Madame de Langlet. He used his influence and connections to cover up."

"What . . . ? You're making this up."

449

Brianne gasped.

"Now old Lavigne's doing it again, Brianne. He thought marrying you would stop Renaud. But Renaud can't quit. He's ill — a pedophile. With all the pressure, Renaud's gone over the edge to hide his assaults, even killing Madame Vasseur and shooting me."

Brianne erupted in sobs.

"You think he'll stop? Forget that Catholic-girl guilt," said René. "*Bon,* we'll point out the residue on your hands and you'll both go to prison."

Brianne's terror-stricken eyes pleaded. *"Non, non."*

"Smart choice," said René.

Thursday, 11 A.M.

Aimée waved to Zacharié as he left the café on sun-dappled rue du Louvre. She tucked a copy of *Le Parisien* in her bag and peered at him from over her Jackie O sunglasses in front of Leduc Detective's building door.

"I explained to Zazie's parents," he said.

"How'd it go?"

"The version I gave?" His mouth turned in a rueful smile. "For reasons of state security, etcetera. The usual smoke screen. I'm only permitted to say blah, blah and apologized for their daughter getting involved. End of story."

For the best and as promised, he'd kept her name out of it. At the corner she saw a flashing glint, heard a car's screeching brakes, a ringing bicycle bell, then shouts as a bicyclist shook his fist at a Renault and pedaled away. A near collision averted. Like yesterday. She gave an inward sigh of relief.

"I owe you, Aimée," he said.

She nodded. "I might take you up on that one day."

"And your friend Saj. For a Rasta hippie, he's a genius."

"Glad you followed his advice." She neglected to mention Saj's scanned addendum copy she'd messengered anonymously to Morbier this morning. Or the description of the Corsican she'd supplied to Beto.

Women with shopping bags stood fanning themselves in the heat at the bus stop. Freshly watered red geraniums from the iron-railed balcony above the café overflowed and trickled onto the pavement, sending out a humid vapor.

"The subbranch in the Ministry offered me a job like the one I did before," he said. "In Belgium, with a flat and international school for Marie-Jo."

Close enough to watch, but not close enough to cause trouble.

"You worked a deal," she said.

The price of his silence.

The 67 Pigalle bus approached, wending its way across rue de Rivoli. Zacharié pulled a *carnet* of bus tickets from his pocket. "Deep down you're thinking I'm wrong," he said. "That it's all wrong. But I can protect my daughter now and obtain full custody. That's all that means anything to me."

The bus shadows blocked out the lozenge of light playing on his face. Ripples of hot air laced with diesel exhaust and lime-blossom scent filled her nose. She felt a flutter as the baby kicked.

"I understand."

"You're just saying that, Aimée," he said, joining those in line for the bus. Then he paused, turned to her, letting people file past, and took her hand. "But I can't live with Marie-Jo like a fugitive. I won't."

For the first time, she really did understand. *"Bonne chance."*

He enveloped her in a hug and patted her stomach.

On the corner she saw Beto shutting a taxi door, pâtisserie box in the other hand. He was staring at her. At them. Zacharié boarded the bus. And when it took off, the taxi had gone and so had Beto.

ACKNOWLEDGMENTS

Thanks go to so many: Dot, Barbara, Max, Jan, always Jean Satzer, Jeffrey Phillips, Ken the Judge, Pascaline Lefebvre of Alliance Française de Portland.

In Paris, Carla Chemouni-Bach; Alex Toledano, Ph.D; Anne-Francoise and Cathy Etile; Gilles Thomas; Benoît Pastisson; Agnès Chauvin at the Conservation Régionale des Monuments Historiques; Jean-Pierre Gauffier; Thierry Cazaux of the Conseiller d'Arrondissement et Délégué au Patrimoine et à la Culture Mairie du 9ème; Valérie Vesque-Jeancard; Marie-Claire, detective privé; Daniel Catan. Boundless mercis to Annie-Laure Assis and Claude Etienne for sharing music, walks and their 'hood; Jean Abou, partymaster; dear Joanna Bartholomew; Denise the photographer; Valérie Mayer-Denarnaud; Areski Garidel of Pigalle; Thierry Boulouque, Commissaire Divisionnaire Chef de la Brigade de Protection des Mineurs; Maryse Leclerc-Joly, Commandant Fonctionnel de Police Chef de la Section des Enquétes; Céline Plumail, Commissaire de Police, Brigade de Protection des Mineurs; Commmissaire Central Laurent Mercier de Police Judiciare 9ème arrondissement; Peter Olson; Monsieur X at Hôtel Drouot.

Nothing would happen without Dr. Terri Haddix, medical pathologist; Dr. Laurie Green, who saves lives; James N. Frey without whom; the Soho family: Rudy Martinez, Rachel Kowal, Janine Agro, Paul Oliver, Bronwen Hruska, who helms our ship, and my whipsmart editor extraordinaire, Juliet Grames; and always to Jun and my son, Tate.